"NO, NOT LIKE THIS, LOVE . . ."

Viveca smacked him away from her in a spark of fury. "I'm the one who dragged you down in a heat of passion. Are you saying I should have been more restrained?"

He laughed uneasily. "All I said was that I wanted to do this right, to woo you and—"

"Woo me! When did a highwayman ever *woo* a woman? You can give yourself airs and a cashmere coat and call yourself a shipping accountant, but you're nothing more than a ten-shilling robber, and you know it, Byrne St. James. Don't feign fancy ways with me!"

"I never meant to insult you. A man of any worth prays to give his lady such pleasure! No, it was my roughness and haste I doubted. It seems we have our roles reversed, my sweet. I'm the one who wants roses and tenderness, while all that matters to you is—how did you put it? Half an hour's sport on the library floor!"

Also by Valerie Vayle

~~~~~~

ORIANA
SEAFLAME
LADY OF FIRE

MISTRESS
OF THE
NIGHT

~~~~~~~~~~~~~~~~~~~~~~~~~~~~~~~~~~~~

Valerie Vayle

A DELL BOOK

For Bill de Andrea,
who deserves Edgar Awards for
his friendship, too

Published by
Dell Publishing Co., Inc.
1 Dag Hammarskjold Plaza
New York, New York 10017

ISBN: 0-440-15710-2

Printed in the United States of America
First printing—April 1985

PART ONE

Ginny

"I went into her chamber for all to take a slumber,
    I dreamt of gold and silver,
      And for sure it was no wonder. . . ."

—"Whiskey in the Jar," late 18th-century Irish Traditional

CHAPTER ONE

April 1746

"Ginny Lindstrom! Missus Ginny!"

Hoofbeats pounded through her carefully furrowed fields. Virginia Lindstrom, a striking blond woman of twenty-two, hesitated in front of her fireplace. She eyed her husband's second-best heirloom musket hanging over the mantel and decided against reaching for it. The horseman knew her name, therefore he could not be an enemy.

She threw her rough woolen plaid around her shoulders and wrestled the bolt back from the door. As she stepped across the threshold she recognized the runty, red-haired man on his frothy horse. "Angus, man, you're in a lather!" she called. "What is it? Has the battle come? Has—" Her hand flew to her throat where a miniature of her grandmother, painted on ivory, pinned her bodice together. "Angus, speak up! Is it me man?" she cried.

He reined in his gelding. Sweat and white droplets from the horse's bit spattered the front of Ginny's gown. Hooves dug in, dirt flew.

"Aye," Angus shouted over the horse's bobbing head. "Bonny Prince Charlie has lost all at Culloden Moor! The sun'll set on a Scotland forever under English rule, wurra the day!"

Ginny Lindstrom caught a damp leather rein. "Angus, me man . . . ?"

Angus spat away from her, hating to break such news to this pretty little widow. He had watched her come to this forsaken plot of ground when she was a shivering bride of fifteen; had watched her mature, bury children, work the ground shoulder-to-

7

shoulder with her tawny-haired husband, Jock. She had helped Angus's wife through five birthings and was always a quick one to kill her youngest hen and fetch chicken soup to the cottage when there was illness afoot. All the folk in these parts knew and appreciated Jock Lindstrom's bighearted missus, Ginny.

"Your bonny Jock's gone, wummin, I seen it m'self, shot full between his blue eyes, he were. Now leave me horse be, I've got to ride on and fetch out me wife and bairns!"

She stepped back, mouth flannel-dry with shock. "Angus—you'd not be mistaking it!"

"Nae, I wouldna. The Duke of Cumberland told his soldiers to take nae prisoners. And they're a-comin' and burning and looting all in sight. Marching right through the countryside, they are, wi' torches and bayonets fixed. Saddle the mare, ye'll just hae time to sling your silverplate and linens into a saddlebag. Ride, wummin! They're not but two farms away, can ye nae ken the smoke? Go, and God be wi' ye, little widow!"

He spurred the gelding. Ginny jumped back. The horse sobbed for air and launched himself across her field—those fields she had struggled so dearly to clear of rocks, had fought to plow with her little mare. . . .

Ginny stared after the man on the horse with stinging eyes. Her Jock, her own man—dead! It didn't seem possible! His child was so newly planted in her that she had only guessed its existence last week, just before Jock had ridden away with the prince's men.

Pregnant, she thought bitterly. Pregnant at last, after the long spell following the death of Little Jock, and now the baby's father wouldn't be here to see the wee one. Pregnant, and now they were riding to burn her cottage down over her head! Ginny stared blankly around her at the place that had been home seven years now, a neat, gray stone cottage with some pink limestone and black bricks Jock had salvaged in Carlisle. They had patched the abandoned crofter's hut together, enlarged it, added the wooden lean-to when they'd acquired the mare and geese to go with the chickens. As well as the tall chestnut gelding Jock had ridden away to this crazy Scots rebellion he so believed in.

She went to the cottage, leaned in the doorway, and wept. Jock with his bonny smile and wide shoulders, shot in the head by one of his countrymen. Jock, so delighted to hear that at last he'd fathered another child to follow their son who died of the cough. And the two stillborn girls and three miscarriages. Jock, who only last week had slept in her arms with his tawny morning beard scraping her cheek, his fingers locked in her hair as their pulses beat together in the first pale peach streak of dawn.

Ginny's head snapped back up. No time for mourning, not now. They were riding for her farm! Her potatoes, her turnips and the rye behind the lean-to—those stubborn, back-breaking acres she and the mare, both pregnant and aching, had carved out of rock and frozen earth at the first thaw. Her chickens. The last goose, the one she'd been fattening for next Christmas. Her mother's worn-out silverplate in the Cedars of Lebanon dowry chest her father had brought back from the Orient . . .

Her head swam. She opened her eyes wide, looked her last at this, her home. Windows set with thin sections of horn to let light in; only one narrow pane was actual glazed glass. There were wooden shutters; few in these parts had them. She was proud of those shutters.

Inherited linens, scrubbed down with lye soap, beaten on rocks in the thin trickle of stream behind the cottage. Her great-grandmother's walnut bed, big enough for four. Jock's great-great-great grandmother's Turkish carpet laid on a battered parquetry table, just as it would have been in the days of the great Queen Elizabeth when it had been woven.

The clothes she had spun, woven, cut, sewn, embroidered; her loom; the cradle still there in the corner where it had stood empty these many months, making a mockery of her womanhood and youth. For too long its presence had said Where are your children to fill me?

Ginny raced to the cedar chest. She threw her shawl down, pulled out a lanolin-rich gray sweater of her husband's. She yanked it on over her head, dug out Jock's best coat of heavy black wool, thinned at cuff and elbows, all the bone buttons sewn on and resewn innumerable times. Last, she pulled on well-worn lambskin mitts and set Jock's tricornered hat on her head over a plaid muffler.

Her little pouch of shillings and one gold Queen Elizabeth sovereign were nestled in the toe of a long-outmoded slipper with paste buckle and red, raised heel. She burrowed in the bottom of the cedar chest for the slipper, found the pouch, and shoved it down the neck of her gown, wedging it between her stays.

Ginny paused in the middle of the room for a last look. There was no time for the silverplate and no way to carry it, anyway. She had no jewels to take. Her only ornaments were her bright blond hair and her mother's lead wedding band, placed on her finger by Jock seven years ago and never once removed—and, of course, she had the ivory miniature. No time for the Turkish carpet now, or her prized linens.

She kicked her wooden clogs away, pulled on her heavy boots without bothering to buckle them. They'd belonged to a great half-uncle killed in the Fifteen when Bonny Prince Charlie's father, the Old Pretender, had tried to march down through Scotland, into England, and onto the throne. That uncle had died just like Jock. And as with fathers so with sons; both Pretenders, Young and Old, had failed at their self-appointed tasks, had been so poorly organized and oblivious to the hearts of the nation that they had fallen into disgrace at the first real test of leadership on the field.

Ginny ran for the long-barreled gun over the mantelpiece, took it down, shoved powder and shot in the deep pockets of the black greatcoat. She considered making a stand, fighting for her pathetic little farm, then thought, *They'd only be the madder after I shot several, and women are always raped in a war.*

She was a better than average shot, but vengeance wasn't as important as escaping with her life, and that of her unborn child. And as for rape . . . Well, it was bad enough with a husband, but to be forced into such a thing by strangers—She shuddered and rushed to the lean-to.

The dappled mare lifted her head from the low manger where she was pulling at the last of her hay. "Not today, Dulcie. I havna a bit of bread nor a turnip bit for you. Be a good lass; stand still and let me saddle and bridle you."

Dulcie complied. Ginny always warmed the cold iron bit in her hands before popping it in the gray mare's mouth, and Ginny was always gentle. But today the bit was put in, cold, and the saddle girth was yanked too tight. The mare shied away from such unaccustomed treatment as well as from the gun strapped to the saddle in its unfamiliar cowhide wrappings.

Ginny led Dulcie to the front of the cottage and scanned the countryside with a mittened hand above her eyes. A gray column of smoke was rising in the dusk over the next hill. Quickly, then. She looped Dulcie's reins over the door latch and ran back inside. She grabbed a threadbare linen towel, scooped up dried fruit, a tin of smoky black tea (it had cost her a good portion of the farm's profits last year), and the last of the dried oats. Then she ran back outside, knotting the bundle as she went.

There were blue-and-red coats in the distance, like tiny marchpane fancies she'd once seen through a shop window.

Except that these pretty marchpane figures had just burned out the two farms up the path.

Ginny flung herself into the saddle, hooked the big towel with its foodstuff over the pommel, and gathered the reins. She clucked at her mare. "Up, Dulcie, up!"

The chickens were spilling out through the open door of the lean-to. They came cackling into the yard, pecking and quibbling. *My flocks,* Ginny thought. *The food I worked so hard to set on the table, my last goose, Mother's silverplate, the Turkish carpet . . . May God damn all wars! My man dead and my home to be put to the torch, my Jock unburied with a load of shot between his bonny blue eyes . . .*

She dug her heels into the mare's speckled flanks. Sweet, spoiled Dulcie leaped at this indignity, galloping across the stern Scottish soil that had grudgingly fed her these many years.

Where will I go? Ginny thought desperately, and then it came to her. Jock had a sister-in-law in Kensington, a sleepy village that London encroached on more every day. Jock had only spoken of his dead brother's wife in hushed whispers, which made

11

Ginny all the more curious, since he admitted the woman was the soul of generosity and concern. Ginny knew less than nothing about this relative by marriage, but family was family, and the woman owned a place called the Black Bull Inn. Everyone knew innkeepers could never find enough good help these days.

Well, the other Missus Lindstrom was about to gain some good help—a fast hand at chicken-plucking; someone good with horses, children, and bleaching bed linens. Yes, family was still family, she told herself, especially in these hard times when any traveler at the door might be a third cousin you'd never met, come to move in for the duration of the year.

Ginny rode south for Kensington and a new life.

CHAPTER TWO

The Kensington of the mid-eighteenth century was as good as connected to London, though Ginny, in her ignorance, had thought to give the latter town a wide berth. Raised in the north, living in small towns and isolated farms, she hated the stench of London with its constant coal fires and rotting sewage in the streets. It was a hotbed of vice—everyone said so—and preachers thunderously condemned the metropolis with brimstone and the lick of flames in every syllable. She believed them, too, going on the finer sensibilities of religion and her nose. Not that she was very clean herself, she decided ruefully, though she had scrubbed her face and arms whenever water had been available. Her one set of clothes had long been coated by the dust of the road, mud caked her boots and skirts, she stank of horse, and the baby was making its presence obvious in a dozen little unpleasant ways.

Ginny rode into the cheery village of Kensington, noticing that the air immediately seemed sweeter, though she was not far from the coal fires of London's heart.

She touched her heels to Dulcie's flanks and rode on, pleased by the look of the village. It was dusty but clean, with green peeping out between freshly painted houses and shops. Several urchins were running on the green ahead, rolling a warped barrel stave between them. Ginny called out to them, "Halloa! Could ye point me toward the Black Bull Inn?"

One of the boys whooped in derision, and they all ran away.

A little farther on she asked the same of two withered old biddies carrying market baskets. They elevated their noses, pulled their skirts aside as though reluctant to sully them on Ginny's

13

presence. *Oh, Lord,* Ginny thought, and laughed. *Geordie Lindstrom's missus runs a bawdy house!*

She smiled sorrily upon realizing that she didn't care. She had ridden hundreds of miles, been pursued by highwaymen, and had eaten little save what she'd brought—oh, that had been gone *days,* and the village was now spinning a bit—and some berries foraged from roadside hedges. Ginny had spent so long in the saddle that she feared she and Dulcie had become a centaur and never again would they split back into two separate creatures. They were one miserable being together, dirty, disheveled, thirsty, bellies crying for food, cramps and nausea increasing with each aching mile.

The mare's heavy iron shoes clopped loudly on the streets. It was still quite early in the day, and most businesses were only now opening their doors to the public. A rooster crowed somewhere. Up ahead a blacksmith raised the thin pine side of his shoeing shed. Ginny could see the red glow of his fire behind him as he readied forge and anvil for another day's work. She could not remember what day this was or when she had eaten last; she only knew that the fire made her think of roast chicken, succulent broths, the pork and brisket she'd never tasted, only salivated after in shop windows.

She reined her little mare in and cupped her hands to her mouth. "Halloa, good sir," she greeted. "I'm a stranger to these parts. Could you help me?"

As he straightened up she saw the cropped ears of a felon. It gave him the fierce look of a dog bred for fighting. "What be ye looking for?" he asked.

"The Black Bull Inn."

He shook his head. "Don't be a-going there, mistress. A bad place, that. Bad men and worse women!"

"I've *got* to go. Me only family's there!"

"All right then," he said, still shaking his nearly earless head as he gave directions to the northeast. "Ye'll coom to an inn wi' a swinging sign bearin' the badge o' the damned Hanover kings— God rot and blast 'em as foreigners and damned fat Germans!

The only decent 'un in the lot's the Prince o' Wales and he won't be king soon enough to suit me!"

Ginny nervously thanked the blacksmith and clucked to Dulcie, who took off at the fastest canter she'd managed in a good while. Perhaps she sensed that the journey was almost over, for she jerked at her bit for more rein, more speed. "It be all right," Ginny told her. "We're almost there. Hopefully Geordie's missus can use another serving wench or chambermaid, because I can't take charity—nor would a woman running her own establishment be likely to offer it!"

She fervently hoped it wasn't too small an inn. May the Good Lord make it a great walloping one with two stories, its own taproom, and a lean-to big enough for at least five horses and two carriages!

Her jaw dropped when she saw the Black Bull at last. It was a three-storied structure with a half-floor above, the plasterwork painted bright blue and the timberwork stark white. The roadway up to it was set with bricks in a smart herringbone pattern, and the stables looked fit to hold twenty nags and half a dozen carriages.

There were tuberoses planted on either side of the brick drive, reminding Ginny of the miniature of her grandmother. It showed a black-haired woman with a sensual mouth; she had pearls and tuberoses in her hair, and the gown she wore repeated the flower pattern. "Mistress of the Night," Ginny's mother had called the tuberose. Ginny didn't know why.

A party of travelers was unloading from a red-lacquered landau with half its leather top down. They ducked low under the old-fashioned arched carriage entrance, for new carriages were higher than the old ones. The horses patiently waiting in their harness were among the biggest Ginny had ever seen. She whistled softly through her teeth and drew back on the reins so that these wealthy travelers might reach their rooms before she made her shabby entrance.

When the last of them had disappeared inside, Ginny clicked her tongue at the mare. Dulcie gave a start and obeyed, plodding on to the stables at the rear of the house. An hostler yelled to her, "Ho, boy! What is it?"

"Is this the Black Bull Inn?"

"Any fool can read that," the one-eyed hostler scoffed. Ginny's ears burned, for no one in her family had ever learned to read—books and news sheets being, her father had said, the provinces of the rich.

Embarrassed by the unintentional insult as well as his mistake concerning her gender, Ginny timidly asked if Geordie Lindstrom's missus still ran the place.

"You mean Missus Caro? Sure thing. Caro's prob'ly in the kitchen a-supervisin' o' the feast frae tonight. Give me the horse and scoot inside wi' ye, if ye got a message for the missus."

Funny, high-pitched voice for so tall a lad, the one-eyed hostler thought, then saw a flurry of skirts and neat, bare ankles as the rider descended. "Uh—nice mare," he babbled as her hat and muffler were removed to present a disheveled and sunburned but still attractive young woman.

"She's one-quarter Barb," Ginny said proudly, rubbing Dulcie's nose. "And carrying a foal due by the first o' the year. I'll rub her down; I can't afford ye doin' it."

"No, missus, that's *my* job! Caro'd have me ears 'f I let guest rub down a horse," he protested.

"But I haven't enough money and I'm not a guest," she answered quickly. "I'm Geordie's Jock's wife." Seeing his blank stare, Ginny fumbled, "Our husbands were brothers. I guess as how that makes Caro and me sisters-in-law."

"Then off to the kitchen wi' ye, and no more o' this currying-your-own-mare rubbish, young woman! Off wi' ye," he ordered, and sent her away with a waggle of the finger meant to indicate the proper direction. Ginny did just fine following her nose. The smokehouse was heaven to pass; the icehouse made her shiver. Bread ovens lined up on either side of the brick walk seemed to point toward the kitchen, a square brick building joined to the inn by a covered passageway.

She knocked at the door, timidly stuck her head in. A mélange of smells pleasantly assailed her nostrils: a whole lamb basted with apricot brandy on a spit that was turned by a dog inside a wooden wheel; hot, smoked hams dripping mustard-clove sauce; fresh, thick coffee cut with cocoa beans; smoky green tea pan-fired in porcelain over slow coals; pickles soaking in copper vats to gain their green color. There were marchpane sweets molded into fantastic forms, and breads brushed with egg yolk for a golden glaze. . . .

Ginny's empty stomach churned. She had never seen so much food in her life. The smells and sounds assaulted her and she swooned. Her knees crumpled and she slid to the floor.

Caroline Lindstrom, twenty stone of massively thewed, pink-faced womanhood, retied her apron and bellowed, "Who in the name of the Virgin's Sainted Mother—"

One-Eyed Jack, the hostler, peeked into the kitchen. "She asked if you were dead Geordie's wife, said she was your sister-in-law, an' now she's fainted all to hell!"

Geordie Lindstrom had been dead these six years past! Caro's mouth dropped open with surprise. "Why, it's Geordie's Jock's little wummin from up rebellious Scotland-way! God's Holy Shroud, you nincompoop, haul her out of the doorway and follow me! And mind you, lads and lasses," she said to those peering out from behind basting, plucking, roasting, and scrubbing, "if there's a single black edge on that suckling lamb I'll spit and roast ye m'self! Now get on with your work!"

Everyone leapt to clear a path as One-Eyed Jack laboriously hefted Ginny up, her long legs dangling and her head lolling over his arm. Ginny was the taller of the two, but Jack threw his shoulders back in a show of strength and followed Caro.

She bellowed for Becka, her best chambermaid, and at the door of Caro's bedchamber the two women took Ginny and shut Jack out. They laid the unconscious woman down on Caro's stack of featherbeds. "Cor, she's thick with road dust," the mistress of the Black Bull observed. "Likely as not she's ridden all the way from that heathen Scotland. Wearing stays, too! I'll loosen these up so she can draw breath like God meant her to. By Satan's scepter, Becka, don't stand there gawking like a yellow-billed loon! Fetch me a basin of warm water and a Turkish towel to wash her with.

Poor child, look at the saddle sores inside those bony knees! She'll be starved when she wakes."

The newly loosened stays told Caro something she hadn't expected—her sister-in-law was about three months pregnant. A good healthy girl, despite her narrow wrists and ankles. They'd feed her and splash her down, and she'd bear bonny enough brats. Clever, too, from the looks of her, for hadn't she traveled in a man's clothes to avoid attack? Not that highwaymen weren't bold these days. Why, one had held up Princess Augusta only last month outside Bristol, in full daylight! And when he'd discovered it was the Princess of Wales, he'd handed back her purse with a merry jest and, doffing his hat, had escorted her back to town!

Caro suspected that the highwayman had been the dashing Jemmy St. James, who had been her lover one roaring night last week and who liked his women big and spirited. *Well,* she thought, *he's come to the right one for that. And let's hope the boy returns for more!*

She brewed a stiff pot of tea while Becka stripped Ginny down to her much-mended shift and sponge-bathed her. When Ginny woke, Caro propped her up on fat pillows stuffed with chicken feathers, lavender, and wood shavings, and helped her drink. The long blue eyes came fluttering open. "I'm Caro, dead Geordie's widow. I ken you're Jock's wife, but I don't know your name," the innkeeper said.

"Virginia. Ginny."

"Well, Ginny Lindstrom, what ails Jock that he'd send his pregnant wife packing off to me, wearing his Sunday-best coat?"

"Jock's dead," Ginny said soberly. "Dead on Culloden Moor where the Duke of Cumberland took no prisoners. They coom wi' torches, burning all in their way. I had but time to saddle me mare and ride south. I buried my only child some time back, and now my house is a burned-out shell. Caroline, I'll cook, scrub floors—I'm a hard worker and strong for all me narrow bones. I can spin, weave, and mend. I can plant anything so's it grows. . . ." She sat up, blue eyes defiant, half-expecting rejection. "I've a good mare, she's a quarter Barb wi' a foal due at Christmas. The sire's a great rawboned Irish hunter wi' blue ribbons at every

18

fair and hunt from here to Kilderry. Foal's yours, and I'll work like the devil. . . ."

"Hush, hush," Caro said, embarrassed. "I'd not turn you out with a babe in your belly! Not even if you darn stockings worse than the stable boy! You're family, Ginny Lindstrom, and Jock was dear to me, so shut your mouth and speak no more of such things. When you're up and around, we'll talk about work, but for now, you're thin and ill. You lie back and take care of the baby you're carrying—and don't worry, here's your money, safe and sound. Found it in your stays where you tucked it for safe-keeping."

Caro *tsk-tsk*ed and shook her head. "Not that what you have will feed you for a single day, excepting the golden sovereign. They say those old gold pieces are purer gold than the ones now, and worth more, so you hang on to it. It so happens I *can* use another chambermaid with common sense. Becka's my right arm, but she can't be everywhere. If you're a religious woman, you won't find the Black Bull to your liking, though. I run a tight house but not as saintly as some, if you get my drift. The girls upstairs see to the gentlemen and them that *aren't* so gentle, and that's their sole job. They keep the rakes occupied and less likely to bother my chambermaids, but it still happens, I won't lie to you. Now you get some sleep. I must be mad to talk business with a worn-out girl who's just been widowed. Rest now, dear."

But before she left the room, she saw Ginny retching into the washbasin. "Poor child," Caro said to herself. "Hope the whole of her pregnancy isn't this bad."

CHAPTER THREE

Once the third month of Ginny's pregnancy had passed—during which time she was useless save for mending and helping brew cordials and tea—her robust good health and humor returned, and she proved Caro hadn't made a poor bargain in taking her on.

It was queer to be without Jock after all their years together. But at least she had to put up with no more of that male madness that fell on him at least twice a week, when he tried to tumble her wherever she stood.

She felt softer toward his ghost than that, but it was no good thinking about such things. Ginny had always been the driving force in their marriage and, as a result, did not fall apart with Jock dead. There was no room for self-pity in her world; the strong said, "That's a damned shame," and went on with their work.

The weak withered and died where they stood.

Caro was far from weak, and her powerful personality and unbending pride lent much to Ginny in those first awkward days. *Why, nothing stops her, or even slows her much,* Ginny would think admiringly. *She took me in like a long-lost sister or daughter, and it never occurred to her I might not be a good worker. She's certain I'll find my niche here—and she'll do her best to see that I do.*

There was security of a sort in the broad, unflinching person of Caro Lindstrom. But sympathy and pity—no. Nor would Ginny have wanted them. *Caro treats me like a child who's stumbled and bumped his head,* Ginny thought. *Instead of saying, "Oh, you poor bairn," and making the child weep for his bumped noggin, she whacks me on the back and says, "You're getting better at walking, laddie!" And far from being shamed for his clumsiness, the bairn's proud he got so far.*

So she was not made to feel an outsider in this fast-paced world where hers was the only northern accent. And yet it was odd to be a widow and alone, and equally odd to be living in a city for the first time in her life. At the inn Ginny was quickly made aware of the differences between city life and farm life. Meat and butter in town were more often rancid than not, and the few vegetables grown in London stank and tasted of the coal fires and garbage amidst which they were grown. Fashionable salons and multi-family hovels alike burned coal—when the hovel dwellers could steal or buy coal, that was.

Poor mothers gave their babies gin to quiet their squalling; it was cheaper than cow's milk, which led to consumptive, spindly-legged children who coughed their lungs out before reaching the end of their teens. The pickles whose bright green Ginny had so admired gained that hue from vitriol baths in copper vats, which sickened diners in medium doses, and killed when overeaten. Oysters, fresh only in February, carried the dreaded typhoid.

But Caro's great passion was food and the wealthy consumers it attracted, so her inn was healthier than most. She kept a well-stocked fish pond in the custom of the old medieval manor, and her courtyard clucked and cackled with geese, capons, and pheasants. She had beds of asparagus and onions laid in because they were cheap, plentiful, and added sharp flavor to food. With Ginny's craving for vegetables at a peak, Caro even had the hostler put potatoes in the root cellar, though she regarded the eating of them with suspicion, as that simply wasn't "done" by Londoners.

It was obvious to Caro after her years of mistressing at the inn that milk was not all it should be, so she never used it unless she boiled it first, which destroyed the taste along with the germs. Oysters and eels she laid on in force during her special dinners for special patrons, and if one or two guests never returned, well, old men often died after a surfeit of seafood, and no one paid any mind.

Ginny observed and learned. Her first lesson was not to ask

questions. Caro had good reasons for things that seemed whimsy at first glance, and she was not accustomed to being crossed. For all her bulk, Caro had an innate love of fripperies, and new trinkets and fine bolts of fabric had a way of simply showing up at the inn. With eyes and ears opened but lips firmly sealed, Ginny watched as mysterious bands of men arrived with dark-draped wagons in the night. They dressed better than average laborers, but their garb seemed tawdry imitations of what the aristocrats wore; they swore, fought, and drank a good deal, and their hair color was seldom the same two trips running. Not to mention their names.

Ginny would nod knowingly to herself as she slipped back to her pallet. So Caro aided smugglers and an occasional highway-man, especially that good-looking Jemmy St. James, already called "King of the Highwaymen." Ginny's morals didn't allow her to disapprove of the working class trying to beat King George II's brutally high tariffs, so she turned a blind eye to the noctur-nal goings-on. Smuggling meant bricks of real black tea, undi-luted by twigs and leaves or sawdust. It brought the inn sugar loaves and delicate chinoiserie, duty-free. Caro had new sheets of jacquard-weave Venetian silk, thick and soft, still smelling of the mulberry bushes that had spawned them. She had enameled glassware from Florence, crystal goblets from Bavaria, kitchen knives from Toledo, leather stuffs from Morocco and Portugal.

Caro resold many things when she tired of them. This year with the extra money she had a cold-water tap installed in the kitchen and then put in a rarely dependable flush mechanism in the "jakes" at the rear of the inn. All it did was empty an over-head cistern into the padded chair with its built-in chamberpot, but lady guests billed and cooed about how chic it was. So Caro kept the porters and chambermaids running up and down the back stairs with buckets of water so that the ladies might say they had used the fancy contraption.

After its unlikely success there was no stopping Caro, Ginny observed with a grin. Caro had a fancier, more thickly padded seat put on the stool and added another water closet on the upper story for her whores and their customers. At last she had to hire a boy whose sole purpose was to run water up and down the stairs for both water closets. At the end of two months he had the biceps of a prizefighter and the disposition of a crocodile. When he vanished one day, Caro had to hire twins to replace him.

Ginny worked as a chambermaid until her pregnancy was impossible to hide, even in the secondhand Watteau gown Caro had found her at an auction. Kings' mistresses had discovered the style's loose pleats allowed them to appear in public while pregnant without showing hugely, and the average woman, whose life was a cycle of births and miscarriages, found the style useful, too. This particular gown was much-mended and altered, with the gleam worn off the glazed cotton, but its pale mauve roses were still visible, and the deep, round neckline flattered Ginny.

No one thought anything of her wearing a dress several decades out of date. Servants always took up their masters' discarded, outmoded clothing and wore them till nothing waited but the rag pile.

Ginny was working in the kitchen when Caro returned from her latest London estate auction triumphantly carrying still more used treasures, a hamper full of dresses of a disagreeable brown hue. She at once ordered One-Eyed Jack, who doubled as a blacksmith, to stoke up his fire, and he obeyed with an expectant gleam in his eye. "Did you buy them rags just to burn 'em, missus?" Becka asked.

"Yes, I did. My mother's granny once told me about her granny's granny having cloth-of-gold dresses in the olden days. About how they reversed the gown inside out when the right side was too worn, like we do now. The difference was," Caro said, watching the fire, "that once *that* side was worn, too, they didn't make rags of cloth-of-gold gowns. Oh, no. They burned them up, melted them down to the gold alone. Come on, Jack, stoke that fire!"

All tasks were dropped at the inn while everyone from the water boys to Cook stood with folded arms, waiting to witness this miracle. "Whot'll ye do wi' the gold, mistress?" someone asked.

Caro rubbed her soft hands together. "Have a bull- or bear-baiting pit put in the courtyard. We already have girls and cards and liquor, so why let the customers go elsewhere for bull- and bear-baiting? I'll get me a fine big bull with horns long as your arms and a golden nose ring, and we'll have folks bring their fiercest dogs to take on the bull. I love a good bull-baiting."

So did the others, and they cheered accordingly. It was not considered cruel to set a pack of savage dogs on a chained bull or bear. There were also traveling prizefighters who challenged the village strongman wherever they went—and Caro was thinking she would like those at her inn, too.

"Where'll you put the bullpit? In the courtyard?" Ginny asked, coming from the kitchen and wiping her hands on the towel that served as an apron.

Caro chewed her lower lip. In that courtyard were the gardens and fowl, all of which would have to be moved. "I can't think where *else* to put the pit," Caro said thoughtfully. "I wonder, could we move the fish pond without too great an effort? Or maybe we should leave that where it is, only cover it when baiting's going on . . . One-Eyed Jack, how's my gold coming along?"

He tapped the fire down and peered into it. Everyone waited with pounding hearts to see the riches with which Caro would build the pit.

Jack shattered the mood. "Missus! It ain't but brass!"

"What?" Caro cried, pushing past the blanched man. There was a stunned pause from the circle of observers upon viewing the embers of Caro's dream, then her pretty face split into a grin. She threw her head back for a brave laugh that made Ginny's heart ache with feeling. "Took for a fool again! Well, lads and lasses, the bull-baiting has to wait a while, eh? But there'll be a good black pudding at dinner if we ask Cook nicely, I wager. Now we must all get back to work and buy a bull another day. Come along, come along."

A fine berlin coach with a handsomely liveried footman was pulling up at the arched carriage entrance. Caro whipped off her apron and the towel Ginny wore as one. Then she signaled for her strongest porter. "God's own eyebrows, move along! We have guests, and filthy rich buggers they are, from the looks of that carriage! Look at the bullion braid on that so-proud footman! And have you ever seen such lacquerwork on the doors?" she asked as they walked.

She bellowed for Becka to spring upstairs and air the best rooms, then launched Ginny along with an elbow.

A man of not quite forty popped out of the berlin as the footman opened the door. Ginny gaped at the elegant green greatcoat, crusty with silver embroidery and dozens of cloisonné buttons. The waistcoat, as per the fashion, was even finer, for it took less material. This one was embroidered all over with Chinese birds of yellow and scarlet on turquoise, the buttons eyed with diamonds the size of peas.

The man's fashionably powdered hair was waved and drawn back into a black silk bag fastened around his neck with a bow— a current fad from the Continent. He had a long, aristocratic nose and amused eyes; Ginny thought his smile honest and mischievous. His knee breeches were elegantly tailored, the double rows of buttons down each silk leg dazzling, and the stockings and shoes—what kind of money this man must have to dress so well!

"Bless my soul, Mistress Caroline," he called out warmly, "is this formal parade the way you greet an old friend?" He had an accent; German, Ginny was to discover later.

"Why, Your Lordship, I haven't seen you in more months than a king has mistresses!" Caro answered. Then, to Ginny's consternation, her unshakable sister-in-law curtsied and dimpled, blushing pink as a virgin bride. What! Caro acting like a schoolgirl? How strange!

"Caro, you are a treat for my eyes as always," he told her. "My friends and I are on official—well, *semi*official—business." His eyes twinkled. "We will be needing some entertainment. Do you still have that temperamental redhead and those two sisters from France? I . . ."

For the first time he took note of Ginny. He swept his hat off and bowed, leaving her no choice but to ape Caro's curtsy. Hers was pathetic, a clumsy mockery of Caro's grace, for Ginny had never curtsied before. She was instantly ashamed of herself.

25

"Caro, my sweet, who is this lily-skinned charmer, this blue-eyed vision of fecundity?"

Caro tartly responded, "She's my dead husband's dead brother's wife, and you'll not be trifling with an honest widow like her. Not over my dead body. Ginny's respectable, not like my girls upstairs. I won't even let her near those hussies."

"More's the pity," he observed dolefully.

His two companions came climbing out of the berlin. "Why, damn me eyes if she isn't a fetching little thing, belly and all," one said frankly, as though appraising a mare on market day. "A bit long-faced for my liking, but skin like fresh country cream! I don't suppose that yellow hair is real, is it?"

"You tug it and see if it isn't," Ginny defended hotly. "I may be a green country girl, but I know all about dyed-haired women and, lord or no, ye won't be a-calling me one o' them!"

When she saw that the lords were laughing and unoffended, Caro ventured a laugh as well, then ordered Ginny inside. "Mind you put out the special sheets and washbasins from Germany and help Becka with the windows. Then get yourself out of their rooms. These gentlemen keep fast company, and you'd lose your virtue sure as you're born, belly or no. They're rich, and His Lordship's an old customer, so if you do see them, don't sass back again! Now hurry! I'll keep them in the taproom a while!"

Ginny went in a welter of resentment and ego. She'd never been openly admired before, nor had anyone talked about her in *front* of her, as if she had no feelings or were some poor milk cow too dumb to understand.

She was not so simple that she didn't know what dangers lay in an upper-class man's roving eye. At least she was not hot-blooded like Becka, and tempted toward the pleasures of the flesh. No, not her. Not until she married again would she have to deal with such foolishness.

She had suspected early on the real reason Caro kept her in the kitchen so much: an inn wench was considered easy to buy for an hour or more, and all the other girls had been here a good long while. Hers was the newest, freshest face at the Black Bull, and it

26

made her a desirable commodity. So Caro was riding patrol on her, knowing Ginny's experience with men to be minute.

Once in a while Ginny wished she were the sinful kind.

Caro kept her tucked away in the kitchen all that weekend and hardly let her out, even for bed, until the berlin and its passengers had rolled away in a cloud of dry, gray dust.

A few minutes later the redheaded whore came downstairs, blasting away in her broad Glasgow accent at Ginny and finally boxing her ears.

"It's not me fault he talked about me blue eyes, bitch!" Ginny shouted back at her and, seizing Cook's big wooden ladle, basted the redhead all the way into the taproom. This caused a welcome stir among the regulars, as the redhead was wearing her stays, two petticoats, and nothing else. A gamester cried, "Two quid on the blond!" and the fight was on.

The redhead was soft from her pampered existence, with men her only exercise, while Ginny had been toting water and tubs of food, fetching valises when the porter was busy, and going up and down the stairs dozens of times a day. And before that she had spent seven years plowing Scotland's rockiest, most unproductive soil.

The redhead fought showily, screeching and flailing with her bare breasts bouncing, but it was no contest. Ginny wrestled her down, threw her over her knee, and administered a fast ten whacks with a hat someone offered her. Then she stood abruptly, dumping eight stone of enraged strumpet on the floor. She dusted her hands. "Now don't bother me nae more, ye giddy bitch! I don't want your customers—*I* work on me damned *feet!*"

The gamester made twelve quid on Ginny and frequently set the redhead on her with wild tales just to make more betting money.

That was the only excitement Ginny knew for a while, barring a brief grease fire in the kitchen, which livened things up for a good quarter of an hour. Ginny was sorry when it ended and she had to go back to baking, kneading, slicing, frying, and roasting.

One rainy night, seven months' growth of child between her and the chopping block, she thought: *Should I ever leave Caro to*

27

marry a glutton, I'm set for life. But till then me feet are aching and me back is shrieking from bending over the sink! I'll swear I've carried this son of mine a thousand years—no girl child would be so contrary as to kick all night long and lie silent all the day when I'm up, anyway!

She leaned against the table—actually a board on trestles—and kicked her shoes off. There, the bread was ready to sit and rise for a while. She'd have to watch the clock and make sure she didn't let it go too long.

Ginny was rinsing her hands in the tin sink when the garden door to the kitchen flew open with a resounding bang. A cloaked and muffled figure entered, shaking himself not unlike a big wet dog. Raindrops flew everywhere.

"If you've a message for Caro, she's up the road with her beau seeing some actors butcher a play by Mr. Shakespeare," Ginny said dryly, for she'd seen the play last night and was certain it had been better originally. "Or if you're a thief looking for the strongbox, I havna any idea where she keeps it!"

"Bless my buttons," he answered merrily in German-accented English as he unwound his muffler. "It's Caro's sister-in-law! How are you doing, little mother?"

He dropped the scarf and hat to reveal his neatly waved hair tied back in a bag-and-bow. Ginny recognized the long nose, merry eyes, and pendulous lower lip of Caro's favorite customer, His Lordship.

Ginny dropped a hasty curtsy—she'd been practicing, with Becka's help—and got back up without ripping her hem for once. "Why Sir, I dinna—I mean, I *did not* recognize ye—er, *you*, I—whyfore are you sneaking in the rear door like a thief in the night?"

He laughed. "I don't wish to track in all over Caro's hooked rugs and those parquetry floors you girls keep so clean and polished. When's the child due?"

Ginny gasped. Men had never spoken of noticing her condition before. It was something polite folk didn't mention. "Oh, come now," he said patiently. "When?"

"Near Christmas, I think, though he feels big for a seven-month child," she answered, feeling as though she confessed to a friend.

"Your husband's?" he asked mildly.

"Your Lordship! There's been nae ither!" she exclaimed hotly, reverting back to her native accent.

He had struggled out of his wet overclothes by now and was laying them out on a bench. "No insult meant, my good woman. I come from a frank family, that's all. My word, you are a fetching thing, *enceinte* or not! You should have a man to protect those trim ankles and long blue eyes! A pity to waste those slender hands and golden locks in the heat and stench of this kitchen. You probably have calluses by now from scrubbing floors on your hands and knees. . . ." He looked her up and down. "Hope for a boy, do you? You're certainly carrying him low."

She blushed, but he cheerfully continued, "Here, here, don't be so bashful! I have children myself, been married some years now to a sweet, gawky thing. She might have been pretty before small-pox pitted her skin, but it happened all the same and made her more timid than she would have been. But for all that, she's a good-natured wife, and I've been there when each of the children came! At this rate I'll have as many brats as you have eyelashes, so there! Now then, do you wish for a boy child?"

"Sir! Everyone wants a son," Ginny replied, delightfully scandalized.

"So they do," he admitted, looking thoughtful—perhaps even sad, she thought. "But my parents are sorry they had *me,* their eagerly awaited son and heir who turned out to be not much of a chip off the old block after all. It peeved them no end." He looked up from his reverie and added brightly, "My sole regret is that I wasn't born twins so I could plague them twice as much!"

Cook came bustling back in before he could admit any more private feelings. Ginny found herself liking this frank, unpretentious man whose clothes were much stuffier than he could ever be.

"Sir!" Cook said. "Why, what a surprise! The redhead isn't busy, if that's of interest to Your August Self, and there's some new French brandy laid down in the taproom."

He bowed to her with gratitude and started out. Halfway through the doorway, he winked back over his shoulder at Ginny. "Boys are naught but grief, as my parents always say to me but *never* to my brother William! If you have a girl I'll bring her a dowry chest and stand as godfather, but I won't lift a finger for a boy. Be a pity if you didn't pass those long, unfashionably slim golden looks on down to a daughter! Godfather, remember! No one else!"

And he went out, leaving bonhomie floating in the air with the scent of baking bread and his shaving tonic.

"You can always tell a gentleman by his cologne, me father told me," Cook said, "and there goes proof. He smells like fifty quid the ounce! Fancy His Nibs taking such an interest in you! He's good as his word, you know, I s'pect he truly will see you churched and all with a girl child. Imagine him flattering you so, and you big as a wagon and him no more mindful of it than a courting boy!"

"He's not courting me, Cook," Ginny answered. "He's just being gallant because he knows I'm sad having a baby alone."

"You could do worse than him, once you have that baby," Cook said knowingly.

And so the seed of temptation was planted.

CHAPTER FOUR

Caro cleared enough money that autumn to put in a bear pit, anyway, cloth of gold or no.

Bruin was arriving by four-horse van from Pontypridd, where his mother had belonged to a traveling show. He had grown too large to control and could no longer be taught tricks, so the owner was glad to part with him. "They say he's a great strapping one—and vicious, by God's teeth," Caro told Ginny that evening. "So now mind you don't go watching the bear-baiting before that child's born. Why, if you see Bruin lop off a hound's ear, it's most likely the babe will be born earless, so quick, say a prayer! I'm off to fetch my bear now."

Ginny nodded. "My mother's cousin ate too many strawberries and had a son with a birthmark the size of a strawberry on his neck, so I'll take no chance. Have a fine trip now, you and the others."

Ginny stood in the doorway, waving good-bye. Because business was seasonally slow, most of the staff was tagging along, on horseback and on foot. She sighed for the dullness of being left alone, but someone had to watch the inn, and she was certainly in no state to travel. Not this big, and a scant month shy of dropping the child. One-Eyed Jack was here, but he slept on bales of hay in the stable loft, snoring to the nesting pigeons in the rafters. He would have to serve as hostler and porter both if there was any business, for Ginny's stomach had her so off-balance she could not lift anything.

With my luck, she thought, blowing out the kitchen lamp, *a party of twelve will arrive, each wanting a hot bath and fresh linen!*

At that moment, in the dark kitchen, air redolent with candied violets and glazed ham from the evening meal, Ginny felt her first pain. All at once the sweet scents were replaced by those of burned bread crusts and congealing fat. Never mind that she had happily sopped her crusts in that very fat two hours ago; she retched now, felt herself sicken.

Women were supposed to time the pains, but Ginny couldn't find Cook's sand-glass or clock in the dark. She hesitated, wanting to climb the stairs to the garret and give birth on her soft old pallet, but suppose guests arrived? Or thieves came to steal Caro blind while the house was unguarded? By God, if she loitered she might drop the child on the flagstone floor right here, like a mare foaling!

Caro had borrowed birthing sheets for her from the woman up the road, but where were they now? Ugly things, stiff and streaked with red-brown, they were beyond use as actual sleeping sheets, except for the first days after birth. And so they were loaned from woman to woman as needed.

Where would Caro have put the awful things? In the linen cabinet? The bottom of her walnut wardrobe? Ginny searched both places to no avail. She was rummaging about when she bumped an expensive goblet off a shelf and miserably watched it dash itself to slivers on the floor.

Last time she'd given birth, Jock had run to fetch one of the old maiden ladies up the road—one of those the Duke of Cumberland burned out of her house after the battle at Culloden Moor. The poor old dear had fainted the moment she saw Ginny lying there with her skirts up and knees apart. Ginny'd had to get Jock to help, him with his great clumsy hands. "It's no different than a mare or ewe, Jockie, and you've helped them lots!" she'd cried to no avail.

So she'd done it all herself in the end, right up to tying off the cord and pumping down on her abdomen to make the afterbirth come out. *Thank the Good Lord for being raised a farmer's daughter!* Ginny thought now, giving up on locating the birthing sheets.

The moon was up now, throwing a globe of silver light with blue bruises like cruel fingermarks onto the surface of Caro's mirror. *A full moon for my son,* Ginny thought. *First night of the full moon. It's an extra good sign if he's born afore midnight and the witching hours.*

Without warning her water broke, drenching her skirts. She groaned aloud. This was her only gown, and she'd ruin it in birthing if she didn't hurry. Ginny scuttled to the main door of the inn, straining her eyes and peering into the damp blackness to see if any of the inn folk were returning yet. One-Eyed Jack would be no help; men never were at a time like this. Like as not he was dead-drunk, too, in the hayloft.

She tripped over him. Jack, faithful to the fearsome Caro's orders, was sleeping on the stoop. What was that he hugged to his chest like a pirate's cask of jewels? Rum! A little round-bellied wooden barrel of rum. He was snoring to wake the dead, and shake him though she may, he didn't budge.

Ginny put her hands over her eyes for a moment, then stepped back inside, loosening her gown and stays. *Big as a barrel, I am. I should have guessed Jock got the child on me in March, not April.*

She couldn't make the stairs. The pains were too close together now. It hadn't hurt like this with Little Jock or the girls she'd had, stillborn. Suppose something was wrong, terribly wrong? For so many months she'd been brave; all of her life she'd been staunch, dry-eyed; now, alone in the dark and afraid Jock's new son was dead or dying, she clung to the newel post and wept.

Then her usual good sense returned. *Get out of the gown, fast, before it's beyond salvaging,* a voice seemed to tell her. Ginny did so, stepping on the skirts and tearing them as she struggled out of the fabric that was weakened with age. Her heavy, wool-linen shift was clammy and uncomfortable from the thighs down. She wished she could take that off, too, but the inn was too cold. There were no fires lit tonight, for Caro had no wood to waste on empty rooms with no guests.

Ginny knelt on the floor, her head on the lowest stair. She fumbled for the brass cuspidor, found it, vomited into it, and immediately felt better. When she lifted her throbbing head, she saw through the long windows that the rain had become sleet, spangling the trees like the silver backing of a looking glass . . .

33

One-Eyed Jack. She should drag Jack inside so he didn't catch his death out there—but Dear God, it was hurting so! She couldn't breathe, couldn't think, and now that her eyes were full of tears, she could hardly see. The pains—

"Halloa," said a familiar voice in the front hall. There was a clattering and thudding; she looked up to see One-Eyed Jack being dragged inside by the armpits. A brass lamp came flaring to life nearby.

"Your Lordship," she acknowledged, and let her head waft back down to the chill comfort of the stair.

"Great Christ, Virginia, what are you doing alone and like this?"

"The bear," she said, and groaned. "No business, so they—they've all gone to fetch Caro's Bruin for the bear-baiting pit. I—uhh—I counted wrong, the baby's not coming in a month, he's—uhh—he's coming any minute!"

"I'll fetch you into Caro's room," he offered kindly, kicking the outer doors shut and throwing his greatcoat over Jack, who was prone and still snoring.

"No!" Ginny wailed. "You mustn't! Her silk sheets—I'll ruin them—"

"*Hang* Caro's sheets, *liebchen,* I'm not dragging a woman and a half up three flights of stairs so she gives birth in my lap! I'll buy Caro new and better sheets!" he said with a laugh, stooping to lift her.

He located Caro's chamber by trial and error and laid Ginny down inside on the silk-covered bed. "Sometimes women are quick as the devil with this thing, and sometimes they're all day and night at it. But don't fear, you're a strong young thing, and for you it shouldn't take over an hour, mark my words!"

He covered Ginny with Caro's most expensive comforter. "That's nice," she said weakly, glad for the strong hand he let her hold on to.

He smiled, stroked her damp hair back from her forehead. "You've never lain on anything this nice, have you? Never had silks or a fine bedstead or waxy tapers in wall sconces giving off

34

the scent of bayberries in bloom. Pretty Ginny, to have had so little luxury!"

Pain after pain gripped her. But she was determined to appear lucid to this dear stranger, and she forced herself to speak. "Don't you worry, Your Lordship, I've done this alone before, and I can certainly do it again. Now if—uhh!—if you'll just go to the taproom and have a brandy—"

She gazed at him in horror. He had removed his waistcoat and was rolling his elegant *charmeuse* sleeves up. "My dear young lady, I have no intention of leaving you alone to bite bravely through your lower lip. I'll have you know I was some assistance at my eldest daughter's birth," he said, bringing Caro's Turkish towels out of the wardrobe. "I'll put a kettle on to boil and be right back."

He did and was. The pains were on top of each other now. When he put a hand out, Ginny clung to it as though to a lifeline. How good he was, how patient and kind and, in his own German way, good-looking—almost handsome, though not tall. Few good-looking men bothered with such kindness, Ginny knew.

"Stop being brave, madame," he told her. "Kick and shriek up a storm. I swear and shout if I so much as stub my toe—*any* man does!—but tell a woman it's birthing time and she muffles her cries in her own shoulder rather than let out one fine, healthy holler! Why, do you know when my wife was having our first child, my parents insisted on being present!"

"What!" Ginny asked, interest pricking her to alertness despite the pain and fear.

"Yes, they wanted to be certain that a son would truly be mine, you know, and not an impostor to be passed off as their—and my —heir. But I was determined to fool them, and I whisked poor Augusta away after dinner."

He slapped his thigh with the laughter of remembering. "So there she was, nine months gone with the girl and kicking me under the dining table to tell me in secret that it was time! We slipped out separately, met in the solarium room. 'Let's away!' I cried.

"Then my old dancing master sticks his head in, overhears,

and says there must be witnesses so my hateful parents can't claim the child was smuggled in inside a warming pan! Why, by the time we had made it into the coach we had two lords, a lady, the dancing master, and a charwoman bundled into the coach with us, and dear Augusta out to here with contractions leaping and rippling . . ."

Unnoticed by Ginny, he was making certain that her heartbeat was all right with his fingers so casually dropped on her wrist, and he watched the movements of her abdomen, too. Ginny swallowed dryly, convulsively, and croaked, "What happened?"

"Augusta gave birth on a tabletop with the cloth on it, there being no sheets quickly available at the friends' house we drove to, and the child was a tiny girl after all, not the longed-for heir. She was so little and hairlessly ugly that only her parents loved her. Of course, we have sons now to inherit, but I like my daughters best of—"

He broke off, seeing her anxiety. "This is it, Ginny, *liebchen!* This is it! There now, don't fight it! You're panting, that's good, work hard for that child—yes, yes, let's draw back the comforter, get your shift out of the way—pardon my indelicacy here, my dear—oh, yes, he's coming along, he's coming along. Don't be so coy, you can't give birth with your knees together! You're a farm girl with more sense than that, and I've seen ladies' bottoms before! Come on, come on, *liebchen*—that's it, that's it, here he comes—no, a girl! I've got her, I've—Drat me, I've let the water in the kitchen boil over!"

CHAPTER FIVE

Viveca Lindstrom was born just after midnight. The towering grandfather clock, waxed and oiled pride of Caro's hedonistic life, was scarcely through chiming before there followed the lusty cries of a newborn child.

Her hair—the one entire wisp of it—and tightly screwed-up eyes were both so dark at first as to appear black, though both would lighten in time. Nevertheless, Ginny took her first exhausted look and said, "Heavens, she looks as though a blackamoor got her on me!"

Caro, Bruin, and company returned home to find mother and daughter comfortably bedded down, and His Lordship sweeping the taproom. The noise of them entering the inn startled everyone: Ginny woke with an exclamation, Viveca screamed, the bear roared outside, and the inn's horses, scenting Bruin, went wild in the stables. "You were born the night they brought the bear home," Ginny would tell Viveca as a bedtime story, and that was all the little girl remembered for a long time about the tale.

His Lordship paid Caro handsomely for the sheets and even promised to bring her better ones. Caro began to argue, then thought the better of it. Anyone could see His Lordship was smitten with bonny Ginny. Perhaps something would come of it, now that this obstacle—she glanced over her shoulder at the squalling Viveca—was born.

"You'll take care of her for me?" he asked Caro, raising one eyebrow.

Caro led him outside of her bedchamber, leaving Ginny and daughter to the admiration of Becka and the taproom girls. "If you'll take her away someday. She's a good girl but green, and I don't know how'd you would convince her 'twas all right, though she's a great deal less easily shocked than when she first arrived at the Black Bull. I think she can be won over, though she's not much for the attentions of men, do you take my meaning? Her husband, my Geordie's Jock, does not seem to have been—let us speak frankly, sir—he appears to have been no lover. Didn't stir her . . . finer instincts."

He threw back his head and laughed. She was more delicate than most in her wording; a woman from Court would have said, "He rolled on and off, and the girl didn't get a damned thing out of it!"

Caro raised an eyebrow at His Lordship. "You be good to the girl. She's my own sister-in-law," she *harumph*ed, as though already reprimanding him for imagined wrongs done Ginny.

He rolled his stained shirt sleeves down, arching one fair eyebrow. "You're still presupposing the lass will go with me."

"She'd be daft not to, next time you come back," Caro said with a guffaw as she threw him his coat.

Ginny hefted Viveca up on her hip and set down her mop, giving Caro her full attention. "A new dress? What do I owe you? You know I need a gown; I've worn this one to a frazzle, but I'll not have you giving me charity."

Caro gestured her into a chair, pushing her ledgers to one side. "I'll have naught for it. It came by mistake with some gowns for the whores and wasn't mentioned on their bills, so I seized it for you. They'll never know, and it's made for your coloring. Hush now, if they hear we've pulled one over on them, there'll be hell to pay!"

The gown Caro took out of her wardrobe was of glazed Indian cotton and was not new, though to Ginny it seemed a thing from a fairy story. Its color was a soft mauve, perfect for her northern fairness. The gown itself was only ten years out of style, with the pleated back that, though derived from the so-called Watteau gown, was much closer-fitting. It lacked a fichu to cover the tops of the shoulders and breasts, but perhaps, Caro mused, that was all for the better where His Lordship was concerned.

"Of course, Ginny, we'll have to rip the lace apron off and raise the bodice enough to make it decent, but not *too* decent. We'll let the hem down for you and put a frill on those sleeves . . . take the bosom up a wee bit, or every rake who comes in the place will be snatching at your skirts. We'll tell the whores that someone left it behind and I made you buy it off me."

Ginny was hardly able to keep eyes and hands off the slick, polished cotton. "I don't have my figure quite back yet from birthing, so let's wait a few weeks on altering it. I need to keep toting and scrubbing so I don't go all soft like most new mothers. And then—oh, Caro, it's lovely!"

" 'Tis glad I am that it pleases you so. Get along now, I have my ledgers to sweat over, and by the way, congratulations about Dulcie's new foal. Pretty little thing."

Ginny smiled. "I hope she grows to be fast; it's in her blood, and I could get more money for her that way."

Thanking Caro profusely, she set off down the hall with Viveca on one arm and the dress on the other. *Good old Caro*, she thought, and then, with a flash of sadness, *Good old Dulcie, too. I'd hate to sell her.*

She didn't want to sell the new filly, either, but supposed she would have to. It cost so much money to keep a horse in grain over the winter . . . but wouldn't she love to keep both horses and breed them to some fine, strong Irish hunter or a Barb stallion! Barbs were worth a lot, and so were the half-Barbs. *And someday,* she thought, climbing the stairs, *maybe I'd make enough off the foals to have a little cottage with some geese in the yard and a few vegetables in back . . . a pond for a few fish . . .*

There was so much she missed from her old life, she realized. Her house had been poor, but it had been her own, with carefully bleached and mended sheets rinsed in the rose water she distilled early each autumn. Her dented old silverplate . . . the Turkish carpet . . .

The redhead passed on the arm of a fancily dressed rake. The two women glared at each other, the rake obviously appraising Ginny. Noting that, the redhead hurried him on upstairs. *Now there goes a woman who knows how to make money,* Ginny thought irritably. *She'll get her own cottage soon enough, I'll wager.*

A seductive voice inside her whispered: *You could, too, with a lot less work. What about His Lordship?*

Startled, Ginny glanced about to see who had said that, before realizing it hadn't been spoken aloud at all. This must be what they call the voice of the devil. *Look,* she mentally told the "devil," *I'm not the floozy sort, I'm a respectable widow—and anyway, I'm twenty-three, past my prime, my waist must be twenty inches by now! And I don't know how to paint my face or talk bawdy or throw exciting glances at a man so as he melts in his jackboots—*

You don't need to do that, her devil answered. *Just see what Caro's done with her old curling iron—lace yourself tight into that pink gown—*

"I'd be too ashamed," Ginny whispered, stopping on the stair landing.

Ashamed of your own cottage and brood mares with a few geese cackling in the yard? her "devil" scoffed. *Think about it, Ginny, just—think about it.*

CHAPTER SIX

Becka giggled and rolled her eyes. "Ginny, first you saved up your coppers to buy Caro's second-best curling iron. Then you cut that lank hair of yours up to your shoulders because you saw the ladies who come here curling up their hair. Then you got that pink dress from Caro, and *now* you're asking me about *men!* Ginny Lindstrom, you prude, if I didn't know better, I'd think you were getting restless!"

Ginny shifted on her dusty, straw-stuffed pallet. She knew the pallet chafed Viveca's tender skin, so she had made her daughter a nest of the old Watteau gown and had to be content with giving her that one small comfort. She tucked the sleeping child closer to her and said, "Yes, Becka, I've gotten restless, all right, for a little privacy and a few of the old things I once had—a home, for one. But as for men . . . well, I miss Jock to talk to and warm me feet on, but the rest—"

"You goose," Becka scoffed. "You talk like we had it rough at the Black Bull! Why, I've served places where the mistress beat me with a razor strap! Caro works us hard, but as she'd say— 'God's shroud!' She doesn't abuse us! If you want out of inn life you'll have to settle for sharing a shack with a sailor who's home every third year to plant another child in you. Or mayhaps some lord wi' a roving eye'll put you in his kitchens for his wife to hurl ladles at. Or mayhaps some poor, half-witted country reuben will take on an inn girl, with her bad repute, and take her home to his sows and one chicken."

"I'm damned well at home with pigs and chickens," Ginny answered tartly. "It doesn't sound half-bad to me. Except for putting up with—*you know.*"

41

"Jock must have been poor stuff on a mattress for you to feel this way," Becka said with a low whistle.

"Here, you two, clam up tight," said a drowsy neighbor.

Ginny waited a full minute before bursting out in a whisper, "Becka. You speak like there might be something *good* in all that male giddiness."

Becka stuck her head out from under the feed sack full of rags and straw that she used for a pillow. "Cor! You are the most innocent thing I ever . . . If you were Jock's first, then I don't expect as how'd he'd be the be-all and end-all of lovers. But if you get one what's been around—why, it can be quite a lark!" She made a shivering sound in the night.

Ginny answered frankly, "It's His Lordship I'm thinking about trying to—attract."

"No sooner said than done, ducky," flipped back Becka, who admired such ambition. "He's had goggle eyes for you all along, wi' his tongue fair draggin' the ground, even what with you full of Viveca!"

"He hasn't been back in months, though."

"Rumor is he's written Caro asking about you."

That was certainly news. Ginny gnawed her lip lightly.

Two pallets down, someone fussed, then drifted back to sleep. At last Becka whispered, softer now, "You wink and wiggle your hips at His Lordship and keep smiling, no matter if his wooing puts you to sleep, because that man has coppers a-plenty to pour into your hands. Maybe he'll set you up in a London house! Think of it, Ginny—a house in town and new dresses for you and Viveca! Now get some sleep!"

Ginny was still thinking about it long after Becka was peacefully snoring.

It was a bright, brisk, late winter night when His Lordship returned to the Black Bull.

What a night, Ginny told herself, descending the stairs to the main hall. She'd tucked in two ladies, their maidservant, hairdresser, and wardrobe mistress, helped the boy fetch buckets of steaming water for baths, then carried the water back down to empty the hip bath. She'd brought up tray after tray of steamed puddings, cold capons, biscuits, and three French wines, including a bottle dated 1699 and smelling faintly of ginger.

Now that all of *that* was over, Ginny thought wearily, she could go out into the courtyard and watch the bear-baiting with the rest of the staff. Most of the snow had been swept away, the rest trampled flat, so her threadbare slippers wouldn't let in too much moisture.

She picked Viveca up out of her playpen-crate. "So you're no longer a blackamoor's baby! Those eyes are as dark blue as a sailor's jacket, and I'm suspecting they'll stay that way. I'm glad your hair's finally gone a pretty strawberry-blond, like you da's. Come on, ducky," Ginny said, and then groaned. "Mama's about to scream with rich guests and talking baby talk to you! Let's go out. You'll like the noise, you always do. There'll be a great hairy bear to shriek at and handsome gentlemen to coo over your yellow curls."

It was the last baiting of the day for the rakes and third-floor whores who trickled downstairs after dark, dotting the gaming tables and taproom with tawdry splashes of color; there would be squabbles and flirting to watch from a safe distance.

Ginny passed on into the kitchen and spotted a heavy plaid of Cook's hanging on a nail by the door. She wrapped it around and around herself and Viveca, remembering how the men of Scotland had folded it here, belted it there, to make a combination kilt-cape. That had been Jock's call to battle with bonny Prince Charlie: "Jock, mon, fetch yaur musket and plaid, we're off tae waer!"

No time to think about that now. Mustn't brood. With a sad smile she carried Viveca outside. *Why, it looks like some pagan ritual out here,* Ginny thought, catching the excitement of the crowd. Her heart hammered against her ribs as though for release. This was the kind of night things *happened* on. Vows would be made and shattered in the heat of passion, money lost or won. She was violently glad to be alive tonight, and slid sideways between groups of wagering men, nearing the pit.

The bear was surly and wanted to sleep. But the chamberlain

who had become his handler prodded him from above with a wooden goad, and Bruin exploded into action as the dogs were lowered in with him. He caught one while it was still in the crate, smashed the box to tinder, and tossed the yelping hound seven feet into the air. One swipe of the paw flattened two hounds. Even with his claws removed, his paws were lethal; one dog lay still and did not rise again.

The dog thrown into the air came down on Bruin's back, much to the delight of the onlookers. "Hoy, hoy, that's it, Freckles! On, Spotty-Dog! Worry the bastid!"

"Another fiver says Bruin'll take one more down!"

"Toasted chestnuts! Get 'cher toasted chestnuts and hot potatoes right here, right here and now!"

"By Jove, I do believe Bruin shall eat the goad stick!"

Ginny stood on her toes. There was Caro, torchlight dancing off the pure serenity of her della Robbia face and the streaming acre of copper satin she wore. *Peaceful, she looks,* Ginny thought fondly. *Angelic-like.*

The image was shattered when Caro roared like a fishwife, "Tear their knackers off, you great bleedin' brute! Virgin's tears, you milksop—make bitches of 'em, each and ev'ry one!"

Ginny laughed to herself. Caro was never dull. Especially not now that dashing Jemmy St. James, the highwayman, was her steady beau. He was a black-haired young cavalier who wore the most gorgeous jackets Ginny had ever seen.

But they were always sooted with powder burns around the turned-back cuffs, or missing gold braid. His waistcoats were invariably minus a strategic button, and the lace at his cuffs was usually limp with misuse. Like Caro he could not afford things brand-new or tailored especially for him, but unlike her, he did not barter—he stole. Noblemen thought it an honor to give up a coat to Gentleman Jemmy and often insisted even when he did not ask: "Here, now, Jemmy, that red coat's five months out of fashion! You take my new black one. Only let me get my military medals off it first—there's a lad, why, it nigh fits you! A smart coat, I was telling the missus the other day, but doesn't quite suit me. Why, Jemmy, you look quite the toff!"

Jemmy never powdered his raven-hued hair, and Ginny and Caro agreed that it made him all the more handsome. With each visit he brought Caro some madly exotic gift; once it was powdered kohl, that deep gray-black substance Egyptian and Turkish beauties painted their eyes with. But it took Caro weeks to figure out how to use the stuff! A thin stick, hardly more than a wand several hairs wide, was dipped in water, shaken off, then dipped in the kohl, which was then rolled on.

Last time Jemmy brought Caro a bolt of bronze-and-black-striped cloth-of-gold. Caro whispered to Ginny that it would make her look like an emir's tent, so the gorgeous stuff became window and bed curtains, transforming a Georgian boudoir into the Thousand and One Arabian Nights.

In fact, there was Jemmy St. James now, Ginny noticed, riding up on his wild black mare with one of his many younger brothers following. "Caro, my dove," called out the splashily dressed Jemmy, "how is Bruin doing with my last golden sovereign riding on his back?"

The bear roared just then as a hound caught him by the ear and would not let go. Bruin threw his head back, cranked it in circles so that the speckled hound whistled around his shoulders like a dangerous halo. "Oh—there he goes!" someone cried.

Whether the ear or the dog gave first, no one knew. But suddenly the hound went sailing up over the edge of the pit. After a thud he went yowling away into the night and never returned.

Jemmy spurred his horse over to Caro, laughing as the crowd sprang out of his way. His mistress caught him as he swung from the saddle, her glad cry of, "Jemmy! Jemmy, my lad!" swallowed up by the noise.

What a good-looking toff, Ginny thought admiringly, *and he loves her, too. Lucky Caro!* For a moment she wished she had a lover like Jemmy, then there came the sound of horses on the drive.

Damn, she thought. Horses mean travelers and more work!

Hiking her skirts up out of the thin dusting of snow that remained in the swept courtyard, Ginny started off toward the covered archway where the carriage would stop to unload its passengers. Her face broke into a frown of confusion as she walked. She'd seen this heavily shellacked coach before—a fancy berlin coach with dock-tailed horses, each wearing a short red blanket with gold embroidered ostrich plumes above a crown. ICH DIEN, the emblem beneath the crown proclaimed. *I Serve.* Ginny, who did not read German nor indeed any other language, thought only that the horses looked quite smart.

It *was* the same red berlin. Why, His Lordship had come back! She sprang forward to meet him.

"Welcome!" she cried. "Welcome back to the Black Bull, sir!"

The red-liveried footman sprang to open the door. Out popped that slight, familiar form, crisp and coiffed as always. "Hello, little mother. How's the baby blackamoor, my goddaughter?"

"Why, she's got quite fair, see how her hair's lightened! But I'm afraid these eyes shall stay black as pitch," Ginny intoned cheerfully.

His Lordship bent over the proffered baby with a smile. "Why, so she *has* got quite fair, Mistress Lindstrom. She'll be pretty as her mother in time, I do believe! Could someone take her for a few hours this evening? I have a place I want you to see. Will you take a drive with me?"

"The lads have all arrived for my friends," she said mournfully. "I fear I have no one to hold Viveca for me, and I cannot leave her alone to wail in the night. Why, I couldna live with m'self!"

His Lordship, who had never attempted a seduction with an unwitting woman, let alone one who was dragging her baby along, faltered. "Why—all right, then, bring her, shall we, *liebchen?*"

The footman handed both of them into the carriage, then gave Viveca back to Ginny. Viveca was loath to let go, having discovered the footman's fascinating lace cravat and wanting to teethe on it.

Peter, the footman, tucked a heavy sable lap robe around Ginny and the baby—as if, she thought, she were a real lady and not some country girl. Then he stirred up a brazier lit with glowing coals and the subtle scent of ylang-ylang. It was warm and smelled delicious in the closed carriage. And the windows had real glazed panes instead of leather flaps to keep out the cold. The lap of luxury, all right. "I've never ridden in a carriage before," Ginny declared as Peter shut the door and leaped back to his perch at the rear of the berlin. "But I know enough to say 'tis an uncommon fine one, with these padded leather seats. And those are the grandest horses I ever did see. German, aren't they? And the gilt door handles!"

"Brass, not gilt. And the lap robe was inherited. I could never afford sable on my own; my allowance is *quite* inadequate."

His Lordship sat back on the padded cushion and took the merest hint of a pinch of snuff. "I've spent some restless hours wondering if you intend to keep working those pretty fingers to the bone, ruining your fine white skin over kettles of boiling water, splitting knuckles and nails kindling wood and scrubbing floors." He paused a moment, then said more softly. "That's a lovely pink gown beneath that plaid, Virginia. I should like to see more of it when we arrive."

Ginny shivered sensuously, for she now knew the purpose of this drive. She said nothing.

At last they were outside a smart medium-size house with a print shop on the first floor. The house was no longer new, but it was freshly plastered and painted, with an aging lady's air of having known better times and expecting to be treated with according respect.

His Lordship led Ginny up the back stairs by the hand, taking her to the prettily furnished third floor. The walls were hung with Oriental watercolors varnished and stretched on frames, and the chairs, bed, table, and settee were of the new, lightweight Chippendale style with their artfully understated decorations.

To the eye of one who knew, financial restraint was evident about the room, but to Ginny it seemed a palace. The furniture was new, if only middle-class, and the wall hangings old, but they were handsomely arranged. And there were windows and window seats everywhere—*So much room and light, so much space to breathe, to think, to have to oneself,* Ginny thought rapturously, hugging herself.

Peter the footman went at once to stir up the smoldering fire, settling two more logs on it. In the meantime His Lordship pulled off his embroidered kidskin gauntlets and, laying them down on the small table, cocked an eyebrow at Ginny. "You haven't said anything, *liebchen*. Do you like it?"

"Why—it's lovely, of course! Such delicate chairs—I love the watercolor panels; why, a real Turkish carpet, like I had in Scotland. . . ."

She knelt to feel its rich nap, thinned by time but still lush. All at once it came into her head that the carpet was not here by accident. None of this was. She must have told Caro and Becka half a dozen times that she missed her red Turkish carpet and silverplate, and here were two fine pieces of plate on a rack over a red rug.

"This place is yours if you but say the word," His Lordship told her softly.

Though she was expecting similar words, Ginny nearly dropped Viveca, who immediately set up an uproar. Her face flamed crimson as she soothed the child, standing and gently bouncing her. At last she looked up from her daughter's tawny head and boldly asked, "How do you ken you're getting a fair shake? I'm not clever and experienced; I might not be worth all of this."

"You're quick-witted, and you catch on to things without trouble." He snapped his fingers at the silent footman, who had been edging toward the door, awaiting his dismissal. "You have nine of your own, Peter, *do* hold the child for Mistress Ginny."

A shiver ran up Ginny's spine. He was making up her mind for her. "No," she said fiercely. "I may be only a dumb country girl, but I'm no king's court whore. *Ask* me, don't presume I'll say yes. I ain't a lady, but I've got some pride."

She drew herself up to her full height, equal to his, and felt her nostrils flare with indignation.

"I—I apologize. I had thought you understood," His Lordship answered gently. "What may I do to make it up to you?"

Ginny was silent, not sure how to answer.

"Let me speak up, sir," old Peter said cheerfully. He turned to Ginny. "See here, you look to be a good lass, missus."

"I'm a good woman. I only slept with my husband, and I don't want to be treated like some slut out of the alleys."

"His Lordship's all right, he means no harm. I've worked for him since he was knee-high on a carthorse, and there's no evil in the man. He *wants* you, is all. He means to make you an honorable mistress, set up wi' your own household, and even get you a maidservant."

Ginny regarded both of them a while, then clutched sleeping Viveca close. This was her chance. Her start toward that house in the country and her breeding farm. A home of her own for Viveca. And sweet Jesus, but she was lonely for an embrace, a kiss on the ear, fond things said at night, the strength and warmth of her own man holding her close to his heart after a hard day's work. "You won't drop her or let her too near the fire?" she asked Peter thickly.

He took the baby, tucked her under his chin, cooed to her. "Just like me own, ma'am, and I've nigh on two dozen grandchildren b'now, too. We'll be happy together. I like the little ones," he assured her.

At last she held out a shaking hand and, ducking her head, let His Lordship lead her into the bedroom. "You're nervous as a virgin bride," he said quietly, closing the door behind them and lighting the lamp.

Seeing Ginny shrink back, he gently put his arms around her and did nothing but hold her a long while, all the time speaking to her in a low, soothing voice as he might have done a halter-shy filly. Ginny leaned against him, eyes shut against his shoulder, fingers knotted in the fringe of her plaid.

He kissed her forehead. "Has anyone told you that your hair is the color of a fine yellow diamond held up to a daylit window? Or that you have the most appealing little mouth, like a curled rose petal? I've often thought of it, imagined the touch of those lips, like pink velvet. . . . Kiss me, Ginny, I don't bite."

He was lightly caressing the nape of her neck beneath the curls with which Ginny had taken such pains, and all for his sake. It felt good. She hadn't guessed a little caress like this could feel so intimate, so exciting. Just his fingertips on her bare nape . . . She lifted her head, opened her mouth beneath his. He tasted of rare old brandy and experience; she gave herself willingly into his arms.

He was kissing her mouth, her throat, and the tops of her shoulders and breasts over the mauve gown. The plaid fell to the floor, unnoticed. Ginny wrapped herself around him, waking slowly to a need she had not guessed existed within her. She caught herself making tiny purring sounds of new hunger.

She couldn't stop.

His Lordship chuckled, pleased, unhooking her gown and easing it down. He then unfastened her stays and took her breasts in his hands—breasts heavy and full, for she was still nursing Viveca. He lightly kneaded them, stooping to lick and suck her swollen pink-tan nipples as they sprang free of her shift.

Then he was pulling down her many layers of petticoat and gown. He knelt like a servant and helped her out of them, with no class distinction between them. "Now you must help me undress," he told her. "I've done it for you, you must return the favor. There's no hurry, Ginny, don't burst the buttons! We have all evening."

He carried her to the bed when they were both undressed, laid her down, petting delicately with just the tips of his fingers until she grew bolder. Jock had never taken this kind of time with her, using the curve of palms on thighs and ribs, the slow, wet kisses, light licking along her inner arms and the throbbing blue-veined pulse point of her wrist. She was hesitant but not passive in return, finding herself eager to learn.

"It's time you learned a little more," His Lordship suggested, shifting around.

"Oh, *that*. Jock taught me *that*," Ginny answered, not impressed.

"But did he ever do it to *you?*"

"Why, how could he? Women don't have the same—*oh!*"

He had parted her thighs. Now he was licking his way in between them. *Uh oh,* Ginny thought, and dug her nails into the nearest pillow. What was this? She'd never—oh, this luscious, wanton sensation flooding her being—she felt soft and hot all over and steered his hands to her breasts, caressing, kneading . . .

Repetitive flicks of his tongue on the most vulnerable part of her, small tingly feelings that were building layer upon layer. Ginny bit her lip, tossed her head with groans and whimpers. There was an expansion of heat and need in her womb—then a convulsion, as though a sneeze had seized her. It tightened Ginny's muscles, made her cry out with needful kitten sounds of bliss and surprise.

She felt queerly shaken for long moments afterward, as though something old and closeted had finally been released—and here she had never even guessed its existence! As soon as she had collected her wits she pushed the nobleman down to return the favor. In this, at least, he should not find her lacking. She knew how to please with a subtle interplay of lips and fingers.

At last he surprised her by pulling her on top. Ginny struggled a moment, but there came that reassuring voice, telling her it could be done this way, telling her she might even find she liked it better. He directed her, taught her to ride him with slow, lazy thrusts of her hips. Ginny soon learned when to speed up and when to draw out the sensation and savor it; when to ride, and when to kneel, relaxed, and let him move the two of them so that she had no control and was only an unthinking body lost in his maelstrom of feeling.

He buried his face between her breasts, holding her by the waist and whispering how good it was, how long he'd waited. "Had I known before what I know now," Ginny told him breathlessly when they at last lay back, "I would have hurried up and had Viveca sooner so we could get on with this!"

He sat up, gathering their clothes from the floor at their feet. "*Liebchen,* I hate to rush us along this first night, but . . ."

Ginny sucked her breath in and laced her stays back up. "I understand, milord. It's late."

He stepped into his boots with a smile. "You won't find a man more willing to do right by you, Ginny. I'll see to it that you have

51

a woman to teach you needlework and a few of the niceties of dressing and coiffing. I'll stand in stead of your dead parents and see to it that you and any daughters of yours have fine husbands, count on that. But not till I'm through with you. Which is a long time off, *liebchen.*"

He hooked up the back of her gown. "And my sons, milord?" she asked bravely.

"Will be acknowledged as my sons. Now let us go back to Missus Caro and break the news, *nein?* Is there anything you wish of me now?"

He had no fear of her being expensive—her tastes seemed simple enough—but sometimes women went wild and bought things they did not want or need, for the simple thrill of buying. "I'd like another dress before moving in here," Ginny admitted, thinking hard. "I-I'd like to look nice for you, and this one's already shabby about the hem and elbows, as I've been working hard in it. Another gown would be wonderful, so I wouldn't shame you."

"That's it?" he asked incredulously. "One gown? You shall have a dozen, all of silk! And buckled shoes with high heels and silver hairbrushes and a fine walnut cradle hung all over with bells for Viveca. Would you like that, my Ginny?"

"Of course I would!" she answered breathlessly, and threw her arms around his neck in rapture. She was not greedy, but neither was she pious enough to turn gifts down. If he offered, she would accept, by God!

He kissed her passionately. Vividly awake to new sensations, Ginny nearly pulled him back down on the bed.

They finally went out and woke old Peter, who had fallen asleep in a Chippendale chair, Viveca happily tucked into his greatcoat with him. As Ginny took her back, Viveca woke and mewed for food. So Ginny loosened her gown and stays once inside the carriage and modestly nursed her child in the shelter of the lap robe. "A pretty picture," His Lordship observed. "Mother and child, like a madonna."

I'm glad of him, she thought, pleased. *I don't feel all that sinful after all. He's good and kind—and I like him a great deal. Wouldn't it be nice to have a husband like this?*

She bit the inside of her cheek in consternation. No use thinking things like that; his sort didn't marry hers. But what a bonny lover he was, and so thoughtful-like; how could she have ever considered such things a sin? He had taken all that away with his gentle merriment.

Someday, she thought, *someday when I have a cottage and my brood mares, I'd like a man just like him all to myself. How very lucky I am! But, oh, dear—I don't even know his whole name!*

"Sir," she said, smiling up at him, "what shall I call you? 'Your Lordship' seems rather formal in the bedchamber, though I would not presume to be more intimate with my betters. It's just that—"

"Presume away, *liebchen.* My family, God rot them, call me Fritz," he said above the squeak of carriage wheels.

"Sir!" came the voice of Peter the footman through the sliding panel at the rear of the coach. "Sir, excuse me, but we are being followed!"

"By whom?"

"A pack of horsemen, sir." There was much respect in his voice.

"Very well, then. Tell the coachman to touch up the horses, if you'd be so good," His Lordship—Fritz—replied.

The beautiful Bavarian geldings broke into a brisk canter.

Highwaymen? Ginny clutched her daughter closer. Not all of them were swashbuckling pseudo-gentlemen like Jemmy St. James. Many, like Dick Turpin, who had been hanged several years back, raped women. She shuddered and crossed herself at the thought. And her with a baby at her breast! Such men had no mercy on mother and child!

"Gaining, sir," came the doleful imprecation from the rear of the carriage.

"Gallop them hard to the Black Bull!" Fritz cried out, rapping at the coach roof with his heavy-headed cane. He glanced at Ginny. "Ordinarily I'd throw them my purse—if they're the St. James brothers they could have my coat as well, and welcome to

53

it!—but other highwaymen can be quite rough, and I'd not have you and Viveca harmed." He raised his voice to an angry shout. "I say, *whip them up,* man! They're bred for speed, and we need every bit of it now!"

Through the glazed windows Ginny caught sight of buildings hurtling past, thinning out as they left the city behind. Not much farther to Caro's—a ways over open road and in five more minutes and she'd see the shop fronts of sleeping Kensington.

Something whistled past the window. "How unsporting," Fritz observed drolly. "Those highwaymen are *shooting* at us!"

There were more bullets *ping*ing past. Then, all at once, they heard a man's cry of pain. A loud, thumping sound followed. The coach sprang forward, lightened. The horses ran as if with new incentive. Neither Ginny nor the lord spoke, but they suddenly clasped hands together, each thinking, *My God, they've killed Peter!*

A second later he released her long white hands. "Have you a second pistol?" she asked, watching him load his.

"What, can you shoot, my good woman?"

"The eye out of a jack of spades at forty paces. Jock would never have left me alone on the farm otherwise. Grant me but a pistol and I'll do me best, though I'm better with a long-necked musket—sir."

"It's *Frederick,*" he answered. "What the—"

They could hear the savage thumming of hooves drawing nearer. There was a low moan and racket at the front of the carriage, then the berlin went careening off across a field. "I certainly hope you *can* shoot, little mother, because it appears the driver's dead or seriously hurt," Frederick told her, flinging off his greatcoat. He handed his pistols and a bag of shot to her. Then he broke out a window with his cane and scrambled out, clinging to the door.

Ginny followed Fritz's lead, smashed out the other window with the little foot brazier. Then she used Cook's plaid to tie the squalling Viveca to her seat so she wouldn't roll and bounce around. Ginny cautiously stuck nose and pistols out the broken window, coolly took aim, and squeezed. It was a good shot though not a true one, due to the motion of the coach; it took the leader's hat away but left him safe.

Her long golden hair came loose in the wind and whipped around her face. A piece of glass bit into her forearm, drawing a long scarlet streamer. There was no time to think of that now. She pushed her hair back as she heard Fritz thumping about on the berlin's roof, then felt a jolt as he dropped onto the driver's perch to take control of the coach.

Ginny was close enough to see their pursuers, close enough to make out foam dripping from the steel bridle bits of horses pushed too hard. She could even admire the leader's Donegal tweed greatcoat. *A handsome coat indeed,* she decided, and put three bullet holes in brisk succession through the front of it. With a soaring cry the man jerked backward repeatedly and at last fell. His horse, maddened with fear, veered off to the left, away from the chase. The body, caught by a spur in the stirrup, bounced behind it over hedges and stone walls.

It was a sickening sight in the moonlight. Ginny felt dizzy as she reloaded and fired again, then thought, *If not him, then me and my baby. And I'll see it done to all o' them first!*

Fritz was screaming, *"Pull up! Pull up, you bastards!"* at the crazed Bavarian geldings. Now he was swearing at them in their —and his—native German, harsh, guttural sounds made by a man trying to save lives. He succeeded in turning them at last, avoiding the open pond ahead.

Ginny was out of shot. She had killed their leader and another man and downed at least two horses by her reckoning. And she had wounded the burly red-bearded man who was reaching for the coach door at this instant, his snarling face spattered with his own blood.

She prayed she wouldn't freeze with fear. If she kept her wits she could live through this and save Viveca. Her child, the most important thing in her life!

The carriage abruptly rattled to a halt, for one horse had gone lame. "Good evening," His Lordship called coolly to the highwaymen. He sounded almost amused, Ginny thought furiously.

How like a man! They would only kill him, after all—*her* they would humiliate and force through horrid acts of sexual violence!

"If you will allow the little lady to hand my coat out to you, you will find my money purse in it. The lady is, I believe, quite out of shot now, gentlemen; the money was never an issue. I only meant to protect her and the child."

Viveca was now shrieking as though she, not Red Beard, was the one shot through the arm. Ginny put the useless pistols down and bounced her daughter jerkily. "Hush, hush! If you make them angrier, they'll murder us all!" she whispered.

She considered putting Viveca to her breast to quiet her, but who knew what that sight might do to these savages? She took up Fritz's greatcoat, lightly tossed his leather purse out to Red Beard, and bundled up in the plaid with Viveca in case they were yanked outside.

A lout had wrenched open the berlin's other door and was shouting, "A toothsome little blond morsel, laddies! Fetching as can be! There be enough for all of us—we can tek our time teachin' her not to shoot at fine robbers sech as us!"

Enough for all of us. In horror Ginny reached behind her, found the walking stick with the ruby eye. The ruby head came loose in her hand. Good Lord, a rapier was hidden in the hollow stick!

She made sure Viveca was securely tied against her chest, then caught up the sword. "Take the gold, lads, but no more or ye'll buy it dear!" she snapped, breathless with fear.

"Blast the silly bint's head off," someone suggested. "The rest will still be in working order!"

"There's no need for that," Fritz answered smoothly. "Look at these horses! Fine Bavarian Creams, each with a pedigree as long as your arm. If you'll escort us to my home the horses are yours, complete with papers. They're worth more with the papers, lads, so think about it. Fetch you five hundred pounds each with their papers, they shall. Look at these fine, strong flanks of theirs and these intelligent faces."

Ginny could smell her own raw fear through his distracting technique. The scent was stagnant in this coach, even with the air

56

oozing in through shattered panes of glass. She could feel the glass cuts on her arms now, and they smarted till her eyes watered. Cold. Terror. *Blood.* She was nearly mad with fear, and even Viveca had fallen ominously silent.

"Say," a brigand abruptly told Fritz, "yaow look familiar, yaow do."

"Yeah, he do. We got us a real swell this time. And he's right, lookit them coach horses, I ain't never seen their like! Big as bulls, they is!"

Red Beard glanced back and forth between Ginny and Fritz as if unable to decide which tack to take. She redoubled her grip on the rapier and tried to look as though she knew how to use it. Her entire body was aquiver with shock. Then it occurred to her that another robber had come running, one whose horse had been shot out from under him. When he reached them, he froze, staring at the berlin's shot-riddled door. "Cor! Great bleedin' zounds —d'ye know who we got, man?"

Everyone fell silent, staring. The runner gasped out, "You got the—*hellfire,"* he blurted, spotting Fritz. "Me own apologies Yer Royal Lordship." He hissed around at his companions, "Bleedin' blitherin' ninnies! Don't you know that German face? *We got us the bloody Prince o' Wales!"*

Frederick Louis of Hanover, Prince of Wales, heir to the crown of England, inclined his head graciously. There was a frantic scrambling as the loyalty of seven hundred years overwhelmed these rough-hewn murderers, and they dropped to their knees.

Red Beard went last, and unintentionally. Still glaring at Ginny, he keeled over from loss of blood and went flat out.

"If you good men will be so kind as to help the lady and child and myself to the Black Bull Inn?" Frederick asked pleasantly. "I would certainly see you rewarded for getting this coach back on the road."

Ginny, pleased and mortified to discover the identity of this man who had taken her in, relaxed her grip on the rapier.

She sat down on the floor of the coach and sagged forward in a dead faint.

CHAPTER SEVEN

Summer found Ginny happily installed in her flat with Viveca and an old woman servant—and pregnant again.

But she was already bored. Not with Fritz. With his *lack*. She wasn't high-quality enough for him to take her public places or even out-of-doors at all. Nor were his purse strings loose enough to have her tutored so that she might become more worthy of the honor, which might have led her closer to Court circles. There wasn't even enough pocket money to let her out to amuse herself, had she known which shops to go to. And, of course, she couldn't read, so she hadn't that means of passing the time.

I would, thought Ginny, whipping her needle past the edge of her embroidery hoop, *have done better as a whore. I'd have money and plenty of loving that way. This way all I get is embroidery lessons, a roof over my head, and a bastard to be born this winter. And, of course, I get Fritz once every six weeks. Or eight. Or . . .*

She was no closer to her own farmhouse and horse-breeding acres than she'd been at the Black Bull! The only difference was that she had the privacy she'd longed for, and she was pregnant again. And she could do fine needlework like a lady now, there being naught else to occupy her hands and time.

She never knew when she might see the prince. Once it had been three evenings in a row; the next visit, two months later. In the meantime she embroidered top sheets and pillowcases. Old Bess, her maidservant, taught her to do Chinese cutwork, and Ginny added that to the one set of linens. She perfected her faggoting and ruching on her petticoats, then went back to work on the sheets and pillowcases.

After that she learned to make thread lace. The sheets gained dainty little scallops, then erupted into festoons four and five rows deep, tied up with little satin ribands. In the windows hung used drapes of imported damask; after bleaching them senseless Ginny buckled down with cutwork and lace and turned the rooms into a giddy riot of femininity.

She set the embroidery hoop down now and scowled at Viveca scuttling across the floor after a scarlet slipper. A baby on the floor and another on the way. *Splendid.* She must have gotten pregnant the first time she looked at Fritz! *Wonderful.* She wouldn't have minded so much on a farm. There would have been plenty to do there: fowl to feed, the pond and stalls to muck out, horses and milch cow to curry. The plowing and planting to do, the harvesting of rye. Now, in a small flat, she had to argue with Bess in order to use her own inn-gleaned cooking and cleaning skills.

She threw her sewing aside. "Bess, I can't take another moment! I'll be embroidering the *backstairs* in a few more minutes! Will you watch the babe while I step around the corner to the bookseller's to look at pictures?"

"All righty, mum," came the age-crackled voice from the cooking room. "Only watch ye ain't gone long, 'case His Highness drops by, unexpected-like."

Ginny scooped up her new-used Chinese shawl and stepped outside, glad for the air, coal-stenched as it was. She loved Viveca and Bess but couldn't bear another second of baby talk or, worse, stories of "When I waited on the king's mistresses." She needed to hear of more talk than mashing up beans for Viveca and the way things had been done when the first George came waddling over from Germany.

She made her way through the sidewalk crowd. Vendors were selling hot chestnuts and potatoes and turnips. Boys in baggy breeches peddled ha'penny news sheets promising scandals galore, while pamphleteers passed out the latest shocking tales of government ineptitude, some of them true. Whores and baronesses strolled, prinked out in the height of fashion.

Then Ginny rounded the corner, and in front of the bookstore she saw the carriage.

It had started life as a normal landau with a roof that could be lowered halfway. There the resemblance ended, for the doors were entirely of amber glass, hundreds of panes separated by ivory spindles, and the body of the coach was buffed tortoiseshell overlaid with an openwork cage of incised gold. Even the spokes of the wheels were wrapped in gilt leaves and vines.

The horses were the finest Ginny had ever seen. The Prince of Wales's Bavarian Creams would look like clumsy oafs next to these dainty beauties. Hitched by waxy, butter-colored harness to the fantastic landau were four perfectly matched Arab mares, each the color of weak tea held up to a lamp.

A crowd was pouring into the bookstore. Ginny worriedly elbowed people aside, ducked under arms, and, once inside, found herself looking down on a breathtaking scene.

A black page boy with slanted eyes that spoke of mingled Eastern heritage knelt with a veiled woman across his lap. She might have been old or young. All that showed of her face were the eyelids, closed, painted with powdered emerald-green malachite and black kohl. The bridge of her nose showed above the veil, and perhaps an inch of forehead was visible over the painted eyes.

She was swathed all over in crisp, golden gauze and vibrant crimson silk. Her slippers were tiny and of flame-colored silk velvet with patterns burned away in the nap of the fabric. There were little gold and silver bells on the slippers and around her wrists and ankles.

Faceted beads of red Baltic amber encasing insects hung about her veiled throat, and more ropes of the stuff were around her waist. Sapphires large as robin's eggs sparkled everywhere, it seemed, mixed with heavy triple strings of waxy yellow pearls.

She lay on a broad length of silver tissue between two turbaned and towering blue-eyed slaves, who wore scimitars and regarded the crowd with suspicion.

Ginny walked up to them, bent a knee in her best curtsy and, for the second time in her life, did not rip out her hem doing so. She bent over the unconscious woman.

The tapering, delicate hand she lifted had never known hard labor, but it did needlework, witnessed by a tiny ridge of callus on the needle finger and another caused by the rim of a thimble. The palm had been painted orange with henna and the nails also tinted with the stuff; they were long nails, filed to inch-long points. There were two rings on every finger and armlets with square stamp-size rubies around the blue-veined wrists.

"Do any of you speak English?" Ginny asked.

The page boy replied in a frantic burble of some unknown tongue.

"They dun't speak it," the bookstore owner said. "My guess is she fainted dead away and they dun't know why, so they brought her in here, damn them. Foreigners be bad for business."

"Nonsense," Ginny replied tartly. "Look at the dozens of people she's attracted. If you had a remotely Christian soul . . ."

The boy was trembling. Ginny cut short her angry words, turned to the page, smiled, patted his slim brown wrist. What had happened to the woman? she wondered. A fit? Stroke? Bad food? She took hold of the limp, tinted hand again; it was warm but not too warm. She bent lower, laid her head to the swell of bosom. Heart was steady if a trifle fast, and the breast over it felt puffy, like the woman had been a size smaller when her clothes had been made, and yet she was quite slender.

Ginny sat up, laid a light hand on the tissue-draped abdomen. Just as she'd begun to suspect! A high roundness had started there. "No worry. She's pregnant, is all," she announced. Sight-seers laughed, broke into small groups, drifted away.

She turned to the footmen with their curved swords and panto-mimed rocking a baby in her arms. They nodded, spoke to each other in a foreign tongue, and made gestures that said, *What now?*

What indeed?

Ginny took the whole parade home with her.

Bess nearly had a fit herself. *"Eee!* Missus, whot've ye gone and done! And these two great blue-eyed savages! They've gone and kilt the woman! *Eee!"*

Ginny threw her Chinese shawl on a chair and pointed to the bedroom, where the white slaves gently deposited their mistress. It was then that she saw the blood.

The page boy saw it, too, and he made a motion of rocking a baby, then motioned the child dropping on the floor. "Bess— Bess, I think he's trying to say she's miscarrying and that she's done it before. We've got to help her!"

There was no one to send for a midwife and no money to induce a midwife to come, Ginny thought grimly. She and Bess would have to nurse the woman themselves. She stamped her foot, shooed the men out of the room. But the page boy caught at her skirts.

"Fee-leep," he told her, pointing to himself. Then, toward the unconscious woman: "Yasaman. *Hasseki* Yasaman—"

"Ginny," she answered, indicating herself, *"Jin-ee."* She shooed Philippe out to where Viveca was drooling on the polished boots of the white slaves.

"Bess, her name sounds like Jasmine. You know, the flower. Yas-ah-mahn, he said. Oh, dear, if only we had the money to fetch a doctor."

"Doctors," Bess scoffed. "We don't need some doctor poking and pryin' at this tiny creature. If you'll boil me up some water and sacrifice some towels, we can make some padding for her, mum. She's losin' a babe, all right. Look at that belly rippling! Fast with those towels—we'll have to hurry."

Yasaman lost the baby. Bess reckoned it was no more than three months along, but she could tell that it would have been a boy. They barred Philippe from the room; in the parlor he alternated between weeping bitterly and trying to amuse Viveca with the fringed ends of his sash. From time to time he rapped on the door and plaintively called out, *"Jinnee? Jinnee?"* Each time all she could do was to answer, *"No,* Philippe."

Yasaman was eventually stirring restlessly. All at once the long eyelids fluttered, then parted to reveal eyes of the purest and most brilliant brown. They regarded Ginny through a haze of silent pain; in response she felt her own eyes mist over with feeling. "I have lost the baby," Yasaman announced in perfect, cut-glass English.

"Yes. A boy."

"It has been a boy each time. Seven times now I have watched my sons slide away before they were born. Why do you weep? We are strangers. I have no tears left."

"I—I, too, have lost many babies, even a son who lived a while," Ginny confessed.

Yasaman tried to prop herself up on her elbows and could not. She sank back against the pillows. "Where am I, kind stranger?"

"London, around the corner from where I found you. Upstairs above a printer's shop. Everyone stood there in the bookstore blithering like idiots and I—I guessed you were pregnant—I mean, 'with child,' and I—I had your servants bring you here."

"They have never been to London with me before; they did not know how to reach my house. You are quite kind."

Ginny blew her nose harder. "You take people in when they need help, that's what me da always taught me."

Yasaman stirred, her wealth of hennaed hair spreading out in a rumpled auburn puddle. "I must return to my house, missus—"

"Ginny. It's Ginny, and Bess here's the one saved your life. No, missus, you musn't move yet."

"She's right," Bess chimed in. "We apologize that the place isn't as you're used to, but moving you now could be the death o' ye."

There was no argument; Yasaman had already slipped away into merciful unconsciousness.

They sat with her the whole night, giving her honeyed lemon water to stop the bleeding. In the morning Yasaman was well enough to write a note and send Ginny in her glass-doored carriage to her physician, an Oriental man with his hair tied in a long black queue. He spoke English almost as well as French and conversed in the latter with Philippe, who had come along carrying little Viveca on his own small back.

The doctor returned with her and spent an hour examining Yasaman, then he took her away in the carriage, which was quite big enough for the afflicted woman to lie down in.

Philippe left his sash for Viveca to play with; it remained a prized possession for some time to come.

When she was older it would cost her the person she loved best.

CHAPTER EIGHT

Ginny was distilling brandy in the solarium when she saw Yasaman's fabulous carriage pull up at the foot of the stairs.

She hurriedly smoothed her hair and untucked the sleeves she had rolled up. She was in her old grisette gown, not actually good enough for guests, but it would have to do. She stuffed her work smock into a cabinet drawer and strode over to the door, feeling the old, familiar pressure of pregnancy at the small of her back.

There were footfalls on the stairs, pattering like light leaves in a breeze. Ginny turned the knob and dropped a curtsy as Yasaman entered the room.

She sensed a quick shadow of a smile behind the veil, saw the Eastern woman make the quick touches to forehead and heart that meant respect. They straightened at the same time, and Ginny laughed. "You'll pardon my lack of grace. I'm no swan and curtsies ain't—aren't—me strong suit!"

She had been about to blame her pregnancy for her awkwardness but realized how tactless it would be in view of Yasaman's loss.

Yasaman held a hand out, shook Ginny's hand as though entering a partnership. "You saved my life."

"Oh, Yasaman, I've been so worried you lost the babe on account of me having you moved!"

Yasaman shook her dainty head, making slender silver bells tinkle around her. "No, my physician said you and your servant saved my life. It is merely a curse of mine that I cannot bring a living child to full term."

Ginny opened the door farther. "Where's Philippe? He was so good to my Viveca . . . she's out with old Bess right now, but

65

they'll be back soon. Please come in. I have some good black tea and a tiny bit of coffee with real bits of almond and cocoa beans in it. It was a gift," she boasted, and then blushed, thinking of the way Fritz had tumbled her after they'd shared a pot of that coffee. He'd been very attentive lately. It had been rather like having a husband around, or at least a determined suitor. Now she probably wouldn't see him again for another six weeks!

Yasaman graciously nodded and snapped her fingers. Philippe and the two white slaves came up the stairs with a large wooden chest carved of sandalwood, that heady, spicy wood so prized by traders. "I wished to thank you but thought money might be taken as an insult, so I have brought gifts to replace what you ruined for my sake."

They threw the chest open and stepped back. Turkish towels were piled inside, each snowy white and inches thick. There were sheets, too, of heavy white silk brocade, thick and soft. Ginny dropped to one knee, rubbed her cheek on the silk like a cat in clover. "Oh, Yasaman, this is so nice I—oh!"

She had just spotted the shift Yasaman had brought to replace her old one. It was of pure silk gauze, fine and sheer as spiderwebs but strong as hemp rope. The low neckline, hem, and three-quarter sleeves were embroidered and reembroidered, white on white, and the lacework was exquisite, set all over with seed pearls and thousands of tiny tucks.

In a separate crate were jars of black currant honey, lush dried apricots, dates and figs, and the fabled candy known as *Rahat Lokum*—Turkish Delight.

"Sweets for you and Bess," Yasaman said, "and there are some jars of herbs I thought she might be interested in. There is also a christening dress for your child, when you bear it."

"If it's a live child," Ginny said impulsively. "I, too, have terrible problems carrying and birthing. I don't know why I did so well with Viveca."

The women sat down at the kitchen table and began telling about themselves. Ginny's tales were of Fritz, the Black Bull, and life since Culloden Moor took her husband.

Yasaman spoke with obvious amusement of her status as official translator and unofficial ambassador from the court of Turkey in the Ottoman Empire. "The sultan," she said, "wants trade between the East and West to expand, but of course no one listens to a woman on business matters, so what I do in addition to translating is invite the English ladies to my house, which is full of our rarest silks, goldwork, silversmithing, and spices. They go home and tell their husbands, and their husbands begin thinking that trade expansion and lower tariffs might be a good idea. This trip I have been sent with some silks to present personally to the queen of your country; fine dress lengths, the likes of which are not to be found outside of my native Anatolia. . . ."

They talked long after Bess returned with Viveca, who climbed all over little Philippe and, in general, made a pest of herself with the good-natured page.

Before she left, Yasaman turned to Ginny and asked very softly if she might stand as godmother to the next baby. "Why, certainly. I'd be honored," Ginny agreed.

"I am Christian, you know. After every night in my lord's bed I go to confession, but I am Roman Catholic and that is unpopular."

"If the baby doesn't mind I won't, either," Ginny answered cheerfully.

"If Bess has any trouble bringing your child you must send for my physician. I have already spoken with him and paid him in advance."

There was no trouble late that winter of '48 when Ginny bore Allegra, her second daughter. Fritz picked the name, as he said Italy was all the mode nowadays, and anyway, it was no more outlandish than *Viveca!*

He could not attend the christening ceremony but sent some silverplate to start Allegra's dowry. Surprisingly the Princess of Wales, sweet, shy Augusta, sent a beautiful layette she had worked herself, and a silver rattle. "What shall I do?" Ginny asked Yasaman on her next visit, wide-eyed with the honor of the princess's gifts."

"We shall write her a letter thanking her."

"I cannot write a word, remember?"

"That is why I said 'we.' I will help you, and eventually you will learn to read and write."

Yasaman kept her word concerning Ginny's education. In less than a year she had her able to read and write the very basics and soon afterward gave Ginny her first book, a leather-bound primer. Ginny all but devoured it, mastering it with increasing skill until finally she sold the rug in the bedchamber to buy herself more books.

She began pointing words out to Viveca, repeating them until her oldest daughter could find the word and say it. Her daughters wouldn't be ignorant, Ginny vowed, and blessed the day she had met Yasaman.

Everything would have been fine save for her own restlessness.

She sat perched in her pretty flat with her needlework and books—and not doing a lick of honest work. Her own cooking, sure, for Bess had begun slipping into senility. And Ginny had sewing and mothering. But she was further away from owning a breeding farm than ever and had barely been able to scrape together the fee to have Dulcie and Darcy, her two mares, bred by a half-Arab, half-Irish hunter.

Yasaman had offered to stable Dulcie and Darcy with her own mares in London in order that Ginny might see them more often and be able to ride them from time to time. Ginny was considering this idea.

And more. Yasaman had given her so much, and she had nothing to return the favors with. Nothing except companionship, which Yasaman was desperate for. As a well-educated woman of rank, Yasaman stood alone in her homeland where women hid behind walls and veils and never spoke directly to men; in London she was a curiosity to be stared at, not confided in. Ambassadors sought her sexually, and their wives often snubbed her.

The last letter from abroad (for Yasaman was on one of her many trips to Turkey) had asked Ginny to become her traveling companion. *Why not?* Ginny asked herself. She had only seen Fritz twice in the last year; the king had cut his allowance again, which left Ginny's household surviving on vegetables, no bread, and very little meat. She felt oddly poor having lost her tiny toehold of near luxury—an unaccustomed feeling for a woman who'd thought herself wealthy in Scotland with patched shoes, pulling a plow.

But, My Lord, she thought, *I would miss Fritz, even as little as I see him now!* She balled her hands into impotent fists. And would he miss *her?* she wondered. She had not heard of him keeping any other mistresses, though she read the news sheets faithfully when she could find them discarded. They were full of the most scurrilous gossip.

What to do, what to do! She wanted him—she missed him—but she saw him so seldom now.

Yasaman's letter had said, "Perhaps you could find a husband among my people, for we do not look down on widows with children; their fruitfulness offers a man every evidence that such a woman will bring him sons."

And so Ginny walked the floor at night, trying to decide what to tell Fritz, what to do with doddering old Bess, whose senility was worse since her fall last May. The flat was too small for two growing girls—no, she couldn't take charity from Yasaman. Decisions!

She sat down on the foot of the bed she shared with Bess and the girls when Fritz wasn't here and reached over to the small bedside table for her jewel box. The only thing in it was the miniature of her grandmother, a dainty oil painting on a sliver of ivory.

Ginny went over to the window with the miniature in hand, tilting it this way and that in the moonlight, studying the tuberoses in her grandmother's hair and in the pattern of lace she wore. She'd asked Yasaman about the tuberose being called Mistress of the Night; it was because the flower's strongest scent rose after sundown. In the language of lovers it signified pleasures in the shared darkness.

Granny, Granny, she thought, *did tuberoses have a special meaning for you and a lover?*

She would have to forget love in the dark in order to make the proper decision.

"Fritz! What a pleasure to see you!" Ginny cried out gladly as teetering old Bess admitted their royal visitor on a raw, blustery February night in 1751.

"I'll put the girls to bed with me on the cot," grumbled Bess, who had gotten used to sharing the soft bed with all those warm bodies; they could afford little enough wood, so the fireplace stood empty this winter. Ginny was making a few pence with her needlework, but it wasn't enough to support them all.

Ginny smiled at the old woman as she trudged off to fetch the girls. Bess was moving and thinking slowly these days, all but helpless, but she was a dear old biddy, the mother Ginny had hardly known, and a kind grandmother for the girls. The thought reminded Ginny that she would have to speak with Fritz about leaving.

She turned back to Fritz, helped him out of his coat. "You look a bit pale, Fritz. Is something amiss?"

"No, *liebchen*. In fact, I'm at the height of my social popularity at the moment," he answered cheerily. "I've been quite busy with my 'alternate court' I've set up at Leicester House to spite Father. His last absence from England with that singularly ugly mistress has done him no good whatsoever. I've been walking out around the town more lately, going out alone—"

"Oh, you shouldn't! It might be dangerous!" Ginny interjected, forgetting her place.

Fritz laughed, warming his hands on his breeches. "No danger at all, sweet. Why's there no fire, it's quite cold up here!"

She bit her lip and put her last precious log in the fireplace, struck a spark, and sank back on her haunches as the flame caught and fed itself on the big log. "Is your father that unpopular?" she asked.

"Well, no one was wild about Mother, either—though she did some good; she had a stranglehold on the old German dumpling, she did! She even picked out his mistresses for him—women older and uglier than herself, of course, so that there would be slight competition in *that* department!" His voice took a more personal tone. "How are the children?" he asked.

70

"Well and growing like weeds. Viveca is four years and a half now, and tonight is Allegra's third birthday. I shall wake them for you—they've only been asleep a little while." So it would have to wait, this talk of leaving. Her resolve was shattering now, from gladness of his presence.

She rose, tightened her rough wool wrapper around herself. When she returned from the bedchamber, she was carrying Allegra and leading Viveca by the hand.

Viveca was sleepy and bored with the rain, for Ginny refused to let her wallow in the mud like the printer's youngest sons. She could already wallop the smaller of the two boys remaining at home and eagerly awaited the day she could do so to the elder, who called her "a damned Scots rebel" and made Red Indian war whoops at her, chanting, "The Duke of Cumberland killed yer da, the Duke of Cumberland . . ."

She had already learned that the Duke of Cumberland, who led the troops that massacred the Scots at Culloden Moor—especially her sainted father—was Fritz's brother. She was only old enough to know that she hated the prince for having such a brother and didn't quite trust a mama who was such good friends with him.

Allegra did not know or care. People doted on her, for she never climbed hedges the way naughty Viveca did, never tore her petticoats or begged to wear breeches like a boy so she could chase dogs and cats more easily.

Frederick had brought Allegra a new pink gown the dressmakers had whipped together especially for her. She was now awake enough to coo about it and mouth thank-yous she could hardly pronounce, but Viveca hung back and asked to return to bed.

Fritz picked the older girl up. "You look sad, my little goddaughter," he said in his thick German accent.

Viveca made no reply, only stared at him with blatant resentment.

"She hates me," the prince told Ginny.

"Nonsense, she's a baby. Babies don't hate! She's just surly about being dragged out of bed. Now *behave*, Viveca," Ginny said, retying her wool wrapper around herself.

Viveca, to her mother's horror, burst out with, "Your brother kilt my da, and I hate you, Fritz, you wicked, wicked man!"

Then she lashed out with both bare feet and dissolved into tears.

Ginny's hands flew to her mouth. She was too mortified to flex a muscle. But Frederick, dear Fritz, held the weeping child close and said, "William was a very bad man to kill all those brave Scots at Culloden. It was a sad time, and I am so ashamed of William! God says we have to love our brothers, but you know, he doesn't say we have to *like* them. After all, don't you dislike little Allegra sometimes? Mmm?" He gently chucked her under the chin.

"So you see, it is that way with my brother and me, too. If Allegra breaks a vase, it is not your doing. Nor is it my doing that William was bad. Now I wish you would be my friend, for your mother and sister are, and I think you're a brave girl to say what you said. Would you like me to tuck you in?"

She nodded, wide-eyed. Frederick winced and pressed a hand to his ribs as he carried her to Bess's pallet—as though, Ginny thought, his chest hurt. She tucked Allegra in next to Viveca, and afterward the two adults stepped back into the parlor, children lulled by the sound of old Bess's snores.

Fritz rested a hand over his heart. "What is it? Something ails you," Ginny said concernedly, forgetting her worries about the future in the face of his illness. She hurried to brew tea for him.

"I was struck in the chest by a tennis ball some weeks back—a great, strong blow 'twas—and I do believe a few ribs were cracked, though the doctors said no. You will have to be gentle with me, Ginny."

His smile was so melancholy that Ginny, hurrying to hand him a mugful of steaming Darjeeling tea, could not bring herself to mention the dire straits she lived in.

"You were good to my girl. I thank you for it. She wants a father badly, and it was good of you to speak so of Jock to her," she told the prince.

He seated himself on a Chippendale chair and sipped hot tea, making small talk. When he was finished, Ginny took him by the hand and led him into the bedchamber. She lit two small braziers Yasaman had given her, filling them with straw to start them and then adding glowing coals from the fireplace. A pinch of precious myrrh powder for scent, and the chamber smelled delightful.

Then she seated Fritz on the edge of the bed, rubbing his temples with eau de cologne. She bent and wrested off his muddy boots, for he had ridden to see her instead of taking his carriage. It made her glad, for once, that her wrapper was of coarse old wool—once dried, the mud would flake off it easily. Fritz still seemed fretful, so she rubbed his feet, too, before peeling off his silk stockings.

The rain had soaked clear through to his waistcoat. "You are too careless of yourself," she scolded gently, unbuttoning the red brocade. "This is the second time you've ridden through the rain to see me, and you never remember to wear your traveling cloak over your coat. I shall hang these things out by the fire so that they may be dry when you leave. You must take better care of yourself, my prince. You're going to be the first broad-minded Hanover to sit on the throne, and the people need you! Frederick the First! Think of it! All the little people in the street will be looking for you to stop those escalating prices! Tch-tch! King Frederick outlaws escalation!"

He gave a low laugh, caught her by the waist. "Hang the clothes up later, *liebchen,*" he urged.

She smiled and set down his outer garments. As Ginny unfastened each remaining article of his clothing, she let light fingertips stray here and there as if by accident, sliding her warm flesh over his chilled body, brushing moist lips against his ear and murmuring enticing moans.

He was preoccupied and responded more slowly than usual, but he obviously wanted her and *had* wanted her for a long time. Ginny let him fondle her heavy breasts and sleek thighs. She gasped at the feel of his tongue snaking across her wanting flesh.

It had been a long while since he'd last visited, and each time he appeared it made her yearn fiercely for a man of her own. One who didn't go home to another woman. One who stayed. And yet —it was *Fritz,* not some stranger, she longed to have full-time.

Ginny kissed him, felt the weary eagerness of his mouth under hers. She sensed that he wanted to be seduced, so she seduced him. She kissed his neck, his shoulders, licked and nibbled her way down. The rigidity of him sprang up against her breast, begging to be taken.

Passionately she applied mouth and fingers, uttering sounds of arousal, bringing him to a fierce peak. His response was intense and made her hunger for a peak of her own. But when she had caught her breath and moved up into his lax arms, sleep had claimed him. In the near stillness of late-night London she heard his breathing, ragged like frayed hems dragged along wooden stairs. It worried her nearly to tears.

He was gone when she rose in the morning, disappointed and swollen with need. Ginny never saw him again.

One month later Frederick Louis, Prince of Wales, died of pneumonia, leaving as heir a young son who would become George III, otherwise known as Mad King George.

CHAPTER NINE

"That's right," the landlord said. " 'Is lungs filt up 'n 'e died. 'E 'adn't paid yer rent in nigh on two years, and I mean to collect yer last remaining pretties to try and get me money back. Unless" —his wolfish eyes flicked over Ginny's shapely form—"unless ye'd like to—*negotiate?*"

The news of Fritz's death had caught her unawares. At first she had not believed it, but now, down below in the streets, she could hear the newsboys crying out to all of London: "The Prince o' Wales is dead! Prince dies, read it here, read it now!"

Ginny yanked away from the grasping male hands. There was a letter opener on the desk behind her; she grasped it firmly. She thought of the twenty-hour days she'd spent at the desk of late, plying her delicate needlework that she might feed the children and keep them dressed. And now this swine wanted to take her *and* what scant possessions she still had after selling the tables, sandalwood chest, and her drapes, pawning the silverplate from Fritz. . . .

Dead. The fathers of her children, both dead now.

Something in her seemed to snap. She swung the letter opener in front of her, hissing like a mother cat. "You'll not take me, nor steal me daughters and the rattles out of their hands! I'll pack and get out right away so you can let the flat to another, but don't you touch me or anything of mine, especially my babies!"

He backed away, eyes round with surprise at her vehemence. "You'll be sorry!" he cried out, bolting through the door and down the steps.

"Bess? Bess, come here!" she cried.

"Yes, mum?" asked the rheumy-eyed old housekeeper as Ginny caught up her threadbare China shawl.

"I must get word to the Princess Augusta to ask for her help! Surely she and the king won't see Fritz's daughter turned out on the streets to starve! It's a long walk, miles away, but—Bess, do not let anyone in while I'm gone. D'ye hear me? *Don't let anyone in!*"

"Aye, mum, I'll lock up." Bess nodded as though she understood, but in her mind she was a young girl again, flirting with a duke at Court—a tall German duke, a friend of the king's, who had lain with her, given her a beautiful son he'd taken away the very morn of his birth . . .

As Ginny raised her skirts a few frantic inches and rushed down the backstairs, the door blew open. Bess, unheeding, danced about the room, singing, "Oh he were fine and tall, he were bonny and strong. An' he were me own true love, O!"

A servant was locking the gates of Leicester House when Ginny wearily stumbled up to him, explaining her plight. He laughed in her face. "The princess is at Cliveden, where Prince Frederick died. An' old George won't do nothing for a bastard granddaughter. Why should he? He's got enough legitimate ones to go around, and there's Fritz's boy George what'll be the next king! The old man don't care about nobody, least of all your sort."

And he cruelly slammed her fingers in the gate, shouting to the crowd, "Look 't her, she's one o' dead Fritz's girls! Whore to the dead prince!"

They stared, made fun of her plain clothing, said no prince ever kept anything so skinny, so drab. But several men, quick to note her honey-blond coloring and swelling bosom, offered her money that they might say they'd had the late prince's mistress with him hardly cold.

Ginny furiously spat at them and turned away. It was lightly raining now; by the time she'd gone two miles the downpour was fierce. In five miles she was chilled and stunned, but a few blocks from home her sharp wits returned.

I'm not down yet, she thought grimly as she turned down the familiar street that led to the printer's house. *There's still Yasaman, or if she's already gone, I can go back to the Black Bull if Caro'll take me with a whole crop of bastards, and no place to stuff 'em but up in the rafters! I was a fool to starve my girls just to stay with a pauper prince—even if I did love him!*

She was frightened but not senseless; she had survived the army at Culloden; she had lost parents, husband, son, lover, her own unsullied name—but she would never lose her daughters, not while she could draw a breath. There would be some way to maintain her family. There *must* be! As she gazed up at the house she saw a string of boys going up and down the stairs carrying her bedclothes and neatly mended dresses. There went her last remaining Chippendale chair.

Ginny hurtled up the stairs, threw a stripling over the rail like a woman possessed. She scored someone's face with her nails, went kicking and punching into the room.

Bess and the girls were huddled on the floor, all of them weeping except for Viveca, who bore the mark of a brutal blow across her face. She lay uncomplaining, eyes crookedly fixed on the ceiling.

Ginny caught up the fireplace poker, swung it at the landlord as he emerged from the bedchamber carrying part of her dismantled bed frame. She missed, sending the brass biting deep into the wood of the door frame. She spat at him; he was no different from the men who had offered her money at the dead prince's house. "Get out or I'll kill you for hitting my baby and robbing me! I'll *kill* you, I *swear* it! I'll kill you—"

"I'll be back with the constables, you slut!" he threatened, backing toward the front door, then running away.

"My baby. He's killed my baby!" she said sickly, and knelt by her family.

A small boy, a friend of Viveca's, stuck his head in. "Missus Ginny? I seen a rented carriage go by. Want me to fetch 'im up so's you can get away 'fore the constables come?"

She gathered Viveca up into her arms. Her daughter was still breathing evenly and was mumbling a bit now. "Yes, God bless

77

you," Ginny told the boy. "I've only one shilling left, but it's yours—here, catch it!"

While Ginny was gathering her few remaining possessions, Viveca came back into herself, fussed, demanded to be set on her feet. "That's my brave girl," Ginny told her. "Now you hang onto Allegra, don't let her go, and I'll throw my last things together. Look, they've left the old spice crate in the kitchen."

She rushed to it, piled in sheets, rugs, earthenware dishes, some honey Yasaman had given them, which smelled of lemon grass, a bit of cold asparagus soup in a jar—the only food she had left. Her best gown and her silk shift were gone; everything was gone.

The jewelry box was broken open on the floor, her grandmother's miniature missing. Ginny's eyes were beginning to fill when Viveca's crackly voice piped up, "Don't cry, Mummy, I got Granma right here!"

And there was the lady of the tuberoses, Mistress of the Night, clutched in Viveca's tiny fist.

Heavy footfalls on the stairs. "Coach waiting, Mum!" called the little boy, gasping.

Ginny cautiously stuck her head out the door. What would she pay the driver with? It came to her in a flash that she had long ago forgotten about the gold sovereign from Queen Elizabeth's days. They had gone hungry through her stupid, neglectful forgetfulness! *But then again,* her ever springy conscience argued, *had you spent it on food, you wouldn't be having it now for the coachman!*

She pried it out of the broken bottom of the jewelry box, again thanking God for Viveca, who had not only saved the miniature but, unknowingly, their passport out of here.

"I have a gold sovereign for you, my man, if you fetch us to Gramercy Park before seven, for there's a ship sailing, and I must meet a lady before she leaves on it for Turkey," she told the coachman as he entered her door. "The crate over there—hurry!"

Neighbors had gathered down below, taking her side against the printer or vice-versa. Some people jeered and spat at a dead man's mistress, but others noted her pride of carriage as she led her daughters out.

The coachman loaded in the spice chest, jamming it on top of the seats so that her daughters had to sit on it. Ginny then drew out the gold sovereign and bit it, scoring it with her teeth to show how very nearly pure the gold was. She dropped it back in her bodice as he nodded. "Seven o'clock? Yes, missus, I'll make me bays fly! Now get in there!"

The horses started up so quickly that everyone was thrown around inside the carriage. Allegra began to whimper. Viveca said, "Your da was a prince, so don't cry—people might see!"

Ginny put her head in her hands. If Yasaman was already gone she would bully the driver into taking her to the Black Bull. If he refused they'd walk. *Somehow.* Alone in the rainy night.

Dear God, Fritz was dead. Dear Fritz, she had loved him a little. Ginny wept a moment, which started all of them sniveling. She wiped her nose on the back of her sleeve, a habit Yasaman had broken her of until now, and shouted out the window, *"Faster, man, faster!"*

They had to catch Yasaman before her ship left! It was that or life at the inn, sweating in hundred-degree ovens, fending off drunks . . .

The miniature was bouncing on Viveca's flat little chest. Ginny stared at her grandmother's face in the light of occasional street lamps and the moon breaking through the last of the clouds. "What'sa looking at?" Allegra asked quickly.

"Granma's picture. Her starched lace cap has a pattern of tuberoses on it, and she has more of them in her hair. Tuberoses grow at the Black Bull Inn in Kensington, darlings, that's where your Aunt Caro is. That's where we lived the night the bear was brought home, the night Viveca was born!"

A tear dribbled down the side of her nose. "Mistress of the Night," she said aloud. "That's what they call the tuberose."

And tuberoses represented pleasures of the flesh, which Fritz had introduced her to. Tuberoses had grown at the inn where she'd met him. . . . Ginny found the handkerchief in her pocket, pulled it out, and blew her nose heartily. She forced herself to gain control, to look out the window.

The night was wicked and wet, despite the clouds dispersing, and both horses skidded at corners, for the rain had made gutters overflow. The coachman squinted up at the sky as he drove and thought, *Man, man, it seems the whole of heaven is a-weeping for the death of one damned prince!*

He took the next corner too fast, thinking what Ginny's gold coin would buy. The horse on the left swung wide, slipped in floating sewage. Whinnying with fear, he lashed out at his teammate, who stumbled. The driver rose on the box, trying to rein them in.

Too late. The horse on the right, rearing, had hooked a forefoot in his yokemate's harness and, three-legged, lost all control.

"What is it?" Bess shrieked. Ginny cried out in fear as the carriage rocked from side to side.

The horses saw the other carriage before their driver did. It was sideways across the turn, for its sole horse had gone lame in the roadway. The matched bays slid sideways into it, then, with a resounding crash, both carriages overturned.

The coachman was thrown clear, his neck broken in the fall. The lame horse was downed and trampled by the others in a shower of splinters and broken glass. His yoke split, flying up and smashing his driver fatally across the forehead.

The passenger in the other carriage had leaped out through the leather flap the moment he saw the other coach careening toward him.

Bess, her back broken, drowned in two inches of rainwater, for the spice crate held her down. It had burst open, spilling forks, earthenware, and sheets inside the carriage. Allegra's teeth-marked silver rattle lay in a pool of broken glass and blood.

It was an hour before another coach entered this shabby street where human carrion lurked, seeking the carriage wreck they had heard in the night.

The elderly man in the carriage rapped on the roof of his landau. "Pull over, there's a wreck!" The coachman obeyed, and the old man sprang out with his footman and coachman, hurrying among the dead to find survivors.

"Two dead men, an old dead woman, a live woman, and a pile

of linens, sir," came the report from the footman who poked around inside the wrecked coaches.

"Well, then, fetch the woman out," the old gentleman said, and the footman obeyed, handing out a limp form.

The gentleman knelt in the mud, careless of his silks and velvets, and took Ginny's pulse. "Why, we must fetch her to a doctor's at once! Come, man, carry her for me!"

Lifting Ginny in his strong arms, the footman carried her to the coach, which then sped away.

Then and only then did a bizarre figure emerge from the shadows. She wore a man's frock coat over a tea gown, with a kimono atop it all; her black hair was frizzled in a style long dead, and a tricornered hat and riding boots rounded out the ensemble. Children oozed out of the shadows in her wake. Then, at a word from her, they fell on the wreckage.

There were spokes to be carried off and melted down, bright bits of leather harness to fetch a ha'penny at market, and horsetails for soldiers' helmets. "Cor, Missus Lee!" cried out a boy. "This here carriage is full o' linens and such!"

"Who's my best boy?" she asked quickly. "Where's Byrne St. James?"

At the age of seven, going on eight, Byrne was the oldest and fastest of the lot. He was inside the carriage before she finished speaking, down through the smashed window into the wrecked seats and guts of the crate. "Missus Lee!" he called out in a reedy voice that would one day be even deeper than that of his famous brother, the highwayman, Gentleman Jemmy. "Missus Lee, there's two little girls under the linens!"

"Dead or alive?" Missus Lee asked in a serpentine hiss.

A tense pause followed, all children freezing in mid-pillage, until Byrne called out, "Alive and whole, though a bit stunned! They're coming around now!"

Missus Lee laughed and clapped her hands together once. The children dropped everything and rushed to gather around her. "Little girls," she told them happily. "Little girls whose mother had enough money to hire a carriage. That means they'll have breeding and manners. They'll be able to get into all sorts of places you boys can't go. You little ruffians will have to help me teach and protect them, for they can bring in big money from all those rich houses that open their doors to lost little girls in good clothes."

A groan rose from the depths of the smashed carriage as Viveca sat, rubbing her head.

Missus Lee chuckled dangerously. "Lads, we're about to meet the two newest members of our band!"

PART TWO

Jemmy

"Well, they threw me into jail without a writ or bounty
For robbing Colonel Farrell on the Kilmagenny mountain,
But they couldn't take my fist, so I knocked down the sentry
And bade no farewell to the Colonel or the gentry."

—"Whiskey in the Jar," late 18th-century Irish Traditional

CHAPTER TEN

London, 1756

"I want to meet your brother, the famous one," Viveca said one more time.

Byrne St. James lowered his spyglass and ground his teeth in the dark. "For the last time there aren't any girls in Jemmy's band. He only trains the best boys, and that doesn't include you."

Ten-year-old Viveca swung a leg over the stair rail in the abandoned house and picked up imaginary reins. "Why not? I bet I could ride just fine! And I can run faster than anyone else in Missus Lee's band. Even *you*, Smarty-Breeches," she said disdainfully.

"But sooner or later you're going to grow up to become a real live woman, and you won't be able to play at this boy stuff anymore."

He trained his spyglass back on the house he was supposed to watch. Viveca swung down off the rail, hands on hips—or what *would* be hips in a few years; she was still as straight and narrow as an arrow.

"What's that supposed to mean, you pigheaded scoundrel?" she demanded. "Does it mean 'real, live women' can't be trusted? Look at me, Byrne St. James! I kept my mouth shut the time the Bow Street runners almost caught you. I never told Missus Lee you held out on her with that ring you stold for your mum before she died. Haven't I been a better matey and closer-mouthed than the other lads?"

He didn't take his eye off the glass this time. Damn the girl, she really was his best friend, but he'd heard enough about growing up to know that it couldn't last much longer. He was thirteen, almost old enough to start training with Jemmy and his other brother Dash, after all. Them and—

He stopped himself. He'd been about to include Benjamin, the St. James brother who'd been hanged at Tyburn these eight months now. Byrne crossed himself and returned his full attention to the spyglass. "Here she comes," the handsome, black-haired boy said at last. "Here comes Allegra with the booty!"

"Any Bow Street Runners around?" Viveca asked. The Runners were a new handpicked police force, and much feared by the thieves who had run rampant until now.

"Nope, coast is clear. Here she comes, looking like an angel in that white dress!"

Viveca lifted her head. White dress. She'd had one to match it till she'd outgrown it this year. Not that she was any wider, but she was tall for her age.

The dresses had been made from their mother's silk sheets. Viveca remembered Missus Lee in reeking tallow light, stitching the sheets into fanciful creations that bore no resemblance to modern fashion but were ravishing all the same.

"She'd better fasten up her brown cape so no one sees her," Viveca snapped, trading her softer memories for the work at hand.

"She is. Come on, Allegra!" Byrne urged, as though the child could hear him. Allegra veered sharply right, hurried down the cul-de-sac, and entered the burned-out hulk of a house where Byrne and her sister awaited her arrival.

Viveca met her at the door. "The sterling and jewels?"

"Got 'em," Allegra answered perkily. "They really believed I was lost. Fed me, tucked me in. Catch, Byrne."

She removed her underskirt full of purloined objects and tossed it to the boy. Beneath the white silk, she wore a boy's knee breeches and scratchy wool tunic; Viveca hurried her out of the white bodice and covered the bright golden curls with a knitted sailor's cap like her own. Once the hue and cry went up, it would be for a sweet-faced girl in white silk—not a grubby little lad in the company of two others.

"Was I good?" Allegra asked as they loped along.

"You know you were," Viveca answered, hugging her.

Byrne glanced over his shoulder. "A light's gone on at the house. Let's run. Wouldn't do to be caught by the Bow Street Runners." Viveca cinched up her breeches with the red-and-yellow sash Philippe had given her, seized Allegra by the hand, and took off at a dead run. She feared the Runners more than God or starvation.

They ran a wild zigzag course, squeezing under hedges, slipping through broken gates. *Damn,* Byrne thought. *I'm getting too big for this, I hardly fit anymore. Jemmy said he'd take me at fourteen to start working the Bristol Road, and it won't be any too soon!*

But who would be his family then? he wondered crossly. Would he have to give up his young friends when he joined Jemmy's band? Viveca and Allegra were as much a part of his tribe as the younger St. James boys he now rode herd over. Mum was dead from having her last black-haired son, and most of them had different fathers; his own, in fact, was probably lying in the gutter tonight, drunk as a lord again.

They raced on toward the split-up point they'd named ahead of time. Byrne found himself irrationally remembering something Viveca had told him: "God doesn't give a damn for poor orphans. So I guess I'll have to work me way up." She loved talking about the horses she'd own, the fancy carriages she'd drive.

Daft little bitch, he thought, and heard the sound of gunfire.

They got him going under the next rosebush, for he was bringing up the rear to protect his girls—Allegra especially, she was so little and slow. Any other boy would have screamed, but Byrne only winced and thought, *Me arse! Some highwayman I'll be, unable to sit a horse without weepin' like an old woman!*

The whining and pinging of metal continued, but he shut his eyes with pain, thought to himself that nothing mattered much now.

There was a sudden yanking on his wrists. "No," Viveca said with a hiss. "Don't you go fainting and dying on me, I won't have it!" She hauled at him until he rose and stumbled along with them.

That's right, don't faint. Who'll take care of the girls then?

He laughed sickly to himself a second later. Viveca need caring for? Why, she was tough as a whore's conscience! She was tugging him along with her, hammering on his shoulder, making him angry, insisting he keep up. "Stop it," Byrne answered. "We agreed to split up when there's trouble so the Runners don't catch the lot of us! Get away! Get out of here, leave me!"

"Quit playing a martyr! You read too many novels, Byrne St. James," Viveca mocked him desperately. "Don't you be a hero! Heroes *die!* And I don't want a dead hero, I want a live friend! Now, you goose it up."

Byrne felt a numbing, red strangeness spread on one side from his rump to his toes. He tried to look down at it, but fiercely loyal little Viveca cuffed him, kept his attention away from it.

They paused around the corner of the Blue Mermaid grog shop. "Get down that coal chute," Viveca ordered. Byrne and Allegra slid down first, and Viveca was about to follow when she saw the blood. There was so much blood. Except for it, she might have joined them, but someone had to stay behind, hurriedly mop up the blood . . .

And leave a fresh trail. Viveca pulled her folding stiletto from her sleeve, drew it across her arm. She gasped with the pain of it; she hadn't expected so sharp a blade to hurt so badly. There. Blood. She rubbed it off on the doorway of a nearby house, ran toward the alley, squeezed out some more scarlet on a dirty headscarf, and dropped it to be found in the alley.

It wasn't an alley at all, but a cul-de-sac. Dead end. Finished by a ten-foot-high brick wall.

Well, she thought, *I've climbed higher.* And, seeking out precarious toe- and finger holds, she crept up the wall and waited. Pursuit was not quite three minutes behind her, snuffling like bloodhounds on the scent. Viveca did everything but stand up on the wall shrieking, "Come and get me!" She scuffled on the loose bricks at the top and finally hefted a brick toward the Bow Street

Runners, bellowing. Then she slid gracefully down the wall onto—

—the roof of a doghouse!

A giant mastiff came roaring out at her. For a moment Viveca froze, an easy target, then remembered she was the only one who could help little Allegra and wounded Byrne. She *must* run. *Must!*

She sprinted across the yard. This was all Byrne's fault! If he hadn't gotten his bum shot up, her baby sister wouldn't be in danger right this very minute. She should have left him behind—anything to keep Allegra safe—but he was her dear Byrne, and he'd been kind to them when no one else cared.

The thought of the constables getting him and Allegra made her cold all over.

The yard was too long, she couldn't breathe, the dog was on her—the knife, get the knife out. . . . There was another dog loosed from the house with a cry of "Sic 'em!"

Shots. They were shooting at her. Viveca kicked the mastiff away as a stray shot picked him off. She vaulted up the last wall, six feet straight up, and not a finger hold in sight. But there was some decorative metal at the top—there! Her slim fingers could scarcely reach. Oh, if only she were older, with longer arms!

Just as she was getting a hold on the wall a steel trap closed around her foot. Viveca screamed and screamed. A bulldog! She'd heard that they never let go.

She wept and shrieked, forgetting how she'd promised herself never to cry, never to show pain. She swung her other foot and kicked at the bulldog as shots whistled overhead.

He only bit down harder. At last she caught hold of two iron bars atop the wall, swung herself up and over with the dog still attached. She jumped, hoping to break his neck or back in the fall.

Viveca landed hard, writhed on the ground in pain and fear. They would hang her—they hanged all thieves who couldn't buy their way out, and age didn't matter. She knew of a seven-year-old girl who'd been hanged at Tyburn—God, God, she was dying—no! Where was her steel nerve that never failed her, the animal

89

courage Byrne so admired? She scrabbled about in the dirt, found a stick, began prying it between the dog's resolute jaws.

"Ho, laddie, you won't loose the brute *that* way. Go on there!"

A deep, masterful voice. Viveca lifted her head, saw something slim and ghostly go flitting past. The bulldog released her and sprinted after it.

A tall, dark horse with a tall, dark man in a violently red-and-gold coat waited a few feet away. "What did you do?" she asked with a gasp.

"Let a greyhound bitch in season out of the kennel over there. Now can you stand, son? Then be quick about it—take my hand, come on, come on," he urged.

She swallowed her tears, accepted the hand up. "Throw your cloak around us and I'll pull my feet up and go small under it," she suggested, bolder now despite the pain and bleeding.

"Why should I?" the tall, dark man asked, though he was complying.

"Because I think you're Gentleman Jemmy St. James, and your Byrne and my Allegra are trapped back there in a grog-shop cellar! Now steady your mare—I can't sit her well with my feet tucked up here!"

"Hush, they're coming!"

Jemmy wrapped his cape around them, trying to make it fall in a natural manner. Then he slouched, pulling his hat down over his face, and wrapping his muffler in a way that obscured his too-well-known square chin and mouth. With any luck, he thought, they might not recognize the mare. He acted none too soon, for at that instant the Bow Street Runners clattered over the wall. Several stayed up there, searching the alleys from that vantage point, while two others climbed down and cocked their heads at Jemmy.

"Gents, an urchin came scrambling over here a minute before you with something that looked like—well, I couldn't be sure what it was, but it might have been jewelry or silver. He took off like the very devil once he shook the dog, mind you, so you'll have trouble catching him, but I think he went that way, back toward Fleet Street," Jemmy said, affecting the London accent of the gentry.

"Sympathetic criminals might have taken him in by now. Come, lads, let's troop on up that way. Thankee, sir!"

Jemmy and the policeman respectfully touched their hats to each other, then Jemmy clucked to his black racing mare, and she set off. "Which grog shop, boy?" came the voice in Viveca's ear.

"The Blue Mermaid, just back there a ways, s-sir."

She was so glad Jemmy had her. She wanted to wrap her arms around him, weep into the strong masculine scents of wool, leather, and tobacco. But that wouldn't be fitting, especially as he thought her a lad.

"I know the place," Jemmy told her after a moment's reflection. "Now what's your name, boy?"

Boy. "Vi— Vivyan," she said, having once heard a gentleman addressed by that name.

"Fine name, has the ring of money to it, and you don't sound bad-educated. Has Byrne spoken to you of my band of highwaymen?"

Her big chance at last! "So he has, sir," she answered swiftly with hammering heart, and touched her cap's brim as grown men did when speaking respectfully to each other. "Mr. St. James— Gentleman Jemmy, sir—I only read and write a *touch,* but I'm fleet of foot and I'd like to learn to ride. I think your band is fine, sir, fine."

"Thank you. Dog took your shoe and a good deal of skin, boy. Why don't we stop a minute while I bind it up?"

He dismounted, took two large pocket kerchiefs from his greatcoat, and bound her aching foot. "Tiny bones for a boy," Jemmy said, and *tsk-tsk*ed. "Get a mite bigger before trying to join up with me, all right? And you'll have to learn to sit a horse, though you're doing fairly well on Black Rose now. Settle on into the saddle, get the feel of it, and I'll lead the mare."

Unexpectedly he reached up and gave Viveca a thumping whack on the leg, which nearly made her faint. "You're a brave little bugger, you are," Jemmy praised. "I doubt Byrne is much braver."

"But he is, sir," she said quickly, thinking of the poor fellow with his bum full of shot.

Jemmy growled good-naturedly with a show of straight white teeth. Viveca loved the growl and the smile that followed; for many months to come she'd turn it over in her head, think that the smile had been all for her, even though he thought her but a cheeky lad. "No more 'sir,' God blast you, this isn't the military! We're not sailing off to make the seas safe for Britain!"

"No, sir," she agreed. "But one never knows, sir."

She thought all men were to be addressed as "sir," for Prince Frederick had been the only adult male in her life, and "sir" was the *least* anyone ever called him.

It was a little dizzy up here on the horse, she thought as Jemmy stopped the mare at the side of the grog shop and went to fetch the other children.

"Now you pop right up there on Black Rose with the other lad. Can't have you losing any more blood," Jemmy ordered Byrne and Allegra.

"Lad? But—" Allegra began. Viveca jabbed her in the ribs with her elbow.

"Aye, and Gentleman Jemmy says if I get bigger as I get older he might take me on! What do you think of that?"

Before anyone could answer, Jemmy stepped back and swore. "Why, my best mare's pregnant! Byrne, remember that chestnut mare of Caro's sister-in-law? I may have to buy her to replace Black Rose for a while when she gets too bulky."

"Darcy was her name," said Byrne as Jemmy began walking, leading the mare again. "Her dam's descended from D'Arcy's Yellow Turk and the Flying Childers. But her owner didn't much want to sell."

A chestnut mare in Kensington . . . Familiar, Viveca thought, yet she didn't know why. She was still bleeding and had her lap full of sleeping Allegra. And Byrne was hanging on to her, too, equally close to falling asleep or fainting.

She leaned back against him, told him he was a good sport. "You nearly died for me," he said.

"Oh, pish, it was no big deal," she said, and heard him chuckle weakly at her brusqueness.

Missus Lee made her soak the foot in a hot broth of mandrake and bitter aloes. Gentleman Jemmy stood by. "A good lad, your friend Vivyan," Jemmy told Byrne, out of Missus Lee's hearing. "Bring him along next year when you join up. Dash and I can use a reliable courier who won't crack under pressure, and I think he's our boy. Now you watch over Matthew and Luke and Dickon and Willy and Skiff and Bartholomew," he added, naming off the St. James brothers younger than Byrne and therefore under his care.

Viveca dizzily counted on her fingers. "Byrne, Dash, Jemmy, Benjamin's dead, and six others. Who's left to round out that famous dozen I hear about?" she asked when Jemmy was gone.

"There was more than a dozen, but three died as babies and one bought it in a shipwreck before I was born. There's Hezekiah, he's a spice merchant, and then there's Bertt, he got deported to the Americas years ago. So, there's your dozen. Now then, I want you to be the one picks the shot out of me arse, not the Chinawoman. I don't trust her witcheries, and you're my best mate. If you'll do it I'll run errands for you while you're laid up."

"If *you're* not laid up *longer*, Byrne St. James," she answered flippantly, though she did not feel flippant and had to force her smile for his benefit.

They hobbled on back to the dirty pallet stuffed with straw that they shared with Allegra and two or three of the littlest St. James boys, and Viveca made him lie down. There was nothing else to let him bite on, so she removed her sash and rolled it up, instructing him to "chomp down on a place where's there's less bullion so as not to scrape your lips off!" Then she took his folding pocketknife and heated it in the flame of the sole, stinking tallow lamp.

"When I'm rich," Viveca said, turning the blade over and over in the flame, "I won't have tallow lamps. They stink fit to make you puke. I *hate* them! I'm going to have lavender-scented oil in

93

tall crystal lamps, and I'll have ivory gewgaws in my hair and gold plates with rubies in the rims. And, of course, I'll have you over for supper every single day, Byrne St. James, and you'll have me to breakfast and fetch me in your silver coach."

"And me?" Allegra asked, still a bit traumatized by the night's harrowing adventures and tearful at being forgotten.

Viveca pulled the hot, glowing knife blade back, looked it over, and stuck it back in the fire. "Why, 'Legra, I couldn't do without you! Who'd wear all those blue silk dresses my dressmakers will make? And who'll be there to drink out of my enameled glass goblets? Now be a ducky and fetch that pot of weird stuff I had my foot in, will you? It ought to be good for ol' Byrne, too."

She dipped the hissing knife into the potion, wiped the soot off the blade, and had Allegra, Skiff, and Luke sit on Byrne while she operated. Each time she popped out another fragment she dribbled some of the mandrake water on Byrne's wound.

When the operation was over, she plopped her foot back in the remaining liquid. The children climbed off Byrne and, gradually losing interest, drifted away except for faithful Allegra. "You were a very brave assistant 'pothecary," Viveca told her. "Most brave of all!"

"I didn't look," Allegra confessed. "Could I maybe have the top floor of your house when we get rich?"

Viveca looked around her at the filth and squalor, and dug her nails into her palms. "For you, anything. Why the top floor?"

"So I can see anyone trying to sneak up on me. And I want a lamp that burns all night. I hate the dark. Oh, look! Poor Byrne's gone green and fainted."

Viveca gazed at Byrne and remembered her mother coming in, soaked with rain or covered with snow, and no one making a peep. But let Prince Fritz arrive damp or overheated from a stroll, and what a fuss! Change his clothes right away! And if he's cold, a hot drink and bundle him up, fast!

An idea came to her. She removed her grimy waistcoat, spread it gently over Byrne's shoulders. "Shh, Allegra, you must let him sleep. Boys are more fragile than girls, don't you know that?"

There would be no graceful running for Viveca from now on. She went from star sprinter of the band to mere kitchen help. The law was looking for a child with a mangled foot, and she couldn't move quickly, Missus Lee pointed out, so she must stay at the house and get things done.

"It's a shame you've outgrown the white dress," Missus Lee said one night, stirring a pot of leathery vegetables and water for the children; she kept the bread and meat to herself. "But we'll make another in a year or so when your hair's grown out and you've changed your hoyden's ways. You're getting pretty, Viveca. We'll have to fix you up, teach you to walk and talk like a lady, have you trained in a fine house."

Viveca didn't like this talk of a "house." She'd seen prostitutes and knew what they were. No more footwork for the crippled girl, all right—she'd be working on her back. "I'm not going to be a whore," she said stiffly.

"But there's such good money in it, my dear. And you're useless for anything else, you know, with that ugly foot. We'll have you educated, dressed nicely. And then, when you go to fainting so that some fine gentleman feels obligated to take you in, you'll have a better chance to go through his pockets. You can blackmail him afterward, too," Missus Lee continued coolly, stealing a solitary glance at Viveca from the corners of her eyes. "Terrible trouble for Cabinet members to be caught with little girls. We'll start you next year."

Next year Viveca would be eleven.

She pretended to work on her darning, thinking: *No, not me!* She wasn't going to be one of those reeking, painted women, those sewer girls. But crossing Missus Lee always led to trouble. If Viveca refused she might have to take Allegra and run away—for their own safety.

She took a final stitch in little Luke's stocking, yelped as she pricked her finger and had to suck it. Hell fire! None of them were going to get rich this way! She cocked an eyebrow at Missus Lee. "Why don't we steal bigger and better things?" she asked. "Less silverplate, more jewels?"

"Jewels are easier to trace and harder to fence, my little moll."

"Gentleman Jemmy doesn't seem to have much trouble fencing the horses and carriages and jewels he gets," countered Viveca, who thought Jemmy was very nearly God.

"He has friends who are smugglers and can take them to France or Spain. I cannot afford such expensive friends, except to get me an occasional fruit of the lotus."

Ah, that was the stuff she took once in a while that made her dreamy and vacant-eyed. They all appreciated nights when Missus Lee became a lotus-eater, for then they were free to run wild.

Viveca wiped her nose on her sleeve and decided that if she was going to move up in the world, she was going to do it without Missus Lee and her reprimanding shooting stick. The old woman carried it like a gentleman of fashion and laid about her with bone-cracking force when she was crossed.

She was being crossed now, and Viveca felt sick in the pit of her stomach at the memory of the last time the stick had come down on her injured foot. So she said nothing else.

Missus Lee eyed her craftily. "My band getting too small for you, precious? You're spending too much time remembering silk sheets and fine dresses, I think. But you must recall that I saved you and your sister and that I own you as surely as a man owns a dog he may beat and even *kill* when it refuses to obey. So do not let your dreams overwhelm you. I think you understand what I mean."

She suddenly hurled a scalding ladleful of broth at the girl. But Viveca had guessed there was a blow in the making and had already ducked to one side. Broth splashed the wall where she had sat propped up a moment ago, but she was no longer there. There was a rustle of sound in the blackness surrounding the circle of lamplight, then the Chinawoman was alone.

The Lindstrom girls did not come back.

CHAPTER ELEVEN

April 1759

"You're certain you're all right?" Allegra inquired anxiously.

Viveca nodded, face ashen above the blue-and-white-striped gown she had smashed through a dressmaker's window to get the week before. She was thirteen and frightened, tired of stealing. She would have given up if not for Allegra. Who would take care of her ten-year-old sister if she didn't?

"You're lying! Your foot still hurts!" Allegra insisted.

"That was years ago, little goose!"

Her little sister shook her dreamy head, blond curls bobbing in agitation. "We should change clothes, you should let me do it, I can still run! And suppose there's trouble? We don't have Byrne to back us up anymore." They rarely saw him now that he was a highwayman.

"Sister, you vex me some," Viveca admitted, then smiled. "Take care of my old clothes while I'm inside, will you? I'll even let you wear my sash, hmm?"

She wrapped it around her sister's narrow waist, knotted it so that the fringe with its bullion tassels hung down past her knee. "Now don't trip over it, ducky. Take care of it till I come back and wear it, all right? And don't look so sad—I know you hate living in the streets, but I'll get us out soon!"

Allegra sat down on the remains of a stone wall near the alley she was to wait in. "All right, but hurry. I'm hungry, and I know where there's an unguarded fish pond."

Viveca gritted her teeth, pinched her cheeks for color, and crept across cobblestones toward the white Palladian mansion she had picked for the evening's heist. She disarrayed the false, dark curls over her arrow-straight, tawny hair, unhooked the top of her bodice—damn! still flat as a dirt street!—and stooped to gather dirt to smear on her cheek.

Then she ran lightly to the door in the dark, carrying her skirts until she reached for the bellpull.

When the long-nosed valet answered, she was clinging to the elephant-faced brass door knocker, letting her weight hang limply from it. "Oh, help me, kind sir!"

Let's see, which tale tonight? Brigands or a carriage wreck? She knew the latter by heart, having been through it, so she used that one. "A terrible carriage wreck—there was a coach stopped in the middle of the road with a lame horse as we came around the corner—oh, terrible! Please send help! My mother, my baby sister . . ."

She even squeezed out a tear or two. *There.* That helped. Peeking up through her lashes, she could see him considering her plight. Carriage wrecks were best: they always got the able-bodied men out of the house to look for survivors, and Viveca figured she could better prey on the women's sympathies if they were alone.

The valet hadn't budged, so she dropped into a feigned swoon, wrist to brow. What was taking him so long to answer?

"What is it, Jives?" called a deep male voice.

Jives disdainfully prodded her with his toe. "Young girl fainting away on the doorstep. Claims a carriage wreck, she do."

"Well, fetch her in, you damned fool! It's our Christian duty, man!"

Through half-opened eyes, Viveca saw Jives wrinkle his nose in disdain and flex his white-gloved fingers.

"Pick her up, Jives! She won't bite!" came the exasperated rejoinder.

"Might as bloody *well,*" Jives observed, and hefted her up.

He held her as far away from him as possible, as though fearing contact with her might bring dire results. He strode on into the family gathering without any further ado and displayed his

98

limp bundle for examination. Viveca clamped her eyes shut, forcing herself to remain lax.

"Why, the poor dear," gushed a voice surely belonging to the mother of the family. "She obviously comes from a good family, with petite bones like that! Commoners don't have those exquisite wrist bones and that finely sculpted jawline!"

Her? They were talking about *her?* Viveca almost glowed. It was an effort to remain limp and not sit up to thank the woman for her compliments.

"It's a nice dress, all right," hotly declared a young miss. "Looks just like the striped damask that Smythe of High Street was making for me!"

Uh-oh!

"Yes," Young Miss continued, "and some boy broke the window in broad daylight and stole it, I tell you! A tawny-haired urchin with a rock! I was *there!*"

Viveca immediately tried to insinuate *curvy, female,* and possibly even *brunette* into her pose.

"Why, I *do* remember the dress," Mother cried out. "It *is* quite like it!"

"Eh, eh?" asked a cracking voice. *Grandmother, no doubt,* Viveca thought. It was time to act fast, before they drew close enough to make out recognizable features, like the distinctive way Smythe had done the gathers for the paniers and the tucks in the bodice.

"Madame," said Jives with many huffs and puffs despite Viveca's light weight, "may I—*oof!*—set the young lady bloody well —oh, no!"

His knees went. Before Viveca had a chance to create a diversion, Jives did so. He stepped backward onto a pair of sleeping white lapdogs and awkwardly sat down on the Chippendale settee.

In the brief silence that followed the master of the house announced he would go look for the carriage wreck, clapped his hat on his head, and vanished out the door.

Viveca sat up, feigning confusion. "Oh, help! There were brigands—why, where am I?"

"Probably in *my* dress," muttered Young Miss, who looked spoiled and dangerous.

"Christ! Going to help the Lord, I am," Jives muttered amid the vortex of swelling female emotion. He sprang for the latch on the garden doors and missed, catching his coattails on two tiny scuttling tables. As Jives whipped around, they swung with him in a giddy three-partner dance.

Good God! Viveca thought. *Have I ever picked the wrong house!* At that instant the little dogs leapt onto her lap, clawing holes in her skirt and exposing the bright lining.

Young Miss jumped up and down in angry excitement. "Maman, Maman! It *is* my dress, I'd know that salmon jacquard lining anywhere!"

"I *bought* this gown," Viveca argued, standing and trying to dislodge the yapping dogs from her wickerwork paniers. Lord! How to get out of this madhouse? Jives was continuing his jig with the tables, Grandmother was swatting at him with an embroidery hoop, and Maman was fluttering to and fro like a demented butterfly.

"Thief, thief!" Young Miss chanted, dancing around in her fury.

"It is *not* stolen. I bought it, and my father's an ambassador, so watch who you call 'thief,' you bloody bitch! I'll break your neck!" Viveca burst out, swatting at the dog and backing toward the bay windows. They opened out onto some bushes, she had discovered when casing the house last night. Bushes were great for breaking falls.

"Did you hear what the trashy wench called me, Maman?" Young Miss shrilled. "Damn it, I won't be called a bitch by a bitch like that! Give me back my dress, you—"

Viveca turned too sharply and missed the bay window. She blundered into an acre of red damask drapes, flailing wildly as Young Miss took careful aim and threw a gilt vase at her. Cloisonné followed, plus an entire set of Bavarian crystal goblets. Viveca, struggling and groping her way through the damask in search of windows, found one at last. A large one, wide-open. She jumped through, taking yards of scarlet damask with her.

She fell face-first into a fish pond. Fat, slimy carp wiggled over her, leaped onto the grass to avoid her. Here was Allegra's dinner, she thought hungrily, and, picking up a flung samovar from its bed of shattered glass, opened it and stuffed a fat carp inside.

Young Miss was still playing tennis with her, lobbing crockery and silver out the broken windows. Viveca held out her torn petticoats, scooped pewter, sterling, and giltware into them. The carp was trying to get out of the samovar, and Young Miss had begun flinging chinoiserie, which broke to bits upon impact, so Viveca decided to give up and leave with the cream of the pickings.

Before she could turn away, she was drawn toward the bushes, where something was making inarticulate snorting sounds. Viveca parted the roses and saw Allegra rolling and kicking on the ground, convulsed with laughter. "Lot of help you were, and me standing on my damned head surrounded by madwomen and carp! Here, take this fish and the loot!"

Viveca ripped off her petticoats and handed them to her sister, who stood up slowly, wiping her eyes. "And give me my breeches, I'm half-naked," she grumbled, changing clothes from the lot carried over Allegra's arm. "Now give me the sack to put all this in, and hurry, there's someone walking over there, and we look suspicious!"

The door banged open as the carp leaped to freedom. *"Help, a thief!"* came an outraged feminine bellow. *"Stop, thief, stop!"*

Viveca and Allegra took off at a sprint. "Why do they yell that? Do they think we're simpleminded and will freeze in our tracks?" Viveca asked. She stuffed her hair under her hat, running at a fair clip for one with a crippled foot.

"Stop right there!" came a steely-voiced order from the dark. It was close, not three yards away, and with it came the sound of a gun being cocked. Moonlight glinted on a badge. The fearless Bow Street Runners!

Viveca swung the petticoat full of loot at the man, screaming, *"Run for it!"* at her sister.

"Look, the sash! There goes the ringleader!" someone shouted as Allegra fled back toward the alley and its man-tall wooden gate.

A heavy blow landed on Viveca's head. She hit the ground, rolled, felt a chain fastened about her ankle, then wrist. There were sounds of gunfire. . . .

She glanced up through a trickle of blood and saw the alley door slam shut behind Allegra as she raced to freedom.

But, wait! The heavy bullion fringe and tassels had caught in the latch! Little white fingers stole around the edge to loosen it—

Shots rang out. There was no outcry, no sound of pain or death. Instead the little white fingers stiffened for a few seconds, then collapsed, making a limp fist. They and the fringe slid down, lower, lower, to the ground.

There were holes in the wooden gate at just about a child's height.

Viveca put both hands to her mouth to swallow down the terrible cry of rage and grief she felt welling up inside her. "It's Newgate and hanging for you, my lad," someone said to her. "And a lucky thing we caught you at last, too. We've been on the lookout. An Oriental woman told us that the brat with the sash was ringleader of all kinds of thieving in these parts."

Missus Lee had gotten them at last, had punished them for striking out on their own. *Why Allegra?* Viveca thought numbly. *Why not me? It was my idea—it was my sash! I've killed her!*

She had two regrets as they dragged her away to the most feared prison in Britain. The first was that sweet little Allegra had died in her place before they could become rich and lead the good life.

The second was that she, Viveca Lindstrom, would not get to kill Missus Lee before they placed the noose around her own neck.

CHAPTER TWELVE

Viveca sat in a corner of the yard at Newgate, cap pulled low on her brow, munching a dried-out orange peel and thinking. The rich continued to live richly, even here; they brought in their servants, cooks, and furnishings, and eventually they bought their way out. The less fortunate gambled, whored, and clawed their way up through heaps of festering humanity to a place of relative safety; the least fortunate, like Viveca, were the young. They sold themselves to the highest bidder or found a protector quickly.

Dressed in boys' clothing, she had been flung in with the men. She was lucky in that a whole tribe of urchins had been brought in that same night, and she was able to lose herself in their midst. There was a great liking for fresh-faced, pretty boys in the men's sector of the prison, so Viveca went to pains to appear as dirty and rough as possible.

There were no blankets for them, and they ate no meat or vegetables, only gray bread—dry, hard, full of sawdust and ground bone meal from charnel houses, mixed in by the miller to save himself money. Stagnant water accompanied this fare, making up the twice-daily meal for those who couldn't afford to frequent the peddlers hawking meats and fresh fruits in the yard each day.

After a week of gagging down brown water and moldy bread, all the while growing feebler on this diet, Viveca decided she had to do something about her state of existence. The noose might be hanging over her head, but in the meantime she still had life of a sort, and that was to be fought for.

She asked around and was told that a prisoner called Great Edward was the best friend to make, that he wielded considerable influence among guards and other prisoners. So Viveca determined to worm her way into his circle somehow.

She was still thinking on it that night when a large, foul-smelling man came shuffling over to where the boys lay whispering or sleeping. He lifted a lantern, let it play among the lads. "You, there—they want to see you a poss'ble pardon," he said. "Seems you know some'un wi' money after all. Follow me."

They were clapping her on the back, congratulating her as she rose with thudding, incredulous heart. *Why, Byrne must have heard,* she thought. *Byrne told Jemmy. Jemmy St. James is the only person in the world I know with money. I'm being rescued by him!*

She clasped her hands together as she followed the turnkey, felt herself grow light-headed with excitement and starvation. Just like the fairy stories old Bess had told her. The prince on the prancing horse had come to rescue her!

She was going to grow up and marry Jemmy St. James, she told herself as the turnkey unlocked a gate, pushed her through, and bolted it after them. He roughly shoved her down a long, cold corridor with murky water running down the walls in stinking torrents. There were stairs that took them deeper. "Are we underground?" she whispered, watching him set the lantern down. An instant later he hurled her to the ground.

She turned her head, sank her teeth into his meaty hand, but he landed a bruising blow alongside her head, dug his thumbs into her windpipe. "Dead or alive, don't matter to me," he said, and laughed wickedly.

He had a knee between hers, and her breeches were torn. Sobbing, Viveca wrenched a wrist loose, tried to shake her knife out of its scabbard. The turnkey seized hold of her elbow and yanked. "Nothin' doin'!"

He was ripping her sleeve to get the knife; it clattered to the floor. "Got ye now," the fat man said, gloating in the dancing lantern light.

She screamed, kept on screaming.

He raised himself on one elbow to unfasten his breeches. Next, he yanked hers down . . .

"Jesus *Christ!* A girl!"

A girl he'd relaxed his grip on. Viveca twisted, lightning-fast, to one side. She caught the knife, flicked the blade out with her fingernail. She wanted to cut him, make him let go. He was so fat, how could she possibly cut him deeply enough to make him stop? He was strangling her. . . .

Then he went limp on top of her, and she couldn't get the knife back. There were running footsteps in the corridors. *"Help,"* Viveca cried out, *"help!"*

They were pulling him off. Freed for a moment, she fastened her clothes with wet hands. Surprised, she sat up, pushed her cap back on her head, and peered down at her hands, red with blood to the wrist. She'd killed him. They'd hang her for sure now. *As good to be shot for a pheasant as for a goose,* she told herself as they dragged her away with kicks and cuffs.

The next day Viveca's sentence was passed.

For the crimes of thievery and murder of an official while in the course of his duty, "Vivyan" Lindstrom was to be taken from Newgate to Tyburn and, on the third of the month, one week from this day, to be hanged by the neck until dead.

She was dragged away to a tiny cell and chained to a post so that she could neither stand nor sit but had to crouch. And thus she was to spend her remaining week of life, shut away in the dark, losing her mind in the filth—

No. She would not go mad. They would not break her. She sang because there was no other way to occupy her mind; when she could no longer remember lyrics of her old nursery songs, she made them up.

The third morning of her confinement, sleepless, losing feeling in her legs, lips cracked and bleeding from singing without food or water, she thought she heard the food slot opening in the door. No, wait—the entire *door* was opening! Sunlight poured in, blinding her, making her avert her head with no sound.

A cultured voice said, "My dear boy, you must know every Scottish ballad ever penned by those noble northern savages. If I hear 'Killecrankie O' or 'The Bonny Earl o' Moray' or especially that monotonous Sheriffmuir refrain—'and we ran and they ran and we ran and they ran'—I shall probably drown you in your tin water cup. Is that understood?"

The voice wasn't angry. Viveca lifted her head, made out the form of her visitor to be male, emaciated, nearly seven feet tall—and holding a large white pocket kerchief over his mouth and nose. "Singing is all I can do chained up like this, and I've determined that they shan't drive me mad before they hang me," she whispered hoarsely.

He said something to a lackey behind him, then turned back to her. "Young man, your speech is quite refined for an urchin. May I inquire as to what sort of parents you had to have educated you so?"

Viveca hesitated only a moment. "My mother was a Scottish widow. Lost her husband at that same Culloden battle you spoke of. She refugeed south, met a man of means, and after she became his mistress, I was born nine months later. In"—she calculated rapidly—"January of forty-seven." There! That made her birth too late to be the responsibility of the man killed at Culloden.

"And this man's name was . . . ?" the incredibly tall man asked.

She decided to act reluctant. "She—my mother—called him Fritz or Frederick. He had a red coach with a crown and ostrich plumes on the door and the motto was in German—"

"Ich dien?" the tall man asked with a sharp inhalation.

"Yes. I believe that was it. What's it mean?"

" 'I serve.' It's the motto of—"

Viveca cut in, "She told me he was the Prince of Wales, but I don't believe it."

"Unshackle the boy, he's coming with me," the tall man said. And so Viveca found herself "adopted."

Great Edward's suite in the prison had carpets on the floor, three and four thick. He pointed them out, taught her the names: *Kerman, Shirvan, Sarouk.*

"We only had a Turkish carpet, and it was kept on the table," she told him. "I had the feeling Fritz never had much money."

"That's true, he didn't," agreed the thin man, eyes piercing behind his spectacles. "Are your legs better now that my masseuse has worked on them?"

Viveca had wept herself sick into the pillow she'd had to hug during the proceedings. "Yes, I can feel them now. Hurts like hell, too, sir. Thank you, sir."

Great Edward nodded and reached into his pocket, pulled out the ivory miniature with that long, haughty face Viveca knew so well. "This was in your boot when we pulled it off you. I believe it might be a Lely, Sir Peter Lely. I shall have to look in my books and find out for certain," he said, and proceeded to do so.

Full of mushroom-and-crouton-stuffed quail, tea, black pudding, and asparagus on rice—all of it taken in minute amounts, for Great Edward said large helpings would make her ill after starving for so long—Viveca nodded pleasantly into her teacup before waking up enough to ask, "Why'd you help me, sir?"

He shook his head. "A starving child sentenced to hang for stealing and for knifing a guard who had attempted rape— where's the justice in that?"

"And you felt sorry for me," Viveca said, confused. "What's pity got to do with life, sir? I doubt anyone's pitied me before— and why should they? I could always take care of me and mine just fine."

"I had sons and a wife. They died," Great Edward said, looking up from his art books. "Had someone helped them, they would have lived. And so I—"

There was a respectful knock at the door. The scholar turned to grant admittance to his visitor, and they mumbled briefly, then the messenger left.

Edward turned to face her with a note in his hand. "What a brave little liar you are," he said, folding the paper up. "Did you think I was an official and that I might pardon you for your feigned noble blood? You're too tall, too old to be Allegra, the bastard daughter of the Prince of Wales by the Widow Lindstrom. That makes you the other child. A brave little liar indeed. You're not even a boy! And you're the child of a northern farmer, not a prince."

He yanked the cap off her head. "Yes," Great Edward said,

"that hacked-off hair might be strawberry blond after a thorough shampooing, and the eyes are certainly dark enough to be called black. You would be Viveca Lindstrom, then, and not the child of a prince and therefore worth saving."

She drew herself up in the tiger maple chair. "Anything was worth a try if it got me out of that cell!"

Great Edward stroked his clean-shaven chin with one gnarled hand. "Yes, I suppose so. Were I facing torture and hanging instead of getting out next month, I'd . . ." He glanced at her sharply. "Is there anyone outside to help you?"

"The St. James boys," she said quickly. "Gentleman Jemmy has lots of money—maybe he'd get me out, let me pay him back later. I know him, I'm friends with his brother. They say if you have money you can buy your way out of anything, even a hanging offense."

"Would that were true," Great Edward said, "then Jemmy would not be in such trouble. You see, my child, he shot a man during a robbery. He's in Newgate this very minute. They're hanging the two of you together on the third."

CHAPTER THIRTEEN

". . . it was an accident, of course, but they'll hang me, any-way," Jemmy said cheerfully. "Oh, don't look at me like that, it doesn't matter. Life's just a here-and-now thing; you take what you want and you pay for it. Fancy you being a girl, anyway. Did you really think you would grow up to join my band?"

He lowered his muscular, booted legs from the table, letting them drop to the floor with a jangling of the spurs he wore, as though still urging on Black Rose, his racing mare.

Viveca wiped her nose on her sleeve and blinked hard. "We'll be brave together, shall we, Jemmy?"

"Of course we will," he answered, and chuckled warmly, a honey-jar-in-a-sunny-windowsill sound. "You just got to go to it like a gentleman with your chin up and a courtly bow and laugh for one and all. Then they'll say, 'Didn't he make a fine end?' And, with my hanging, it'll now be more of an honor for people to be robbed by my brothers. They'll say, 'Why, you look just like that Gentleman Jemmy, and wasn't he a fine lad? Some end he made, eh? Here's me purse, lads. Don't spend it all one place!' "

She drank in the beauty of that young male face, swallowed hard, acted brave. "Did they say that when they got your brother hanged?"

He poured her a pewter tankard of sherry, then added some more to his half-empty one. "Sure they did, sweetheart. Ladies loved me for looking like Benjamin, you know. And they feel the same about Dash, and it'll be Byrne after him."

There were footsteps outside the door, then a morose-looking guard stepped in without knocking. Behind him waited a company of armed men. "Jeremy St. James and Vivyan Lindstrom?" he asked gruffly.

Jemmy waved the guard away like a fly—or tried to. "Get on wi' ye, man, you can't touch us till Tuesday!"

The morose man regarded him evenly. "Not true, St. James. We're expecting trouble from those wild brothers of yours, so we've moved the execution up two days."

Jemmy's jaw went chalky along the edge. "All right," he said at last in a low voice, and reached for his hat. "I'll make myself ready two days early, is all."

Behind him, among the men in the hall, Viveca saw a guard of Jemmy's exact size and build with the same black hair and eyes. This man was perhaps six or seven years younger, with a narrower chin and a nose that had plainly been broken at least once, but the face—the face might be Byrne in another ten or twelve years—or it might have been Jemmy at about the age of twenty-eight. Viveca gawked so at the man that at last he winked, put a finger to his lips, and shook his head violently. He must be the famous Dash St. James. *Must* be!

Her heart wanted to leap out of her narrow chest. "The *lad* comes, too," the guard insisted, while Jemmy argued with him.

She stepped down hard on Jemmy's foot. He wore boots and she had little strength after her confinement, but there was no mistaking the deliberateness of the act. Jemmy raised an eyebrow at her. "I'm coming along. Not to worry," she said almost gaily, but what she thought was, *Can they do it? Can they really save us?*

When Jemmy persisted in arguing with the turnkey, she put a hand on his arm and pinched him. "It's all right," she said bravely, in a lad-to-lad-about-to-die-together tone. "In fact, Jemmy, my boy, I feel as though we have a great deal of . . . *brotherly love* going for us at present."

At last he looked away from the turnkey, saw his family. "Why, yes," he agreed, brightening. "Let's go then."

There was another dark-haired young man at the rear of the seven guards. Viveca could not be sure, but she thought that it might very well be Byrne.

He fell into line alongside the brother who must be Dash, with his startling resemblance to Jemmy. And there was a third guard who looked to be in on it, a slim, elegant-looking young chap with a thick mustache—only the mustache didn't fit quite right—and his long blue eyes were absolutely beautiful. Even a fast application of theatrical makeup and dirt couldn't disguise the basic fact from a woman's knowing eyes:

The guard between the two St. James brothers was a woman! The long blue eyes lit on Viveca with the same start she had just felt: the shock of recognition.

They went on down the corridor into the noise and bustle of the yard, where the other prisoners fell silent, realizing what was happening. The men removed their caps, one by one, in salute to the king of highwaymen. On the other side of the fence, the women set up a wail for the beauty and still-lingering youth of Jemmy going to the gallows at a ripe thirty-five years of age. Spurs clinking, he strode along, winking, blowing kisses to the keening women, looking, in his gaudy clothes, like a lord with plenty of money but no taste whatsoever.

Viveca trooped along behind him, trying to breathe steadily. When? When would they make their move? Now? Or outside? Before the gallows? Or were there reinforcements there? Dear God, they just might cheat the hangman after all!

There was a sturdy little open wagon waiting at the gate, with an armed driver and a man sitting next to him holding a long-barreled musket across his knees. Both wore their caps pulled low across their brows, as though, Viveca thought, shielding their faces from the light of day—or recognition.

She and Jemmy were roughly bundled into the wooden Death Cart. A white-haired minister climbed in with them, reading in a monotone from a creased leather-bound prayer book. But he was reading in *Latin*. Viveca looked more closely at his clerical collar and saw that it was Roman. Why, a priest. What a shock! They were a rare sight, indeed, being quite out of favor, with the Church of England so firmly entrenched on both throne and conscience.

After a moment she realized that Jemmy was staring goggle-

111

eyed at the priest, too. His face was white, very white beneath the healthy tan; she wondered what shock of recognition had just been dealt *him.*

Her knees were knocking together as they chained her wrists, but she noticed that it was the disguised woman who did it, and the key was not turned far enough to click the lock shut, despite a show of bustling efficiency. The woman did the same thing with Jemmy's chains, but he continued to stare at the priest, oblivious to all else.

They jolted off as a crowd began to gather. Viveca made small talk with the guards, figuring out rapidly who was and wasn't in the rescue party. Two St. James boys, the girl, and possibly the priest. And the driver?

Yes, for just then the driver sang out, "Highwaymen after us!" and whipped up the horses so quickly that everyone was thrown onto the floor of the Death Cart. Viveca pulled herself back up, glanced in front of her. Those were no ordinary cart horses. They were fine animals, and they were running like the wind. Heads were beginning to pop up all over the cart, but someone—could that be Byrne? His voice sounded so deep!—yelled to keep down, for they were being shot at.

Surely it was a ruse, wasn't it? She wanted to be sure she stood a chance on her own, so she unscrewed the bayonet from the musket of a distracted guard and slid it down her boot, one hand hovering over it, ready.

The cart went rocking around a corner. Viveca looked up to see a roof, then abruptly realized that they had just driven into a stable.

"Ho, there!" the driver called, standing up and hauling back on the reins. The horses skidded to a stop as everyone else, bumping heads together, also stood.

The stable doors slammed shut. Two burly brigands with muskets were coming toward them. And Byrne, Dash, the driver, and the girl were aiming their own weapons at the other guards. "Climb out real easy now," Dash St. James advised the guards and driver's assistant.

The driver's assistant hesitated. Viveca, sensing trouble, unobtrusively drew the bayonet from her boot and waited, muscles coiling for the jump.

The man sprang at Jemmy, who saw it coming and ducked. Viveca tripped the man, held the bayonet to his neck. "It isn't sharp, so cutting you will take extra work," she said, her words like hisses. "Drop your knife—*drop it!*"

He opened his hand, let it fall away. The driver stooped to retrieve it. "Good work, boys, but you could've warned me," Jemmy sang out, springing over the side of the Death Cart to the ground.

"We just found out from Great Edward this morning that they moved up the day of execution," Dash said, letting the two men at the door take charge of their prisoners and quickly bind their hands and feet.

There were horses waiting, saddled, bridled, impatient to be off. Viveca recognized the slim black head and arched tail of Black Rose, Jemmy's famed racing mare. She turned to Byrne. "You're all grown," she said wistfully.

He grinned broadly. *"You're not!"*

The girl guard ripped her mustache off and laughed. Black curls fell from beneath her hat—strong, wavy St. James hair. She stuck her hand out, gave Viveca a firm handshake. "I'm Lilly Carlisle, Jemmy's daughter. I've heard all about you from Uncle Byrne."

"Get on your horses!" Dash barked. *"Hurry!"*

A strong hand seized Viveca under the arm as Jemmy yanked her aboard Black Rose. "Let's go!" he shouted, then, to Lilly, "That's my girl!"

The priest waved to Jemmy and slipped out through a side door. "Why did he come along? Is he really a priest?" Viveca asked as Jemmy prepared to spur his mare.

"Yes, he's really a priest," Jemmy said tersely. "He's also my father. Gee up, Rose!"

The horses, clattering out onto the street, were met by a volley of gunfire.

Byrne, with an exemplary coolness belying his age, picked off the leader of the government troops and shot him between the

113

eyes. Then he reined his black colt in between Black Rose and the gunfire, protecting Viveca and Jemmy long enough to throw Jemmy a long-barreled pistol and a heavy musket. "Everyone scatter! Thin out!" Jemmy shouted, and reached over affectionately to cuff brave Byrne on the ear in thanks.

Then the gunfire was worse. Byrne was winged, and Lilly Carlisle was grabbing his horse by the bridle and taking him down an alley.

Viveca felt something shoved into her hands. She looked down to see the long pistol there. "Kill anything that moves," Jemmy ordered tensely. A moment later a volley of shot ricocheted off a tin feed tank and nicked Black Rose's haunch. The mare reared straight up in the air, all four iron-shod hooves leaving the ground.

She came down, fishtailed. Her left shoulder almost brushed the ground, throwing Viveca halfway off. Shots rang out perilously close. Jemmy's fingers were digging furrows of pain in her shoulder. "Hang on, damn you! Hang on, girl!" Then the mare was up on her hind legs, flailing like a boxer at the surrounding foot soldiers.

Not six feet away a man crouched in between storage bins, taking careful aim at Viveca. But the mare was bobbing, blocking his shot. Viveca hung low on the plummeting ebon neck and squeezed off a shot. She felt queerly disturbed as the man fell back in an arc of crimson. He'd tried to kill her. So why did she feel like this?

Jemmy was no damned help at all. He was leaning his full weight on her, and she seemed to be the only one shooting. And why was Black Rose so wild? Like Jemmy had no control over her at all.

Then a loose rein snaked past her cheek, and she understood: Jemmy was dead or seriously wounded.

There was an explosion of red off the mare's shoulder. Black Rose was hit! Viveca wondered how badly as she desperately clung to the heaving neck. She swung a foot free, kicked the mare again and again, and at last Black Rose turned, galloped wildly down the alley Byrne and Lilly had disappeared into. She stumbled over a rubbish pile, and in that moment Viveca caught one rein, then the other.

She reached for the slumped Jemmy. He was breathing, all right, and his pulse was racing, but damn if he wasn't shot through the chest. There was blood, but there wasn't time to stop and see how much. Moving him might kill him, but given a choice between that and recapture, she thought he'd urge her to take the risk. She reined in the mare, yanked off Jemmy's silk muffler, and used it to tie the two of them to the saddle.

Jemmy said something. Or did he? She urged the mare on with sharp toes and a flap of the reins. "Caro," came from the wounded man's cracked lips. "Caro. Black Bull."

Black Bull? That must be a tavern or grog shop somewhere.

They galloped out of the alley. Viveca's eyes went around in consternation. There was a fruit market there, and a cart blocking their way. "Up, Black Rose," she babbled, not knowing if that was the proper word to make a horse jump. "Up, Black Rose, up!"

She felt the mare's muscles gather, tighten, and compress. Then she gave Black Rose another three inches of rein, smacking her on the rump with the flat of her hand.

The racing mare rose, stretched herself into a curve of night-black heart and muscle. Oranges and apples flashed below, and heaps of blazing green limes. She came down neatly, like a dancing girl, hooves smacking onto cobblestones. Merchants fled, screaming, overturning their own wheelbarrows in their hurry.

Down the cobbled street, around a corner, into a cul-de-sac with a fountain. They raced back out past three Bow Street Runners blasting away on their whistles. Viveca grappled for the musket trapped beneath her leg, wrestled it free, and fired a shot to clear their way. It only brought more gunfire whistling vengefully around her ears.

Blood. Jemmy was bleeding freely now, and the mare's shoulder streamed scarlet. A crossroads loomed ahead, and Viveca did not know which way to go. She was exhausted and discouraged.

Caro. The Black Bull. She took her sightings on the sun,

squared the mare for the west and Kensington. Several false turns later she was certain they were on the road to that quiet hamlet.

A startling thought made Viveca's head shoot up. *Caro. The Black Bull.* Jemmy had asked to go there, and the mare knew the way, just as she would had she been there many times. *But Jemmy had never said the Black Bull was in Kensington.*

How had she known? Viveca wondered dizzily. There was a mist in her head, swirling, with many images caught there, all the faces speaking at once. At last she singled out her mother from the maelstrom, that scarce-remembered blur whose features she had once known by heart. She heard her say, "Your Aunt Caro in Kensington . . . you were born the night they brought the bear home to the Black Bull in Kensington." Caro . . . the Black Bull . . . Caro . . . she hurt, she hurt. *I've been shot.* . . .

Flowers. She saw flowers—were they tuberoses?—growing on either side of the private road, under the signs whose lettering she couldn't read. Signs with paintings of a rearing black bull.

A big blue house . . . but there seemed to be no one in the yard of the inn. Black Rose cut across the courtyard as she had done a thousand times. Viveca, who did not know the mare had been taught to wait at Caro's bedroom window, thought they were about to ride right on past the building. Her head sagged on her chest.

She fainted.

Hidden by the curved side of the old Tudor house, Black Rose was unseen by the hostlers and gamesters emerging from the inn. She pawed up some tender green shoots of grass and waited, as she had been taught to do. Trusting, in the manner of all domestic animals, she hung her weary head, blood streaming from her shoulder wound, and waited for someone to feed her and take the heavy load from her back.

PART THREE

Viveca

"Well, the gold and the silver on the ground,
It looked so jolly
That I gathered it all up and brought it to my Molly.
She promised and she vowed that she never would deceive me,
But Devil take the women! for they never can be easy."

—"Whiskey in the Jar," late 18th-century Irish Traditional

CHAPTER FOURTEEN

Kensington, 1762

"She's my mother's horse, Byrne St. James, and I'll jump her higher if I want to!" came the outburst as Viveca touched her heels to Blackamoor's flanks.

Caro Lindstrom sighed disapprovingly and sat back in her new Adams chair, which was highly unstable beneath her bulk. She called the chambermaid for a pitcher of lemonade and was glad of it a minute later when she saw Great Edward emerge from a carriage. "Hello," he greeted, bending over her hand and kissing it as if she were some fine lady. "You're looking lovely, if flushed, Missus Caro."

"Thank you, Mister Edward. It's those wild children that have me riled again—not Byrne, for he's a good lad, but that Viveca! Sixteen now, and fast-talking! She's been uncontrollable since Jemmy died. You're the only person able to talk a lick of sense into that girl, and I wish you could take her to London and put her to work more than twice or thrice a week like you do, not that I'm not grateful or don't love her, but—"

"I know," Edward said, folding his long body onto another small chair. "It's just that Viveca's something of a wildcat. But her reading and writing has come along splendidly, and she's making a fine secretary for me. Now, it's none of my business, Missus Caro, but you and I are getting to know each other better, and I feel I should ask about this mysterious mother of Viveca's. I mean, I know Viveca thought her mother was dead for years, but—"

"Her mother's remarried twice and has gone off now on a long

119

honeymoon with the last one, off to Roosia or some such wild frontier. She sends money each month for the care of the horses and gives instruction on their breeding and training, but no return address, and I don't know how to contact her, to tell her the child lives!"

"I have the impression Viveca's decided her mother doesn't want her."

"Ginny would want her, if she only knew! She was so battered in that carriage wreck, Ginny was—when she came here, she was a ghost of herself. She was only half-healed when she staggered off to find her daughters, and she lived in the streets, starved, searching for any clue of them. I couldn't get her to give a hang about her health or looks; she just wanted her children. At last she nigh died of hunger and cold, and weakened enough for me to catch her, and I contacted her Turkish friend, Yasaman, that she'd told me about."

"Would Yasaman know where Ginny is now?"

The lemonade arrived. Caro poured for both of them, watched Great Edward take an approving sip. "I'm hoping so. She's not in London anymore, but I got her address this summer and wrote her at long last, so we'll see."

They both turned to watch the horses at the sounds of a fresh outburst between the riders. "Mind your own damned business!" Viveca shouted at Byrne.

"You think riding astride like a man and swearing like one will make you tougher?" he scoffed. "You sure have a lot to learn!"

She reined in Blackamoor. "What I am," she said, indigo eyes flashing black fire at him, "is the best damned bagman you and Dash ever had, Byrne St. James, and you'd better not forget it!"

Then she touched her heels to the dark bay mare and was away over Caro's fledgling yew hedge.

Byrne shaded his eyes against the sun, squinting. Viveca was soon shouting, "Watch this one, Byrne!" And he did, though he'd seen it a hundred times. She was galloping the mare hard. Just as expected, she dropped from sight in a flash, hanging on the far side of the horse. Then all at once Byrne sat forward in Black

Rose's saddle, jaw dropping. For, damn it, Viveca had just reappeared—*under Moor's belly!*

She hung down there, dangerously close to the pounding hooves, and even at this distance he thought he could see her jawline going white with tension. Then she was up and over, back into the saddle in time to guide the walnut mare over Caro's yew hedges and the fence she'd raised two notches. Moor took it like the trooper she was, light as a filly, not a mare who had borne two colts and ought to know better.

"Watch this!" came the shout again. Baffled, amazed, and angry enough to haul her off the horse and spank her, nineteen-year-old Byrne could only sit and watch as she aimed Blackamoor at the stone wall dividing the carriage drive from the brood paddocks. It was too high for any horse, even a trained hunter, to take cleanly, and for a moment he started to shout, afraid she would be killed. Then that damned Moor hooked her hooves over the top and practically walked up the wall, dragging her hind legs and buttocks clumsily but making it nonetheless.

He never figured out how Viveca stayed on. There they were at the top, looking outrageously pleased with themselves, as though they had done something quite wonderful. Then Moor decided she'd had enough and rocketed off the wall, dumping Viveca flat in the tall grass.

Byrne rode toward her, fuming. "You crazy little numskull, I wish I was your father so I could paddle your backside for such a dangerous stunt! You might have broken that mare's legs, not to mention your own fool neck! When are you going to learn you're not twelve anymore? It's time for you to start being a lady, not a foulmouthed hoyden pulling Red Indian pranks on such a valuable mare!"

Byrne bit down the rest of his angry words as she looked up at him from the corners of those nearly black eyes and said, "You're only mad because you care. You can scowl all you like, Byrne St. James, but I think it's true. And I can't help doing my horse tricks. They're all I've got with my crippled foot so much worse since Newgate. I can't run, I'm too old for games with children, and I'm not able to go to dance class and learn all the latest sarabands and such like Edward suggested. Besides"—she cast a sly, sidelong look from those sloe eyes before continuing—"besides, when Dash and I were unhorsed at that last holdup, wasn't it a good thing I taught the Moor to come at a whistle? And what with Dash getting a leg up on her, wasn't it good that I can Indian-ride so that I was able to cling on to the saddle girth and her neck till we got clear?"

"You're right, of course," he answered coolly, "but you could try acting more feminine sometimes, like Lilly." Byrne pondered the comparison he couldn't avoid making. Lilly was good at being a girl, while Viveca—well, Viveca was a figure at last, but she still spat and swore like a sailor. He adored her and, at the same time, dreaded being seen in public with her.

Byrne reached a hand down, extending strong fingers. Viveca grasped his wrist instead—he heard stitches pop in his new stocktie shirt—and hauled herself aboard with little effort. She fastened her arms around his waist. "I'm sorry, Byrne. I don't mean to be cruel in worrying you so. It's just that I have things weighing a mite heavy on me mind."

There was the queerest twinge around his heart as she settled on Black Rose's rump, rubbing her face between Byrne's shoulder blades. It made his insides feel as though they'd turned to treacle. He angrily told himself that he was a fool. He loved her, always had, and during the past year that love had mingled with being *in* love.

Viveca and her unthinking virginity! *And* her damned dreams. Rich men expected to marry virgins, and she wanted to be rich someday, so she was saving herself for some fat old man or debauched, foppish rake. The silly chit thought she could use her maidenhead to barter her way into society.

And here he was, eating his heart out in the background, unmindful of the dozen women he'd had by now, any of whom would have done desperate things to have this quiet, handsome youth back in their arms. *Hellfire,* he thought sourly, *she carries on like we're still eight years old and have no gender!*

Byrne glanced back over his shoulder at her. She was looking up now and smiled as he headed the black mare toward the stables. *What eyes! A man could drown in those pools of ink; could fall right in and go under without a struggle,* he thought. Especially when the eyes were paired with hair that, when clean, was blond with some light brown and pale copper. And she was filling out at last, though she'd never be the hourglass type. *Tall.* She was tall as the stable boys and taller than Caro by far, though, like Shakespeare's Rosalind, she was only "high as his heart," the St. Jameses being a long lot.

It wasn't that he thought of Viveca in purely sexual terms. She was still his best mate, closer to him by far than any of his own brothers. He'd rather ride with her than Dash or any of the tarts he knew. He even preferred her company to that of the tavern keeper's daughter, and he'd been her first—she hadn't been like the rest, who did it for pay or just so they could brag they'd tupped the best-looking St. James lad.

He still felt friendly with Viveca, and they still poured out their hearts to each other—well, once in a while—but they weren't telling as much as they once had. . . .

"Viveca!" someone shouted.

His head snapped up. They were no more than a few yards from the stables when Caro came breathlessly racing around the corner of the inn. She had gone a queer pink color, as heavy women sometimes did in the heat, and her hair was escaping its pins to fall over her magnificent bosom. "Viveca, darling, dear girl."

Caro was nearly overcome and sat down on the stoop gasping. Great Edward came striding alone behind her. "What is it?" Viveca demanded tensely. "What is it? Why is Aunt Caro so upset? Is it—is it—" She gripped the front of her grass-stained shirt. "Oh, Sweet Savior, my mother's dead!"

"She's doing quite well," Great Edward said, "and she's sent your aunt to fetch you."

"Why couldn't Mother fetch me herself? *What* aunt?" Viveca demanded, sliding off the horse's rump.

"Your mother is *enceinte.* With child," Caro explained as Edward helped her to her feet. "She can't travel, she's too far along.

123

And—and your mother's friend, Yasaman, is your aunt now. Your mother married Yasaman's brother, Hasej."

There was a carriage in the entranceway. Viveca could see it if she craned her head. She began running toward it, her mouth dry. *Yasaman.* She didn't remember much except the name and a gentle cloud of frankincense . . . a carriage with glass doors, amber-colored . . . the tallest coachman she'd ever seen.

A woman was standing on the stairs, a tiny little creature swathed in blazing blue silk with ropes of walnut-size pearls and lapis lazuli. Her eyes were more heavily painted than any Englishwoman Viveca had seen, touched with ground green malachite and sooty kohl. Like a deer's eyes, and none too pleased with what they saw: a ragged boy-girl urchin with bare feet, elbows coming through her shirt sleeves.

There was grass in Viveca's hair, and green stains all over her rump and knees. She smelled of the stables, and there was a bruise on her cheek from a tree Blackamoor had tossed her into last week. She looked worse than lower-class—as bad as the beggars back in Yasaman's Anatolia. That this—*this* should be Ginny's daughter!

She's tattered, and she smells like a barn, Yasaman thought, her innate fastidiousness revolting at the scent of straw, clover, perspiration, and horse. *She's not even a real girl. She's something in between, without a gender! She's picking her nose and spitting on the ground!*

No woman in Yasaman's homeland would be so uncouth, so mannish. The worst of Turkish women did not soil their hands on horses, did not wear men's clothing, did not slouch and spit—this creature couldn't even stand up straight!

Yasaman was filled with a sudden, unreasoning fury. For *this* her dear friend Ginny had ruined her health, almost starved herself to death. Looking for this scruffy little—

"You must be Yasaman," Viveca said, and spat again. Even Byrne, coming up behind her, winced. She wasn't usually this rough-acting; why was she putting up a front now when she needed to be at her best?

"Where's my mother?" Viveca demanded.

No use in mincing words with her, for she looked as though she would brook no excuses. "At her home in Turkey. She has been having premature labor pains for six weeks now," Yasaman said frostily. "Travel could injure, perhaps even kill the child. *Or* your mother. I received your Aunt Caro's news that you were alive just as your mother arrived back from the Russias. She wanted to come for you herself, but Hasej and I pleaded with her not to risk herself and the child. She is overcome with joy and excitement and wishes you to come to her at once."

Some of Viveca's false reserve buckled. Eyeing Yasaman's beautiful clothing, she murmured, "I could learn to stand Turkey if I got to wear pantaloons like yours, and them—I mean, *those*—curly-toed slippers. Just so they didn't slip from the stirrups, that is."

Edward, Caro, and Byrne all gathered at several yards' distance, sensing that the interview was not going well.

Poor Yasaman, nearly overcome with revulsion for this shabby creature, wished she had brought her pomander from the carriage to wave in front of her nose. "I remember you as a child," she managed to say at last. "You and your sister. Two little angels with golden curls and primrose-colored dresses. I doubt you recall me."

"No. I guess I don't," Viveca admitted frankly, slouching and cramming her hands into her deep pockets. "But I remember—*Philippe!*"

He had stepped from the carriage, and though he was grown to manhood, she knew him at once and launched herself across the stoop to embrace him.

Byrne, observing, blazed with jealousy.

Viveca abruptly stepped back. "Oh, hellfire! I guess that wasn't proper of me. Hullo there, Philippe. The sash you gave me—I lost it when they killed my sister. I'm sorry, I knew you trusted me with it."

He smiled, made a sweepingly graceful bow. "It is of no consequence; it was yours to lose. My only regret about it is hearing of the demise of the little Allegra. I shall get you another sash if you wish."

His French accent was a delight; the voice light, soft, rather high. With a chill Viveca remembered hearing Great Edward speak of male singers who were castrated in order to maintain their purity of tone for choirs. Philippe was slim as a rail and not male enough in his movements. She wondered, had this terrible thing indeed been done to him?

"We can put you up for as long as you need to become acquainted." Caro approached Yasaman in a nervous huddle of words. "You and your footmen and eunuch."

Philippe, watching Viveca's face, saw the effect of those words. "Do you think me a freak, then?" he inquired in that languid, lilting voice.

"Oh, dear, I feel terrible that anyone would have hurt you so! It makes the colts *miserable* at first!"

"Do not regret it," he said, smiling. "I can do much except father children. My pleasure is not completely removed, you know."

No, she *didn't* know, though she was a little surprised at his candidness. Viveca looked at him again closely. She expected eunuchs to be obese, tittering things with soft hands and softer bellies. Philippe was slim and hard as a tightly braided whip—and she suspected he was as flexible, too.

She heard Yasaman say to Caro, "Thank you, but we must be going at once. There is a great deal of work to be done with her."

Work? Viveca thought, uncomprehending. *Going at once?* What about her horses—and Byrne, Caro, Great Edward . . .

She looked up just in time to see Byrne turn heel and stride into the stables with a rigid bearing to his shoulders that spoke of anger. "But, I can't leave now, so suddenly," she said stiffly. "These people here, they're my family. 'Tisn't fair I should be torn from them with no warning, no chance of good-byes. I don't remember you, I hardly know who you are. I do want to see my mother, but I don't like leaving this place. The Black Bull is my home!"

Yasaman squared her shoulders and managed to give the impression of looking down her nose at Viveca, though Yasaman was by far the shorter of the two. She knew soap was expensive, and water—clean water—often hard to come by, but still, the child did not have to reek of manure and sweat. Yasaman knew that English people did not bathe often, and she had always considered this a barbarity.

But this sloppy little baggage was Ginny's long-lost child, so she must force herself to be pleasant. The clothes would need burning, of course, she decided, studying the girl. Her complexion looked sound enough under the dust and sunburn that had turned it an unbecoming crimson; she had no blemishes, nor had she been marked by smallpox like so many young girls. Her height was, like Ginny's, above the ordinary, but not grotesquely so, and beneath the baggy male clothes was the intimation of a blossoming figure.

The girl's hair—well, it was quite terrible, though it might be a pretty color when clean. *If I teach her posture, how to dress,* Yasaman thought, and found herself brightening. The child swore and spat like an old salt, but at least her command of the language was fairly sound.

She felt better already and managed to smile at this ragpicker-child. "You and I are aunt and niece now that your mother has married my favorite brother. I am your family now. I do not intend to demean your relationships here at the inn. But your mother has suffered too much for the sake of the children she lost, and childbearing is no longer so easy for her. It will ease her mind to have you there. And you have siblings now."

Viveca gave a great start and began dusting herself off furiously. "Where? Get them off me! I must have picked them up when Moor threw me!"

Philippe was laughing soundlessly, but Yasaman was horrified. Caro smiled sadly in bleak appreciation of that emotion. "You must think me a poor substitute for a mother," Caro intoned softly, "but the fact of the matter is, she's been her own parent for ten years now and never yields to suggestion. *Never.* And I'm not the type to bend and break others to my will for the sake of appearances. She's old to make over, but it isn't making over she needs—it's making a little *smoother,* is all."

Yasaman inclined her head slightly to show that she respected

127

Caro's opinion. Then she said to Viveca—who hated standing there like a mare in the show ring while everyone discussed her, as if she had no ears nor mind—"Siblings are brothers and sisters, dear, and you have several now. And your mother is very anxious to see you after so long."

Viveca looked at Caro and said, almost apologetically, "She's my *mother,* Caro! What else can I do but go now?" Then she turned to Yasaman. "Just answer me one thing. Is she—has she—"

"She has converted to Islam in order to marry the men she has married. She says it is all one god, anyway, and that perhaps He will not be offended if she merely calls Him by a different name."

There was a moment of awkward silence before Great Edward stepped forward and placed a bony hand on Viveca's shoulder. "It's growing late. Perhaps your aunt would agree to waiting until dawn before setting out?" He raised an eyebrow at Yasaman, who reluctantly nodded after a moment's thought.

"Good," Edward said. "That will give Viveca time for a ride on her favorite mare, a chance to adjust herself to this move, and to say good-bye to the lads."

Caro picked up her trailing skirts a few inches so she could walk, and announced that cold drinks from the icehouse would be served on the balcony immediately. Then she flew off to stir up Cook.

Yasaman turned to Viveca. "You and I shall become better acquainted on the journey. For now, go see your friends."

So Viveca ran to the stables after Byrne.

He was in the hayloft, lying on his back with his long hands behind his head. There was a stable cat on his chest, playing with his shirt strings. It took fright and fled, trailing a string, as Viveca approached.

Byrne didn't seem to notice at all. He remained as he was, staring up at the ceiling. So she plopped down next to him, picking a piece of hay from a bound bale and playing with it. "I'm leaving in the morning," she said, studying the piece of hay. When he made no response, she looked at his face. "Maybe you could come along."

"I hardly expect so," he answered gruffly. "You know what A-rabs and Turks do to highway robbers? They bend the tops of four trees to the ground, tie a man to them, and then let the trees spring back into their natural positions. No thankee. We only got hanging in England nowadays, and I don't mind that *nigh* as much. I'm not a complete clod, you know. I understand you have to go. Especially as it looks like your mum married rich and you always wanted that life. Eating off gilt dishes and having a house full of windows to show the world the window tax didn't mean anything to you. That's what you've always wanted, isn't it?"

He sat up, irately brushing bits of straw off himself. His loose shirt slid down, baring the top of one shoulder where a bullet had creased him last autumn. Viveca impulsively put her fingers to the scar. "I've hurt you and I didn't mean to," she said thickly. "You were my real da, and my mum, too. We were always there, looking out for each other, weren't we? Fancy me keeping apart from you, thinking that because you were a man now, you weren't as trustworthy as the old Byrne I'd growed—*grown*—up with!"

She kneaded his shoulder gently, hating the thought of what that raised scar had felt like when new, remembering the hurt it had given him and the crude way she'd had to stitch him up like an old shirt. But Edward said it had saved Byrne the use of that shoulder muscle.

"I'm tired of stealing," she said slowly. "I don't mean I look down on it, I just mean that I'm tired of *being* looked down on because of it. I want to be as good as everybody else. Look at Philippe, compared to me. He's better educated, better dressed, more couth—why, Philippe could go anywhere and be accepted. But he'd have to leave me out in the alley and throw me scraps, don't you see? I want to be as good as Philippe. Don't scrunch your forehead up like that, Byrne, I'm not a-going to elope with Philippe. They gelded him, for crying out loud!"

Byrne was suddenly sitting up straight as a board. "That's horrible! And these are the people you're going to go live with? Well, did it ever occur to you that *I* want out, too? Do you think I wouldn't like to be some bloody gentleman with a pack of hunting hounds and valets and footmen scrambling at the sound of my voice? But I'm a highwayman. I was *bred* to be one. In ten years or maybe twenty I'll end on a rope or die of my wounds the way Jemmy did. I can't even read or write, and no one will teach me without money."

"You great lout," Viveca answered, "you've got some silver to spend for lessons. And even if you didn't Great Edward would—ahh, but now that you're nineteen and a man, you're too proud to ask for help. Byrne, don't let that stand in your way."

Byrne sighed. "Mayhaps you're right. But things'll be different for you. Your rich mother'll dress you up and find you a wealthy lord to marry, even if he's Turkish and you don't speak enough of the same tongue to pass the butter at the dinner table."

Viveca wrapped her arms around his waist, miserably plopped her head on his shoulder. "I can leave anything behind, Byrne. I can leave the memories of Allegra and Jemmy, I can leave Caro, Dash, Edward, even the Moor—but you! You don't know how I missed you after you first went off with Dash and Jemmy, and my sister and I struck out on our own. I can't imagine a world with no Byrne St. James riding on my left, guarding my back, and me his. Seems as though I've lost everything I ever cared about, and now that I'm getting something back, the price to pay is *you!* Doesn't seem fair, Byrne. Not at all."

She lifted her tousled head and smiled through tears at him. Byrne saw nothing but the beauty in that smile, ignoring the patched hand-me-downs, the straggly hair. She was his Viveca and she was wonderful, and he didn't give a fig if he died of it, he had to kiss her right now.

As he leaned into the embrace, Byrne felt ashamed for presuming upon that virtue she so doggedly clung to. So he gave her just a light kiss on the lips and drew back. To his surprise Viveca remained in the same position, her expression bearing no anger. She fastened her fingers in the thick black hair falling over the nape of his neck and gasped out, "Byrne, what if it's the last time I ever see you . . . ?"

She lifted her face to his, drew his head down. Her nose was sunburned and peeling; there was straw in her hair. She was a thousand times more beautiful than his city girls with their too-soft skin and scent of violets; he loved her with an intensity that made his bones ache as though with a terrible ague.

He was Byrne, and she trusted him not to hurt her. She felt the first probe of his tongue in her mouth, shivered in confusion. Then he was stroking the back of her damp neck with light fingertips, reassuring her. She kissed him back, discovered it felt good. Felt *wonderful,* in fact. What a funny, fluttering feeling in the pit of her stomach, like soft little birds in a coal chute.

She was responding. Byrne's toes curled in his boots. This was better than he'd dared hope. She had a long, expressive mouth, made for kissing and sassing back. How often, when she'd angrily spouted off at him, had he wanted to take her in his arms, kiss her like this!

He wasn't the most experienced lover in the world, but he could tell when he had a girl too enthralled to quit. *Me,* he thought, *I'll be her lover, her husband. She's not peddling her maidenhead off to some rich old lord if I can help it. I'll keep her with me; we'll go on working the road together.*

He was terribly confused, and it made him gentler than he'd ever been, even with newborn foals and a dying Jemmy with pneumonia-laden lungs. Viveca was breathing like a runner, clinging to his shoulders and fervently returning his kisses. He slid a leg between hers, rubbed against her. With surprise and delight he felt her return it, arching against him, catlike. Most girls didn't react this strongly. She was digging her fingers into his shoulders, ribs, now thighs. "Don't stop," she said breathlessly when he hesitated. "No, no—don't stop, Byrne, please . . ."

He slipped his hands under her rough riding shirt. Viveca quivered as his palms cupped her breasts, rubbing the nipples to hard points. She peeled her shirt off, cupped her breasts, "fed" herself to him as his dark head lowered to her golden skin.

She had a sunburned *V* down the front where her shirt had been worn with no cravat. But the rest of her was a soft golden-white, pale blue veins showing through creamy breasts that rose, firm and full, against his hands. Byrne hadn't guessed her body was this mature, nor that she was so ripe for the pleasures of love.

"Touch me, Viveca," he urged huskily. "I like it, too. Don't be afraid to touch me."

She began stroking him, sliding her hands down the open neck of his shirt, helping him out of it an arm at a time. The scar on his shoulder—she kissed it as though she could take away memories of that old pain. He tasted of sun, a thin film of salty perspiration, and smelled of clover, leather, old linen. Man smells. *Home* smells.

He bent, rubbed his face against her creamy breasts. He sucked one nipple, then the other, and finally licked the palms of his hands, rubbing them faster and faster over her nipples until they stiffened and glowed a hot pink-red with excitement.

Now. Now he wanted *more.* But not to hurry her; no, he would never risk hurting or frightening his Viveca. He kissed the open pink mouth, drank in its curves and corners, its secret softness, the sweet taste of her eagerness. When he first tried to unbutton her riding breeches, she hesitated a moment, so he moved against her, let her feel the throbbing, needful rigidity of him through their clothes. He shifted so that he was pressing against the most sensitive part of her body. She's seen stallions cover mares; she knew what would follow if she let it. Byrne waited to see if she would back away, but she only pulled him closer.

She was uttering small, breathy sounds of arousal and uncertainty. Byrne reached down, stroked her through her heavy breeches and, finding no resistance, unbuttoned them.

Viveca wound around him like a snake—and damn if he didn't feel like Adam forgetting himself and taking a bite. He undressed both of them, spread their shirts beneath them that they might have something to lie upon in the scratchy straw. "Do you like this?" she was asking, licking his throat. "Am I doing this right? Or do you like *this* better . . . ?"

No coyness, no pretending to struggle, no needing to be overcome. He'd never met a girl, even among the whores, who didn't like to pretend she'd been overpowered. It was more exciting this way, with Viveca's need as frank and fascinated as his own. He

132

felt larger than life, a god, and struggled to remove their heavy jackboots and breeches.

Her skin was even whiter here, and she smelled deliciously musky. He wanted to devour this pliant, throbbing body, make her whine and sigh with ecstasy. Thank God for the whores, thank God for the tavern keeper's daughter. Without them he wouldn't know how to please the person he loved most.

"You're beautiful," Byrne told her. "You are the most beautiful woman I've ever seen; a duchess couldn't touch you for beauty. I love you, Viveca, more than anything on earth. I'll make you happy."

He lowered his mouth to her cool, burning flesh, felt her shudder at that first so-intimate touch. There was no shyness, no pushing him away, no snapping about sin. Only a fierce need and acceptance. Byrne licked her, touched her, stroked her, made the sensations build. He watched her reactions, guessed what was good and what was *not* good for her. *This,* for instance, made her gasp and quiver while *that* brought only a faintly annoyed stare at the ceiling. Here, more of *this* . . .

She was growing hotter against him, more frantic, the intensity building. "Oh, no, no, no," she murmured. "No, no—God, God —oh, Byrne—oh! *Oh!*"

The force of it brought her arching up off their crumpled clothes. She pulsated, cried out with the force of the peak. Her hard, pink nipples stood straight up, and a faint rash broke out across her chest. Even before the rash was gone and she had sunk back onto the straw, she was clutching at his shoulders, wide-eyed. "Oh, please, Byrne, please . . ."

She was eager, but she was also a virgin. Byrne penetrated gently, a measured stroke at a time. There was no resistance of a stubborn maidenhead, though the difference between her and the whores was at once obvious. She didn't seem to be in pain, though she was rigid with tension. "There," he soothed, "is that all right?"

"Doesn't hurt. It's supposed to hurt," she said nervously.

"You've been listening to old wives' tales. I think girls only bleed if the man's too rough or if they're the sort who sit in a chair all day. You're firm as an apple, Viveca, not like city girls; they're flabby. You have muscles from riding—you're so slim, so supple. . . ."

He was up on his elbows, moving faster. And, indigo eyes wide, she was looking up into his own black-eyed gaze, smiling until the next thrust made her say "Oh!" and catch her breath.

Mustn't rush, Byrne thought. *Draw it out for her, make the first time so good that she never goes anyplace else.*

It was difficult to remain gentle. She was sinking strong white teeth into his shoulder, panting, moaning out his name. Byrne forced himself to think of a night's work and grooming down his colt Blackberry afterward—it wasn't working. He didn't want to lose control, but she was thrusting back with each stroke, twining herself around him. Her hips were bucking like a wild mare's.

Harder, faster . . .

Viveca, clinging to his neck, gave a single, triumphant cry and sagged in his arms. Byrne stared, unseeing, unhearing, as he joined her. Then they collapsed in the straw, a tangle of arms and legs. "Marry me, Viveca," he managed finally, catching his breath. "Marry me and stay here. We'll raise racehorses together. We'll breed your Godolphin mare, the Moor, to Black Rose's colt, my Blackberry. Think of it, Viveca, think of our own horses on acres of grass. We can do it!"

He moved the miniature of her great-grandmother, kissed her between her breasts, and laid his head there to listen to her heart.

He didn't see the tears forming in her eyes as he fell asleep like that, safe, cradled in her arms. The tears had dried to nothing when Viveca heard her name called from below. She dressed hurriedly, laid Byrne down, and climbed down the ladder from the loft. Lilly Carlisle was waiting, as darkly beautiful as the St. James boys. "Byrne?" she asked softly.

Viveca jerked her head up at the loft. The older girl put an arm around her shoulders. "You've been crying, hain't ye? I just got back and heard you're leaving in a few hours. I'm sorry, Viveca."

"So am I. I'll miss everyone so much, but it's my *mother,* after all these years of being separated, and—and it wouldn't be right not to go see her."

134

"Maybe you'll be back then," Lilly said softly.

"Maybe. But whether I am or not, there's something I've got to do first," Viveca told her solemnly. "It's kind of a sign—a pledge. Wait for me, will you? I'll be right back." And she climbed back up into the loft.

When Byrne woke, he was alone and covered with a blanket against the cool night air. Later Lilly described for him how Viveca had driven away with Yasaman, face set like a death mask, Moor tied behind the coach.

There was one small bit of comfort in it. Perhaps she was running away to a new life where she'd have the riches she'd always craved, and she would forget what had passed between them—the shared childhood, the unexpected passion. If it made her happy he would let it be. He would have no regrets.

But deep inside he suspected she would never be happy as an ornament and brood mare for some rich man.

Besides, he thought, hugging himself against the early-morning chill, *she's given me something that proves she'll be back someday. If she returns as plain old Viveca I'll be happy fit to bust. But if she returns as a lady with a footman and a husband, I won't go near her. I'll just send the gift back to her that she might keep that part of her heritage. But I won't interfere in her new life if it proves to be all she truly wants.*

For she had given him more than affection and a roll in the straw; she had left him something she valued above diamonds and had never let even dear Allegra handle.

Hanging about his neck was the ivory miniature of her great-grandmother, the woman of the tuberoses, the very flower that scented the air around him at the moment.

The Mistress of the Night.

CHAPTER FIFTEEN

Angora, Anatolia (Turkey), *Ottomon Empire, 1761*

Wealthy, elegant, and beautiful, Ginny Lindstrom nervously awaited the arrival of her eldest daughter.

Ginny had been considered a marital prize of great social stature for Hasej, for not only could she read and write, not only was she beautiful, not only was she European and therefore rare in these parts, but she was also a wealthy widow with two fine sons from her first Turkish husband. Riches, beauty, and fecundity—a catch for any man, the locals reasoned, and the fact that she was several years Hasej's senior did not lesson her appeal.

Pacing tensely in the doorway of her white marble mansion, she looked nothing like the woman who had left England in despair so many years ago. Her hair, glossy with oils and herbs, was twisted and wound around her head in the manner of blond Circassian harem beauties. Her palms, soles, and fingertips were hennaed a bright orange, and her eyes were painted in a manner no Western woman would have considered seemly.

Silks, rubies, embroidered undergarments of the finest, filmiest cotton—she was as gorgeously decked as an empress, and yet she took no pride in her appearance this day. Never mind that she had finally put weight back on after the harrowing birth of her last son—she was still afraid she might look wan and mistreated to Viveca, who, according to Yasaman's letters, was a highly critical youngster.

Oh, Hasej, she thought, twisting her hands together. *You're the man I always longed for, the "man of my own" I always wanted to love and be loved by. And yet—did you make a mistake by advising me to have my daughter come here? She might be more comfortable with me in her own territory, but that would have meant delaying our meeting.*

She clasped her hands together, offering a quick and fervent prayer to any deity who might be listening: *I want my daughter to like me.* Silly to be as nervous as a girl with her first suitor. And how must poor Viveca be feeling, yanked away from the only home she remembered, dragged across land and sea to see a mother she no longer knew? *I'm older,* Ginny thought. *I'm not so angular as she remembers, if she remembers at all. My Scots brogue is gone at last. I'm Moslem now, heathen to her. I've wed a man nothing like her father.*

Hotheaded, passionate, amazingly gentle Hasej, who had comforted her when she woke weeping in the night with the old nightmare of the carriage wreck and her lost daughters. If someday Viveca could find a man like him . . . Allah speed the day he returned from this business trip he had wisely taken to allow mother and daughter time alone together!

Dust on the road ahead. She turned her gaze from the gleaming whiteness of her house, relieved by the courtyard and its tropical greenery. "Lady, not to squint," a slave admonished. "Deepens those lines at eyes, it's the only time they show. Don't you make them worse."

In other households a slave would have been whipped for such effrontery, but Ginny was a kind mistress, and her servants and slaves doted on her, convinced that her health and beauty did them much credit. "All right," Ginny replied mechanically, but inside she clenched and swirled with frightened nausea. Her baby. Her eldest child, who had shared those hard times in London—how they would talk about those times and laugh! How happy she could make this beggar child, this child of the streets!

Here came the coach, drawn by two white Barb geldings. It was turning into the paved drive, circling the fountain. Footmen were springing to hand out darling little Viveca and cool, serene Yasaman . . .

Wait a minute. Something was wrong. Yasaman's conical hat

was on sideways, veil ripped. Her silks were rumpled, splotched with stains and perspiration, and she was losing a curly-toed slipper.

And who or *what* was this caterwauling little baggage she was hauling out by the hair? Rumpled, patched clothes, lank hair—ugh! Ginny could even smell the creature!

Wait, the urchin had indigo eyes. *Mashallah!* It must be Viveca!

The girl went sprawling at Ginny's feet. Inscrutable, delicate Yasaman, in the coarsest gutter Turkish, spat out what she thought about the unwashed English, how she felt about vile girl-children who snorted when they ate, refused baths, and had never heard of cleaning their fingernails. She had spent almost a month with this—this "traveling barnyard," and she was going straight up to her rooms "for a bath or twelve" and perhaps even a pinch of opiate in her sorbet.

She had *never,* she blasted, suffered such indignities in her life. And worst of all—here she scratched furiously at herself—the beast was *infested!*

Yasaman tore her hat off, tromped on it, and stomped furiously inside with a bevy of handmaidens and Philippe, who looked stunned.

Ginny raised an eyebrow as the tall ragamuffin sat up, scratching an armpit. "It would seem that so far the family reunion has been less than successful," Ginny said softly, hiding her disappointment. She helped Viveca up, gave her a swift kiss on each cheek. "Welcome home, darling."

The girl wiped her nose on her stained cuff and spat on the mosaic entryway, square into the eye of a Byzantine dolphin. "I don't think we much belong together after all these years, and Yasaman and I spent the entire trip at each other's throat. Hasej's messenger reached us at Naples to say the baby was a boy and you are fine. You *look* fine. Not much like I remember you. You're prettier. Taller. And you didn't get *old.*"

Then this brave, belligerent little thing burst into tears. Ginny folded her daughter in her arms and almost immediately felt an urge to scratch herself.

"There, darling, you may stay here as long as you wish, but I shan't keep you here against your will. What is it you would like?"

"I'm tired of being a thief and so raggedy. I thought you might help make me into a lady, but Yasaman swears it can never be done. She was so angry with me, she spent three hours confessing to the priest aboard ship. I'd like to get civilized, dress and act properly, and do you proud. I can read and write well enough."

This urchin wanted to be a lady! The idea wrung at Ginny's heart. And then she glanced down and saw the dirty, bare feet. She snapped her fingers at her maid. "Slippers for the child. Viveca, feet are not to be bare here. That is considered unclean."

"Well, hellfire, I left my jackboots in the loft at the Black Bull!"

Yasaman must have tried, unsuccessfully, to wrestle her into some sort of footwear. Ginny smiled weakly as the servant returned and worked to ease Viveca's feet into jeweled slippers. "You're my size in slippers, that is fortunate. Quit crow-hopping, darling, she will put your slippers on your feet if you will only *let* her."

"I've always put on my own boots," Viveca said resentfully. "I'm as capable of bending down there as the next person."

"Ah," Ginny said, wagging a forefinger, "but you want to live as do the wealthy, and the primary rule of the wealthy is: Never do anything that someone is paid to do for you."

She turned to her page boy. "Please tell my maid to draw a bath. And locate the cedar and lavender and eucalyptus oils to kill the lice and fleas. Have them also prepare mud packs and depilatories."

It had all been said in Turkish, and Viveca stood on one foot, scratching her hip and wondering what was happening. "Now, upstairs to bathe," Ginny said brightly, slipping her arm through Viveca's. "My husband, Hasej, is away, and we women shall have the run of the house. Won't that be fun?"

Ginny cast off her outer robe as she walked. Before it could fall, a servant caught it. The same happened with the three veils and under robe, leaving Ginny in slippers; full, gathered trousers;

139

and a short, sleeveless kind of jacket thing that was very shocking.

Crikey! Viveca thought. *Now that's money! Someone to pick up your clothes as you drop 'em!*

Ginny propelled her through a beaded curtain into a tiled room with a big, sunken box in the middle. "What's that?"

"The bath. I hate to rush you, darling, but we shall have to talk later when certain things have been taken care of. Someone call in Mama Roxelina, please."

And, to Viveca's shock, her mother stripped and sat in the sunken tub while her servants twisted knobs so that hot water flowed down into the tiled bathing place. They were scrubbing her with rough-looking sponges and she stood to let them rinse her. Now she was climbing out, and two women were drying her off with sheet-size cotton toweling.

They were taking Viveca's clothes off. She shrilled about it, closed her eyes, and crossed her arms in front of her. "Relax. There is nothing obscene about the body or its workings here," Ginny's voice soothed. "Let them bathe you, and then we shall be oiled and massaged. And then the *real* work shall begin."

Ancient Mama Roxelina, a black-swathed, one-eyed crone, came in. "Open your eyes," Ginny directed her daughter. "Now get into the bath, darling." She turned to Roxelina as her daughter was flung into the bath and descended upon by a troop of maidservants eager to remove the dirt and smell from this English savage.

Roxelina looked over the wailing girl as she was dunked and dunked again in a flurry of sponges, suds, and brushes. "No scurvy, no severe emaciation or worms," she observed. "The teeth are good. There is a scalp condition, but that merely comes from never brushing or washing the hair. Colorless henna and oil massages will quickly clear that up."

"Anything else?" Ginny asked quickly.

"Yes," Roxelina answered, brutally frank. "She does not know that she is just barely with child."

"Will you take care of that?" Ginny asked, not skipping a

breath. "If she wants to be a proper lady she cannot do it with an illegitimate child clinging to her skirts."

The old witch-woman considered the suggestion a moment. "It will be long before her next child. And she hasn't the look of heavy use; I would say one lover. A black-haired man with eyes as dark as hers. He loves her greatly. She has no pox, no disease you need worry about. Nothing except the child and—"

Roxelina itched frantically at her shoulder. "Damn!" she said, and left the room. A moment later she stuck her grizzled head back in. "Inoculate her against smallpox as soon as that other matter is taken care of."

Viveca was subjected to a thorough oiling to kill the fleas and lice, then a massage that left her feeling like a jellyfish. "Too many flea bites for the depilatories," a maid told Ginny. "It would irritate her skin unduly, and, beneath it all, she does have very lovely, very fair skin."

Ginny scowled as the masseuse began work on her. "She's also pregnant, as you no doubt heard. Bastards are one thing in England and quite another here; with no lord to protect her she would be an outcast, despite my money. If there's one thing I've observed it's that no one minds concubines here, as long as that's what they are—*kept* women, not whores or gullible young girls like my daughter, who was probably seduced beneath some hedge. Tell Roxelina to hasten with her potion for bringing on the child."

"Could you speak in English?" Viveca asked suddenly. "And do they have to touch me? It doesn't seem right."

"Darling, I apologize, I was merely making—arrangements for your future. Now, why don't you tell me about yourself?"

Through mud packs, hair trimming, oil treatments, and a light dinner of fruit and broiled veal served on the shaded veranda, Ginny learned of her daughter's life. At last she understood the girl's roughness and felt her own heart stirred. If only she had found her daughters when they were all in the streets of London, the two girls with Missus Lee and herself alone!

"Now, then," she told Viveca at last, clearing her throat, "there will be no more spitting on floors or even the ground outside. Ladies do not do that. And you will be given handkerchiefs to use when your nose drips. You will dab, not honk into it like a goose. And you will not put one ankle up on your knee like that, do you understand? Spine stiff, both feet on the ground. You will not slouch, scratch your nose, swear, throw things, or pick your teeth."

"But everyone has to do most of those things sooner or later!"

"Then I advise you to retire to the water closet for them," Ginny said with narrowed eyes, as if threatening.

"Maybe I don't want to marry after all!" Viveca sniffed.

"You shall marry and marry well."

"Aunt Yasaman isn't married!"

"Yasaman was head concubine to Mustapha Sultan and is still his respected adviser. She is a mature woman of wealth and power, free to do as she chooses. Now come along."

They scrubbed out the sweet oils they'd rubbed in earlier, then trimmed Viveca's hair again until it was barely shoulder-length. Removing all the damage of dirt, wind, and sun left her hair a curious, soft, cat color, floating lightly around her face. It had never floated before, had never been this luscious, pale apricot hue. And thick! Viveca could not stop looking into the mirror in astonishment at this tall stranger, wrapped in silk, with sparkling skin and cleavage like a woman. The hair—oh, the glossy hair! It was worth everything they'd put her through.

Ginny floated back into the room, caftaned and elegant, as they plopped Viveca into a chair and attacked her nails—all twenty of them—with soft sticks and files. "Drink this. All of it," Ginny directed, and handed her a steaming mug.

The brew was bitter and hot, but Viveca gagged it down. "It's dreadful. What is it?"

"Medicine," her mother answered mysteriously. "Now observe what the maids are doing. You will never let your fingernails get dirty and ragged again. You will keep them shaped and not too short," she directed as Viveca's fingertips were buffed to ovals of a fragile opalescence.

Ginny studied her daughter. Same long face as Ginny, herself. But her own pale blue eyes were navy-coat blue on Viveca, and

142

the young girl's hair was an ashy blond-brown-copper. Her eyelashes looked an inch long and were brown enough to show up without eye paint. She was not yet Ginny's height, but she was close enough. And her figure would be better after losing this early pregnancy.

Viveca gasped suddenly. "I think my courses have started! Hellfire, I'll ruin these clothes of yours! I'm sorry, Mama, I-I've never had these gripping pains before."

An hour later it was all over. Viveca had been violently ill and frightened until Ginny broke the news. "I won't die then," Viveca said weakly, lifting her head from the basin her mother held.

"No, you'll only be sick a little while. It's normal. I'm . . . sorry, Viveca. But you're still a baby yourself, and I couldn't let you throw your life away on a bastard child. Not when we both have such hopes for your future."

Now Viveca lay silent in her wide white bed with its mosquito netting draped all around. Ginny tried to get her to talk but to no avail. At last she went out, leaving the door ajar and instructing one of the servants to sleep on a mat outside Viveca's room in case she needed anything. She looked back in to murmur softly, "There will be other children later, darling. When you're ready for them."

Alone, Viveca stared at the whitewashed ceiling with its frescoed border of squares and diamonds. Byrne's baby. It would have been Byrne's son or daughter. She allowed herself a moment's fantasy of maternal joy, then snapped it in half. Babies weren't like foals. They weren't standing half an hour after birth, trotting in two hours, and weaned for life at six months. Her mother was right; she was still a child who knew too little of the world and its folk. She only knew the harsh things, the life of the streets.

But to lose a baby . . . Byrne's baby . . .

Byrne. She mustn't think of him now or she'd be crying. She had to stay here, become a lady, be so wealthy that she never went hungry again. No more stealing, either. She could return later and surprise Byrne, but she and Byrne wouldn't be fit company then, would they? If she became someone who danced and prattled about dresses and card games, what would he see in her to love? If she became a social success what would she have in common with a highwayman? He seemed doomed to the rough life—living and dying a highwayman like his brothers. If he could only learn to read and write, find honest work, but where was the thrill in a desk job? How could a man find ledgers interesting once he'd looked down the barrel of a pistol aimed at him —and lived?

She dug her nails into her palms. *And how will I bear luncheons and tea parties after having those same pistols aimed at me? I've lived with the noose over my head for so long; can I really survive without that horrid excitement, that constant fear driving me onward, forcing me to keep moving?*

She remembered hunger, trying to keep Allegra up and moving one snowy night when they both wanted to lie down and freeze to death. The awful fight against their own lagging bodies . . . sleeping huddled with a pack of strangers in Newgate, striving for a little warmth . . . torn clothes, ladies in carriages laughing at her.

I will do it, she thought fiercely, fists pressed together. *I don't care what it costs me inside.*

I will *be a lady!*

CHAPTER SIXTEEN

Angora, 1763

"Well? What do you think?" Ginny inquired of Yasaman as a maidservant approached, bowing low with a tray of fruit sorbets.

Yasaman smiled behind her veil. "One cannot tell her foot was ever injured. The rebreaking and setting that the surgeon did— miraculous!"

"No, no, I meant the dancing."

Yasaman leaned forward, lightly hennaed elbows coming to rest on the balcony rail in a most un-Eastern fashion. "Philippe is a very light dancer, very lithe, quite quick on his feet."

Exasperated, Ginny said, "No, my daughter!"

Yasaman smiled. "She has gotten much more graceful. Her figure has filled out nicely, too. A definite improvement over when I saw her last . . . a year and a half ago? The surgeon had just fitted her with that porcelain tooth, and he was about to rebreak her foot when I left. And what was it, a year or so before that when I brought her here?"

Ginny took a spoonful of her nectarine sorbet, savoring it and swallowing before she chuckled. "In those days she was, as her father would have said about a rambunctious horse, 'all brass and full of vinegar.' The change is in more than appearance, Yasaman. I think, when you speak with her, that you will be pleased to note a change in attitude and manners."

The perspiring violinist continued to play, but the two young dancers finally stopped and left the courtyard, laughing at some shared joke. Ginny watched them go, heart full of anxiety. "What troubles you then, if she does so well?" Yasaman asked.

"She's restless. She's absorbed all that my tiring women and I can teach her, and I believe she's homesick. She's had a few suitors around these parts, and none of them landless, but the only one who got so much as a watery smile from her is that half-Scots, half-Turk boy who keeps serenading her at midnight. And you know Hasej, he's never seen the beauty in bagpipe music. No, my girl wants to go back to her own people, and that means London—the cesspool!"

She shuddered slightly. "My memories of it are repellent, but it's home to her; they speak her language there. And she and Hasej are getting on each other's nerves. She keeps advising him on his horses. . . ."

Ginny gazed down at her abdomen, swollen with a six-months' child. "I am not fit to travel, and Hasej would not permit me to go, anyway. The twins have discovered the opposite sex with a glee bordering on *maniacal*. Khurrem is just old enough to be jealous of Viveca, and—

"Will you escort her back, Yasaman? Will you do me the greatest of all possible favors and let her live with you in London till she's married? I know the two of you have not always gotten along, but since you left Philippe with her, she's quieted down. She isn't quite ready to be on her own, and I'd like her to have some wedge she can use to gain admittance into polite society. Because, while she's content to have a counselor and a friend, she balks at having a mother."

"But I love you so!" Viveca's voice broke in. She and Philippe had shamelessly eavesdropped, which, as Philippe had explained to her, was one of the few sinful pleasures he was willing to encourage her in.

Viveca hurried to her mother's side, dropping to one knee and kissing Ginny's hands. Philippe entered languidly and seated himself on a cushion at Yasaman's feet, where he proceeded to peel grapes for her.

"I know it's been difficult for you, Mother," Viveca hurried on, "but don't think I'd leave you eagerly. It's just that this is *your* world, *your* place, where you've found peace and joy . . . and it isn't my world at all. I miss black puddings and pianoforte music

146

and hearing cockneys squabble over which of the king's mistresses is the ugliest. I love you, truly I do, and I'm forever grateful that you've civilized me, but I'm out of place here."

Yasaman graciously held out a hand and drew Viveca near to sit on the edge of the balcony rail in front of her. "There is no need to convince anyone. She has already decided that you may go back when you wish. And if there will no longer be bad blood between us I shall invite you to live with me so, while not being mothered, you will at least be chaperoned."

Yes, she thought, regarding Viveca, *the girl is* taller. And lushly curved, not the scrappy boy-beast she had dragged here by the scruff over two years ago. The indigo eyes were lightly touched with kohl, the flushed cheeks faintly dusted with rouge, the shine taken off the straight nose with expensive rice powder. And Viveca's hair was long, lush, strawberry blond. Why, the girl had become a beauty!

"You are looking well," Yasaman said sincerely, pleased at Viveca's progress from urchin to lady. "Perhaps the three of us, with the aid of the household seamstress, might make you a traveling trousseau of some modest sort."

Viveca looked from Yasaman to her mother. "Then it's settled? I may return to London with Yasaman on her next voyage?"

"Yes. Now run along and speak with the seamstress, dear," Ginny directed. "And take Philippe with you; he has his ears cranked out to hear everything Yasaman and I say. And you don't have to apologize for wanting to go."

Viveca caught Philippe by the sleeve, pulled him along after her. "Seamstress, bah," he said as they started into the house. "You know what I think you should do first? Go see Mama Roxelina. You have dried lentils rattling around in your head where a brain should be if you think to make such a move without consulting her. She can tell your fortune, see your future—"

"That witch-woman would get herself hanged or burned at the stake if she lived anywhere but in Turkey."

"No one *alive* misses a chance to have their fortune told. Who do you think you are fooling? You're just frightened because Roxelina knew you were pregnant before you knew it yourself."

She glared at Philippe, aghast. "Are there *no* secrets from you?"

"None at all. What I'm trying to tell you, is: Any virgin with bad enough luck to get herself with child the very first time had better be an ex-virgin smart enough to consult that old witch before taking such a long voyage. Otherwise you're likely to have triplets before we make it halfway across the English Channel!" Before she knew what was happening, he had her by her heavily embroidered felt jacket and was hauling her out the door and around to the back of the house. "Philippe! Stop! What are you—"

Mama Roxelina was in the icehouse, directing removal of a large chunk of ice for more sorbet.

"I've brought her," Philippe said, and, releasing Viveca, bowed low.

"Then you have wasted your time, Monsieur le Frenchman, because until she is ready to listen, I will not waste my breath speaking to her."

Viveca's mouth fell open. "Well, hellfire! I don't want my bloody fortune told, anyway," she snapped, and turned away.

"Not even where it concerns your husbands?" asked the old woman in a wheedling, yet mocking, voice.

Viveca came to a sudden halt. Husbands? More than one? She pivoted slowly on one flat leather heel and cocked an eyebrow at the wizened old crone. "Yes," Roxelina said, *"husbands.* More than one but no more than two. And both the best-looking men in London. Now what do you think of *that,* eh?"

"I think perhaps I'm interested now," Viveca said coolly. "Perhaps I even misjudged you. After all, you did know about the child."

The old woman walked on into the house, signaling them to follow. She came to the reading room with its white-enameled bookshelves and crewelwork chaises on white-on-white patterned rugs—a room whose only color came from the cracked leather spines of thin, expensive books on the many shelves.

Roxelina sank onto the plushest sofa, sitting like an aged crow amid a snowy field of cushions. "Shall I tell her what I see in the past first, so that she believes, my fine-feathered Frenchman?"

Philippe nodded once, sharply. The crone turned to Viveca. "The father of your child was dark, dark as my gown, and yet fair as the sun. A dark man without the darkness in his heart that kills so many in his trade—the trade of other peoples' belongings. He will not sink into the wine scupper as will his brother, the one with the odd name . . . not his birth name. *That* starts with a *w.*"

Dash St. James's real name was Walter. Viveca felt the fine hairs on her nape prickling.

"But don't grieve for the child we took from you," the old woman continued. "He would have killed you in coming. Too large and you too small, and turned to be a breech birth and strangling on his own cord—that child was not meant to be. I did not tell this to your mother; she needed no added strain at the time. The price to pay for saving your life is this: Your next children are far, far ahead in the future. You will give up on bearing a living child, and so you will be surprised to find your womb quicken at a time when all seems death and loss about you."

The room was full of evening's lengthening shadows, and it seemed to Viveca that this old woman with her time-ravaged face could actually *read* those shadows. Death? Loss? A child only when she had given up on having one? What an odd tale.

All at once Roxelina barked, "Doubt, ah, there is always doubt. And yet it is the very nature of the Scorpion to toy with the Unknown and lift the veil covering the future. So do not doubt too much this time, Scorpion, for you never know whose curiosity in this matter is stronger than yours. . . ."

She gave a chuckle that was more of a wheeze. "*His* curiosity is strong, little girl. Both of these husbands are curious, and neither is what they appear to be. You will mistake strength for weakness and weakness for reliability. You will blind yourself to so many things, you will let the ground beneath your feet crumble before you admit the tragic mistake you have made. It is the placement of planets in your house of Leo that makes you this way, though

149

in Sagittarius you are saved by your own good humor and courage."

No, Viveca thought, *it isn't the shadows she squints into for her
answers—it is my face. Why, she's reading my features.*

At that Viveca rose from the doorway where she had sunk
down on her haunches, rose and crossed the small room to kneel
at Roxelina's feet. Viveca lifted Roxelina's withered hands, bones
sticking up to press whitely against crackling parchment skin,
and laid them on her face. "Read me," she said simply. "I won't
fight anymore."

"Bah, you will always fight. It is what makes you live. A fair
man, a dark man, both will love you too much. I think you worth
neither of them, myself. You will come back here with the golden
girl, though I doubt I will still be here then."

Roxelina began struggling to get up from the cushions. "But
you haven't told me anything," Viveca cried out. "Who is the
golden girl? And when will I be back?"

"You will be back when England faces a revolution of her
colonists; you will be back when that which you believed lost
forever returns; you will be back when your black stallion is
beaten by one horse and one horse alone; you'll return years from
now when all of this is clearer to you. Now let me up, little
girl—"

"Not yet, Mama Roxelina. More!"

The crone hesitated. "There is little more. I could tell you all
of it, and you would not change a thing, so why waste my
breath?" One of her sticklike hands came to rest on Viveca's
head. "I see you riding the night like a Fury, your clothes dark, a
gun in your hand, or is it a sword?"

"But that's the past, Roxelina, that's when I worked with the
highwaymen."

Again that dried, dusty wheeze of a laugh. "Your past is your
future, little girl. You will be poorer than poor and richer than
rich, and you will not get what you want but, child, you will get

150

what you need most—though only when you think it lost. Now let me past."

"Why, she spoke in riddles," Viveca murmured softly when the old woman had gone. "I wonder what she meant? I wonder."

CHAPTER SEVENTEEN

On Yasaman's next trip to London Viveca accompanied her. With her came three fine Barb mares and two Arab fillies, the pride of Ginny's breeding stock, as well as a half-Barb yearling colt and the colt that Moor had been carrying when they left England.

In with their breeding papers Viveca carried signed deeds and notarized statements giving her two hundred acres adjoining Aunt Caro's land, enough money to build the needed stables, and two thousand pounds in gold to be put in various trusts and properties as her dowry and the dowries of any daughters she might bear. To top it all off Ginny had given her all of the breeding stock in Kensington that Caro had kept for her these many years, with the stipulation that Caro pick and keep the five best mares in exchange for her faithful aid.

Young, beautiful, propertied, Viveca cried most of the way across the Mediterranean to Marseille. She pouted through France to Limoges, cheered considerably at Orléans, and made a complete recovery at the coast, only to remember, as the boat cast off, that she might never see her mother again. Then the sadness came back.

She was also worried about her old life coming back to haunt her while she tried to climb society's rungs; and after the way she'd left him, would Byrne and the boys welcome her at all? She thought not. And what about Caro and Great Edward and Lilly . . .

In mid-Channel a shipful of bawdy, raucous sailors passed within spyglass-and-hailing distance. "Ahoy, there, with the strawberry blond hair! Marry me!" came the first offer.

Viveca perked up at once, lifting her chin from the rail with an audible snap.

"Halloa, Red!" shouted another sailor, hands cupped around his mouth. "Come dance in Rouen with me!"

The offers slid indecorously downhill after that, until the other ship's quartermaster reclaimed all spyglasses and cuffed the sailors back to work.

Philippe, who had observed the proposals (and propositions) along with Viveca's wordless but glowing-faced response, knocked at Yasaman's cabin door and went in. "We'd better get her married soon—a passing shipful of sailors just tried to get her to elope!" He sobered as he eased a folded sheet of paper from his waistcoat. "Mistress, she *does* need marrying. I have begun listing the landed and/or titled sons of British gentry who would consider marrying a girl with money and land but no family. They're not so caste-conscious in London these days, you know. Too many lords from fine old families have lost their fortunes in this war or that and have had to let their sons start business firms. I could read them to you alphabetically. . . ."

"What would I do without you?" Yasaman asked, laughing.

Viveca bent over her needlework, feigning absorption in it as old Lady Jane Holland went off on another delightful tirade. She liked the old woman immensely better than Lady Sarah and the nieces who were calling. In the four days she had been at Yasaman's newly redecorated house, Lady Jane had been the only truly interesting caller.

And there had been many, many callers, for Sultan Mustapha III was a man shrewd in the ways of trade and travel; political conditions in England did not change quickly enough to favor him, so he released just enough Eastern luxuries to tempt the palates of the English. His own trade agreements with Manchuria brought cottons and rare teas to England along with Turkey's spices and silks; now that he had let trade with his country tighten up again, everyone was clamoring for Yasaman's attention. In fact, even the misogynist Turkish ambassador had come to Yasaiman for aid in dealing with Mustapha and these capricious English unbelievers!

In addition, there was a deepening vogue for things Eastern, and Yasaman fit that vogue. She had also gained several close friends during fifteen years of visits to this country, so newly turned over, in 1760, to the priggish and dumpy George III.

"I'm serious," Lady Jane said, and snorted, a sound that younger women would have been ostracized for. "The fat Hanover king is so prudish and circumspect that the Court's gone hog-wild trying to make up for his behavior. Necklines are lower than ever, exposing—"

"Please!" snapped one of Jane's nieces, crimson-faced.

Viveca hid her smile as she thought of Philippe, surely listening at the keyhole.

Yasaman asked, "Has the king passed any legislation on morals?"

"Legislation?" Lady Jane roared. "All that softheaded, sauerkraut-guzzling German fool has done is churn out proclamations against vice and permissiveness!"

As Lady Jane spoke her spectacles rattled on the tip of her nose. "And you know who encourages Farmer George? The worst of the gamblers, the most shameless seducers and hussies from among our own ranks. As the Good Book says, 'And Jesus sat Him down by the waters and wept.' Jesus *wept!* Those very voices clamoring for law and order belong to the same folk whose eyes nigh fell out with watching the coronation when Queen Charlotte's train was too heavy and kept yanking her gown down to her waist, exposing her—"

"Aunt Jane, *please!*" pleaded the grand-niece.

"Jesus wept, girl, don't interrupt me. And don't act so pious; I heard what you said about the Churchills yesterday. No, I will not 'hush up' in front of young Viveca; girl's lived on a farm, she knows what goes on. Farmer George is a damned sight better than his grandfather, mind you, but just as useless as that charming young Prince Fritz, his father."

Viveca's jaw dropped. She had nearly forgotten about Fritz, the man who'd fathered her sister, Allegra—who, had she lived, would no longer be simply a dead prince's bastard but the King of England's half-sister!

"Viveca, darling, please pour more tea for Lady Jane, I cannot quite reach," Yasaman said smoothly. "Now, Jane, as I was not at the coronation, perhaps you would be good enough to tell Viveca and myself about it?"

Viveca poured, cranking her ears out another notch.

"Well, Yasaman, William, Lord Talbot, was *quite* the hit of the hour. He's Lord High Steward of the royal household, you know, and the Lord High Steward is supposed to ride his horse into the coronation hall and make his obeisance—a horse in the hall, mind you! Jesus *wept!* But since no one is so disrespectful as to turn his back on the sovereign, the horse has to be carefully trained to back away from the throne."

"But what went wrong?" Yasaman asked mischievously.

Lady Sarah began laughing so hard she nearly spilled her tea. Jane continued her story. "Talbot trained the horse so well that the damned beast refused to go foreward! It *backed* into the hall, *backed* up to the throne, *backed* around the hall, and there's Willy Talbot shrieking out obeisances over his shoulder! Some folk called it 'one horse's rump facing another'!"

"And a large jewel toppled from George's crown during the ceremony," the snooty Lady Sarah said, pulling on her gloves, a signal that it had grown late. "Some people think it a very bad omen for his reign, and I suppose it *is*—the horse certainly thought so!"

Viveca watched and listened, hastily smoothing her skirts before she stood. It was one of only two gowns she owned, a ready-made one that Yasaman's servants had attacked last night with basting thread, steel pins, and heated irons, letting out the seams over the bust, taking in the waist. She couldn't wait to get to a dressmaker tomorrow.

Yasaman seemed to read her mind, for she began asking the ladies who they might recommend for Viveca's gowns.

"Madame Avenel," answered Lady Sarah, buttoning her little kidskin gloves. "No one else is acceptable for ball gowns this season. She is, of course, unaffordable, but it's worth wearing day gowns by some underling in order to have an evening dress by her. Of course, all of my gowns are by her, and I don't care if I break my husband in the process—anyone who can't afford Madame Avenel has no business in polite society. So you run your sweet little niece over there in the morning and say I sent you."

On the way out the door old Lady Jane dropped back by Viveca's side. "Don't think I didn't notice you listening and cleverly keeping your mouth shut, my girl. Now, don't you believe Sarah about the ball gowns. There are plenty of seamstresses on Threadneedle Street who can make very cunning copies of an Avenel gown without impoverishing your purse. I like a young lass with enough wit to laugh into her sewing over my barbs and witticisms. You'd do quite nicely for my third grandson, William, by the way."

The old woman cackled, then added, dead serious, "You know, you put me in mind of someone, I can't think of who. Why, it's the Baroness de Gwyn, I suppose. You're lucky—it's quite fashionable to have her type of peaches-and-cream beauty. She is so *au fait* with the court, and you do rather resemble her. Farewell, dear, and remember: Grab beauty sleep while you're still young."

Out she went, cackling into the sunset. "Oh, dear," Yasaman said breathily, leaning against the wall. "Oh, that Jane Holland. She makes me laugh till I sob."

"She says 'Jesus wept' like other people say 'God damn,' " Viveca observed.

Yasaman dabbed at her eyes with the hem of her veil. "No, Jane says *that* when she means it, too. Now let's choose the invitations we wish to accept and politely refuse those we find uninteresting. Then supper and early to bed—heavy schedule tomorrow, all those fittings for gowns, fabric shopping. And, I'm sorry, but Madame Avenel's out of the question, she'd bankrupt you."

Of course Viveca could not sleep after all that. Invitations, accepted and refused, danced through her head while damask gowns dripping Irish lace seemed to hang on a rack just over her head where she could not reach them. At last she fell asleep only to dream she stood outside a banquet, dressed in burlap, while everyone laughed and pointed at her.

She woke hours ahead of time, punching her pillow into a more comfortable position before sinking back on it. *Damn!* she told herself. *I have the land and the horses, so why not raise my stables alongside a little house where I can live alone? Why do I feel I have to reach higher? Do I think marriage to some minor lordling will remove the taint of being a Scots rebel's daughter and an urchin who once robbed to eat?*

Or was it that she needed a title and husband to remove the traces of a highwayman's love from her soul? Viveca had known no lovers since Byrne. She had strange, erotic dreams sometimes . . . they reminded her that she was no longer a child, that she wanted a man, a man of her own, not some thief in the night.

In the morning Viveca's eyes were so puffy from lack of sleep that it took cool cucumber slices laid on the lids to bring the swelling down. After that, she dusted her nose lightly with rice powder, rubbed on barely enough rouge to simulate a healthy blush, and, checking out her recently dyed eyelashes in the looking glass, decided she needed no kohl. It would not do to appear too heavily made-up on her first city outing.

The household breakfasted lightly on tea, buttered toast, and fresh fruit from the greenhouse, then a footman came in to announce that the carriage was ready.

They dropped Philippe off at the printer's, for he was overseeing the engraving of Yasaman's new calling cards. Then they drove off toward the dressmakers' district. Viveca peered out the glass doors of the carriage. "Is this Threadneedle Street, or do men nowadays just consider it fashionable to walk about with bolts of fabric on their heads in place of hats? Such a racket out there—why all the excitement?"

Yasaman called for the coachman to pull up, and a footman sprang to hand them out of the carriage. "It looks like an auction at the Maryland and Baltic coffeehouse! They carry tobacco, cotton, sugar, and rum from the American colonies, and other exotic things from the Russias. We haven't time to attend just now; we need to get you fitted."

Viveca *ooh*ed and *ahh*ed over fashion dolls in the shop windows—slipper-size mannequins cunningly dressed in the height of fashion from France. Some shops had watercolors of the latest fashions pasted up in their windows. Women edging in through open shop doors passed the dolls from buyer to buyer, exclaiming over each fringed wig and smart set of sleeves, only to moan, "But it is so *nouveau,* I know Madame Avenel will never make it for me."

"The silly cows!" Viveca exploded as they left the fifth shop in a row. "Why don't they tell Madame to go to the devil and then get a dressmaker who will follow the fashions from France and Italy and adapt them to make each lady look her best? I never saw a sillier herd of babbling brood mares in my life! Say, who's that little man across the street? He looks so despondent."

"Probably a new dressmaker who can't get any business. Look how clean his shop is and how the windows sparkle."

"To Hades with the sparkle, Yasaman. Look what's *behind* the window!"

It was a bewitching two-tone navy-blue silk taffeta that looked black in the creases and folds. Together the two women crossed the street to see the man's pasted-up watercolors of suggestions for the material. He had raised the usual neckline, filled in the open bodice with pleats and beadwork instead of the bows everyone now wore, and had made the paniers smaller and set them lower, so that the greatest fullness came at the hips and not the waistline. The skirts were gathered up every foot or so to show ruffled petticoats.

Viveca felt her mouth water, and she saw that Yasaman was equally taken by the sketches. Slack-jawed, Viveca turned to the little man, who had sprung to his feet. "Good morning, could you help me?" she asked.

"Certainly, dear. Madame Avenel's shop is just across the street and back toward the coffeehouse about seventy paces."

Dismayed, she said, "This is one of Madame Avenel's outlets?"

"No, no, I only meant that . . . no one *speaks* to me unless they want directions to *Madame's,* so—"

"Hang Madame Avenel! Where's your mistress?"

He drew himself up to his full height, considerably below hers. *"I* am master of this shop."

"Good. Grab your measuring tape and your pins, then, because I'm wild about your sketches. I need a ball gown in two weeks for Lady Sarah's ball, and I need half a dozen day dresses and some morning gowns, but I'm not rich, mind you, so most of it will have to be mere chintz. But I will want two good evening gowns to knock the heels off their shoes!"

"Well, dearie, you could knock me over with a bloody *feather!*" he exclaimed, hand on hip. "No one goes *anywhere* but to Madame's, or else to her copiers, but you dare to want something fresh, something scrumptious, something oh-so-Continental? Oh, we could start *fashions* together, you and I! We could get London out of its clothing rut. Now don't you *go* anywhere, dearie! I shall fetch my sketchbook and dolls and . . . oh, *do* come in, dear, and your *houri,* too. Help yourself to the coffee, it's what the French call café au lait." He scampered off.

Yasaman, gazing about, said, "I think you're safe here. I can go to the auction knowing you're as good as chaperoned."

"But he's a *man!* I thought it was unheard of to leave a girl alone with a man, especially one we've just met, and who ever heard of a male seamstress—er, seamster?"

"I, er, uh," Yasaman delicately groped for words, "think he's, er, um, uh, like . . . uh . . . Philippe."

"Good God, do you mean they gelded *this* one, *too?*" Viveca roared, upsetting her cup of café au lait.

"Hush, darling," Yasaman directed, mopping up the coffee with some material scraps from the shop's waste bin. "No, I meant he . . . ahh . . . Viveca, you were in Turkey, you remember there were eunuchs and concubines of both sexes. Why must I spell it out? I think he's like Philippe in that he is not adverse to the charms of other males. Except in Turkey, boys are a side dish. In this case I suspect they're the entrée."

The tailor returned, trilling and warbling like a crazed nightingale. He was unwinding a bobbin of lace as he walked, letting it fall in festoons about Viveca. "Now, mind you, I haven't much stock because there's been *no* business, and I've gone through *all* my money *just* keeping the door open, but I know where I can get more of this and some peach damask that would be *lovely* with your hair and skin but on *no account* should you wear a green unless it's moss or emerald. My, my, the current necklines just don't suit a healthy, strapping girl like you at all. They're for those *bustless* wonders at court who—"

Yasaman, in a choked voice, announced that she was returning to the Maryland and Baltic, and fled at a run.

"My," said the little man admiringly, "those foreigners can *scurry,* can't they? I suppose it's those curly-toed slippers they wear, light as feathers. *Goodness,* but you put me in mind of someone, I can't think *who!* That *baroness,* that's *who!* A Welsh baroness she was, the spitting image of you. I saw her just last week coming to pick up some gowns from Madame. She is *blonder* and less *'strawberry'* than you, and not *built* so well. My dear, I shall build a clothing *empire* on the strength of *my* taffeta and *your* cleavage! I'm Terrence of Threadneedle Street, what shall I call you?"

"Viveca. Plain old Viveca Lindstrom, not Lady or Missus or anything," she said, pleased that he offered his hand and shook hers. Like partners. Like conspirators!

160

CHAPTER EIGHTEEN

The gown was dazzling. An iridescent watered silk moiré that looked blue, then black, then both. It was cut with a deep, scooped neckline, close-fitting bodice, and three-quarter-length sleeves.

"What God has granted, let *no* man disfigure," Terrence had said in explanation of the comfortable bodice. "With a figure like yours it would be a *crime* to squish and smash it all flat, dearie! I've put in enough boning to support you, and I've raised the neckline enough that you don't fall out, but no steel corsets and bosom flatteners for *this* dress and *that* figure, *please!*"

There was a tiny edging of dyed-to-match lace, gathered all along the neckline, with more, wider lace at the turned-back cuffs. Terrence had gotten no sleep for two nights while he stitched tiny black sequins into the lace, and he had even gotten some matching lapis-and-gold earrings for her at auction.

Viveca stood now in the open carriage, wearing the gown, unable to sit for fear of crushing the silk. She wore one of Yasaman's most fetching shawls, a blue-and-gold fantasy of dragons and warriors, and carried a black feather muff that dangled stylishly from a satin strap on one wrist. "I'm sure I'll do you or the dress some disservice tonight," she whispered to Yasaman.

"Nonsense. You are enchanting."

"I could throw up in a *closet!* I should have worn some insipid pastel and been like all the others my first time out. I have a bosom, I'm not flat and smooth and nice across the front like the other women. My neckline isn't cut all the way down like theirs. The paniers are smaller, I'm too different, I—"

"Here, dear, let me get that tiny speck of kohl—there! Perfect!

161

You shall be the belle of the ball, just as Philippe vowed!" They had pulled into a horseshoe-shaped drive lit with torches in the hands of footmen, who helped them out of the carriage.

"Did you see the footman's eyes?" Yasaman whispered as they climbed the stairs to the house with its pseudo-Ionic pillars. "Didn't his face tell you that you're beautiful?"

They stepped into Lady Sarah's house, the most modish dwelling imaginable to Viveca. It was light, airy, filled with fragile-looking chairs that she knew were by Adams and Hepplewhite, the masters of sleek design. All the breakfronts, highboys, and settees were of the currently fashionable tiger maple or cherry, stained a deep, rich orangy-burgundy color, like strong tea in a glass pitcher. And the *walls,* Viveca marveled—the walls were covered with Japanese watercolors of chrysanthemums, dragons, and clouds!

The only clue that this had once been a Tudor mansion lay in the carving of the black oak ballroom and minstrels' gallery, and Lady Sarah had even brought that up to date by covering the exquisitely grained wood with buttermilk lacquer stained a pale saffron to go with her new Florentine drapes. The orchestra was clad in yellow and white to coordinate with the rest of the room, as was the hostess.

In fact, as Viveca gazed around her she saw much yellow and white. And washed-out blue and pale pink and a weak, bleary mint green. Nothing dark, even on the men. Every dress might have been cut from the same pattern, they were that alike. Each was so décolleté as to actually expose nipples when a lady took too deep a breath, and each was worn over a steel or leather corset that pitilessly smashed the breasts to nothingness, waists laced so tightly that all women stood or sat fanning themselves and swaying with dizziness.

The men noticed Viveca first. She saw their smiles, some lecherous, some genuinely pleased with this fresh new creature. Her neckline was at least three inches higher than any other, and yet, because she was not tied flat, they stared at her cleavage. She felt her pierced ears redden.

And then the women saw her. Dancers halted in midstep, conversation ceased, the orchestra's strings fell mute. Lady Sarah, about to greet Yasaman, took one look at Viveca's dress and veered away.

Oh, the men approved, all right. Each impudent glance told Viveca that. But women ruled the roost, and women obviously did not approve of someone who dared to dress differently—and better and more modestly. Why, she wasn't even painted like the rest of them, red cheeks and lips on a dead-white face. And, as befitted an unmarried woman, she had not powdered her hair, which meant the men were giving that glorious peach topknot wistful glances, longing to loosen it, bury face and hands in it. . . .

My God, Viveca thought as the silence of the room began smothering her, *they're snubbing me merely because I went to a different dressmaker, because my neckline and sleeves aren't the same as theirs, because I wear dark blue instead of one of those damned pastels that would never suit me!*

It was now quiet enough to hear a pin drop. One did. Terrence had forgotten it while hemming the gown, and now the report of steel on waxed parquetry floor sounded like cannon fire to Viveca, though she knew no one else was aware of it.

Leave now, some craven part of her begged. *Yes,* she answered herself angrily, bravely, *leave now and give up my dreams, my hopes of a future at some social strata above that of pig farmers and highwaymen. Go back to riding boots and patched breeches, a life with thieves.*

The ghost of Allegra's voice in the back of her brain asked, *And when you have the fine house you dream of, may I live on the top floor?*

The roaring silence was too much. She and Yasaman stood out together in the crowd, and that was the worst of it—she had disgraced Yasaman, who had forgiven her all her early truculence, taken her in, and treated her like a daughter, a sister—and now she had ruined everything for Yasaman, too.

No, she mustn't cry. Tears would make grotesque tracks in her eye paint, publicly displaying her acceptance of defeat at the lace-mitted hands of these slayers of girlhood dreams.

Pop! went the dreams; *smash!* went the fantasies of happiness and plans for her future. Like soap bubbles hitting a stone floor, they left a mere rainbow froth where they had once been.

Someone spoke through the rivers of blood pounding in her head.

A man. She swallowed hard, fought tears again. "I beg your pardon, sir?" she asked stiffly, unyielding, a tigress at bay and unashamed.

He was perhaps in his mid-twenties, with sparkling china-blue eyes and hair so fair as to appear silver without benefit of powdering. His shoulders were broad, his height slightly superior to hers; his bearing spoke of the military. "I said, my lady, that perhaps you might favor me with a dance."

"You mock me, sir," she answered hotly, and began to turn away.

"I never mock the whitest arms and reddest lips at a ball. Particularly when they belong to someone bold and spirited enough to dare to be different!"

He was, she saw upon turning back to him, surely a newcomer, for there had been only pastels when she entered the room, and yet this gentleman wore a black frock coat. "Maestro!" he called, and signaled the orchestra leader to strike up a tune. Viveca numbly felt Yasaman relieve her of shawl and muff, then she was swept out onto the slick parquetry floor on the arm of this Adonis, this Apollo.

The orchestra leader mopped his brow and signaled for the dirgelike Handel saraband.

His fingertips scarcely touching hers, the man in the dark coat led Viveca to the center of the ballroom. *Now* must all those months of Philippe's coaching pay off, *now* must the skirts of her gown be cut just so or else she would back over them and stumble. Everything must be perfect and precise, for the eyes of two-hundred she-wolves and their consorts were fastened upon her, awaiting failure.

Viveca's partner was light on his feet but not foppish about it. His clothes were expensively tailored but not flashy, as were so many others. In fact, his black frock coat was rather plain. He did not look at all like the others with their glaring waistcoats and gem-studded buckles, yet he plainly had good breeding.

"Smile," he whispered. "Don't give them the satisfaction of knowing you're upset."

"They're all waiting for me to stumble," she answered from between gritted teeth, for the entire room full of guests still stood watching.

"But you shan't, shall you, because *I'm* the dyed-in-the-wool stumblebum tonight—despoiler of ladies' satin slippers, faller-into-punch bowls, smasher of demitasse cups."

This time Viveca *did* smile—she couldn't help it. "Surely you jest, sir."

"Would that I did! Father demanded his money back from the dance instructors at least twice that I know of . . . but you! You're so light on your feet. Where did you learn this step we're doing?"

"In Turkey," she answered dryly. "From a black eunuch."

"Good old Philippe!" he exclaimed, to her surprise. "You must be Yasaman's niece! What a relief. My grandmother, Lady Jane Holland, has been trying to push me into your arms, and I've been resisting, since, never to my knowledge have spunky old beldames had good taste in young ladies. But she surprises me this time. I wouldn't have run and hid had I known you were like this."

"Like what?"

He chuckled. "Young. Gorgeous. And gutsy enough to stand up to a roomful of the old battleaxes. Uh-oh—see, I told you I trod upon toes from time to time, but you wouldn't listen. Next time just smack me with your fan and tell me that God only meant for *one* of us to walk on your feet!"

They laughed again, startling all observers except Yasaman, whose smile was hidden by her veil.

"You weren't here when I came in," Viveca accused lightly as she curtsied and he bowed at the end of the tune.

"I most certainly was, and gaping in openmouthed admiration."

"But I saw no black coat."

"Of course not," he answered cheerfully. "I went out and swapped with my valet so you wouldn't feel so all alone. Worked, too, didn't it?"

She laughed helplessly as he helped her up from her curtsy. A man with spirit and wit amid this crowd! Who would have expected it?

After that Viveca did not lack for a dancing partner, for many were anxious to squire her now that the ice had been broken. By the end of the ball even the women had unbent to speak to her, several asking, in whispers, where she had gotten "that too, too lovely gown." It made her wonder whether the next ball would be overrun by women in dark taffeta dresses.

She and Yasaman were on their way out when Lady Jane's grandson approached again. "Lady of the tuberoses," he said cheerfully, in reference to the tiny white buds in her coiffure, "may I call on you soon?"

"Please do."

"Very good, I shall send my man over to consult with Philippe on the proper hour, because Yasaman says he is her master of protocol and nothing may be done properly unless he approves."

"You young rascal, Philippe will approve," Yasaman told him with a laugh. He kissed her little hennaed palm—something he could not do with Viveca, for they were not well enough acquainted—and the two ladies went on out.

"You know who that was, don't you?" Yasaman asked as they were handed into the glass carriage.

"Jane Holland's youngest grandson."

"Sir William Holland. If you still have your heart set on a wealthy man with a heavy title, you should know that he's only the third son of a duke, and that both brothers already have sons."

"Well, money and a title would be grand, but hellfire, Yasaman, I couldn't marry a man I didn't like, and Sir William's got a friendly way about him. He swapped coats with his valet so there'd be someone else in unfashionable darkness."

"That was exceedingly good of him; be glad he has his family's prestige to back him up on such an act. Lady Sarah's eyes nearly popped out, and do you know what?"

"What?" Viveca asked, fanning herself and slumping, not caring if the dress wrinkled now that her evening was ending.

"I will wager you five bob that she rushes to see your revolutionary Terrence first thing in the morning!"

Philippe was waiting at the door with a face like a thundercloud. "Visitor for you," he told Viveca.

"Oh, good! Is it a big woman with the face of a Renaissance madonna?" Viveca cried out eagerly, casting her fan, shawl, and muff to a waiting maid.

"Not bloody likely," answered Philippe, whose English had expanded to include the vernacular. "Go look in the library."

Well, it wasn't Aunt Caro, then, Viveca thought, puzzled but still excited. She caught the double doors to the library, flung them wide-open. A man stood there, leaning on the mantel in front of the fire, absently fondling a Meissen goatherd statue.

He turned as she entered, and Viveca had to catch her breath. He was the very image of Jemmy St. James, only broader through the shoulders and longer-legged, topping Jemmy—had he lived—by half a head. His features were sharper than either Dash's or Jemmy's, which oddly served to make him handsomer, more expressive.

There was even a resemblance to Lilly Carlisle, though there was nothing feminine about this man. Viveca thought giddily that the resemblance must lie in their unthinking beauty and pantherlike grace: a beauty that was ageless, genderless.

It was Byrne St. James. Byrne, and a man now! Without thinking she gave a glad cry and launched herself into his arms.

Behind her, Yasaman firmly latched the doors and said to Philippe, "I am *not* one to sit in on reunions."

"No need," Philippe agreed merrily. "I'll listen at the keyhole for you."

Byrne unfastened Viveca's fingers from the collar of his stylish wool coat and stepped back. He was dressed like a merchant or clerk, in somber colors albeit good fabrics. His eyes said he liked what he saw in her, but she sensed anger there, too.

"I missed you!" she blurted out.

"Not too much, apparently. You've been back for most of a month and have done no more than send a brief note to Caro, leaving everyone to wonder what's gotten into you to so forget her."

She wasn't prepared for a scolding; had she been a cat she would have laid her ears back. "I haven't forgotten anyone, and I told Caro I'd be out as soon as things settled in around here."

"You're settled enough to go parading about in your fancy new gowns, sucking up to the aristocracy, though."

Her temper flared up. Narrowly controlling it, she put resolute hands at her waist and answered, *"This* from a man swathed in silk and cashmere himself? You look like a damned courtier, and yet you have the nerve to rail at me for my pretensions! What's the objection to my life-style, anyway? Is it my ambitions, my wanting to get out of the gutter? Just because you're stuck with no education and living a life on the turnpike, robbing and—why the devil are you laughing at me?"

"Business has been good, my beautiful simpleton, but it hasn't been the business you think. I've a job."

Her delicately tinted mouth fell open. "You . . . it . . . I—"

"Yes," he answered, savoring her discomfort and settling himself more comfortably against the mantel. "After you left I apprenticed myself to Great Edward, learned to read, write, work figures. I keep the accounts for a shipping firm now, and an honest one at that, apart from a little smuggling on the side, but we all do that, even Caro, what with the tariffs so high and all. Even George III's family brings back contraband from abroad, so don't try to turn your lip up at me. I have a job now, and all your sneering won't make it less than honorable."

Viveca said nothing. Could two and a half years really change a person so much? He seemed so—so polished, so deliberate, in such control. And, oddly, he seemed to dislike her. So why the visit? She was glad to see him—oh, *God,* she was glad; she wanted to hug him, kiss him, clasp him to her heart and speak of the old days, the good times they'd had together.

"I thought you'd come out to the Black Bull," Byrne continued. "Not so much to sully yourself with your lower-class relatives and former friends but to get your new stock settled in. I imagine you'll keep Blackamoor here, but surely you'll send her colt out to Kensington?"

"And just how do you know about my new stock and the Moor's colt?" she asked defiantly.

He shrugged lazily, masterfully, in an almost insulting manner. "Have you already forgotten I'm a shipping accountant? You crossed the Channel on a ship belonging to my employers, the Cheney, Meddows and Grey Lines—*La Dona del Fuego III.* I inventoried her. Christ, did you think I wouldn't know the Moor when I saw her? I'll wager *you* don't know her anymore—ladies of quality with social pretensions seldom ride scrappy little half-Arab mares that climb garden walls."

"Why are you being so vile? Why are you angry with me?" Viveca demanded, rubbing her arms as the chill of the room settled in on her.

"Because you never thought of coming out to see poor old Caro, who's missed you like the devil. You never thought to inquire about Lilly, who loved you like a sister and who's miserable now. You obviously never gave a thought to Great Edward nor me and Dash and the others."

"You blithering idiot, d'ye think I didn't dwell on the past? Well, Jesus wept and so did I, Byrne St. James." Something of the street urchin she had been crept into her speech, making Byrne smile as at a victory. "But I havna the time to live in the past. It's all over now, and I thought it best to get on with my life and not go troublin' any of you."

"Meaning it's more important that you find a rich lord to wed. Can this be the same Viveca who never wanted to grow up, refused to become a woman? For someone who felt that way, I'd say you have the feminine arts down pat. Right down to the last heaving inch of cleavage! You mustn't pant like that, just because your stays are so tight. Shall I call Philippe in from his listening post at the keyhole and have him loosen your stays so you can draw a decent breath? You're turning an unflattering shade of red, my dear—goes with the new hair color, though. But watch it with the henna, I hear tell more than a tablespoon of it makes dun-colored hair like yours go orange as a Caribbean sunset."

"And where would you be getting information like that but from the whores and sleazy innkeepers' daughters you still associate with?" she shouted, then turned around and added, "Philippe, damn you, get away from that keyhole or I'll have your guts for garters!"

"Very ladylike, indeed. Wouldn't the young fops who adored you an hour ago be flabbergasted to hear you shrieking like a fishwife now," Byrne mused coolly, pushing back his fine cashmere coat to put a hand on his hip. "You sound just like the runny-nosed brat I knew who palmed cutlery and picked fistfights all over Dirty Lane and Rogue's Acre. More like the real Viveca now!"

"Damn you, I'm *not* that Viveca now!" she railed, and discovered, to her chagrin, that she was on the verge of tears of rage—and even closer to taking a swing at his infuriating face.

She thought it over. And then she *did* swing a punch at him.

He blocked it. She'd guessed he would, for even back in the days of Missus Lee's band he'd had the fastest reflexes of anyone she'd ever seen. Adulthood hadn't slowed him any. Viveca, angrier than ever, launched herself at him, only to discover it was impossible to fight, dressed as she was.

Byrne caught her, only to be met with a hail of blows on his shoulders and chest. She couldn't even punch him decently as in the old days. Still she struggled uselessly, trapped in her voluminous skirts, imprisoned by the very finery she wore.

Byrne pinned her against him. It was as much embrace as restraint. "No, don't," he said suddenly. "Don't fight me, I'm not the enemy."

"Yes, you are! You railed at me for Caro's sake and never said *you* missed me at all. You came here to mock me, and I won't stand for it," she insisted, muffled against his broad chest.

"No, I only wanted to hurt you as you've hurt *me*. An argument isn't what I want at all. I only want—*you.*"

Her memories of the interlude in the hayloft with him hadn't been mere daydreams after all, then. For two and a half years since then she had been rebelliously celibate, not certain what to do with this unwanted desire he'd unlocked. And here he was now, holding her so close, she could feel his bones and muscles fit against hers as if notched with this embrace in mind. A chill crept up her spine. He released her arms, and she watched them creep around his neck as if she had no will to stop them. "Damn you, Byrne St. James," she murmured, using his full name as she had in their childhood days. "What am I to believe—that you love me, hate me, or only want to use me like a taproom whore?"

He drew her harder against him, let her feel the throbbing force of his desire. She limply let him tilt her chin up so he could gaze into her smoldering eyes. "If I told you the truth of why I'm here, Viveca, you wouldn't believe me, you stubborn, beautiful . . . kiss me. I don't give a damn for yesterday or tomorrow, only the moment, the moment with *you*, you thickheaded, pride-blinded, beautiful—"

He kissed her. Not hesitant like the boy he'd been but with the strength and passion of the man he'd become in her absence. For once in Viveca's life someone's will was stronger than hers—stronger and yet not cruel or harsh. There was a gentleness born of this new strength and maturity in him, a gentleness running neck and neck with blazing desire.

She kissed him back, parted her lips to hot sweetness and the insistent fire of his tongue caressing hers. The kiss seemed to sear them together, like burning fuses entwined for an explosion.

They had been apart for over two years and were in a library, not a bedroom. He would have picked her up and carried her to the settee, but she was breathlessly untying the stock-tie at his neck, untucking it, running her hands along bone, muscle, and the fine, silky hairs on his chest and stomach. Byrne shuddered, lowered his head to her long white neck. He found the pulse point there, sucking it greedily while she moaned and gasped in his muscular arms.

"Oh, please!" she managed between kisses. *"Please!"*

And she pulled him down onto the hearth rug, heedless of her expensive gown. He was unhooking the front of it, opening it, struggling with her whalebone stays and corset strings.

Byrne wanted them to be naked and in a bed, but Viveca had waited too many years already. She pulled him down on her, sinking into the thick wool Tabriz rug. She helped him raise her heavy skirts, impatiently twining long, creamy legs around his as they both tore at the buttons of his breeches.

The shock of penetration made her cry out in surprise. At once she dug her fingers into his back, urging him on. They surged together, Viveca crying out in excitement. The heat of the moment took them, drew them on as Viveca arched against him, mewing in ecstatic amazement. Byrne had never had a woman react so strongly, not the most seasoned whores, not the most enthusiastic virgins. She was bloodying his back now, thrusting up against him, moaning his name, calling for him to go deeper, harder. . . .

She rose with the crest of it, then broke and broke. Byrne could not control himself any longer. Lost in the flaming silk of her being, he let the peak of passion drain him. They shuddered together, strained, clenched, sagged down into the rug. When they had caught their breath, she heard Byrne whisper, "No, not like this, love . . . I wanted to court you, carry you to some grand four-poster, not tumble you dishonourably on your aunt's floor as I would some whore."

Viveca smacked him away from her in a spark of fury. She sat, climbed to her feet as she hurriedly fastened her gown. "Whore! Who are you calling a whore?" she demanded, pushing her bedraggled hair out of her eyes as a shower of hairpins clattered onto the hearthstone.

"I didn't call you a whore. I said I'm sorry I treated you like one instead of courting you as you deserve to be——"

"Being sarcastic again, are you? *I'm* the one who dragged *you* down on the floor in a heat of passion; are you saying it was whorish of me not to be more restrained? That I was cheap or ill-bred to experience this as strongly as a man—or stronger?"

He laughed uneasily. "You're pitching a fit over nothing. I never insulted you; all I said was that I wanted to do this right, wanted to woo you and——"

"Woo me! When did a highwayman *woo* a woman? You can

give yourself airs and a cashmere coat and call yourself a shipping accountant, Byrne St. James, but you're nothing more than a ten-shilling robber, and you know it! Don't feign fancy ways with me, I know all about you men, all you want is half an hour's sport on the floor, so don't pretend it meant any more than that to you. *Especially* don't pretend it at the expense of a woman who did it honestly, willingly—if stupidly!"

Byrne fisted his hands. "I'd knock a man's head half-off for saying such a thing. But being as you're only a pigheaded, uppity bitch who doesn't know an honest emotion or a friend when she meets one, I'll let it pass. You take my compliments and twist them to bitterness and bile. You've turned a beautiful feeling sour because of your touchy pride. And suppose I *had* compared you to a whore? What's the harm in that? They may be coarse, my lady, and not so refined as you, but neither are they as two-faced. It wasn't your enthusiasm that displeased me at all—a man of any worth *prays* to be able to give his lady such pleasure! No, it was my own roughness and haste I doubted. I wanted silk sheets and flowers for you, a candlelit night, but I was wrong. It seems we have our roles reversed, my sweet. *I'm* the one who wants roses and tenderness while to you all that matters is—how did you phrase it?—half an hour's sport on the floor!"

Byrne strode forward, brushing against her so hard that she spun into the wall. He threw the doors open, which sent Philippe, bent at the keyhole, reeling into the potted orange trees. There was a pause, then Byrne leaned forward and, seizing Philippe by his coat front, yanked him out of the orange trees and plopped him back onto his feet.

The urbane Philippe, rarely at a loss, caught Byrne's tricornered hat off the wall hook and sailed it to him. Byrne snagged the hat one-handed, shoved it on his head, and stormed out the front door.

On the threshold he hesitated, fishing a cloisonné jewel box out of his coat. "Catch," he said sourly, and tossed it to Viveca. Then a corner of his mouth lifted with sardonic humor. "A friend left it with me for safekeeping once. In case she ever shows up, you might give it to her."

She'd been the best catch in Missus Lee's band, but her reflexes were dulled by emotion and the lateness of the hour. Viveca scolded herself, thinking soft living had ruined her as the box ricocheted off a wall. Then she caught it, banging her head on a jasper pillar in the process.

Inside was her mother's miniature, the Lady of the Tuberoses. Before Viveca could say anything, the door banged shut behind Byrne. Philippe, standing on his toes, peered out the glass in the door, saw Byrne fish another jewel case out of his pocket and fling it into the rhododendrons lining the brick walk.

Viveca sank down on the steps to the second floor, cradling the box, confused, angry, hurt. Damn him, what had he wanted from her? No matter what she said or did, she managed to anger him! When she'd first held him, a fire of affection and desire had stirred within her, not merely passion's heat, but the old flames of family feeling, of *partnership* between them. He'd made her think all her hopes of snaring a lord were a mistake and that she belonged with him—and then he insulted her, stormed out as if she mattered not at all.

The front door opened again, then closed with a light *snick* of sound. Viveca glanced up to see Philippe insinuating his way toward her. He took her hand, pressed his best handkerchief into it. "Mop up your kohl before it runs down into your gown," he suggested kindly. She hadn't even realized she was weeping. "He had another jewel box with him and threw it in the yard. I have brought it in for you," he told her, and laid it in her lap.

Viveca opened it. Inside was a small, very nearly perfect sapphire mounted on a gold band set with square-cut diamonds. She stared from it to Philippe with an unspoken question in her eyes.

"My guess," the handsome eunuch said wisely, "is that this is not the product of his highwayman days, nor is it the sort of thing to be purchased with stolen loot. It would be larger, gaudier, more flawed then, bought or stolen for size and effect rather than for perfection and taste as is this ring. It looks to me like the sort of thing purchased by a man who has looked long and hard for it and spent a year's pay buying it. It's a pledge, I think. The sort of betrothal gift a man brings to the woman he truly loves. I'm sorry I misjudged him."

She sprang to her feet. "Hellfire! That's why he was so mean— it's because he still loves me! Why couldn't the fool just come out and say it? I've got to get Moor saddled! I've got to go after him—"

"No, you can't ride after him! In the first place, it's too late and the roads are full of footpads and highwaymen. A lone woman would be raped, perhaps murdered. And it wouldn't be right to wake the coachman or footmen this late. No, you must wait until morning. Don't sulk, Viveca. What man ever talked sense after a fight? He needs time to cool down so the two of you can talk reasonably."

She relaxed in the grip he had on her shoulders. "You won't ride after him with me, then."

"Some defense *I'd* be—the two of us together are only half the size of the average footpad!"

"You're right," she said, and bit her lip. "He will need to cool down before we can talk. I'm glad you pointed that out to me. He never *could* talk straight after a fight."

He smiled, releasing her. "You'll see I'm right in the morning when he's not so angry and loves you again. Now up to bed and I'll send the maid with hot chocolate."

She blessed Philippe's good advice until morning, for in the morning it was too late. In years to come she would think, *What I wouldn't give to have ridden after him that very night!*

CHAPTER NINETEEN

"What do you *mean,* he's gone?" Viveca asked, feeling her heart stop.

Caro Lindstrom stepped back from the embrace, wiping her hands on her apron. "Why, sweetheart, 'tis just as I said. Byrne's gone. He mentioned, oh, must have been five months ago or more, that the shipping firm was after him to go work in their Caribbean offices. So he blew in here like a nor'wester last night, packed his few good clothes, and left on a ship bound westward an hour before dawn."

Viveca plopped down on a three-legged milking stool in the kitchen and said a word so vulgar that even Caro jumped.

"What happened, my girl?" her aunt asked gently.

Viveca told her. Caro gave her bread dough a final pinch and covered the loaves with damp towels to speed their rising. Then she washed her hands and removed her apron, giving Viveca time to finish her story. At last she said, "Bullheaded, the two of ye. That boy made up his mind you didn't love him, and now he's gone. Fair broke Dash up, it has. He never stopped believing Byrne would go back to that disgraceful robbing with him, and now Byrne's gone and Dash feels right lost. Mayhaps he'll quit that dirty business now, 'specially with the way he drinks as of late. Like a fish, he does, swilling it down. It'll be the death of him, that and women lining up to say they've been had by the famous highwayman! And him with no more sense than to injure his brother's ghost!"

"What do you mean?" Viveca asked anxiously. "Jemmy's ghost, you mean? And what of Lilly and Great Edward?"

Caro studied her hands awhile. "Well, Great Edward's health

is no good, but we all know that. He's quit his profiteering schemes, started breeding cattle. Doctors told him he needs country air and good cooking, so he's been a steady boarder here for some time. Now the old sot's asked me to be his missus."

"Aunt Caro! That's grand!"

Caro blew her nose. " 'Course, he's no Jemmy, no fancy-free young buck with long black hair and a romantic way about him, but I'm not a young woman anymore, and he's a steady sort. We get on, we do . . . it's not like it was with Jemmy, but damn me if I don't think I love this long, lanky heron of a man!"

Viveca smiled for her aunt's good fortune and tried to forget her own bad luck. "And Lilly, Jemmy's daughter?"

"Well, her da's ghost has been offended, it has."

"Why? What do you mean?"

Caro leaned on the sink pump. "Dash had no respect for that child being his flesh 'n' blood, and of a tender age. He toyed with her affections, led her down the primrose path. He got her with child and then dropped her like a hot chestnut. I offered to keep her on as chambermaid here, but she said it was too close to Dash for her—said if she stayed here he'd like as not turn her child into a drunkard or robber like the rest of the St. James clan. So she's took herself and the babe off and is living and working in some sweatshop doing sewing and pattern-cutting. Lord, there must be a hundred of them crammed into a room not big enough for fifteen, hardly making enough to pay for stale black bread and water."

Caro's usually gentle eyes flashed fire. "I'm afraid for her health, nursing that baby, so I pretend I just happen to be in the neighborhood and have leftover food, and I take her meat pies and bread in a hamper, or some clothes for the babe. She's too proud to accept anything else. Byrne tried to drag her out by force, and she hit him over the head with a lead pipe and called the constables on him." She sighed. "When I think of the prettiest black-haired creature ever to come out of that no-good clan a-wasting her eyes squinting over needlework in the dark, and her and the child like to die of scurvy and consumption with no food

. . . but damn it, Viveca, I can't drag her back, I've tried! And now Byrne's gone, too."

She was sobbing into her apron. Viveca stood, held her aunt. "Caro, Caro, it's all right. I'll go see if I can't talk some sense into Lilly. And I've been such a sluggard about visiting. . . . I'll come out to Kensington more often, we'll have picnics like we used to, and you can come for dinner at Yasaman's and we'll go to the theater and see some shocking new plays. Now, would you like that?"

Caro looked up gratefully. "You're a good lass, you are, to think of my feelings when here you must be dying of a broken heart over that stubborn, mule-headed Byrne! Those St. James boys, they'll break a poor woman's heart, they will. Been like me sons, the pack of them, since Jemmy died. And you and Lilly like me own girls." She blew her nose into an embroidered handkerchief. "Well, I can't help Lilly for the moment, but I can help you in a small way. You wrote last week to ask if I could still get silk at rock-bottom prices from my smuggler friends. The answer is yes, so tell your dressmaker he needn't pay those cutthroat prices in town anymore, just let me know what he wants and send him on out."

There was a pause, then both women stared at each other. "Aunt Caro, are you thinking what I'm thinking?" Viveca asked.

"Yes! If your dressmaker gets enough business to need help—"

"Then I could send Lilly to him and it wouldn't seem like charity, and she could get out of that dreadful place—"

"Hello, what am I interrupting?" asked a clipped, educated male voice. Viveca whirled to see Great Edward, thinner and grayer than before, enter the room. She hugged him, bringing Caro into a three-way embrace. "Edward, when's the happy day?"

"As soon as your aunt agrees to make an honest man of me."

"Oh, you!" Caro scolded him, blushing with pleasure. "Get along with you, now, I have to drag Cook in here to help me finish dinner. You two go off and talk breeding horses or something, I'll be out soon."

After lunch and a long chat with the two of them, Viveca woke

178

her manservant from his perch on the veranda, and they rode back into the city. She stopped by Threadneedle Street for a chat with Terrence and found out that nearly twenty women had come clamoring for gowns like hers. "I refused, of course," he said merrily. "Told them there are *no* copies at Terrence of Threadneedle. Each woman shall have her own most flattering fashion. And then I charged them quadruple what I charged you, and they all went away *ditheringly* happy. I'm nearly *mad* with all this measuring, cutting, fabric-hunting. I so desperately need help."

Viveca responded breathlessly, "I have a friend stuck in a sweatshop, making ready-made clothing. I think she's good, Terrence, she was good years ago, used to make clothes for all of us at the inn where I lived, and she's desperate. She'd probably work just for a roof over her head until you can afford to pay her."

He leapt up, throwing his sewing down on the cutting table. "Splendid! Let us go fetch this paragon!"

"Well, there's a baby, too."

He eyed her wisely. "My dear girl, there always *is* in these cases. Let's hurry!"

She regarded him warily. "What in the world will a confirmed . . . *bachelor* like you do with a baby underfoot? You'll stuff her in the samovar!"

He yanked his coat off a hook by the door. "Nonsense, I'm the eldest of fifteen, I know all *about* babies. *No one* baby-sits like Terrence does! Now let us fetch your dear friend!"

It was late that night when Viveca arrived back at Yasaman's house. Yasaman and Philippe were just leaving to attend dinner at the Turkish ambassador's house, for they had given up on the tardy Viveca. She waved at them to go on, too weary and disappointed about Byrne to want a formal dinner.

Her maidservant met her at the door, saying two of the St. James brothers had been by to discuss building her new stables; she had forgotten Luke and Bartholomew were studying architecture—the first of that highwayman brood to go to school.

And, more important, her maidservant hurried to say, a footman had left a note bearing the Holland family coat of arms. She ran and fetched the thick, creamy-colored envelope for Viveca, who quickly ripped it open.

Sir William Holland wished to know whether he might attend tea tomorrow, or as soon as it was convenient for her "graceful, glorious self." It was signed, "Yr. Obediante Servante, Most Respectfull & Admiring of You, Sr. Wm. Holl."

She pressed the note to the starched bodice of her riding habit. Damn it, she thought fiercely, *why not? Why shouldn't I enjoy myself while Byrne's gone; why shouldn't I keep company with a dashing young man?*

And suppose Byrne never came home. Or worse yet, *did.* Was there any future for them together?

She ground her teeth and said to the maid, "Please be so good as to shake the footman awake, he's in the parlor. And ask him if he'd trot over to Sir William Holland's at once to tell him that tea is at two o'clock sharp tomorrow afternoon."

CHAPTER TWENTY

She greeted William in the small dining chamber, wearing her new white chintz tea gown, its tiny blue flowers offset by her blue-black eyes and the miniature around her neck. She had no other jewelry save for the lapis earrings Terrence had scrounged for her at an estate sale, so she made do with a few hothouse tuberoses in her soft chignon and blessed her dressmaker. With such a lovely gown her lack of jewels wouldn't be noticeable.

William bowed low over her hand, so low that his silver-gilt hair, caught back in a black silk bow-and-bag, stirred and nearly escaped its moorings. *My God,* she thought irreligiously, hand to her bodice. *He really is a damnable handsome man, with hair so fair he never need powder it!*

He straightened from his low bow. She was relieved to see that his china-blue eyes were twinkling. "I considered the usual compliments," he said frankly. "You know, gushing about your eyes, your figure—then I considered the usual gifts, chocolates, flowers, and I took the liberty of inquiring about you and learning that you enjoyed reading and horses most of all. Well, I could not lay my hands on anything about horses, but I thought this might interest you."

From behind his back he brought out a leather-bound volume on the excavations at Pompeii in Italy. Viveca thanked him eagerly, took the book, and opened it to see that it was illustrated with hand-colored prints.

"Sir William, this isn't proper. I mean, chocolates and flowers don't cost nearly what such a book as this must have—"

"The lady of the tuberoses wouldn't approve if you refused it," he answered, *tsk-tsk*ing.

"I—I beg your pardon?" she asked, feeling stupid.

"The relative in your miniature. She *is* a relative, she has the same determined jaw, the defiant eyes—she'd approve. No woman with that much strength and character in her beauty sat around munching chocolates and sniffing gladiolas. No, she was a reader, I'm sure of it."

Viveca chuckled, pleased. "She's my great-grandmother, and a regular old rip, judging from the low neck of her frock and all those flowers in her hair. Tuberoses in the lace of her gown if you look closely, too."

He stepped closer, his breath stirring her hair for a moment. "If you are inviting me to look closer then *you* are being improper. I like tuberoses. You wore them in your hair at the ball, did you not? I looked up tuberoses in the dictionary to discover what they represent. They stand for the pleasures of the flesh."

"Oh," she said, blushing all the way from her bodice to her hairline. "I didn't know that. I wear them because of the portrait miniature—and because I like white flowers. These are so cool and waxy, they don't wilt like other blossoms, and they smell strongest after dark—at an hour when the petals have dropped off every flower other ladies might be wearing."

He stepped back, and she was aware that he watched her seat herself on the satin settee. Would he try to sit on the settee next to her, which was considered quite racy? *Hellfire,* she thought *irritably. As if I were a virgin or something! I've got to be so bloody proper!*

He sat across from her. "The tuberose is also called Mistress of the Night," William added, almost as an afterthought. "It seems fitting when I recall how you looked sweeping into the ballroom —chin up, daring them all to condemn you, your alabaster skin splendidly set off by that midnight-blue gown and the flame of your hair studded with snow-white flowers. It should have seemed delicate, demure, pure. Yet there was something challenging about you. Something mysterious, too, for why would a young woman dare be so different at her first ball? It said you cared enough to be there but not enough to be another of those paper silhouettes, turned out by the thousands."

He laughed, a warm, unaffected sound. "I said to myself, 'Will, do not let the slim neck and tapering hands fool you. She isn't one of those swooning, tittering fools. This is no lilting lily-girl with drooping head and colorless soul. She stands there, defiant, magnificent, strong enough for two, strong enough to bear the weight of the world on her back and never disappoint anyone—the kind of woman who is courageous, spirited, worthy of worship. A woman of mysteries.' "

Odd talk for a suitor. And surely he was courting her for her body as well as her mind, despite his talk of souls and strengths, for his eyes devoured her figure as they spoke.

"And you want to unravel the mystery?" she asked, thinking that must be his sole interest in her.

"Of course not," he answered, looking surprised. "Mysteries are whole in themselves and not to be tampered with. I am not one of those who believes in stripping away a woman's many secrets and bringing her down to a common level. No, a woman is to be worshiped as an equal in mind and a superior in heart, soul, and appearance."

Viveca chuckled, amazed at his reply. "You have revolutionary ideas, Sir William. I've never heard the like. Most women have no wish to be worshiped, no urge to be stuck high upon a drafty, lonely pedestal, solitary and hungry for companionship. A woman wishes to be an equal, working shoulder-to-shoulder with those she treasures."

In his smile she saw, for a heart-wrenching moment, a ghost of Byrne's admiration of her spirit—an admiration that could never hope for her pride to bend enough to allow true partnership. So why shouldn't she allow this rich, handsome, *interested* man to worship her, if that was what he wanted? If he wanted an Athena she would climb up on that pedestal in Grecian robes and let him lay his empire at her feet.

Wouldn't she?

It was three months later, while Terrence was pinning her into a new gown, that Viveca received the news.

Lilly entered the shop, her baby Charlotte on one hip, a heavy bolt of Genoese damask on the other. "Oof!" she cried out cheerfully, letting the tissue-wrapped bolt land on the cutting table with a resounding thump. "Terrence, I'll finish pinning Viveca. You trot yourself on over to Garraway's for that auction. Fabrics galore, and dirt cheap, too."

Terrence seized his coat and hat. "Missus, I leave you to Lilly's capable hands—follow those pleat-lines *close* now, Lil—I'll be back soon. After all, I can tell when you're trying to get rid of me so that you two can gossip behind my back."

"As if anyone's a bigger gossip than you," Viveca told him, smiling.

The door banged shut behind him. "Lord, just so I don't have to hear any more about the Churchills' family squabbles," Viveca commented, shaking her head. "Lilly, unpin me a tad and help me down off this milking stool. I need to catch my breath and have a sip of coffee."

Silence. She turned around to see Lilly watching her, white-faced, baby pressed to her heart. "Lil, what is it?" Viveca cried, concerned for her friend.

"Byrne's married."

Viveca stood stock-still a moment, then wobbled on the stool. Lilly put a hand up, hauled her down quickly. Blackness. The room was dark and spinning. She felt a breeze on her back: Lilly must be unpinning the gown so she could breathe. Viveca groped for support, felt her friend's arms go around her. "Jesus, Lil. Jesus *wept!* When did you hear this?"

She was vaguely aware of baby Charlotte on the rug at her feet, playing with her shoe buckles.

"I was at Caro's just before I went on to the auction. Dash was sunk down in his cups, celebrating. Goodness, he slurs so badly when he drinks that it was an effort to get a sensible word out of him. He said Byrne had married some planter's daughter up in the Colonies. That's where their convict brother Bertt is, too. I guess Byrne went to visit him and met this girl. I'm sorry I sprang it on ye so rough-like, Viveca, but hellfire! I scrambled back here after buying just one damned bolt like I'd promised Terrence. I wanted to get back to you, let you know what happened. Don't look like that, Viveca, you're tearin' me heart in two!

"Byrne's gone and married now, and you're free to do the same, you hear me? You marry that nice Sir William next time he asks, 'cos girls like us don't get such a sterling opportunity every day."

Viveca's vision slowly cleared. She could see Lilly's trusthworthy arms around her and the sprigged grisette gown her friend wore. She could see the pinned seams on her own arms and, beyond them, the shop windows where sunlight streamed in bravely as though the world had not ended.

"Why—why, you're right, Lilly. It's a miracle William asked. I don't have much money or a lot of land; I have no family, no social connections. I've had incredible luck making it this far, haven't I?"

"That you have, and Sir William's the one for you, ducky," Lilly said, giving her a fierce squeeze before releasing her.

"He's . . . different, though, Lil. Kind of dreamy-like at times. Wants to worship me," Viveca said slowly.

"Well, you let him. And let him cover you with silks and jewels and ermine, too, if he likes. You hold your hands open and take all you can get."

Viveca swallowed hard. The hurt was immense and yet she wouldn't have to sit and wonder about Byrne now. That quick he'd gotten over her. Just that quick! "Lilly," she began, "you remember that day . . . the escape?"

"That day we met? Sure I do. We've changed since the gang helped you and my da escape the noose. All of us who were there that day have changed aplenty. I'm a respectable seamstress; you're monied, with breeding stock; Dash is a falling-down, maudlin drunk; and Byrne's gone off and become an accountant —and married! There ain't no going back to the past, Viveca."

"No. I guess there isn't."

"Damned right," Lilly answered, turning away from the window to face her.

Viveca looked at her friend, wreathed in white light pouring through the shop windows. Made her look like an illustration

185

she'd once seen of the Angel Gabriel, who brought tidings. Only this Gabriel hadn't told her she was God's chosen mother but that Byrne, her Byrne, loved someone else and had married—and that she'd be a damned fool not to get on with her life and do the same. Thank God for Lil!

"Pin me back in," she said hoarsely. "I've got an engagement to agree to."

She married Sir William in April 1764 during an eclipse of the sun. Looking back on that day always made her wonder why, with such a bad omen, she had gone ahead and married, anyway. Hurt pride? Need for her own home? The realization that being worshiped could prove pretty balm to a wounded ego? Her genuine, though sexless, fondness for the bridegroom?

There were other omens for that marriage, she realized years later. That very year the king's uncle, dead Prince Frederick's brother William, Duke of Cumberland, "the Butcher of Culloden" who had ordered the troops to massacre her father's regiment, died.

Before his death he had brought about the breeding of two of the greatest racehorses of the eighteenth century—indeed, of all time. First there was King Herod, and then the magnificent Eclipse, born this April Fool's Day of Viveca's wedding; "Eclipse the Undefeated," who had yet to make his mark on the track.

And on Viveca's life.

Racehorses and dying dukes were not on her mind this day, though. She thought only that it was amazing how many people had shown up and what fabulous gifts they had given her and William; William, who could not seem to take his eyes off her in her gorgeous wedding gown.

The dress was a confection of silver damask and charmeuse with a bushel basket of seed pearls adorning the stomacher and sleeves. Viveca herself had made all thirteen yards of the feather-fine silver lace at the cuffs, neckline, and hem of her shift, its soft gathers allowed to peek out from under the gown. Later she would realize those thirteen yards had been unlucky for her.

She said her vows at the altar of St. Paul's with conviction, for she cared for William, despite his unworldliness, and surmised that he loved her with an urgency bordering on obsession. She had never heard of a man so attentive to a woman's whims, whose every wish was to spoil her, bring her any little thing she admired in shop windows.

All too soon this ceremony of stained glass and solemn promises ended, and the big star-ruby betrothal ring was on her finger forever, "till death did us part," as the vow went. William lifted the veil for one of his fevered kisses that always, oddly, left her as untouched, as unfeeling as a nun. She thought then of how she had told him before accepting his proposal that she was not a virgin and how William had merely smiled and said, "My angel, my Athena, neither am I!" Odd answer; odd man.

Down the cool, darkish nave of the church now, the only light coming from sun strained through colored glass and half a thousand beeswax tapers. *I'll never have another stinking tallow lamp in my house when I'm rich,* she had told Allegra. *Our home will be alight with beeswax tapers and lavender-oil lamps.*

Dear God. Thinking of the dead on her wedding day. She started to cross herself, then stopped, for as Lady Viveca Holland she now had the attention of a churchful of people.

They burst out into daylight on the front steps of the church, momentarily blinded. Blinking, Viveca threw her arms around William's neck, promising "to be the best damned wife you'll ever have, sir!"

"I do love you, my goddess, my life," he answered passionately, and kissed her again, to the delight and applause of the onlookers.

As they stepped back from the embrace, she saw over his shoulder a badly lathered horse, standing with legs splayed and head hanging. A little bubble of anger burst in her that anyone would ride a poor beast so hard, so heartlessly . . .

. . . and then she recognized the horse. Black Rose's son, Blackberry. She had named him herself five years ago.

His rider had frozen halfway up the stairs, hat in hand. He was tanned dark as a Red Indian or quadroon, emphasizing the gleaming blue-black of his hair and the stark whiteness of his even teeth and crumpled shirt. His velvet coat strained across his broad shoulders, laden with the dust of the road. He looked as if he'd ridden hard and fast. From Kensington, she guessed, where he'd gotten the news upon returning from his ship at Gravesend or London.

The expression on Byrne St. James's face said he had not expected to arrive too late. But why? Why should he be here when he had a wife of his own—a *wife*, damn his eyes!

She met his astounded, defeated stare with triumph on her face, an unspoken slap that said, *There now, take back your own medicine and be as hurt as your marriage hurt me!*

"What is it?" William asked, taking her firmly by the elbow and hurrying her away to the waiting landau and team. "Someone walk over your grave, love?"

When she shuddered and said nothing, he handed her into the carriage, though he did not climb in himself. "William, why aren't you—"

"I'll be a little late to the wedding feast, but trust me, my empress, I'll not be late for the honeymoon."

She stood up in the carriage as he started toward his horse. "But, William. Where are you going?"

"Why, my angel, my pet, I thought you knew that Herod is running in the ninth at Ascot today. I have three hundred bob on that horse, and I have to see whether he's made me a winner or a loser. Driver, take her ladyship to the feast hall at once."

For one horrid moment, for a few heartbroken seconds, she almost called out to Byrne. He was no more than ten yards away, leading his weary horse down the street, away from her, out of her life. But she forced herself to remember that Byrne had a wife now and that he had scorned her, Viveca, to marry that wife.

"William?" she attempted a final time, but he was lost in the rush as the crowd, spilling from the church, spotted her carriage and began flinging flowers and rice.

There was no further glimpse of Byrne and Blackberry. It was as if the street had swallowed them up.

Then she heard the outcry of the crowd and, glancing up, saw a menacing black silhouette cover the white sun overhead.

PART FOUR

Byrne

"So next morning I woke at the hour of six or seven;
The redcoats stood around me in numbers all uneven.
        I then produced my pistols. . . ."

—"Whiskey in the Jar," late 18th-century Irish Traditional

CHAPTER TWENTY-ONE

West End, London, 1766

"What do you mean, it hasn't been paid for?" Viveca asked, folding her parasol and handing it to Stuart, her page boy.

What do you mean, it hasn't been paid for?

She stood in the doorway of her half-finished mansion, under construction these two years of her marriage while she and William ran up exorbitant bills living in a suite at Tallman's fine London hotel.

In those months William had often brought jewels home for her; jewels he bought on credit, jewels Viveca wound up paying for herself when creditors became too clamorous. William also brought friends home without notice to attend intimate little dinners for nineteen. That meant calling in a caterer or at least an assistant for Cook, usually running up considerable expense.

Three of their footmen had just quit, claiming they hadn't been paid since before the wedding; Cook was continually begging her for pocket money; and little Stuart was forever tugging at her skirts to say there were more Bad Men at the door wanting Missy's money.

Viveca stood now in the broad, burled walnut doorway of her unfinished house with its killingly fashionable West End address. She looked, unseeing, past the thirteen-foot lapis and jasper columns, the doors and built-in screens with their linenfold paneling of fine Spanish mahogany. The parlor just beyond with its mosaic ceiling taken from a Roman ruin in Italy. The parquetry floors.

"Nothing but the best for my bride," William had said with a heart as large as she imagined his father's purse to be. And so she had ordered her furniture from Chippendale, Hepplewhite, and the modish Mister Robert Adams. Waiting in crates were little scuttling tea carts, latticework Chinese chairs, mahogany breakfronts, matched cherry highboys, settees, daybeds, sofas. Their huge canopied bed had been personally designed by Robert Adams himself.

She longed to move in here, to live in this house with its cunningly concealed brick drains and china water closets, its frescoes, and trompe l'oeil paintings that made it impossible to tell where wall ended and ceiling began. The paintings of her horses by Stubbs were waiting to hang in the hall, portraits of her and William by Reynolds, the sterling and Dresden and Meissenware . . .

"I said, Your Ladyship, that Sir William, he ain't paid us in a long while and we can't go on no more," the workman repeated.

"Very well," Viveca answered stiffly, pulling her lacy mitts back on and taking her parasol from Stuart. "I shall have Sir William go over the accounts with you this evening, then."

The foreman clutched his cap to his heart, smearing the grime on his smock. "But, Missus, he glances at 'em for two seconds and says to do what I see fit. And then he leaves! And I got a crew o' men here wi' no food in their bellies, nor their families', neither, and I can't afford to replace the hammer I busted last week."

A sensation very close to horror gripped Viveca's heart, but she kept her mask of coolness on. "I'll look at the accounts myself, then, shall I?"

"Oh, Missus! Much obliged Missus . . . er, Yer Ladyship. So good of you, really 'tis—"

"Aye," piped in another workman. "Lady what keeps racehorses got to know where the accounts stand so as she can keep them horses running and winning for us. We all pooled our last shillings and won on your Godolphin colt at Ascot last February. A ripping good colt he is, mum!"

"Thank you," she said automatically, frozen inside as she accepted the ledgers from the foreman. "Stuart, darling, be good

192

enough to run over to that coffee shop and bring something back for the gentlemen and ourselves."

The workers lowered their heads. "Missus, we ain't no gentlemen."

"Well, you are to me. You treat me with greater chivalry than any of those upper-crust louts we entertain. Oh, and Stuart—see if the proprietress will make up some of those delightful new things John Montagu, the Earl of Sandwich, has come up with. You know, have her slice meat and vegetables thin and put them between two pieces of bread."

"Aye, mum, sammitches, they're called."

"Good of you, mum, we—we ain't et much in a while," the foreman said nervously, kneading the brim of his cap against his chest and avoiding her eyes.

"I thought you had credit at the coffee shop?"

"Not no more. The bill there ain't been paid since sixty-five. Now don't you go ordering meat in them sammitches, missus. Meat be awful high this year."

"You've been working half-starved. I can see what you all look like," Viveca cried out angrily. "By God, man, the least I can do is get a warm cup of tea and some food in each man's belly. Now please have someone help Stuart carry the food. Here's my purse, use it all if need be. Don't give me that hangdog look, man, I trust you. If you weren't trustworthy you'd have stripped the place bare and gone months ago. When you get back, I'll be in the library working on the accounts."

Viveca laid her coat across some crates and sat down in the library with the ledgers. She hardly noticed when Stuart came in and cut up her sandwich into bite-size bits, pressing the food into her hand, making her eat, holding the porcelain teacup to her mouth while she drank.

When the awful truth was out and the ledgers shut, she gathered Stuart onto her lap and hugged him hard. "It's bad, missus? It's awful?" he asked.

"What makes you think that?"

"Because you get that funny look that means tears with any other lady. Like when you're thinking of them babies you lost

193

and you're turning sad. Don't be sad, missus, you're too pretty to be so sad."

"You little flatterer! Now run and fetch the foreman for me," she answered tartly, setting him down and watching him race off. Great God in Heaven, even a ten-year-old child spotted trouble before she did.

She rose slowly, dusting her smartly pleated coat and day gown of the same rose-colored cashmere. The foreman entered in a moment, respectfully tugging his forelock by way of salute, and agreed to come to the hotel that night so the two of them could talk to William.

"She's a plucky wummin," he told the others when she had gone, "but she ain't caught on to the whole truth yet, she ain't."

The worst was not over for Viveca. Missus Tallman, the hotel owner, met her at the door and asked that she step into her office for a moment. William had not paid her in eleven months, Missus Tallman said, and everyone from the brandy importer to the bootblack was hounding her, demanding their shares. Viveca said she would speak with her husband as soon as he came home and, stiff-lipped, climbed the stairs to the bridal suite. "By Sunday, or it's out you must go, Your Ladyship. I'm sorry, but that's the way it is," came the landlady's voice behind her, echoing up the stairwell.

At the top of the stairs Viveca had to pause for breath. "Goodness, I must be getting fat, my stays are cutting into me so," she told Stuart. "Why the frown? Oh, hellfire, William hasn't paid *you*, either, has he? And your poor mother with all those children to care for. Why didn't you tell me?"

"Missus, you had enough on your mind," he answered dolefully.

"Well, you and I will sit down and figure it all up and have you paid tonight." A sudden suspicion stabbed her, and she glanced sharply down at Stu's bowed head. "Come now, what else do you know that I don't?"

He stared at his feet. "Just that Sir William, he gambles some."

She stooped to pat the little silk-clad shoulder. "But *everyone* gambles, Stu."

194

He frowned up at her. "Not like Sir William, missus. If two dogs strike up a fight in the street, Sir William, he bets on the outcome. Prizefights, horse races, wrestling matches, he'll bet on anything. I once seen him wager on how long it would take this farmer's horses to pull their cart clear of some mud. He ain't a bad 'un, Ladyship, he just caint keep his hands off his purse strings! He even bets the maid what time you get up after a late-night party."

"Thank you, Stu. No, don't look embarrassed, I mean it. They always say the wife is the last to know."

"Oh, no, missy," he answered hurriedly as they walked down the carpeted corridor to the bridal suite, "they say *that* when there's another woman, and there'll never be no other woman for the sir, he's just mad for you, we all know it and smile about it. Gambling isn't like cheating on a *wife,* Missus V'ica."

"But cheating doesn't cost this much money," she told him, sadder but wiser. "Now let's sit down so I can figure your wages, get you paid, and send you home to your mother with a meat pie and some rolls. I need the evening alone to speak to my husband."

It was after midnight when William returned, scented with rare aged port and citrus tobacco. He came smiling through the double doors at her—"My angel, my goddess!"—as he pulled a velvet jeweler's box from his coat.

"No gifts," Viveca barked harshly, sitting up and letting her copy of Mr. Fielding's *Tom Jones* drop to the Aubusson carpet. "I had to pay for the last five necklaces myself, and you have damnably expensive taste."

"But, why are you angry? My goddess, I fail to comprehend your rage—"

"And the house, William! It's not paid for, *nothing* is, not the servants, not the hotel—"

"Well, then, sweetheart, I fail to see the problem. Pay them!"

Once her jaw would have dropped open in shock. But Viveca was older now and had greater control over her features. "Why should I? *You're* my husband, *you're* the one with money."

William's knees seemed to give way. He sank into the wing

chair that was twin to hers and, taking a silk handkerchief from his pocket, passed it over his brow. "Viveca." He said her name slowly, dully. "Viveca, I have what my father gives me for an allowance to cover my gambling—one hundred pounds a month, no more and no less."

Her jaw still did not drop, but the bones in her face stood out, pressing white and stark against her skin. "You—your estates—" she stammered.

"Angel, I had to sell them ages ago to cover my drinking and gambling debts. I'm not that much a *drinker,* mind you, but when it's my turn to pick up the tab for sixty at the club . . . why did you think I had money?"

She rose inch by stiff inch from her chair. "You're the son of a duke, the brother of an earl! Your clothes are so expensive . . . my betrothal ring . . . your horses and servants—"

"The betrothal ring was from my dead mother's store of jewels. That was a favor to me from my father. I'm the youngest son, Viveca. My brother the earl has everything, and my other brother the viscount, the rest. I'm only a baronet. I cover my clothes out of my winnings when I can, and the rest of the time I have old things retailored—this jacket is five years old, love! And as for my six horses, they were my legacy from Mother, and I've sold all but Jack. I haven't cost you anything for my personal upkeep, Viveca, so why have we a problem?"

"You don't seem to understand! I'm not rich, either!"

His china-blue eyes went round and wide as saucers. "But—but—but—"

"I had a good-size dowry from my mother, but I spent half of it for my wedding dress and trousseau and getting the stables raised and finding help for my horses," Viveca said. "Hellfire, William, I can't even *touch* the rest, it's in trust funds and special accounts. I spent over *five hundred pounds* paying off the bloody jewels you brought home. What remains is for our daughters, William—the dowries—if we manage to *have* daughters! Jesus *wept,* William! Did you marry me for my money?"

He stroked his chin thoughtfully. "No, my love, but I do seem to have taken it for granted that you were rich. Your Aunt

Yasaman is wealthy, and you dress so well and own such expensive horses."

"Christ's blood, William, *look* at me," she cried out desperately. "What jewels do I own that you didn't bring home for me? Rich women own jewels and furs, William, and all I have is my Lely miniature and the earrings Terrence picked up for me. That's why I always wear tuberoses in my hair—I can't afford gems. I find most of Terrence's material for him through Aunt Caro, and I make my own lace and do my own embroidery, so Terrence just charges me a pittance, especially since I made him famous. The horses all came from my mother. Oh, *Lord,* William! And you tell me you haven't a brass farthing!"

"Just my hundred pounds a month, love."

"That's more than a hairdresser makes in ten years, more than a common laborer earns in a lifetime, and you've been spending it on gambling and—and . . ."

She gestured toward the accounts she'd spent the earlier part of the evening going over. "God's bones, William! We owe *fifteen thousand pounds* on a house we haven't even lived in; eleven thousand on the house itself and four on furnishings. And we've run up a bill of over three thousand pounds here at the hotel, and now you tell me *we can't pay!* William, we have to come up with that money or we'll go to debtors' prison."

"But I know Terrence charges a thousand quid for a ball gown, so I presumed—" William said, as if he had not even heard her.

Viveca leapt across the short space separating them, caught him by the shoulders, and shook him until his teeth rattled. "Don't blither at me about ball gowns. I paid fifty quid apiece for them and not a shilling more. And I haven't had a new one in over a year. I've had to modernize the old ones myself. Everywhere I go there's someone telling me, 'We haven't been paid, Ladyship.' William, we've got to go to your father. Perhaps we can work out a loan with him."

". . . so I kept gambling, thinking to make some of it back," he whispered.

Viveca drew back, saw the glaze of panic in her husband's beautiful blue eyes. "William?" she asked shakily, her voice a mere croak. "William, have you lost money at the gaming tables?"

"Not much. Two or three. I was going to ask you for the money soon."

"William, two or three hundred more pounds at a time like this," she exclaimed hotly.

"No, love . . . two or three *thousand*."

Viveca did not scream, though she wanted to. She placed both hands over her mouth, pushed the scream down, back down to the turmoil it had escaped from. She sank down to the floor, feeling that familiar queasiness and light-headedness of the last week closing in on her.

"No, darling." William was kneeling at her side, tearing his hair, beseeching her not to cry.

"I'm not crying," she answered flatly. "I don't cry anymore. Never. I outgrew it. No one's ever going to make me cry again. I've faced the worst there is to face now. . . ." The loss of Allegra, thinking her mother dead, poverty, starvation, committing crimes, climbing and clawing this far up, only to discover that Byrne had fled her to another woman and she was married to a gambler whose children she continually miscarried.

Horrors swam through her head: She saw the horses being taken from her, the still-crated chairs and highboys going up on the auction block while she went to Newgate again—this time for being unable to pay her debts. Would they chain her once more in the room where she could not sit or stand but would have to crouch by the hour until sensation left her limbs and she was lost in filth?

She had not realized how quickly her possessions and way of life could be taken from her; she had thought herself above the law now that she was rich. But she wasn't, was she? They'd take her away and . . .

The eyes she turned on William were wild, unknowing, an animal's shocked, cornered gaze. The face of a vixen lifting her head as the hunter cocked his gun.

"Why, I shall go see my father and brother at once," William blurted out, though he had never willingly talked business to either in his entire life. "They'll know what I should do. Yes, I'm certain they will. You—you just stay here. I shall take care of everything."

William is really frightened now, she thought blankly as she let him pick her up and settle her in her favorite wing chair with a lap robe, tucking her solicitously in. *Fancy William getting efficient at this late stage of the game!*

Why did he always panic so if anything went wrong? she wondered vacantly. He must think her to be some unassailable tower of fortitude, because when she was shaken, William immediately reverted to a childlike stage of helplessness. But tonight, for the first time, he seemed to realize matters were serious and that he must act the man. He would settle things as a husband should. Yes. Things would be all right.

He did not come home that night, nor the next day. It was the second night following before he returned.

Viveca greeted him at the door, face and nightgown rumpled, eyes ringed with the bruiselike shadows of fear and fretfulness. "Darling, are you all right?" she cried, flinging herself into his arms.

"Why, yes, I always am. Don't tremble so, my love, my goddess. You know I can't bear to see you upset like this—I've been at the gaming tables."

He said this quite casually as he took his hat off and sailed it onto the nearest tea cart.

"Why were you at the gaming tables?" she asked stiffly, pulling back from him.

"Well, Father and my brother agreed to help us at fifty percent interest."

She sat down hard, crestfallen. *"Oh.* Well, with them making such ludicrous offers we can't expect any help, can we?" Her shoulders sagged.

"We already have. I've signed the papers and all that," he said, pleased with himself.

"But we could never pay off that kind of lending rate!"

"But we already *have* most of it. I've had a very good night at the tables and again at Ascot today."

"Really? And what did you put up for your stake?" she asked disbelievingly.

"Our breeding farm."

Almost before the words had left his mouth she was upon him. Thank God she was not tiny like Yasaman; thank God she was not bird-boned and underweight like Lilly. She caught William by the shirt front, knocked him to the floor. Her mind was filled with a moment of blackness, then a moment of red, like rivers of blood roaring ocean-loud in her ears. She backhanded him once, twice, three times.

The maid and footman materialized to pull her off him. William rolled limply away, gasping, sputtering, choking.

"We were discussing finances," Viveca told the servants with a kind of joyful savagery. "I was showing him what happens when a husband dares risk the business his wife and her mother have spent most of their lives building up from nothing. Surely you've had discussions like that yourselves?"

"But, mum, all a wife's property belongs by right of law to her husband!" the maid answered, shocked.

"If he buys them, they're his, or if I die without leaving them to my aunt and mother, then they're his. But until that day they're *mine*, damn you! *Mine!* They're all I have, all I've *ever* had!"

The servants fled, shutting the door behind them. "I didn't realize the horses meant so much to you," William said, slowly sitting and placing a hand against his throbbing left temple.

"I would lose the house, our furnishings, my books, even my family and friends before I would part with the farm. *My* farm! How dare you call it 'ours' when you've never put a lick of work or one shilling into it."

"But surely you understand that marriage entitles a husband to his wife's possessions."

"I refuse to accept that. *Christ*, William, the simple solution to all of this is for you to stop gambling, and we'll sell the house, put the furniture, rugs, and dishes up for auction, and pay off our debts. If there's anything left we could build a cottage on the farm, perhaps."

He shook his head. "Would that it were that simple, my love. Do you think I've never tried to quit gambling? We live in an age when card games are played in every parlor for money—even you and your lady friends gamble at tea parties. And dice fit so easily into a pocket, and there's always a horse race, a bull-baiting, five quid to put down on a team of mastiffs matched against a bear. It's all so easy, don't you see, Viveca? Too easy, because everywhere one goes one is surrounded by money and the games that can quickly make and lose it."

"I—I guess it must be like people trying to quit drinking when they live above a gin shop," she said slowly, comprehension stealing in.

"It's a disease, Viveca. Eats away at me like smallpox. In its own way it is as much an addiction as what I feel for *you.*"

She shivered; there was something unwholesome in the way he said that, as if she were a pipeful of opium from the East—or a pack of cards, cut and waiting to be dealt.

"No other woman could ever mean to me what you do," William continued, standing and taking her by the hands. "You represent all that is noble and fearless about the whole of womanhood. You're not afraid of things, as I am; you meet troubles head-on and conquer them by sheer force of will. I've used you to hide behind, I know, for I lack your confidence, your purity of spirit."

Purity? Nobility? What was this rot he spouted while she stood with her heart cracking? He spent too much time mooning over statues and paintings when he needed to be brushing up on his mathematics and bookkeeping. And how to make a living— Great Mother of God, the man had never done a lick of work in his life!

He needed something to do, that was all. Goodness, why hadn't she thought of that earlier? She'd beg him to help with the horses; that ought to puff him up with pride. William knew and liked horses; it might be just the thing to save their marriage.

He pulled her back into his arms. Viveca noted that his breathing was quickening. At a time like this! Well, there was no insult in being lusted after by one's husband, even if at times he did make her feel like a beautiful, abstract object he had coveted, purchased, and now caressed with the delight of a collector.

When it came to fanning the smoldering embers of William's desire, Viveca knew she had to do little. The right look, a mere touch on his arm or face, and he wanted her. She had never heard of a man so obsessed with a woman, and while it was flattering, sometimes the obsession unnerved her.

He was picking her up now, booting the bedroom door open in his urgency. Then he was laying her down on the bed, undoing the pearl buttons on her nightgown. "I need you so very much, Viveca." He breathed it in her ear, like an invocation for mercy to the goddess he sometimes claimed she was. "You mustn't despair, you mustn't give up on me. I couldn't make it alone, couldn't survive—I'd kill myself rather than be without you!"

He had her nightgown open. She felt his lips, then fingertips on her breasts. It made her feel fiery inside. Anxious. Hungry for much, much more.

She had never been the aggressive lover with him she had been with Byrne. Somehow she was a little removed with William, a feeling that dated back to her disappointment that wedding day when he had ridden off to the races and left her to face a reception hall full of strangers. She had been unable to ignite sexually with him that night, for anger and the earlier rejection had made her withdraw into herself, and William was not an experienced enough lover—or sensitive enough—to realize that she had been hiding ever since.

Besides, he always hurried her. He always kissed her, then went directly to her breasts, carelessly scraping her nipples with lace and cuff buttons, which further made her shrink back inside herself.

He stroked her ribs, then thighs. Not clumsily but too quickly, barely letting her feel pleasure before moving on. He turned her this way and that, and now there *was* clumsiness. When she tried gently to direct his kissing and touching, William ignored her efforts in his haste to possess her.

It was confusing, frustrating. "William, darling, I like it so much better when you do *this.*"

Was he suddenly deaf? Grossly uncaring? Or did he think if he persisted in his own fashion that she would eventually like it? And yet, in a way, she did like it, for there came a few moments, sooner or later, when he caressed her breasts just so, or hungrily dove between her legs, licking and touching, and she began to respond.

Those moments were upon her now, for he was lying between her thighs, touching her. Then he rose on his elbows and she knew he wanted to make love. *Perhaps,* she thought, *I could use my mouth ..ntil he loses control—and then, afterward, when he's less anxious, he'll last longer with me.* For William's lovemaking always took a maximum of three minutes, no matter what.

She was a tall woman, and voluptuous, with the strength that came from handling horses; she knelt up quickly, pulling William with her. Before he could shift, she was kissing him, running her hands up and down his body. Then, while he was still kneeling up, she bent, drew him deeply into her mouth with slow, sensuous strokes of lips and tongue.

William enjoyed it massively; she *knew* he did, and yet it always seemed to unhinge him a little, as if this were something wives shouldn't do. *But he does it to me,* she thought. *Why won't he let me pleasure* him *this way?*

This time she thought she had him too excited to stop. He was twining his fingers through her hair, gasping, moaning out her name, then, abruptly, he swung her down. She gasped as he thrust into her.

This was the part she liked best, these few moments they were in perfect sexual harmony. The fevered rocking together, the clutching and groaning, clasped together like drowning swimmers. She never felt closer to William than she did at these times, for she knew him as a lover far better than as a man or even a human being.

It was over. She was just loosening up when William cried out and sagged on her, giving a few final thrusts. Two minutes from start to end—and just when she had begun enjoying it.

Why was she stiff and sore? Why had the motion made her so nauseated?

William kissed her pink mouth and the tips of her swollen breasts, telling her how much he loved her, how grand it was to see her in a haze of sexual ecstasy (*Is that what it was?* she thought wryly.)

Why can't I love him the same way? she asked herself. Why couldn't she forget the wedding-day desertion, the money and gambling problems, and be one of those impetuous, passionate women who let nothing interfere with their enjoyment of the intimate senses? Why couldn't she overlook his foibles? *Weak,* she thought bitterly as he rolled off her and burrowed his head in the crook of her neck. *He's a weak, spoiled little schoolboy who can't wipe his own nose without me. And I'm that schoolboy's fantasy come to life—a strict mother he can seduce.*

What an unwholesome thought; it made her shiver.

He was stroking the new fullness of her breasts, and she found it uncomfortable. As she lay frowning to herself, William raised his head. There were some things he was neither slow nor weak about. "Don't look so puzzled, my dear. Surely a woman who's had two miscarriages can tell when she's pregnant again?"

CHAPTER TWENTY-TWO

West End, London, Autumn 1767

The empty house echoed with each footstep.

Viveca stood in the nursery, the only room where furniture remained. And what furniture it was! She ran a finger along the gleaming brass of the hanging cradle, rocked it gently. The satin comforter was dusty now, the eyelet-embroidered pillowcases and sheets yellowing at the edges.

"Now come out of there," Lilly scolded gently, coming up behind her. "Thinking about Cecilia will do no good. After two miscarriages, at least your last pregnancy ended in a live birth, so you know you can bear a healthy, living child. 'Tisn't your fault Cecilia caught pneumonia. My Charlotte took it, *too,* Viveca. We both lost our little girls, but we'll get over it. We have to. At least I still have my new baby, little Simonne."

Viveca swiftly hugged her. "I'm so thoughtless. My loss was a newborn I hardly had a chance to know, but Charlotte . . . you'd had her, held her, loved her these almost three years, watched her grow, only to lose her."

Lilly wiped her eyes and smiled. "Let's have no arguing over who lost more to that pneumonia. We've both recovered—or have started to."

"And you look fine and prosperous," Viveca said generously.

"Why, I am prosperous," Lilly answered, shoving her sable muff up on one arm to free her hands, which she rubbed vigorously together. Her breath came out in filmy white clouds that rose slowly, suspended in midair above them. "Terrence and I have such a booming business that we've taken over half an acre on Threadneedle Street with six cutters, two pinners, a sketch artist, and three 'prentices under me. I'm a full partner now since I designed that gown for the queen on her last birthday, so it's Terrence and Carlisle now on the signs and receipts. And I'm in love with little Simonne's father, Viveca; he's a handsome French *comte*. Of course he can never marry me, but—Oh, I'm babbling on and forgetting you. It's rude of me to talk about my good fortune when you've had none."

Viveca shook her head as they slipped out of the nursery, arm-in-arm. "Now, Lilly Carlisle, don't you go apologizing. I'm glad of your fortune. As for me—I've had to sell this place, and that's that. I have a nice little house for William and me. It's about a fifth this size, in Kensington near the farm and, to tell the truth, Lil, this mansion is gargantuan. More like a temple or monument than a home. I was never happy here. I was always too aware of struggling to pay for it. I'll feel positively blessed in a place we can't lose without real effort."

"You just see to it that your husband doesn't *make* that effort. Now let's get you back to the shop and into that emerald gown that needs finishing. Aren't you going to have the footman box up the cradle?"

"It was sold with everything else. I'll have that old woodcarver in Kensington make another, if there's ever need," Viveca said with a tight-lipped smile.

The coachman waited at the carriage block, hand on the door of the dressmaking firm's little berlin coach. He handed the women in, climbed up on the box, and the coach jolted off down the street.

"Funny how things work out," Lilly said suddenly, burrowing down under her lap robe. "Would you believe I've Luke St. James working for me now? Wouldn't seem proper calling him Uncle Luke, as he's six years my junior. Anyhow, he did such a good job on your barns, I've gotten Terrence to hire him for expanding the shop a fourth time. I don't hold it against the lad any longer that he's Dash's brother—or Byrne's."

"I've been scared every time I go to the Black Bull that I'll

206

bump into Byrne there, but I never have. What's the big mystery about his whereabouts?" Viveca asked.

"I gather he got himself in some legal trouble and fled north. We could ask Luke."

Viveca shuddered. "I'm not about to ask. All that's over and done with. I've got a husband now, and Byrne has himself a wife."

Luke was at the shop when they arrived. It gave Viveca's heart a twitch to see him. Of course, his shoulders were narrower and he wasn't as tall, but even from behind, the resemblance to Byrne was startling. The St. James family was the only case she knew of where human breeding ran so true. Most of the boys had different fathers, but they all had the same mother, and they all bore her black-haired, sloe-eyed good looks, and her legginess and height, as alike as the black colts or fillies Black Rose threw like clock-work every year and a half. Black-haired sons; ebony horses. They went together well.

Terrence was *ooh*ing and *ahh*ing as much over Luke's biceps as over the blueprints he was supposedly looking over.

Viveca called out, "Terrence, dear, hullo. Luke, good to see you. Did you get the business I sent you?"

He took her hand, shook it. Up close his face was more like Dash's than Byrne's or even Jemmy's—more even, more forget-table, but, she supposed, considered more handsome than the cragginess that made Byrne so unforgettable.

He answered, "Yes, Viv, and I should give you a commission, too. I got two barns and a house out of it. Say, Caro's a mite sore at you for not visiting lately. She says it's been since before you had the— She says it's been a long time."

He was aghast at mentioning the baby, but Viveca was able to squeeze his arm and smile. Her talk with Lilly had made her strength return. "You tell her I'm all better now, and I'll be out Sunday, come rain or shine. I've got to get over losing that baby and my house someday, and I might as well start now."

Luke shook his handsome head and said, as if no one else were present in the shop with its scents of dyed silk and café au lait,

"My brother was terrible broke up when he heard about the baby. He said you always loved children so."

"Well, you tell Dash that was sweet of him," she answered automatically, for her train of thought had already moved on to the emerald wool gown awaiting hemming in the fitting room. She slung her traveling cloak over a chair and followed it with her cheap rabbit-fur muff and hat.

"No, Viv, I didn't mean *Dash*, I meant *Byrne*."

She sucked her breath in too sharply, turned slowly around to look at Luke. "And how are he and Mrs. St. James doing?" she asked with false sweetness.

"Jesus, Viv, me mum has been a goner for years."

"I meant Byrne's *wife*, knothead," she answered irritably. Funny that a boy as bright as Luke could be so dense!

He looked pop-eyed. "Wife?" he asked. "Huh? Byrne ain't married, Viveca. He always said if he couldn't have you, he wouldn't marry anyone else. Viveca? Viv? Jesus, Lil, but she's gone a queer color. She's not pregnant again, is she?"

Lilly bounced a tiny box of pins off his arm from across the room. "Why, you young scoundrel. Byrne is *so* married. Dash himself told me about it two or three years ago. Drunk as a bloody lord, Dash was, swimming in his wine bottle. Said he was celebrating Byrne marrying some planter's daughter in the Colonies."

Luke stared a moment, then relaxed, slapping his thighs and laughing. "Great God Almighty, Lil, you don't know shit for shakes about geography, do you? Byrne went to the Caribbean."

"So? We figured he traveled," Lilly burst out.

"No. Did you forget the brother we do have in the American Colonies, the one who was deported years ago and finally worked hisself free? No, it was *Bertt* got married to the Georgia planter's daughter. And when the old man was a goner, they inherited the whole place, lock, stock and barrel."

Bertt, Byrne. Almost indistinguishable names, especially when spoken by a drunk.

"Lordy, lordy," Terrence sang out. "Catch her, she's gone a dead fish-belly color. Viveca? Lady Viv, are you all right?"

She slapped everyone's well-meaning hands away from her. "I'm fine," she barked.

"Hellfire!" Lilly exclaimed. "Viveca, Dash slurs so when he drinks. I forgot Bertt was over in the Georgias, I thought he said 'Byrne.' Oh, Lord, girl, you needn't ha' married that gambling wastrel of a—"

"Stop it, Lil! He's my husband, I won't hear anything against him."

"Oh, God, you must hate me for that mistake," Lilly whispered, and fled the room in a flash of chintz skirts.

"God's *mother*," Luke whispered breathlessly. "Viveca, that's why you married that sissy baronet—you thought Byrne had got someone else for keeps. We always wondered and he wouldn't speak about it, and now they've accused him of embezzling at the company, and he's gone back to the highway life in Scotland. He said it didn't matter since he didn't have a wife and family to go honest for. Especially when he'd been honest all along and they'd accused him of thieving. It sure was a mystery to all of us why you'd marry another when you'd always been so far-gone on Byrne."

"Everyone knew it but me," Viveca answered no one in particular. No tears. No groaning. The wrong husband tied to her by law, guilt, and affection. Her only live-born child buried six months ago. The man she loved, wronged by her and by his employers, driven away to the cold, rocky Northland where she herself had been conceived—a country Ginny had spoken of with genuine horror in her voice. A country where women pulled the plows and children starved by the thousands—raped and aching Scotland, broken by the English. And her love, her friend, was exiled there.

She lifted her head, her mind clearing. The gaze she turned on Terrence and Luke was cool, even-keeled, controlled. "I'll take that green gown home and whip up the hem myself, Terrence. I'll be needing it now. I've worn out my last decent day gown, and now I'm wearing grisette and rabbit fur like some stepped-up servant girl or old hussy."

"Gown's done, but it took some work," Terrence scolded, "because you've dropped so much weight since losing that child. You haven't been the same ever *since,* dearie. I have to press the rest of the seams and finish the neck ruffle, and then I'll run it by your new place tomorrow night."

"You're an angel."

She let Luke help her into her thin cloak and then took up her rabbit muff. "Thank you for the news, Luke, I—please tell Caro and Edward I'll be on out Sunday and that we've slaughtered the last pig, so I'll have a good ham to fetch along and . . ." Viveca chuckled self-mockingly. "Why am I asking you to take a message? I won't live but two miles from Caro now. I can tell her myself on the way home."

They watched her close the door and head on out into the crowds on the street, looking oddly shrunken in stature.

"Laddybuck," Terrence said firmly, so that he caught Luke's brown-eyed gaze in his own, "if you have an ounce of sense in your entire system—"

"Yes," Luke answered, "I'll send word to Byrne as soon as possible."

CHAPTER TWENTY-THREE

London, 1768

"You've been an angel about having to live in that little place and make over your old gowns," William said gently, folding Viveca's hands in his.

She smiled weakly as the carriage jolted along. "I'm only sorry that you can't afford to keep up with your fashionable friends. I'm afraid that while I prosper in the country, you're miserable."

That much was true. She was utterly at home rooting about in her vegetable garden or hand-breaking the colts herself. But William knew only the occupations of an aristocratic gentleman, which meant he was useless.

Viveca's plan to have William help with the horses had been a fiasco. He panicked at once, thinking it meant that her strength was slipping and she wanted him to carry the whole burden for them. Her jockeys had lost every race that week William was in charge; two mares turned up pregnant, and William had no idea which stallion in the neighborhood was responsible; and two of her four hostlers quit. Then the first barn developed a leak in the roof, and William tried to fix it himself.

He had fallen off the ladder, wrenched his back and broken both legs. Even now he had to walk with a cane.

That had been the end of *that* experiment. Viveca had gone back to running things, and she did it so well that now they could afford a maid and a coach with driver again. Her horses were their financial saving grace.

William had taken up the gentlemanly arts of oil painting and hunting.

He was trying so hard; Viveca knew he was. Never a complaint from him, never a moan about how she kept him on so short a lead that he could not socialize. Yet he *did* socialize to some extent, for he often disappeared for hours at a time and returned smelling of tobacco and brandy. On those nights that he appeared jubilant she bit her tongue, but when he came home minus his watch or coat, she feared for the safety of her breeding farm and thus their future. One night he limped home afoot, minus faithful old Jack, his hunter. Viveca saddled the Moor and rode to buy back Jack, for William loved that old horse.

William smiled at her now, squeezed her hands lightly. "There's a chance you'll be presented at Court with me early next year. Would you like that?" he asked, and bounced uncomfortably against her as the coach hit a pit hole.

"Oh, William, you *know* I would!"

"You'll need a new gown, of course, and myself, a new suit. I wonder if Father—"

"No," she answered swiftly. "Don't ask him, William."

Viveca would never forget the humiliation of scraping and scrimping to repay that murderous loan. It wasn't unusual for a parent to charge interest on a loan to a son, but to talk poor, unbusiness-headed William into paying fifty percent! She had worked her fingers almost to the bone repaying the Duke of Wynford and his eldest son, the Earl of Gillingham. Sold everything she owned but her precious horses, and then had been forced to auction off an entire spring crop of foals—the best, most promising foals ever, the result of careful and expensive cross-breeding.

She'd had two King Herod foals in the lot, and Herod's stud fees were astronomical. Well, no use crying over spilled milk. The foals were gone, and this time her mares had all been bred to a son of the famous Matchem.

Her colt Baronet was racing now, and Tuberose, the colt Moor had foaled in Turkey, was soon to run his first race at Ascot.

She suspected it had been one of Black Rose's sons who had gotten Tuberose on the Moor, because Tuberose was pitch-black; only in certain light could the seal-brown bay coat beneath be

212

seen: his mother's deep brown hue. He'd make her money. She felt in her bones that he was special, that he was *fast*.

"Whoa up, there! We're at Gillingham, sir and ladyship," the coachman announced, breaking in on their thoughts. The coach clattered to a halt.

They went in to fetch William's sister-in-law—the Countess—and her daughter, for they were all attending the theater together that evening. Viveca was glad the earl, William's brother, wasn't home. He looked down on her; his wife had been baroness in her own right before marrying him and becoming a countess, and he made it plain to William that Viveca was beneath the sacrosanct Holland family.

The four of them piled back into the carriage, Viveca thankful they'd finally been able to afford having windows installed in the carriage in place of leather window flaps. The coachman lit the brazier, which they could only afford to use when there was company in the coach, and the foursome huddled under their lap robes, chatting about the upcoming play.

At least three of them did. William smiled from time to time and remained silent, his smile so sad that it tugged at Viveca's heartstrings. *He knows he's a failure,* she thought with sudden desperation. *I must help him find some new way to regain his self-esteem. I do love him in my own way despite himself, but it's not hot and fiery like he wants. And he's finally realized that.*

She gripped his hands fiercely with hers, trying to put some heart into him, but his fingers were lax in hers, untrying, effortless. God! She could forgive all faults in a husband if he was only a fighter! But William took everything lying down, hardly noticing the world was trying to roll over and crush the life out of him. She had to be husband *and* wife in this marriage, and yet, in the eyes of the law he was head of the household and could dispose of her property and chattels at his whim. Thank God he had more heart than that.

Thank God he remembered she'd tried to choke him for betting her horses.

Soon everyone was lulled by the scent of frankincense from the brazier. There was a steady *thrum-thrum-thrum* of the coach horses' hooves, and the passengers felt quite warm huddled under their lap robes. Soon the niece drowsily quit prattling about her beaux and the countess began snoring. William continued to stare out the window with the face of a man doomed.

Thrum-thrum, his heart went against Viveca's side. *Like the monotonous beat of hooves on the road,* she thought sleepily.

But wait! Those hooves were too many, too fast. The sound of pursuit by a pack of riders, perhaps?

She jerked herself upright from William's shoulder. Just then the coachman whipped up the horses. "What is it?" the countess shouted.

"Highwaymen!"

The cry chilled the blood of everyone but Viveca. She felt a thrill, a rush of excitement tingling through her bones right to the marrow. Her heart felt warmer, lighter, buoyed up with excitement. "Well, lash up the bays, you dolt!" she shouted at the driver.

Viveca turned to the countess and her daughter. "Take off your best jewels and only the best. But leave a few trinkets on—highwaymen aren't stupid. If they see three women dressed to the nines with nary so much as a pinky ring between them, they'll know we've hidden the best, and you certainly don't want a pack of ruffians searching you!"

"Great heavens! Do you think they'll catch us?" the countess bawled.

"Of course. Four nags hauling a carriage can't go as fast as ridden horses—and highwaymen ride racehorses whenever they can steal 'em. Now give me that diamond tiara and those rubies and let's see . . . they'll expect us to cram them down the back of the seat, so we'll have to think of somewhere else. . . ."

Viveca glanced about her, deaf to the terrified squeals of her female companions and the black looks of her husband. "You're ungodly cool about this," William commented.

Viveca ignored him. "I believe I'll pry this loose hinge on the window open a bit and . . ." She dropped the handkerchief-wrapped jewels down inside the carriage door after flattening the tiara a bit.

"They shan't board us," William cut in on her thoughts abruptly as he removed his brace of dueling pistols from beneath his coat.

"Don't be a fool. They outnumber us badly, to judge by those hoofbeats."

"Aye, and I've a coachful of women to protect!"

"You mustn't shoot or they'll open fire," she told him sternly. "Highwaymen ofttimes try not to kill if they can avoid it. But let me have a pistol—we can each keep one, then we'll throw them the countess's cheap topaz and my faux pearls and your niece's garnets. They'll be in Gravesend with their loot before they realize they got poor pickings. We'll only shoot if we have to do so in self-defense."

Hoofbeats surrounded them now. The countess screamed as a scarlet coat swung by within two yards of the window. William at once lunged forward, broke out the window with his pistol, and opened fire.

"You'll get us all killed!" Viveca snapped, lunging at him.

A woman screamed again as bullets tore through the wooden door—a reedy, falsetto sound of metal boring through cheap mahogany and metal. There were more shots from the highwaymen. One tore into the padded leather seat near Viveca's knees. She felt a quick, searing line drawn on her flesh there.

She closed both hands on William's wrist, making his next shot go wild, up through the top of the coach, but he was still too much stronger. Viveca caught him by the lapels at the same time she tromped down on his toes. This distracted him enough that he turned toward her; she seized hold of his cravat and felled him with her strongest punch to the jaw.

"What's the matter with you?" William's sister-in-law shrieked.

"They'll probably kill us for firing. Perhaps it isn't too late—if I can convince them—"

She threw her skirts up, grabbed a handful of pale pink petticoat, and tore. She then waved this unlikely surrender flag out the broken window, ducking back in case they tried to fire again. "Driver, pull up. *Pull up!*" she cried out.

215

When he did so, she straightened her skirts and cloak and, pistol in each hand, stepped out into a circle of masked dark men. "Gentlemen, I can shoot the smile off a jack of spades at fifty paces, so I suggest a truce. You outnumber us, but I can take at least two of you with me before I go. Now then, my lady friends shall toss their ear bobbles and rings out to you—tied in a kerchief—and you shall please be so good as to gather them up and leave at once, or I shall kill two of you before you can say George the Third. And I believe I shall start with the two tallest ones."

She brought the long-barreled pistols out from under her thin wool cloak.

"Why do we even bother?" asked the tallest highwayman in a patient, familiar voice. "She's doing all our work for us. We could have stayed home in front of the fire, toasting our toes, had we but known this minx was so eager to help!"

He dropped his mask to reveal the handsome, saturnine features of Byrne St. James. Next to him, Dash also dropped his mask, and of the three other riders, at least two more were their younger brothers. Viveca's heart all but dropped to her feet. Should she cry or laugh? she wondered, trying not to stare at Byrne.

"The ghost of Gentleman Jemmy St. James! He is robbing me again!" William's sister-in-law shrieked, and fainted.

"Hellfire. Not a decent jewel in the lot, and I hear the bloody constables coming," Dash groused, digging through the little hankyful of gems. Whistles blasted, and shots came whistling up the street toward them.

"Viveca, how's the roof holding up on the barn?" Luke asked cheerfully.

"What are you doing with them, and you an honest builder?" she asked irately. But all she could think was *Byrne! Byrne's here!*

"Business is poor in winter, and I've a wife and a flock of ewes to feed," Luke answered, unoffended.

"Not a decent jewel in the lot," Dash repeated, still pawing the poor topazes and garnets. He raised Viveca's pearls, rasped them over his front teeth. "Hell's bells, Byrne, these ain't even real! Viv

216

Lindstrom, you've fallen on hard times to be wearin' such poor-grade stuff—and you married to a fancy-assed baronet, too! Doesn't he keep you any goddamned better? Ought to be ashamed o' himself, makin' you wear such trash. Not a jewel in the lot," he scolded.

"Not true. I see the jewel for me," Byrne said suddenly as the constables neared.

He touched his heels to Blackberry, urging him forward.

Viveca whirled to face him, still stunned by his presence. Her banter with Luke had served to hide her muddle of emotions at the sight of Byrne. *Up north,* they'd told her. *Probably Scotland.* What the devil was the man doing here? And oh, God, the constables were so close. . . .

Byrne leaned half-out of the saddle, caught her under the arms. Viveca felt her feet leave the ground; he was trying to lift her aboard his horse. She reached for his face, intending to tweak his nose until he let go, but Byrne was too quick. "Don't do this— they'll hunt you. . . ." she attempted.

He had her facedown over the front of his horse, and there wasn't much she could do about it except quit struggling, because he urged Blackberry into a canter, then run, and to fall could mean death.

"I hate you, I hate you! Byrne St. James, I'll *kill* you for this," she threatened in a hiss.

Hooves clattered on cobblestones as the other highwaymen scattered. She heard shots pinging and whistling past them. "You won't kill me, Viveca, but the Bow Street Runners and their friends might. Get a leg over before you land on your head, woman."

Woman. Had it been that long? He'd called her "girl" last time.

She deliberately ripped her gown in order to straddle the stallion. Something still remained of the trick rider she'd been; she found it easier than expected to get from an ungainly face-first sprawl to an upright position. Then Byrne pressed against her, leaning forward, and she bent low over the black horse's neck, presenting as small a target as possible. "Why have you done

217

this?" she shouted angrily, though the thrill of the chase was coming back to her.

"What, held you up? I confess, darling, that one carriage looks much the same as another to me. I wouldn't know your coat-of-arms from that of Fat Georgie the Third. But once I recognized you I knew we had to risk speaking. Luke told me the real reason you married What's-His-Nibs."

They urged the colt on like a precision team, lightly dusting his flanks and shoulders with feet and hands. "I thought you were married," Viveca admitted in a yell over her shoulder. "And—and he was good to me, gentle-like, at a time when my pride had been sore-struck by you—"

"Next thing, you black-eyed vixen, you'll be telling me that you 'love him in your own way.' Isn't that the line? The line that means you're *fond* of the bloke, but there's no fireworks?"

"Don't mock me. You and I were children together, and I thought William would be an adult—"

She could have bitten her tongue off for giving Byrne that opening. Viveca fell irritably silent as the constables clattered up the street behind them. "But he's *not* an adult, is he? You have to wear the breeches in the family, paying the bills, making the rules," Byrne accused.

"Well, I would with *you,* too."

"No, darling, it would have been a *partnership,* each helping the other and yet being able to stand alone if necessary. Though damn your black eyes, I've always needed you too much."

Her eyes filled with glad tears. "I need you, too, Byrne," she admitted.

"What? *Louder!*"

"I need you, *too,* you thick-skulled, blithering, long-leggity—"

"I get the idea. Well, we're not children anymore, Viveca, and William's not your husband—not tonight, anyway. It's just us again. You still ride like a starving jockey."

"I have to. They'll hang you if they catch us," she answered.

Then there could be no more talking, for he had given the black stallion his head. Blackberry steadied, then burst into action as he realized he had been released from the masterful grip on his reins. He jolted forward, surging like a rocking horse. The ground roared beneath them as he broke into sweeping, twenty-foot strides the constables' horses could not touch.

Viveca felt one of Byrne's arms steal about her waist. She was still angry with him for risking her life this way. And yet . . . to her astonishment she was leaning back into the embrace, molding her body to his. She had not felt this alive in years: the wind tearing through her hair, shots whizzing past, night frost stinging her bare throat before melting.

Byrne was letting her know that he still wanted her. After the missing years, the misunderstandings, he still cared. She had a husband left behind on that snowy street, but Byrne was holding her and she could pretend it was their wild, impetuous youth again, risking death as collaborators, co-conspirators, partners in crime and lust.

Blackberry gathered his muscles under them. Viveca, fore-warned, clutched the streaming black mane, knotted her fists in it. She gently squeezed with her knees as Byrne did the same. It was partly to hold on and partly to tell the stallion: *Yes, jump!*

He sprang up and over a wooden gate. They rode south, turned, rode north, circled a cul-de-sac, emerged, and fled. And still the distant sound of pursuit dogged their hoofbeats.

"Wait! I recognize this neighborhood. We're near Threadneedle Street, Byrne. Go east at this intersection," Viveca shouted sud-denly. "There's a place we can hide."

"Thank God," he said without much force. The strong arm around her waist slackened.

The watchdog at Terrence & Carlisle knew her well and, after some preliminary woofing and snuffling, let them into the rear yard.

Viveca shut the gate behind them, chose a small window at eye level and, wrapping her hand in her muffler, punched the glass out. "Now here, Byrne, let me get out of these cumbersome skirts and you can boost me up. I'll climb on through, then unbolt the door for you. Now shoo that horse off; they'll recognize Black-berry in an instant, and if he lurks about, he'll lead them right here."

Byrne dismounted, leaned against the back of the lean-to, breathing heavily. "Afraid I can't boost you up, my little minx. They got me just after we went over that wooden gate."

He slithered down the wall and lay in the snow, neck bent oddly.

Viveca caught him, checked his pulse and breathing. He was too bundled up for her to tell where they'd shot him. First she would have to get him inside, out of the cold, and remove his layers of cloak and coats.

She kicked off her outer clothing and several warm petticoats. Then, clad only in a thin silk-cotton chemise and one underskirt, she whistled Blackberry over to her. He wasn't happy about letting her stand up on him, but he obeyed.

Viveca pushed up off the horse. It was a tight fit, but she squeezed through the window.

She landed on a shelf of fabric bolts, and the shelf promptly broke under her. Viveca tumbled with a landslide of fabric, then rolled and came up, breathing hard. She lunged at the door, yanking back the bolt with both hands.

Byrne lay crumpled up a yard and half away; she caught him under the arms, yanking for all she was worth, and finally succeeded in dragging him indoors.

She left him in a pile and hastily scooped up her discarded skirts to sweep the yard clean of telltale hoofprints. Blackberry had fled; she hoped he didn't lead their pursuers here. Then she seized a hammer off a packing crate, pounded the window frame partway back together, and tacked her torn cloak over the missing pane of glass.

The whole repair took under five minutes. Viveca knew that with the delay she might be risking Byrne's life, but she was equally risking it should she leave an obvious trail and signs of a break-in.

She knew there were lamps in the front of the shop, so she crept out to steal one, and something to light it with, though she waited until she was back in the storeroom to do so. Wouldn't do a damned bit of good to have come this far, only to let a night patrolman spot a lamp burning at so late an hour.

Thank goodness Lilly was a full partner and no longer lived in the shop. Viveca would not have entangled her in this night's adventure for anything. Aiding a highwayman made Viveca as guilty as if she robbed carriages herself; she and Byrne would swing from twin nooses should they be caught.

As the lamp flared to life Byrne sat up, swinging wildly about him and calling for Jemmy. Viveca rushed at him, pinned his arms down lest he knock over the lamp and set the building on fire. "Hush, darling. It's Viveca, it's all right, you're safe."

He looked around to get his bearings and lay back. "I thought it was the day Lilly and Dash and me came to spring you and Jemmy from Newgate. . . . Jemmy's father came along, the old priest. I was angry with Jemmy that day . . ." He folded his fingers over hers, smiled weakly up into her face. "I was angry with Jemmy for almost getting you killed, V'ica." He said her name as he had done the first few weeks they'd known each other, before he could pronounce it.

"Where are you shot?" she asked gently, unfastening cloak, coats, sweater, waistcoat.

"Up high, thank God. Above the heart, don't think they got a lung. It . . . seems to be in the fleshy part by the shoulder."

She took the knife from his boot where she knew he always carried it (left boot; in a sheath just above the ankle) and cut his shirt and coat away. "Lie on your side now . . . that's good, that's good, hold it right there . . . it's a lucky man you are, Byrne St. James. That bullet went clean through and didn't stay to fester."

"Hope there's no fragments left in me," he said, and winced as she lightly probed. "Be an angel and pack it to stop the bleeding, will you? I'd fix it myself, but I go all muzzy-headed when I sit."

"No wonder. You've a cold draft blowing through you, laddybuck!" she joked feebly.

She melted and boiled snow over the lamp, used it to cleanse the wound and slow the bleeding. Then she began packing the wound with lightweight, absorbent silk—the fabric that breathed most naturally and would allow air to circulate around the wound so it didn't turn gangrenous. "Why did you boil the water?" Byrne asked.

"Mother's Turkish doctors said it keeps infection away. They think there are things in the water that need to be killed so they don't cause gangrene."

"Funny opinion."

"Well, they always boiled Mother's birthing sheets and bandages before using 'em, and they did the same when they had to open my foot up."

"Tell me about that," Byrne said, desperate to have his mind taken off the pain.

"No, that's too grim. Let me tell you about Baronet's last race. . . ."

As she talked and mopped up blood, she shoved the used rags behind her so he wouldn't know how much blood he'd lost. He was going to need plenty of red wine and red meat to get his strength back.

"Treat you well, this husband of yours?" Byrne asked suddenly. What an awful color he was!

"I said he was gentle, didn't I?"

"Said in that tone of voice, it means he's *weak*. Had you meant he's a gentle man but plenty strong, you would have mentioned the strength first. Doesn't beat you or cheat on you?"

Viveca gave him an exasperated look as she went on with her nursing. "Where's the man could lift a hand to me and not be flattened?" she demanded crossly.

"Yes, and where's the man would need other women once he'd had you? You're more beautiful than ever, Viveca. Black-eyed and copper-haired . . . you've filled out, you're not a scrawny little boy-girl anymore."

She was finished. She hid the last of the bloody cloths from him, pulled his shirt and waistcoat together over the bandages, and covered him with his cloak. She retrieved his coat and her skirts for herself to wear against the chill of the unheated shop.

"I'm sorry about the child," Byrne whispered in the flickering lamplight.

"She should have been *our* daughter, Byrne, yours and mine,"

222

she blurted out, and choked down the tears. "But you had to be cool and hard that night at Yasaman's; you had to attack with your harsh words, never knowing or believing what you meant to me."

"I know that now. But you were a bitch, V'ica. Proud and painted like a puppet. I hated seeing my natural, windblown Viveca like that. I refused to believe you were growing up and needed to be allowed to do so. And now, well, I know how loyal you are; you can't walk out on your husband now. You've shared too many years, too much pain. The lost babies, the rising and sinking through society . . . unless he was dead or the relationship gone beyond all mending, I know you'd never walk out on him. And yet I wish you would come away with me."

The dutiful wife or the wild highwaywoman? She ducked her head, eyes shining, and said, "Yes, I'm afraid that's the way I am. But, Byrne, though it's late—too late for you and me to ever make it right—I want you to know you're the only one I've ever truly loved."

"You admit it at last! And when did you discover *this,* Lady Viveca? About the time the bullets came whistling about your careful coiffure tonight? Christ! You always were a slow learner."

"Yes, Byrne," she agreed, smiling, and lay down with him. They both laughed. Twined together, dirty, cold, exhausted, one of them wounded, they slept the sleep of the dead for several hours.

At last, rested and hungry, Viveca rose. She tried to open the door to get snow to melt for drinking water but discovered it wouldn't budge. *The hinges must be frozen,* she told herself, pulling her battered bodice and powder-burned skirts closer around her for warmth. *Brr,* she'd have to see if Terrence still kept a heavy work smock here and if there were any sweaters in the wardrobe. She needed to get Byrne warm, fast. This much blood loss in cold weather was doubly dangerous.

When she went into the front room, she had a shock. The windows showed only pure whiteness beyond their pasted-up sketches. It had snowed all night, and the drifts were as tall as she was or taller. And on top of a layer of snow so wet, its own weight had packed it down. The search for her and Byrne must surely be called off for a while.

She pried the front door open a crack and scooped snow into Terrence's new Queensware-by-Wedgewood cups. Then she shut the door again and smacked herself on the forehead. Here they'd been hungry and thirsty all night, and Terrence kept a stock of coffees, chocolates, and butter cookies for his customers. How could she have forgotten?

There was also firewood in the office and a ceramic stove from the Continent—quite shockingly ahead of time for England, where people persisted in vainly trying to heat hundred-room mansions with fireplaces.

It was nearly dawn, and Terrence sometimes worked this early, so if any constables managed to struggle through the snow to the door, she would claim to be a pattern cutter arrived early for work and awaiting her employer's orders.

With that alibi in mind, Viveca stoked the stove, started a pot of strong Darjeeling tea, and went back to wake Byrne.

It wasn't as difficult to wake Byrne as she'd feared. He looked much better this morning, though the smudges of pain beneath his eyes spoke of blood loss and troubled sleep. "Look," she told him, seating him in Terrence's overstuffed leather office chair, "this is where your niece Lilly works. Here—here's the tea, don't scald yourself, and I heated some butter cookies."

"Oh, quit clucking like a mother hen. I'm not some mentally enfeebled child. Break the bad news to me now."

"We're frozen in, *snowed* in, too, and your damned horse headed for the hills hours ago. Every trooper in this section of town is probably looking for us, but they shan't have any luck in this kind of snow. Our trail's safely covered by me and the weather. And if Dash has half a brain in his drunken arse, he won't go near the Black Bull for weeks."

"They know it's our headquarters now, anyway, so we've been avoiding it. We're in the process of buying another house in Bromley."

They greedily ate all the cookies and drank two pots of good, strong, auburn tea. "I feel much better now. All the same,"

Byrne said when they had finished, licking their fingers like naughty children, "we'd better get you back soon, so they don't lynch every St. James lad within a hundred miles. Granted, they'd run out of rope eventually, but . . . You look pretty like that."

"Like what?" Viveca asked, self-consciously putting her hands up to her disheveled hair.

"Oh, all tousley and undone. Like the urchin you were when I first loved you."

"I had to clean up considerably before anyone but you knew I was under that dirt. But you liked me, anyway. Do you remember what you told me last night? That we weren't children anymore and William wasn't my husband—at least not at the moment. Byrne? Do—do you still want me?"

Byrne reached for her hand, drew her onto his lap. "Wounded or not, there's enough of me left to want you right here and now. Is the answer yes, Viveca?"

Trembling with desire, she felt herself nod, then whisper the forbidden word of consent. *"Yes.* Yes, Byrne, I want you, too."

She cupped her hands around his face, lifted it, parted his lips with hers. He tasted of sweet dark tea and the age-old strength of men; a strength without brutality, tempered with gentleness. Something inside her seemed to tremble, remembering how it had been between them, knowing that Byrne's kind of loving, unlike William's, would not leave her empty and aching.

There was no rush to his wooing, no hurry to fall on her, have his way, and call it quits. He continued to hold her on his lap, kissing her, murmuring endearments and do-you-remembers in her ear. Then he was lightly licking the edge of that same ear, sweeping her pale apricot hair back to nibble her long, white, swanlike neck.

Viveca unfastened her bodice, unbuttoned her transparent chemise so he could reach her throbbing flesh. She unfastened his shirt once more, easing it open in order to caress his broad brown chest and uninjured shoulder.

His hot mouth was on her shoulders, then her taut, sloping breasts. Her nipples, a deep pink-tan, were unbearably swollen with need beneath his lips. Byrne stroked them, licked them, made slow circles around them with his tongue until Viveca shook and gasped. He then found a place between her left breast and underarm that, when stroked, made her cry out for more, shuddering in his arms.

In the cold morning, lit only by the pale peach approach of day and a glow from the stove, her skin was white as the tuberoses she favored, and as fragrant. She arched this way and that as Byrne touched her, and her eagerness in lifting her petticoat and exposing the full of her sexuality both shocked and pleased him.

"Is it like this with your—with William?" Byrne asked almost savagely.

"No, never—*oh!* Never, and besides him and you, I've never had any other man."

That amazed him. This voluptuous white body had writhed in *his* arms only; the long, pink mouth became wet and quivering with passion for him alone. No hordes of admirers had sampled this pulsating paradise of womanhood; her indigo eyes smoldered, half-closed in ecstasy, for him and him only. The man she married had never given *this* to her, this slow, deliberate favoring of her magnificent body and heart.

Viveca thought hazily, *I have never once known it to be half this powerful with William.* No, only with Byrne had she moaned and wriggled like this, sighing in expectant bliss as his fingers found her, stroked maddeningly in the same soft place. He was making love to her with his hands alone, touching her, stroking her long, sleek thighs, drawing her nipples into hard, red points. And always, *always* he returned to the damp heat between her legs.

He played her with consummate skill born of love, lingering at each chosen place. A spot on the inside of one elbow made her moan as he licked it. Her hips began to buck, then she reached down, to guide the movement of his hand between her thighs. She was impossibly hot and moist all over, perspiration glazing her skin in the blueness of dawn.

Byrne slowed, drawing out her sensations when she would have urged him on to immediate completion. He understood her years of agonized frustration and so led her on and on, always pausing if they drew too near the brink. Her passion increased until she had no mind, no rational thought process, only this ravenous, throbbing need.

Then he sent her crashing over the edge.

Viveca sagged slowly forward, face contorted, then began arching back. Drawn out taut as a bow with the arrow fitted to it, she felt the fire explode, explode . . . again and again.

Whimpering, she arched up a final time, then returned, gasping, to earth.

He touched her lightly, and to their amazement, it happened again, for the aftershocks had not died out. Viveca twitched, crying out. Byrne observed with fascination as the rhythmic pulsation gripped her, clenching and unclenching the body sprawled across his lap.

He was excited by her pleasure, and pleased that his nights with the whores and trollops had made this possible for her. There had been many other women in his life once he'd thought he could never have Viveca again; he blessed every one of them now, for teaching him what women liked.

Suddenly Viveca slipped, eellike, from his arms. She pushed his feet apart with a mischievous grin on her face and knelt between them. She reached for the buttons of his breeches. "What are— *oh,*" Byrne said.

She took him lovingly into her mouth with an eagerness that said she enjoyed it. It had never felt like this for Byrne; a perfunctory act with whores and shop girls, even the most eager hadn't acted as if it pleasured *them,* too. He wound his fingers through her thick, strawberry-blond hair, lightly guided the bobbing head.

It did not take him as long as it had her, for seeing her excitement had already brought him close to an inescapable climax.

She rose afterward, poured the last cup of tea for them so that they handed it back and forth, savoring kisses and the dark sweetness of the bottom of the pot. Then, locking his gaze with hers, Viveca pushed his knees together and climbed onto him.

She dropped a leg over either side of the armless chair, steered him into her, and began moving.

227

Every thrust felt good to Viveca, who quickly lost herself in the sweet, hot tension of the ascent. Climbing, climbing . . .

Byrne bent her back over his arm, kissed the tips of her breasts, then brought her back forward. They kissed deeply, passionately. When the kiss ended, she loosened his black velvet hair ribbon, drew strands of his dark hair through her mouth in ecstasy.

He gripped her hips, matched her thrust for thrust. He watched her face with its look of limp surprise, the fine, delicate tawny eyebrows arching, wet mouth forming an *O*, eyes half-open. Never had he seen such an expression of delight and suspense. Then she grimaced as the peak began closing about her. Too much . . . too much . . .

Release. Within seconds he followed her quiet, shuddering release with his own soaring fall. They were left radiant, exhausted, clinging together like drowning children. All words were superfluous, so they said nothing, only held each other.

There was a sudden and thunderous hammering at the front of the shop. "Halloa!" cried a deep male voice. "Please answer at once, sir or missus. We're tearing the neighborhood apart for fugitives."

Viveca sprang up. "Byrne, quick, in the dressing room there, and draw the curtain!"

She hooked up her bodice, straightened her skirts, and stumbled to the door. The musky scent of lovemaking clung to her. Would they notice? She secured the few remaining pins in her hair, deftly winding it back on top.

Two constables had dug through the drift and were forcing the front door open. She slipped the bolt back, helped them pry their way in.

One was holding a list, apparently descriptions of her and her "captor," for he studied her, then the list, then her again, and asked, "Be you Lady Viveca?"

"Why, yes, I am, I—"

"The baronet, your husband, said you might be here if you had managed to escape, because it was the closest familiar place. We saw the smoke from the stove and didn't know if it was you or the shop owners."

228

"Are you all right, missus?" the other constable asked swiftly.

"Of course, my good man. I shot the old rascal with my husband's pistol and escaped," she said, pointing to the blood on her bodice.

"Where did you shoot him, ladyship?"

"Over by Dirty Lane, I believe. A very bad part of town."

"No, ladyship, I meant, what part of the body?"

"Right through the side," she lied, slapping herself just above the waist. "About *here*, I think. If the old codger isn't dead of a shot through the kidneys, I've lost my aim, gentlemen. He had hold of me by the skirts at the time—well, you can see what kind of damage he did them—but I got clean away and left the aging gent for dead on his bay."

"Uh—*bay?* We heard it was a black horse, mum."

"Goodness me, no," she answered, heart hammering, and she forced a tinny laugh. "It was a dark enough bay, though. I can understand someone mistaking *her* for a black. No, gentlemen, I breed horses, you know, and this was a rough-headed Irish hunting mare with white forefeet."

There—that ought to throw them off the trail of a shoulder-wounded young man on a black stallion. She had them now. They were scratching their heads in confusion when Lilly stomped in wearing snowshoes.

"What's going—*Viveca!*" she cried.

Viveca lunged forward, embraced her, and whispered, "Play along." She stepped back, smiling, then said, "I was kidnapped by highwaymen last night, Lil, but I'm fine now. But I fear one of those highwaymen has been injured and forced to hide out. I turned the stove up too far when I escaped to the shop, and I fear there's a *long, black burn* in your dressing room. A *burn* that isn't in very good shape."

Lilly reared back with sudden understanding in her eyes. "Of course, Lady Viveca, don't you worry, I'll fix that *Byrne* up so well, you'll never know it was here. You needn't worry. Now run along home."

She picked up a broom and shooed them out, her face unnaturally pale with worry and excitement. Viveca heard a sound that might have been the shop door being bolted, then the scurrying of early-morning tradesmen on the snowy street blocked out anything else. "Gentlemen," she heard herself say limply, "please see me home, I-I've had quite a night of it."

PART FIVE

William

"Some take delight in fishing,
Some take delight in bowling,
Some like the fields or the sea that goes a-rolling,
But I take more delight now in the juice of barley,
Then to courting pretty maids
in the morning bright
and early."

—"Whiskey in the Jar," 18th-century Irish Traditional

CHAPTER TWENTY-FOUR

Kensington, October 1770

"And who is this?" Philippe asked as a long black equine head thrust over the box-stall door at him.

Viveca leaned on her pitchfork and swept her hair back from her eyes. "This is my prize, my winner, my Tuberose," she said fondly, and reached out to rub the stallion's velvety muzzle. "And he'll have competition soon from my own stables—Moor's had a Matchem colt now because Matchem's won so many races; hellfire, but he's made his owners rich! He's a grandson of the Godolphin Barb, and Moor is the Godolphin's daughter, so it's actually rather close breeding, but the colt will be worth it."

"The bright red one down at the other end?"

"Brick Road. He'll start at Ascot this spring. And next year my other Matchem colt, Matchless, starts."

She impulsively kissed Tuberose between his flaring nostrils. "I love this animal, love his stupid, unthinking speed and courage. He has not been defeated once, did you know that? Not once. He'd run till he died of it, if I let him. He isn't intelligent; all he knows how to do is run. But he's brave and fast, and we would have lost everything if not for his winnings. I'll breed him in two years, but in the meantime all my mares are now with foal to King Herod. Which cost a fortune!"

"I won twenty bob on Herod yesterday. You're doing well to afford having him cover your mares."

Tuberose let loose a mighty sneeze that considerably dampened the front of Philippe's embroidered waistcoat. The elegant eunuch made a face and whipped out a handkerchief to blot the material.

"Oh, dear, I'm sorry. I'll pay to have it cleaned," Viveca offered.

"Don't fuss. I came out here to find out how you're really doing, because Ginny and Yasaman suspect you're not telling the whole truth in your letters. You have too many empty stalls here; how much stock did you have to sell to pay off William's debts *this* time?"

"I buried dear old Dulcie last year," Viveca said, returning to the bale of hay she'd been attacking when Philippe arrived. "I didn't breed her these last five years; she was too old and frail. But she loved it when the neighboring children came over to learn riding on her. But there's still Darcy; she was foaled the same year as me."

She jabbed hay with her pitchfork, tossed it over the box-stall door into Tuberose's manger.

"What I'm saying is that I've got Moor, Darcy, and the Barb mares Mother gave me, my three racing stallions, four big, rowdy yearlings from the mares who foaled last year and were then sold. I auctioned off five pregnant mares, and then there's William's Jack, the chestnut gelding behind you, and I guess that's it."

Philippe made no pretense of control. "Viveca, you had forty brood mares last time I was out here, and a field full of foals. Do you mean to tell me"—he counted on his fingers—"that you have only thirteen horses left? You can't run a successful racing farm with only a baker's dozen of stock. And I don't even want to *hear* about your damned dowry money. I imagine he gambled *that* away, too. And still he clings to you like a fungus, like feeble mistletoe strangling a strong oak."

Her dark blue eyes seemed to dance with fire. "That's enough, Philippe. He's my husband."

"That doesn't mean you owe him financial support."

"He *needs* me, and he's quit gambling for good—"

"Just like he does every year at this time. When are you going to free yourself, Viveca? When I think of Byrne St. James wasting his life for lack of you, and of you letting William drag you down,

I'm so angry I could strangle someone. At least let me tell your mother so she can send you some—"

"Good God, no. Do you think I'd take her money again and disappoint her? By God, Philippe, William's my husband, and I'll see him through."

And so the rift began between her and Philippe, just as the abyss of noncommunication had opened with all of her friends who criticized the well-meaning, if ineffectual, man she had married. The maternal love she would have showered on children and friends was poured into her relationship with William, for the children were always miscarried or stillborn, and now she had not even been pregnant in two years.

Not since she lost the six-months' child that might have been Byrne's as much as William's. Her husband had known about Byrne, she was sure of it; she had seen it in his eyes that morning she returned home. And yet there had been no guilt, no questions. She had lost much blood during that premature birthing, and William had never once left her side, overcoming his own horror of her weakness for the sake of mopping her damp brow, holding her hand when the contractions came and the dead child followed. "No more," the midwife had told them. "I don't want you trying again before a year is up. It could kill her."

She couldn't explain to Philippe that poor William had been close to a kind of madness at that point. But she found herself remembering . . .

"Mama Roxelina," Philippe said suddenly. "She told you that it would be many years before you bore live, healthy children. She was right. And she said you would marry more than once. Is that why you hang on so determinedly to William? Because you think someday he'll widow or divorce you and then you won't be responsible for his fate? I've seen Roxelina's predictions come true before."

"She said I'd bring a golden girl back to Turkey with me. When did she say I'd do it?"

Philippe's café-au-lait skin went an ashy gray. "She said it would happen when England's colonies revolted, when your black horse was beaten—"

" 'By one horse and one horse only.' She said I'd have something I believed long lost. It'll never happen; Allegra was the only golden girl in my life, and the horse isn't foaled who can whip Tuberose. Now please go, Philippe, I've work to do."

He backed away. "All right, but just remember: Roxelina told you about your black stallion before you *had* one. And you can cut me dead for daring to speak against your precious William, but I'll still be your friend. I know you're just blinded by your own stubbornness, your insistence on being responsible for the man you should desert for Byrne. But Byrne's too honorable to ask it, and you're too honorable to *do* it. But, by God, I keep hoping you'll see the error of your ways."

He stormed away then, and she felt truly alone, for one by one she had alienated them all. Was pride worth so much, then, that it was better to be proud than have those she loved near her? Was breaking a miserable marriage *that* dishonorable? Was she hiding, childless and impoverished, behind William in order to put the blame on anyone but herself?

She had made a mistake—a major one—in her life. Now how could she rectify it? *How?* How long would Byrne wait? And why hadn't she heard from him since that night in the shop? If only William would tire of her! If only she could make a success of the farm!

If. *If!*

Viveca and William, dust-coated, reined in their horses at a tavern near the track where they had just watched Tuberose race.

The tavern looked to be packed with racing followers. "Would you rather stop someplace better?" William asked, lifting Viveca down from the sidesaddle on Moor's back.

"We can't *afford* a better one, William. Please throw Moor's blanket over her while I go get us a table."

She hobbled inside, for she had snapped a heel off her riding boot this afternoon and been stumping about like a peglegged sailor ever since. There was one ale-stickied table near the wall, so she sat down at it and signaled William as he came in. She heard a tipsy Irish voice raised in celebration of some sort over

236

near the taprail, and she had to shout at her husband in order to be heard.

"What's going on with the Irishman?" William asked good-naturedly. That was one of the things she appreciated in this man no one else could love: he was never cross, never short-tempered, even when she picked fights and sniped at him in exasperation or weariness—which she was doing more often than she liked to admit lately. William may not have been a good lover, but she still missed the physical intimacy they used to share, for they slept in separate beds now and there was not so much as a hug between them. That restraint, too, made her appreciate William; he so feared to get her with child again and risk her life that he ruled his easily aroused urges with an iron will—the first time she had seen him truly strong about something.

And yet, perversely, she sometimes wished he would take that chance, for what was risking death in childbed compared to the dangers of riding with highwaymen and having bullets whistling through her hair? But William continued to follow the midwife's advice, uncomplaining, while the handsome edges of his face blurred from strain and strong drink.

"Aye, and sure as God made little green apples, I tell ye, it's no idle boast," came the determined voice. "Oh? Ye won't bet? Then let me finish me song!

"I first produced me pistol and then I drew me saber,
Sayin', 'Stand and deliver, for I am a bold deceiver!'
With me ring-dum-a-doodle-un-a-dah . . ."

At the highwayman's phrase, "stand and deliver," Viveca nearly choked. She shot a glance at William to see if he'd noticed, but he was looking away, trying to spot the Irishman in the crowd.

A serving wench came bumping and grinding her way over to their table, breasts hanging out of her gown. She shoved them in William's face and asked what he'd have.

"Two ales," he answered, pushing his chair back to be free of

237

her quivering cleavage. "What's that wild Irisher going on about?"

"Has got hisself a hoss in a race tomorrer, and the drunket bastid claim he kin name the finishing position o' every hoss in the race!"

William licked his lips, but his attention wasn't on the preening serving wench. Viveca watched his hands tighten on the table edge with that familiar old gambling urge. The girl abandoned her efforts and moved away to get them some ale and crumb cakes. *Ahh, this is a sad come-down from eel canapés and fifty-year-old French wine,* Viveca thought.

"They don't know you here, my husband, so they won't take your bet on credit. Calm down, William . . ." she attempted. The Irishman continued:

> "Well, the gold and the silver on the ground, it looked so jolly
> I gathered it all up and brought it to me Molly!
> She promised and she vowed she would not deceive me,
> But Divil take the women!—for they never can be easy!"

"Now, Captain O'Kelly, you cannot be serious," someone was scoffing at the tap rail. "Surely you haven't a snowball's chance in hell of guessing where every horse in that race will be at the end."

"Aye, I can predict the finish, and we'll put it on paper and into the care o' someone we all trust. Then we'll open it tomorrow, lads and colleens, and just you see if the captain doesna know his horses. Now, then, if you don't like my singin' o' 'Whiskey in the Jar,' maybe you'll like this one better—"

His companions drowned out the captain's fine Irish tenor in their haste to vote the tapster as the most honest man they knew.

"Old Hans it is," O'Kelly agreed, and called for pen and paper. Honest Hans suggested the Irish captain use the empty rum closet to write down his bet. O'Kelly emerged in mere seconds, chuckling to himself, and handed the folded paper to Hans, who locked it in his strong box. "Now, then, gents and ladies, let's take those bets."

"By God, I do believe that man knows something he hasn't told the others," William exclaimed, bright blue eyes hot with gambling fever. "Viveca, if you would let me have the money just this once . . . I know you've five quid on you."

"Jesus wept, William," she snapped wearily. "I've been training those damned horses twenty hours a day, fighting with the jockeys, practically getting trampled by Brick and Tuberose and the Baronet. I want to go home after this ale. My back's aching fit to burst. You know damned good and well that this is the last five pounds we have for the month! The last strip of bacon's hanging in the smokehouse, and the vegetables in the cellar have sprouted and gone bad. We have to feed ourselves *and* the horses on this money, and I haven't a shilling more to my name."

When the sluttish serving girl returned, thrusting her sagging bosom in William's uninterested face once more, he asked her if she'd seen Captain O'Kelly make bets before and if he knew horses.

"Oh, Lawd, suh," she answered, laughing, "he's bought hisself a half interest in some hoss used ter belong to the Duke o' Cumberland. He says he'll soon make enough to buy the whole hoss."

"The Butcher of Culloden! He bred Herod, probably the fastest horse alive today—" William began.

"You forget my Tuberose beat him," Viveca said coolly.

"Tell me about Captain O'Kelly's horse," William urged the girl.

"He ain't run before. Name's Eclipse 'cos he was foaled in the eclipse o' sixty-five."

"During our wedding," William said in an aside to Viveca, then, "Go on, girl! There's a shilling in it for you."

She accepted the coin, bit it, and inserted it in her cleavage. "This Eclipse be a big, ugly, rawboned brute. I seen him. Why, his shoulders is higher than me 'ead, and he's a long, bony face with a white blaze and one white rear leg. *Mean,* they say, mean as the devil!"

She distributed their crumb cakes—Viveca wrinkled her nose at the stale cakes—and their mugs of ale. Viveca was about to pay her, digging into the purse in her pocket, but William stopped her.

"No, darling, I'll get it," he said, and fished out his last pence.

When the tap girl had left, Viveca said softly, "Why, William, you really are struggling to avoid gambling. I fear I misjudged you; you had money in your pocket and used it for refreshments instead of gambling. Thank you so much; it renews my faith in this effort you've made."

Uncaring of the company, she quickly kissed him. In return, William embraced her with a fervor he had not shown in months, and after a half minute of such, she had to slap his hand off her hip. But lightly—it did her good to know he still found her attractive.

"Perhaps later," she told him, smiling. "It's been a long time. Perhaps it will be safe now."

He kissed her on the forehead and excused himself to use the water closet. She watched him disappear into the crowd, and her weariness resurfaced when he stopped at the tap rail before returning to her.

"What were you asking of the tapster?" she inquired suspiciously.

"Whether there is a safer way for us to go home. We have to pass some rough neighborhoods." He smiled innocently.

It did not occur to her to doubt him until they were halfway home. Her nose began to itch, and when she fished in her pocket for a handkerchief, she discovered her purse with the five pounds was missing.

"William, I've been robbed! It must have been that serving girl—"

Her husband turned to face her, twisting in the saddle. Even by moonlight she could read his expression: guilt. Chagrin, shame, *guilt* on the drink-ruined features. "*You* did it," she shouted furiously. "You took it when we embraced; you wagered it on that damned man with his damned horse—our last five pounds and now we haven't money for food, and I can't pay for grain for my racers. We haven't so much as a crumb of bread at home and only half a dozen rotting potatoes. We'll starve and we have no lamp oil, you cad! You lying, thieving, honorless bastard!"

"My love, my goddess . . ."

His sickening, overblown endearments—how they nauseated her! He reached out for her arm, reining his gelding in alongside the Moor. Viveca was carrying a walking stick; without thinking she lashed out at him with it. There was a solid, horrifying crunch as the weighted brass head smashed across William's wrist. Viveca, disgusted with both of them, gave Moor her head.

"No," came William's cry in the distance, "I'm right this time. You'll see I'm right. . . ."

He seemed to fade away. Moor turned a corner and half-reared in sudden panic. Too late, Viveca saw that this was not a street but a cul-de-sac with no outlet, only a shoulder-high brick wall at one end.

And footpads lying in wait.

One lunged up from the trash heap he had hidden behind, yanking at Blackamoor's bridle. He dragged the bit hurtingly across the mare's sensitive mouth, and she panicked. For the entire fourteen years of her life no hand had been laid on her except in love and gentleness; angry and frightened, she lashed out with an iron-shod hoof, creasing the man across the temple. There was a sudden surge of blood, then he fell back on the alley floor, eyes frozen open.

Viveca yanked the sword from her walking stick, letting the wooden cover clatter to the ground. She laid about her with the sword like a Fury. The thin blade of tempered steel sliced through one man's arm and nicked another in the neck. They collapsed, shrieking.

Others had hold of her cheap grisette skirts. The coarseness of the gown allowed them fingerholds, so she hauled a leg up, slashed through the yards of material. Freed from too much encumbering fabric, she clung to mane and saddle as she endeavored to swing a leg over and ride astride.

In that moment she glimpsed an even more frightening sight: William sitting on Old Jack at the head of the alley, mouth open, pistol still in his coat. He had not entered the fray at all and, in fact, his puffy face looked paralyzed. "Coward," she shrieked at him as rough hands seized her ankles, tried to drag her down. "Coward, coward!"

She could not fathom his shock, nor the frightening awe he held her in at that moment, for, of six men, she had already disabled three. And as he watched she kicked another in the face, sent him reeling over backward.

Then more footpads poured out of broken doorways, at least a dozen. Viveca was dimly aware of hands plucking at her, of a knife that sliced her thigh. Then a pistol fired as William regained his senses. The shot distracted the footpads for the moment Viveca needed.

The brick wall rose before her. Could she still take it?

She turned the Moor toward it, shouted the trick word, *"Fly!"*

And to the observers it seemed that the dark mare did just that. She arched up into the air, scrambled up the wall to the top.

Viveca looked down over the rear of the bricks into nothingness. The wall had once been part of a house, now demolished, and the place had been stripped down to its very cellars—some twenty-five feet below.

They could not make the jump and live. In another moment the robbers would be scaling the wall, for, despite her cheap clothes, they'd seen that Viveca wore her miniature and betrothal ring, and Moor was worth plenty, whether roasted on an open spit to feed these starving miscreants or sold to a breeder.

Byrne would have fought his way to her with only his fists if necessary but this useless dandy she was married to . . . ! For the first time she hated William, loathed him with a marrow-heating intensity that gave her the final burst of energy she needed, for the footpads would kill her and William to get their horses, her ring and miniature, his watch, unless, dear God, he'd wagered his watch on Eclipse, too.

With the burning cold passion of a scorpion, she put her heels to Moor's flanks.

The gallant mare left the wall in a rush of courage and blood lust. She scented gore and fear; she felt the excitement about her.

She came soaring down where Viveca directed her—atop the would-be thieves.

Men shrieked and bellowed, limbs snapped. Moor lurched, clawed for footing, regained it. Viveca, half-in, half-out of the saddle, waved the thin sword about her madly.

They scattered before her like wheat in the wind, those who could still run or crawl. She started past William in her determination to smite them, punish them. "Tell them 'twas the Mistress of the Night defeated you single-handed!" she roared out as the last of them dug into refuse heaps and broken-out cellar windows.

William tried to follow, tried to catch Moor by the bridle. But both woman and horse were aflame now and easily escaped him. Blackamoor raced for home, bobbing unsteadily. *She must be hurt,* Viveca thought, her head clearing. She tried to rein the fiery mare in, but Blackamoor had the bit in her teeth and sped home.

There was a brittle snap as the mare faltered. She went down in a heap, pitching Viveca into the road not fifty yards from their front gate.

Kensington and home. How had they covered so many miles so swiftly? *Moor,* Viveca thought dizzily as she struggled to her knees. *Moor's injured and yet ran all this way to please me.* Blackamoor, her first horse, her lead mare.

The mare struggled to stand but could not. One foreleg flopped uselessly, the ankle spinning in what seemed a complete circle. There was dark blood everywhere, coming from the mare's nostrils and heaving mouth, too.

One of the brigands had stuck a knife in her chest. And she had fractured a fetlock leaping down from the wall, only to tear it the rest of the way through with her galloping.

Viveca lifted the trembling ebony head to her lap. "There, lass, there, my darling. I won't let you suffer anymore. Here comes William with a gun. It'll be all right, Moor, my Moor . . . you're dying for me, you great fool horse; you love me so much you ran yourself to death with a pierced lung and only three legs. . . ."

She had never needed help so much as she needed it now. The

fall to the road had left a dizzying lump on her head. There were cuts and claw marks all over her. And, most important, her friend from those confused teenage days was dying—dying in sobbing, shuddering agony. "William," she said dully as he dismounted, "shoot her for me. Put the pistol's muzzle right behind her ear. I'll hold her head."

He loaded, trembling, and held the pistol out to her, unable to shoot Moor himself. A final blackness seemed to come over Viveca's heart then. On this, too, he had managed to disappoint and betray her.

Viveca rose, bent over her beloved Blackamoor, and shot her. The valiant horse shook, then eased in death's impartial grip.

Viveca dropped the gun at her husband's feet. "You're not completely useless after all, William; you can bury her for me. And you had *better* bury her; if I hear the butcher got her, I'll kill you with my own hands."

And she went inside the tiny cottage they had built on her dower lands after their farmhouse and one hundred acres had to be sold for his debts.

She woke to the cool, metallic clinking of coins. A shower of silver and gold seemed to be falling out of the sky at her. Was she dreaming she was Danäe, the Greek heroine visited by a god in the form of a firefall of gold?

Viveca sat, rubbing her eyes. "What is this?"

"Captain O'Kelly's horse won," William said, smiling as he sat down in the chair next to the rickety bed. It was a terrible old bed; she'd salvaged it from a trash heap last year. The chair, too; its caning had shredded, and her husband could barely sit on it without falling through. He'd been drinking, for she could smell it, and his eyes were bloodshot with excess.

He continued. "I placed my watch and two pounds ten shillings on Eclipse. The rest I used to back the Captain's bet. And Eclipse won."

She was suddenly awake, interested despite herself. "And the captain's bet?" she demanded.

"You know the rules of racing," he answered, folding his hands over his stomach as his smile broadened. "If the winner finishes two hundred and forty or more yards ahead of the nearest competitor, the rest of the horses' finishing positions are not even posted."

Her mouth opened in a soundless *O* of understanding.

"Yes," William answered gaily, leaping up and shaking her by the shoulders. "Captain O'Kelly's slip of paper said, 'Eclipse first, the rest nowhere.' The others were half the length of the track behind, or more. I was the only one who bet with O'Kelly on his knowing the finish, and as Eclipse was a maiden racer in a field of experienced runners, hardly anyone but me and O'Kelly bet on the nag in the race itself."

"How—how much did you win?" she asked, stupefied.

"Somewhere around five hundred pounds, all of it in gold and sterling. And if Eclipse keeps winning this way, I think we should set up a private match race between him and Tuberose. There's money to be made off that Eclipse."

He fished a jewel box out of his pocket. "No," she said, waving him away. "No more overpriced jewels bought on credit!"

"They're little star ruby studs for your ears, paid for with cash at Garraway's auction. And I brought you a bolt of blue silk velvet. I didn't spend too much. Don't be cross, dear, but I had to bring you a gift. Oh, Viveca, my goddess, my angel."

He threw himself into her arms. "Don't send me away—I'd die without you, I would kill myself should you turn your back on me! I've tried so hard to quit drinking and betting. You're all I have!"

Has anything really changed then? she thought with a lump in her throat. *How long will the money last this time? How long will he need me, and how long will I so desperately need to be needed?* She didn't feel love for him anymore, only pity and contempt. But he needed her, and if she could buy her horses back . . . No word from Byrne in two years . . . Her horses . . .

Greed. She was overcome with a painful combination of greed and loneliness. "I want my dowry back, William," she said firmly, holding him at arm's length. "I want every blessed shilling repaid. And I want a horse for every one of my horses that I had

245

to sell. I can't stop you gambling, but if you win, I can claim my share of it. And we can work together to curb your drinking."

He agreed, and she thought that she had either done a very greedy thing—or a very sensible one.

CHAPTER TWENTY-FIVE

Kensington, 1771

They built a fine new house on the land adjoining Caro's property and bought sixteen brood mares, for William continued to bet on Eclipse, and Eclipse continued to win.

So did Tuberose, at least until he was matched against Eclipse. People called it the "Race of the Century," and afterward Viveca mollified herself by reasoning that it was no great shame to own the only horse to come so close to Eclipse at the finish line.

Several of the mares Viveca bought were heavy with foals sired by the great Matchem; the rest of her stock was bred to Tuberose and Eclipse. Soon she had colts by the four greatest racers of the day, and, some said, the century: Herod, Matchem, Tuberose, and Eclipse. Funny how the Duke of Cumberland had taken her father from her and yet provided her a thriving farm and house through his horses.

William wanted to shower her with gifts, but Viveca insisted on very shrewdly investing the money, with Great Edward's sterling advice. She worried about Edward; his health was failing and had been ever since they had met during their Newgate incarceration. Would Caro again lose a man she loved?

Money seemed to be everywhere. Moor's last colt, half-brother to Tuberose and sired by Herod, brought a record price at auction. Viveca let William have the money with the stipulation that he invest it. To her surprise the pacifying gesture did more than renew his self-faith, for William turned out to be uncanny about investments, always seeming to know where to place money, when, and how much. In fact, the challenge interested him so that he neglected the tap rail and gaming tables and became known as an investor whose leads were a sure thing.

They dressed in gold-shot silks now, and velvets and furs fit for an empress and her consort. William's stickpins were flawless bean-size diamonds, and Viveca had sapphires to match her blue-black eyes and the many new gowns Terrence and Lilly made, struggling to keep up with her requests. Viveca and William were looked upon as fashion leaders, and soon there came the invitation for the Court presentation that had lapsed when their finances had tumbled so low.

Many men sought Viveca, yet none won her. Married to a man she could not respect or feel passion for, barren of the children she wanted, separated from the man she loved, she pined. Her only satisfaction came from work, and she found comfort in keeping too busy to mourn her losses.

She wore men's clothes to break her horses herself, not trusting them to some stranger's whips and goads. "She has a touch, Her Ladyship does," men said admiringly, and the womenfolk added sadly, "Anyone that good with foals would be a wonderful mother; if she only had children, poor dear."

To own a Lindstrom-Holland colt became a status symbol. Soon people were not only asking her to serve as professional trainer to their racers, but also pleading for her to break in their riding mounts as well.

She wasn't the only one prospering; there was no need to curse herself for staying with a loser, for William made great progress in business. He hadn't made progress as a lover, though. Viveca was now past the danger zone of a year's duration for avoiding pregnancy, but ever since the night of the footpads' attack when she had called William a coward, he had been impotent. She found it something of a relief not to have to endure those lightning-fast grapplings in bed; and yet she missed the physical closeness of him. To be so young and yet live like a vestal virgin! If there could be no Byrne in her life, then there would be no romance at all, no sweetness in the dark. She would not dishonor William's name; there was still that much feeling in her for him.

And so she immersed herself in her work and social outings.

At parties she turned the wittiest phrases, wore the most sumptuous gowns. There was a kind of branched velvet they called Holland cloth in honor of her, and Lindstrom blue was still popular from her first ball. Women came to her for advice on clothing and men; children shyly sought her out to ask if she would help their parents find a good pony; and men, rebuffed by her sexually, soon realized that she was a boon companion for hunting and consulting on all things equine. She could answer their questions concerning horses, and her husband could help them on investments.

She and William were to be presented at Court for her first time in late summer. But there was some trouble brewing in the American Colonies, and William's regiment, of which he was captain, was one of the first to be activated.

"What will you do?" Viveca asked as soon as he told her.

"Why, there is no question of going or not going. I shall, of course, lead my regiment. Don't worry, my angel, there won't be any fighting. We're only going to act as constables, no more. I expect to be back within the year. The only problem it poses is that you shall have to run the investment firm while I am gone. Do keep Great Edward as a consultant and partner; he's invaluable, but then, you know that; you're the one who recommended him to me. The other complication is that your debut at Court must be made before I leave, which shall be sometime in the next three weeks. You'll have to have your gown made quickly."

He began to say more, then hesitated. Viveca waited with a slight frown. "What is it, William?" she asked as he threw his coat over a settee back and began to pace along the hearthstone.

"My angel, I know all about you and the highwayman, that Byrne St. James. And I fear I allowed a very evil thing to take place."

"What do you mean, William?" she demanded tersely.

"You told me before we married that you weren't a virgin, and I didn't mind. No, 'twas not important; why shouldn't a woman have her *amours* just as a man does? But I did some inquiring, oh, of your aunt Yasaman's servants and the staff at the Black Bull, and I reasoned your lover must have been this Byrne fellow. He returned from the Caribbean when we were newlyweds, and I had already sensed a dissatisfaction, an uneasiness about you. I have always loved you very greatly, you know, and I frankly feared the competition.

"In short, I made the mistake of asking my father if he could use his position and money to influence the shipping line to transfer St. James to some other country. Instead he had the man framed for embezzling and then reported to the authorities that this was the St. James highwayman they had been seeking. Your friend was then forced to flee to Scotland, wondering all the while how this could have happened."

"How—how horrible! At last I understand what happened!"

Poor Byrne, to be used so! She clasped her hands in her full skirts, crushing the damask.

William stopped pacing. He leaned against the mantel awhile, as though consulting with the caryatids and mermen carved there, then turned to face her. "I didn't know this for a long time. All that mattered to me was that my rival was out of the way. Then there came that terrifying night he kidnapped you, and I feared you would never return. But you did . . . and you were radiant as you'd never been, even when a new bride."

He drew his breath in and let it out slowly, toying with the ugly Staffordshire dogs on the mantel. "I sent for him and he was gentleman enough to come, though he must have suspected it was a trap. I was suspicious, too; I was sure his pack of brothers lurked in the bushes, waiting to murder me at a moment's notice. The long and short of it was that we both agreed we should put no pressure on you in making your choice between us. I said that if three years passed and I had not managed to decently provide for you and make you happy, then I should give you a divorce. And he agreed that instead of rushing in he would leave you alone to make your own decision."

William smiled sadly. *He has aged these last years,* Viveca thought, noting how lusterless the silver-gilt hair had become. She saw again those fine, feathery lines at his eyes and mouth, the bloat of drink and dissipation. He was at this moment the oldest young man she ever beheld, and he was only in his early thirties.

"So," William announced, and cleared his throat. "So, the

three years shall be over this coming year, and while I am off in the Colonies you shall have time to think it over. It's obvious to me now that this marriage is over, *has* been over a long while, only you were too brave to admit defeat. We have been friends, mates, and strangers in these long years together; I should like to be friends again at the end."

Viveca was above and beyond astonished. It took her three starts to speak. "But, William! You always said you couldn't live without me! You said you'd die, and so I went on clinging and drowning both of us in guilt and grief. I would never have held on so determinedly had you but told me—"

"No one actually dies because someone leaves him, my dear, misguided Amazon. He might blow his brains out because he is without a soft place to land any longer; he might drink himself to death, refusing to accept the truth. But this business you were good enough to help me start has proved to me that I can stand alone. Odd, isn't it, how I leaned on you so hard that you forever tried to find me a niche to fit into, digging this place and that for a square spot that this round peg would fit into. Well, my sweet, I have found it at last, thanks to you, though I believe I shall go with the regiment before I slip again and wager away everything we've fought for all these years."

"Will you . . . will you be all right on your own? Able to stand without falling back into your gambling patterns or drink?"

"I don't know," he answered frankly as she surveyed the bloat of liquor and sleeplessness at his jowls and thickening waist; he, who had once been called the handsomest man in London! Poor, confused William. Not an evil man, merely a weak one whose ambitious family had conspired to destroy his rival for her affection.

"You and Byrne never were rivals," she said suddenly, passionately. "I made a marriage contract with you, and I stuck to it faithfully until that one night—that one, reckless night. It was unplanned, what happened between Byrne and me, and I came back to you at once."

"I believe you, my dear. Now, then, by this clock it is nearly six, and you have an appointment at seven at Terrence and Carlisle for fitting your gown for Court. Do run along." He held up a hand as she opened her mouth to speak. "No, do not attempt to thank me, or worse, apologize. You have nothing to apologize for. We are neither of us perfect, and as a result things worked out the way they did. The fault is mine for hanging on—and a little bit yours for not tossing me in the street when you should have, for you encouraged my weaknesses. You are too loyal, Viveca, my sweet. You do not know when to let go."

"It's time for me to let go *now,* though, isn't it?" she asked, sadder but enlightened at last to this baffling man she had married.

He rang for the maid, requested Viveca's sable coat, along with her expensive new ermine muff and tall hat *à la russe,* as the Parisians called it. William helped her into them, then kissed her on the cheek and saw her out to the waiting carriage.

She had plenty to think about on the way to Threadneedle Street, not the least of which was the fact that her men had gone behind her back to make their pact. She didn't like being lied to that way, having things hidden from her as though she were a child. And yet . . . and yet Byrne, as always, had known her very well when he'd told William that instead of rushing in he would leave her alone to make up her own mind. How cunning they were, these men! How devious and terrible . . . and how easy to love, despite their flaws.

Try though she may, Viveca could feel nothing but an aching, frightened relief at the thought of leaving William. It was as though someone had slipped the bolt on a tigress's cage—the cage where she had paced, lonesome and narrowly confined, for far too long.

Soon enough she saw the familiar sign, TERRENCE & CARLISLE OF THREADNEEDLE, and cheered up.

The shop's major business had ceased for the day. Customer traffic had ground to a halt, and lamps were low except for the interior office—Terrence's new office, with etched glass walls a person could look directly through. *How the shop has changed!* Viveca thought, rapping softly at the locked front door and peering in. *When I first came here, it was hardly more than a closet with a few pasted-up watercolors.*

Lilly was in the glass office with another woman, and the turbaned head above that wing chair over there could only belong to Philippe. Who was that woman with Philippe? Viveca wondered. She was lovely.

Lilly heard the knock and rose, striding toward the door with recognition on her face but without the usual pleased smile of camaraderie. No, it was a look of awe. Viveca, who had waved the coach away as soon as Lilly rose from her chair, cocked her head in wonderment.

The words **Lilly** spoke upon opening the door made her raise an eyebrow.

"Good evening, Your Grace, we—we hadn't expected you."

And damn her if Lil didn't drop an averted-face curtsy!

"See here, Lil, what's all this flattering nonsense?" Viveca asked rather more sharply than she meant to. Ahead of her, Philippe and the little beauty were laughing and flirting. Yes, Philippe flirting—and with a *woman!*

Lilly Carlisle straightened with an audible snap of her backbone. *"Viveca?* Hellfire, you scared me! Out there in the dark I thought you were the Duchess de Gwyn. You're dressed so like her—"

"Haven't you mentioned her before and said I looked like her? She used to be the Baroness de Gwyn, right?"

"Yes, her husband is a duke now, ambassador to Russia, and she dresses in their mode, with cocked beaver and sable hats and those great, flowing coats like yours."

"I wore this for Terrence's approval. If he hates it I'll burn it all. Aunt Caro says I'm too tall to wear a tall hat."

Lilly gestured in dismissal of that statement. "Nonsense. Now let's fit you for your Court gown," she said, slipping an arm through Viveca's. "Any stipulations besides it having to be white and silver?"

"I don't think so," Viveca said, letting herself be steered toward the office. "Lilly, where is your little Simonne, and tell me, who is that fetching little woman with Philippe?"

At that, Lilly's blue eyes twinkled. "Simonne's home in bed. But come and meet Philippe's friend."

Philippe and the woman rose from their chairs. There was something odd about how the woman slid from her chair, something a trifle gauche in her movements, something mildly coarse in her features. She looked strangely familiar, too.

Lilly mischievously supplied, "This is Lady Viveca, and this is—"

"Terrence of Threadneedle Street," the small woman said, and whipped off her powdered wig to reveal Terrence himself!

Viveca was too astonished even to blink. But after a full half-minute her senses returned, and she collapsed on the settee, chuckling.

"Is it that funny?" asked Philippe, who loved a good chuckle.

"Oh, dear! It reminds me of how I used to dress as a boy when I was young—and Terrence had me so completely fooled, I was standing there wondering if 'she' was your mistress, Philippe!"

Terrence reached into a desk drawer, pulled out a soft cloth and unguents, and began removing his makeup. "You're not going to ask, darling girl, why I'm dressed like this?"

"Oh, I'm curious enough," she admitted brightly, "but it's none of my business. Yasaman told me all about—er, you know. She said that sometimes certain men like to dress up in, er, you know. Now, then—how *is* everyone?"

"We're fine. But are you really getting divorced?" Terrence asked. "The word came through a hairdresser who knew one of your servants, the usual grapevine."

"Funny, I just found out an hour ago *myself.* Yes, it looks like a divorce."

Philippe, murmuring condolences he did not feel, poured her some mocha from a tall golden pot. "How far we've all come since my first visit here," Viveca said thickly, watching the graceful spout of the pot bend over her Meissen cup. "Terrence had a dented old tin samovar and some chipped stoneware cups. Yasaman still lived in London half the year, and now she's in Angora forever. This place used to be a hole in the wall and now it's a palace. Lilly's gone from highwaywoman to fashion designer; Philippe, who used to be a page boy without a single serious thought, is now the bookkeeper here; and I'm getting divorced from a man I never knew."

"I'm glad of it," Philippe said almost savagely. "I was beginning to think you'd cling tight to wifehood until it killed you, William, *and* Byrne!"

Byrne. Byrne, whom she had not seen in years. Byrne, her fellow thief, who had worked to become a respectable businessman and been forced back to thieving. And she, herself, had gone so far, risen and fallen so many times. Gulping down tears, she held a hand out to Lilly. "I was so cruel to all of you. I wouldn't listen when you tried to warn me about my marriage. Can the three of you forgive me, be my friends again?"

Lilly took Viveca's hand. "We were always your friends. You were just too distraught to see it," she answered kindly.

CHAPTER TWENTY-SIX

Hampton Court, February 1772

"Don't be so nervous," William whispered. "You are by far the most beautiful woman here, and your gown and hair are perfection. So what troubles you?"

"Everything," Viveca glumly answered as they stood in the palace corridor, waiting for their names to be called. "There's a long line in front of us, and I'm sure my hair will wilt before I meet the king and queen . . . you're leaving tomorrow for the Colonies . . . all three of my stallions have important races this week—"

"Captain Sir William Holland and the Lady Viveca," rang out the herald's voice.

"Damned ninnies got the cards shuffled—we're not supposed to be called for another eight minutes," William said in a whisper, elbowing bosomy dowagers out of the way. Viveca, caught by his hand through the crook of her arm, was propelled along by his speed. She stumbled through the loitering crowd, trying to kick her train out of the way.

Then they were pausing before the doorway, straightening themselves with final flicks of gloved hands at hair and buttons. Viveca gave her train a quick kick of the ankle, and it went rippling stylishly behind her, just as in all her portraits.

They entered a regatta of powdered wigs afloat on a sea of silver damask and white taffeta. Viveca's fingers trembled on William's arm. She had never been among royalty before, only a few baronets, mere sirs and ladies, never these great peers of the realm. It was the first time she'd had her hair powdered, for though she was renowned for flaunting her strawberry-blond locks, Court protocol demanded whitened hair on one and all. William, drat his luck, needed no such artificial—and troublesome!—means for his silver locks.

King George and Queen Charlotte sat far ahead on a raised dais. At least they *must* be the king and queen, for they sat on chairs of state on the dais. But the king was shockingly and plainly dressed in a brown frock coat and breeches, old flat shoes. And no velvets, ermine, or crowns!

This must be why they called him "Farmer George"—the plain clothes and the puttering he did in his vegetable garden. And the queen! *Hellfire, my gown outshines hers ten to one,* Viveca thought, confused.

It outshone *everyone's.* He was subtle, that Terrence, and so was Lilly. They had not gone in for ostentation, choosing instead to use sumptuous, unfigured white silk velvet lined with swishing china silk and buoyed by stiff taffeta petticoats so Viveca would have that costly rustle as she walked. She wore none of the loud-looking silver lamé or charmeuse of the others, and her gown was edged simply in pristine white satin cord.

The neckline was rounded because a square neckline would overemphasize her square jawline. And, as with her first ball gown, Viveca's neckline was slightly higher than those of the Court beauties, who revealed nipples and even some armpit. The filmy lace at her bodice and the wider stuff gathered in festoons at her three-quarter-length sleeves had been bleached as white as the rest of her ensemble: white dress, white shoes, white silk hose, white hair ribbons, hair also powdered not a pale gray but a virginal white.

She had not tried to cover her suntanned skin with white lead paint as had the others, their clownlike color made even more frightful by blood-red lips and cheeks, with blue veins penciled in on their bosoms. They looked like rotting corpses compared to Viveca's sun-ripened freshness.

The gown and her hair were scattered with seed pearls and mother-of-pearl sequins; she wore her miniature and diamonds, a small, square-cut choker and dangling earrings. Next to the overpainted countesses and baronesses with their gaudy emeralds and rubies flashing against gowns crusted with diamond dust or worn—shockingly—over no petticoats to show the shape of their legs, she looked a vision, summer prettily wearing winter's clothes.

They had reached the dais at last. William bowed, and Viveca sank into a carefully rehearsed curtsy, taking pains not to lean forward and reveal an indecent amount of cleavage. On rising she discovered, to her horror, that William must be standing on her skirts. No, worse than that, his spurs were caught in her hem, and the moment either of them moved, he would rend her garment from hock to withers and back again.

She dug her fingers deeper into his gloved wrist, refused to let him budge. "Rise, my dear," Queen Charlotte whispered kindly at long last.

"Your Majesty, I fear I must not, for Sir William's spurs are caught in my train."

"What, what, hold on there, young woman," said King George III, sovereign lord of England, Wales, Scotland, and at least *some* parts of Ireland. He came huffing down off the dais and disentangled her, handing her back up with a country gentleman's rough friendliness. "Got spunk, doesn't she, Charlotte, what, what? Anyone else at this cattle show would have been too cowed to speak up as she did. We like her, eh? Looks damnable familiar, too. Lady Viveca, was it? Have you relatives in Scotland, lass, what, what?" he barked pleasantly, holding her by both gloved and trembling hands.

"Why, as a matter of fact I *am* from Scotland, Your Highness."

He turned to Charlotte, and the two portly people smiled fondly at one another. "The spitting image of our Duchess de Gwyn, what, what?" he remarked.

The queen stepped down alongside him. By now the entire Court had droned to a roaring silence.

Queen Charlotte smiled beatifically up at Viveca. "Why, yes, dear, she most certainly is. Her hair is perhaps as fair as the duchess's beneath the powder."

"Majesties, I have never met the Duchess de Gwyn, though my dressmaker has said there is some resemblance," Viveca admitted humbly.

"Your dressmaker?" the queen asked, then took in Viveca's gown with a quick, searching stare. She brightened. "Why, that's a Terrence and Carlisle gown, isn't it? Goodness, but that Terrence is a card, isn't he?"

"What, hoy, what's this, what, what?" the king broke in, reaching for Viveca's miniature. She felt William unclasp it, watched him offer it for the king's inspection while the Court buzzed with speculation. "Quite a bit of my half-sister about the eyes and jaw, don't you think, Charlotte, what, what? Though this gal in the painting has dark hair."

"Your sister? But I thought—" Viveca's head was swimming. "You asked if I was Scots, Your Highness, and I am. But isn't de Gwyn a Welsh name?"

"Her husband's Welsh, dear girl, but the duchess is half Scots and the rest pure Hanover. Here, herald," he said, raising his voice. "Fetch my half-sister from Maman's sickroom, what, what!"

A few moments later a voice rolled out, *"The Duchess de Gwyn, Countess Feversham, Viscountess Hemstead, Baroness Bredon, Jura and Norwich!"*

A lovely young woman was hurrying toward them. Perhaps a few years Viveca's junior, she was not dressed for a Court function. She had on a simple, square-necked Terrence and Carlisle house gown of brilliant blue bombazine over a high-necked shift, her ash-blond hair loosely, becomingly netted back from her face. She wore little paint, only a touch of kohl at her pale blue eyes.

She was several ghosts to Viveca: the face in the ivory miniature, her mother Ginny, herself in the mirror—and, most shocking of all . . .

The two women stared at each other, wide-eyed, openmouthed. The duchess reached out as if to touch Viveca's face, to explore this near twin. But she stopped, hand in midair, fearing to disturb this ghost of the dead.

"Duchess de Gwyn, this is Lady Viveca Holland," said the king. "Lady Viveca, my half-sister, Allegra, what, what?"

Viveca did something she had always regarded as the silliest, weakest thing a woman could do: She fainted.

"Yes," said the dying dowager Princess of Wales, Frederick's widow, the king's mother. Her voice was raspy and pained with the cancer in her throat, but she still smiled at the Lindstrom sisters. "Yes, 'twas me took in little Allegra. I was outraged when I discovered that the poor Lindstrom woman was turned away from my gate. A destitute woman with two little babies, and my Fritz the father of one of those unfortunate girls."

Here she paused to cough wrackingly. Allegra quickly leaned forward, sponging her stepmother's face in the golden lamp glow. *How good she is,* Viveca thought gladly. *How kind and loving, how like Mother.* Viveca had been admitted to the sickroom so Allegra could talk to her without neglecting the dying princess, who took such comfort from her presence. William, realizing he was not an integral part of this poignant reunion, had been given permission to return home.

"I thought you were dead," Viveca said to her sister. "I saw the bullets go through the gate."

Allegra set the sponge back in a china basin. "I had stooped to unfasten the sash when it got caught in the gate, and thus the bullets went over my head. But I thought it safest to play dead, so I went limp—I was sawing through the sash with my knife when Missus Lee arrived."

"What!" Viveca exclaimed, knotting her fists in her lap at the mention of that hated name.

"That woman," said Princess Augusta, "had followed you two in order to be certain you were killed or captured. After the constables dragged you off she found Allegra, trapped, and was about to kill her when Allegra cried out . . . you tell her, dear."

Allegra squeezed her stepmother's hand with deep affection. "I said, 'Don't kill me, I'm the Prince of Wales's bastard, and they'll pay you at the palace.' It was the only way I could think of to stay alive, you see. She didn't believe me at first, not until I began

260

to talk about his carriage and clothes, then she grew curious. And greedy. She was hoping they'd pay her if it was true, and if I'd lied, I suppose she would have knifed me."

The dowager princess Augusta said, "So Missus Lee brought her to the gatekeeper at Leicester House and made such a racket that I finally came down. You see, I'd been looking for Missus Lindstrom and you girls for a long time, and Allegra was able to talk to me about Fritz in a most convincing manner."

Here she was halted by painful coughing and had to let Allegra finish the tale. "I also told her all about Missus Lee, and Princess Augusta had the soldiers arrest her and take her away. But Missus Lee had the little knife I'd been using to saw through the sash, and she tried to get away. She attacked a soldier—and he shot and killed her in self-defense."

Viveca drew a sharp breath. "So *that's* why no one in the street knew what had happened to her. My friend Edward had people searching and searching. But Allegra—" She could not prevent the note of hurt creeping into her voice. "Why didn't you come looking for me in Newgate?"

Princess Augusta said raspily, "I went with a small company of troopers to Newgate and Tyburn—even though Missus Lee had sworn you were dead. But neither prison reported a small girl brought in that day, at least not a blond of your age. Where *were* you, Lady Viveca?"

Viveca went weak and sank down in her chair. "Good Lord, you missed me because of my disguise. I was wearing boys' clothes, and they thought me a lad when they caught me, so I went *on* letting them think it. And if I'd been in the women's quarters you would have found me. To think of all that pain for nothing! But, Allegra, why didn't you try to contact Aunt Caro in Kensington?"

Allegra's forehead puckered. "Aunt who?" she asked in puzzlement.

"Of course, you wouldn't remember her. You weren't born until Mother moved to the city, and I only remembered her because of tales Mother had told us, but I guess you were too young

261

then. So you were raised *here,* Allegra—here, so close to me, and yet I never knew it."

Allegra signaled her to rise, then bent and kissed the princess's forehead. "I will be back in a while, dear," she told her step-mother.

"Yes," came the scratchy, pained voice, "you girls run along, you have much to discuss. Lady Viveca, I'm glad, *glad* she has you now that I shall be gone."

They went on out, Allegra signaling to the maidservants in the corridor. She quietly asked someone to send the king to his mother and instructed the maids to attend to Augusta's every wish. Then she took Viveca by the hand, led her to a small solar-ium with an oriel window through which lamplight and moon-beams poured.

"Mother?" Allegra asked at once. "You said something about Mother before we went in to see the princess. Mother's—"

"Alive, yes. Now sit down and don't be shocked, but she's converted to Mohammedanism and lives in Anatolia in the Otto-man Empire. She looked and looked for us; she was pregnant again by Fritz at the time and lost the baby through starvation and exhaustion from living in the streets searching for us. Do you remember Yasaman? No, I didn't suppose you would. Mother's Turk friend. Yasaman took her in, and then Mother married a Turk. Now she has a whole crop of kids by the handsomest man you ever did see."

She had worried that Allegra would react violently to discover-ing her mother had turned heathen, but Allegra only asked, "Is she happy? Is everything good for her?"

"Well, she's fine now, and wealthy, and breeds horses and raises the cutest little brats you can imagine. But, Allegra, she never got over losing us. Sometimes we would be at breakfast or talking in the evening and suddenly the tears would course down her face. Then she'd say, 'I'm so glad to have you back,' or, 'If only Allegra had survived, too.' I felt it was all my fault when you 'died,' I—"

"No, no, you mustn't. If not for your wild schemes, I should

262

never have been taken to Augusta, as a result of which my life has turned out like the fairy tales you used to tell me."

They sat on glossy Chippendale chairs, each reaching across to hold the other's hand.

"Your marriage is good?" Viveca ventured.

"Oh, he's a widower, much older than me . . . as much a father as a husband, but that suits me, I was never feisty and solitary like you. They didn't force me to marry, they let me pick my own husband. He's a kind man, a strong man, and I have a daughter, a son, and my husband's girl by his first marriage. And Russia is so wonderfully untamed, so barbaric. I love it, except the people are extremely superstitious, so God-fearing. Someday we'll come back to England, but in the meantime I enjoy the snowy steppes and cocked fur hats. And you, what of your life?"

Viveca released her sister's hands and sat back. "Well, dear, two out of three Lindstroms didn't do so badly. I married a very kind man who's a gambler. We starve one year, and the next we can afford to gild the windowsills and wallpaper the dining room with Spanish leather! We built a house and had to sell it—'twas a palace, really. We lived in a cottage once, and I liked it there. Now we have money again, and I own one of England's best breeding farms, and every day I wake to wonder if he's wagered away all I worked for these last seven years. He's going off to America now with his regiment. And after years of thinking I'd have to stay with him forever, it finally seems we'll divorce. I believe I just might marry Byrne St. James if he comes back and is fool enough to ask one more time."

"Byrne is still around? Oh, tell me more—tell me *everything!*" Allegra urged, and so they sat until morning, sharing tales of love and disaster, triumph and loss.

The same morning that William left, promising the divorce was already in progress, Viveca packed for a trip to Anatolia and closed the house up after placing her trusted servants with friends.

She and Allegra had a farewell breakfast with Caro (Viveca was thrilled to see that Caro and Allegra got along famously;

saddened to learn no one had heard from Byrne yet), then they set out together. At first they savored each shared moment, for after Anatolia, Allegra would have to return to the Russias and they might not see each other again for years. In fact, Allegra had only made this last trip to London unexpectedly to visit the fading Augusta, who died within days of Viveca's presentation to Court.

"Won't your husband be furious with you for staying away so long?" Viveca asked as they boarded ship.

"How *can* he be? I expect that the longer he is left to his own devices among those thick-ankled, *screamingly* devout Russian Orthodox Muscovite women, who do not so much as let you touch a *pinky* unless you're married to them, why," said Allegra perkily, "I *do* believe he'll be more sure than ever that I am an absolute *prize.*"

They laughed heartily together at that one.

From the docks at Gravesend to the coast of Anatolia, Allegra's excitement made itself evident in further breathless chattering; she carried on, nonstop, all the way from the British port to Ginny's front door, making Viveca understand that there could be too much of a good thing. She heard more than she could possibly want to know about Allegra's little daughter, Augusta Rose, who was afraid of her own shadow. She was subjected to tales of nasty little Trevelyan (who sounded a proper scoundrel) tackling the empress's last tame tiger, breaking priceless Ming vases, and shredding ermine hats. Viveca thought he needed a good spanking, not such glowing praise.

There followed the details of Katerinka's harpsichord lessons and *all* of Allegra's newest clothes.

How many hundreds of miles Viveca had spent hearing about silk gowns and velvet gowns and ruched cotton chemises and ruffled dressing gowns and . . . Then there was the subject of ermine versus martin: "Only royalty should wear ermine or else it's just too, *too,* don't you agree?" Allegra unknowingly asked Viveca, who had recently spent fifty pounds on an ermine hat and matching muff.

And, "Women under forty should never wear rubies, especially *star* rubies, that pinkish-red color sucks all hue from a woman's skin and makes her look like old parchment!" Allegra exclaimed.

"Look," Viveca said, changing the subject and twisting her star ruby ring to the inside of her hand, "there's a caravan with a white camel."

Then they were almost there, each plodding step of the way punctuated by a running fashion commentary, Allegra insisting green dresses always looked cheap. By that time Viveca had made up her mind to unpack her emerald moiré and wear it their first evening at Ginny's.

She was wrung out with exhaustion by the time they arrived, nerves snapping like frayed reins. Allegra wondered aloud at Viveca's shortness of temper, and Ginny and Yasaman did, too, until the end of the third day when they came out onto the balcony to find Viveca hiding in a bamboo chair. "Is she asleep yet?" Viveca asked dismally.

"I had Roxelina put opiates in her sorbet. We shall have blessed silence for a good twelve hours," Yasaman answered tartly. "She is a dear child, but . . . a gaggle of geese at feeding time could not raise so much ruckus!"

Ginny sighed as she sank into the chair across from Viveca's. "I've heard how women over forty shouldn't wear white, how blondes ought to let themselves go gray naturally—and I stood there with dyed blonde hair in a white caftan all the while, as over forty as one could get!"

"How about the little boy, Trevelyan, and the tiger?" Viveca asked with great weariness.

"That child! A pity the tiger didn't eat him!" her mother exclaimed.

"I admit I've wanted to bounce something off her little golden head ever since we passed through the Loire Valley," Viveca said, then hesitated, listening to her own words echo in her mind. *Little golden head, the golden girl . . . the colonies revolting . . .*" Viveca sat bolt upright in her chair. "Everything Mama Roxelina told me has come true! I must speak to her again!"

Ginny shook her head sadly. The old seer had died early that winter, she said. "She predicted that you would go to the Americas, didn't she?" Ginny asked her daughter.

"I hope not. William is there and I wish to be free of him."

"She said you'd go, nonetheless," Ginny answered, smiling. Then her expression softened. "Has it been that bad for you, my dear?"

"It's been no more than I brought upon myself with my urge for social climbing and wealth. Allegra seems to have done all right, though."

"You could drop that girl into a snake pit and she would emerge unscathed," Yasaman said, shuddering.

"Yes," Ginny answered with a diabolic grin, "she would *talk* the snakes to death!"

PART SIX

Mistress of the Night

"As I was going over the Kilmaganny Mountain,
I met with Colonel Farell and his money he was counting.
I first produced me pistol and then I drew me sabre,
Saying, 'Stand and deliver, for I am a bold deceiver!'
With me ring-a-dum-a-doodle-un-a-dah
Whack-fol-the-daddie, O!
There's whiskey in the jar!"

—"Whiskey in the Jar," late 18th-century Irish Traditional

CHAPTER TWENTY-SEVEN

The coast of England, September 1772

Home. Home at last!

Viveca leaned on the ship's rail, feeling a lump of sentiment tighten in her throat as the chalk cliffs of Dover came into view through the night's approaching fog. Dear old, foggy old, rainy old England! There would be an entire herd of foals awaiting her, born in the spring after she left. Philippe had written to say the other mares had been bred to Herod, Tuberose, and Eclipse, as she wished, his letter many months old by now.

And more important letters were tucked in the bodice of her silk-wool gown: "My love, I have finally received your letters. I will be waiting for you. . . ." Her Byrne, her laughing playmate since early days, her lover, her friend.

"Would you like the ring to be rubies or emeralds or diamonds?" he had written.

Her reply: "Sapphires, and big as chick peas or small as pinheads does not matter. Would you wear a wedding ring from me?"

The answer in his next letter was: "Sapphires. But I want mine big as chick peas, and with a pair of tasteful ear bobs. I've been hanging around Terrence and Lilly's dress shop too long waiting for you to get back!"

She took one of Byrne's letters out now, reread the postscript: "Viveca, as you well know, Kensington is not the safest place for me. Would you consider the Westlands, toward Wales, where there is still good grazing land to be had . . . or even the Americas? If not, tell me. But please consider it—the noose makes a poor cravat for a bridegroom."

"Small boat approaching!" the lookout cried, breaking into her pleasant reverie. A few crew members scurried past at the quartermaster's instructions, calling out to the small boat. There was a commotion toward the stern, then the captain was called. He exchanged words with the people below in the little boat, then turned toward the posh passenger cabin. The quartermaster caught up with him; Viveca overheard the words, "Young Lady Holland," which she was often called to differentiate between her and William's grandmother.

"Over here, Captain," she called out. "What is it?"

They strode toward each other, her steps as long and purposeful as his. "Evening, Ladyship," the man said, nervously touching his hat. "Got a lady in the dinghy down there just cast off from Dover, says she has to see you at once. Claims she's your aunt. Now excuse my saying this, and please recollect that it's uncommon strange to get callers aboard ship so close to home and that I gotter look out for wreckers and pirates trying to get on board, but she don't look like no auntie o' yers."

"I have two aunts, both related by marriage, not blood. One's a big, buxom woman with a country accent. This must be her."

"No, mum, this un's a little thing with a veil, all got up in breeches like a Turk."

"Yasaman!"

"That's what she called herself, Yes-A-Mum, much as I could understand her behind that veil."

But she had left Yasaman in Angora with her mother! How could Yasaman have beaten her back to England—and why would she insist on casting off from Dover instead of waiting for the ship to dock?

"Please," Viveca said, clearing her throat faultily with fear of the worst. "Please, could I borrow your cabin to speak with her? I fear—I fear the news may be very bad, and I would not disturb the others in the passenger cabin."

"Yes, mum, you go right on in, and if you need it, the brandy decanter's in the upper right-hand desk drawer. I'll fetch your little *houri* aunt to you straightaways."

A sailor escorted her to the cabin, saw her in, shut the door on his way out. Viveca considered the brandy, but she had never been a coward, nor needed artificial courage. So she stood and waited until she heard the soft shuffle of heelless slippers outside. She sprang to open the door, only to have it flung open in her face. "Allah be with you, Allah be with you," came the falsetto chant from the veiled and cloaked figure to the crewman who had accompanied her. Then the woman slammed the door, shutting the sailor out.

Allah? But Yasaman was a *Christian!* Old habits died hard; when traveling, Viveca still carried a wrist dagger, much as she had when a street urchin. She drew it now. It never occurred to her to scream for help. She was too curious about this deception —she wanted an answer first.

She dropped into a fighting crouch as the veiled figure whirled to face her. "Jesus *wept,* dearie, will you drop that thing?" came the urgent, deep-throated whisper, as her "aunt" began to unwind her many veils. "I hate sneaking up on you like this, but we held a council of war and agreed a woman might get aboard far more easily than a man, what with all the moonrakers about at night, all those wreckers waiting to prey on so fat a fish as a merchant-passenger vessel. Lilly would have come, but the silly chit broke her ankle last week, and so I said, *'Boys,'* I said, *'do* let me go!'"

The veilings dropped to reveal the handsome, slightly sardonic features of Terrence of Threadneedle. He yanked off his ear bobs and stood there frowning as though aware of how silly he looked in a woman's gauzy wrappings, eye paint, and slippers—and a man's bobbed forelock, braided queue, and hairy chest rising above the costume he was tearing his way out of.

"Strip, darling," he directed curtly as Viveca just stood there staring at him.

"Why, Terrence, I never knew you *cared!"* Viveca answered with a coy coo, then: "Why don't you tell me what's going on first?"

271

"You and I are leaping through that little round window over there and swimming to our boat, which is now waiting somewhere to the left—er—south. Or is it called—"

She lunged across the two yards separating them and grabbed Terrence by the shoulders, shaking him until the rest of his gauzy silks fell away and he stood there in eye paint and knee breeches. "Terrence! For God's bleedin' sake, tell me what's happened!"

He reached up, laid his hands over hers. The absurdly painted eyes were not at all humorous. "In the seven months he's been gone, William has gambled away *everything* the two of you own. The property was all claimed this morning, and the officials are waiting at the docks in Dover, Gravesend, and London to arrest you and throw you into debtor's prison."

She must not scream. This couldn't be happening to her again! Her horses, her house, furniture, her land—*her horses!* Dear God, her racers!

She put both hands over her mouth to prevent any sound from escaping. Terrence hurriedly pushed her so that she sat on the edge of the captain's desk. He gave her a moment to absorb the shock before adding, "I'm sorry, dearie, to have given you the news so roughly, but there's no time to spare, not with the docks only three miles away and the constables waiting with their warrants and such. Can you get your jewels from the passenger cabin?"

"I'm wearing them in a pouch under my skirts," she answered blankly.

"Clever woman! Byrne broke into your house and took the rest of your jewels; he and Philippe are waiting below in the boat. Lil, God bless her, broken ankle and all, has horses waiting on the cliff. Now shed those skirts and let's go!"

Viveca tried to think of an alternative, but there wasn't one. Debtor's prison. The officials wouldn't care that the horses were hers, not William's; it did not matter to them that she'd put years of labor and grief into building the farm up from nothing. She and Terrence would have to swim for it, and that was that.

She urged him to unhook her gown, then, in chemise, with one petticoat drawn up between her legs and tucked into her waist-band for modesty's sake, she threw open the porthole.

"Damn!"

The fog was like split-pea soup. "What if we can't find Byrne and Philippe in this fog?" Terrence wailed. "It's gotten much worse."

"Then we shall swim three miles. After you."

"Oh, no, dearie," he said with a stiff bow from the waist. "Ladies first."

"As you wish, *'Auntie,'* " she said, and stuffed the little man through the porthole.

There came, she thought, some comment about his not being able to swim; she waited for the telltale splash, then followed him down, throwing their clothes as she went. Let the captain wonder! Behind in her cabin remained her trunks of clothes and breeding papers for the five Arab mares in the hold of the ship. Perhaps she could get them back later. But for now . . .

The water closed over her head. It was cold, *too* cold, and dark as ink. Viveca rose, exhaling as she went. She surfaced easily, tossed her head to clear the water from her eyes, and realized that it made no difference.

Because it was the darkest night in the history of the world, and the fog was thicker than an Irishman's wool sweater.

"Terrence? *Terrence!"* she shouted. Almost instantly she was rewarded with a muffled word from nearby that might have been *"glymphh!"*

Viveca struck out in the direction of the sound, found Terrence kicking and swallowing water not fifteen feet away. She dragged him to the surface. "No—no, don't fight, Terrence! Relax, or I can't keep us afloat. *Relax,* I say, or I'll crown you! There, that's better."

She got him to float on his back while she kept him in a kind of headlock, determinedly paddling in place.

"Whistle," the dressmaker said. "That's to be the signal. A repeated whistle—I can't do it myself, not with a mouthful of salt water."

She could feel fear in the tension of his body, for the poor man was rigid with terror. "Something will come nibble my toes," he fretted as she began whistling. "Some leviathan, some gorgon of the depths will rip off my legs . . ."

She began to laugh then, and she couldn't whistle while laughing. "Wait!" he cried out. "Oars!"

"Oh, thank God, I'm getting a cramp in my—"

He struggled then and clamped a hand over her mouth as a faint yellow glow neared. "There's no lantern aboard our boat," Terrence hissed.

Viveca treaded water, watched the lantern nearing. *"Terrence,"* she spoke from between his fingers, "I don't know if it's constables, wreckers, or just local fishermen, but we've got to submerge, to keep from being discovered. Just for a minute, then I'll bring us up behind them. Now draw a deep breath."

An instant before she went under, she saw that the Dover lighthouse no longer winked reassuringly through the fog. Then there was the steady, furtive sound of oarlocks muffled by rags, and she knew—she *knew*—the ship she had just left was in grave danger.

Thank God Allegra was back in Russia by now; thank God she had left no one she loved behind on board ship—*Jesus wept, Lindstrom,* she told herself crossly. *Where would you be had your friends thought of naught but saving their own hides? You've got to get to Byrne's boat, fire warning shots, let the ship know there are wreckers about!*

She inhaled powerfully, sank beneath the bitter-cold waves. The ocean was churning, and not only due to the wreckers' oars. A storm must be coming up.

She had to force Terrence down with all her strength. He fought, for he was still afraid of the water, but she dragged him along. Her strong kicks took them beneath the boat and away.

Viveca was a Georgian and therefore little troubled by conscience; five wreckers in a boat against the lives of all aboard ship was nothing. And Terrence—well, Terrence would just have to excuse her risking him.

She shot up to the surface, rocking the tiny boat above her. She brought Terrence up, let him gulp some air, then slipped an arm over the boat's stern, rocking it violently. The men in the little boat were howling with fear. "Some sea monster has us in its coils!" She tipped, wrestled desperately—and dipped the boat just far enough for the waves to do the rest.

The boat spilled the wreckers into the black sea. It went keel-up; at the same time she heard axes biting into wood nearby, above the screams and curses of the drowning men. So they had companions who were already chopping into the merchant ship to cripple her!

Someone clutched at her ankle. She made sure it wasn't Terrence and began to shove the man away. But wait—he was holding a still-dry musket over his head. . . .

Viveca punched him hard in the jaw. He gave her the gun with no further ado. She cocked it, shouted, *"Wreckers, wreckers!"* in a stentorian voice, and fired the gun. Enough of this now. Let the ship look to itself. She had to rescue Terrence.

Who needed no rescuing at all. When she had put his hands on the side of the boat, he had stayed there. As soon as the boat went keel-up, he climbed aboard and now perched, straddling the keel, kicking away anyone who came near.

"Having a good time?" she asked.

"I should say so. I think I drowned some bloke who was about to shoot you."

"Terrence!" she exclaimed admiringly. Would he never cease amazing her? What a friend to have! "How did you do it?"

"I stood on him until he quit kicking," he replied, then, "I shall have to rush straight to the confessional when we get home, I feel so naughty!"

There seemed to be some air left under the boat, so it would stay afloat a while longer. Viveca leaned on it, pointed it toward what she thought must be shore, and began kicking with the tide.

But the temperature of the water was worsening—getting cripplingly cold—and this was only September. At least it wasn't January, or they'd both be dead. "You're remarkably chipper for a woman with no home left," Terrence said, and she saw that he, too, had rescued a gun.

"I-I'll w-worry later. For n-now we've got to reach sh-shore," she answered wearily, teeth chattering.

The boat was sinking. "Hang on to it as l-long as possible, Terrence, shore can't-t-t be much farther."

There was a huge *whoosh*ing sound just then. The black-and-woolen night about them was suddenly alight with orange heat.

The wreckers had successfully driven the ship onto rocks and set fire to her!

The upended rowboat scraped sand. Terrence slid off, began dragging Viveca ashore. They knelt, retching from cold and exertion, in the sand. Viveca turned her head toward the fire, saw a fight going on. One of the men involved was tall and black-haired and familiar. "Terrence. I think they're trying to rob Byrne," she whispered as thunder rolled far above. "They're choking him!"

They blinked back salt water and peered at the inferno. "Why, so they are," Terrence said coolly. And, drawing a bead on the wrecker who held a knife at Byrne's throat, he shot the man through the back of the head. He then coolly blew the smoke away from the barrel. Meanwhile Byrne had taken on someone else, gained a gun—Viveca recognized the ship's captain at his elbow, fighting on his side. Trunks were being unloaded from the ship, livestock driven ashore in a wild stampede.

"Where'd you learn to shoot like that?" Viveca demanded of Terrence.

"I come from a starving family with fifteen brats. Before I made dresses I was the best bloody poacher in Yorkshire. Let's go."

She still had her wrist dagger, so she drew it. They staggered toward the fire, saw that the battle between wreckers and ship's crew was evenly pitched.

Above the screams and flames came a war whoop such as small boys and Indians made. Down from the cliffs rode Lilly, driving their horses before her. Led by Tuberose, who would run as long as he thought there was a race, they smashed through the outer ring of wreckers. Unfortunately Lilly was also leading the constables down on them. And it had begun to rain, half-extinguishing the fire.

In a moment the tide of battle had turned against the wreckers. Viveca struggled through the thrashing crowd to Byrne's side, tugged at his sleeve. He whirled, caught her up in his arms with a look of rapture and surprise. "Wreckers caught us—are you safe? You're safe! I've got your ring."

"I've got yours, too."

They chorused, "Sapphires big as chick peas!"

He found his coat lying on the sand, bundled her up in it. They found Philippe, then Terrence, and began edging their way through the swordplay and gunfire to Lilly and the horses. "Horses." Viveca exclaimed suddenly. "I have five mares in the hold of the ship. I have to have those mares, they're all that's left me now. Tuberose! How did you—"

"I had your Aunt Caro sign some papers, and Edward forged the rest so it would appear you legally sold Tuberose and Matchless to Caro—that way they couldn't be claimed when your estate and farm were taken," Byrne explained.

"You must have worked quickly," Viveca said as they reached Lilly and the horses, and she caught at Tuberose's reins.

"I had to. Your entire life's work was at stake. You and Lil wait up here, I'll find the mares and drive them up toward you. I'm safe, after all; this time they're looking for Lady Holland, not the St. James lads. Up with you!"

He boosted her easily into the saddle, took three horses, and vanished into the crowd with Philippe and Terrence. William never would have been such a help. William hadn't half the guts to dive straight into trouble like this. "Lilly!" Viveca cried out, leaning out of her saddle to take her friend's hand. "Thank you. You were clever to drive the horses down into the fight."

"Thank goodness you're safe. I could see some of what happened from the cliff above the fog. Oh, here comes Terrence. Uh-oh, the constables are on his tail; they must think he's a wrecker."

She drew a long pistol and coolly shot off the lead pursuer's hat.

A moment later Byrne threw open the door to the ship's hold. The mares came lunging and smashing their way out through the wreckage. There were only four; Viveca wondered why, until she realized the rear of the hold was still deep in the water. One mare must have drowned when the wreckers chopped the belly of the ship open.

It was a mad scene, lit by the burning ship, which sputtered in the rain. Constables gained control of the battle and began shackling their prisoners in the fog while sheep and cattle ran about, bleating and lowing. Casks of wine broke open, spilling their red grapes' blood onto the white sand. Smoke billowed; the fog whitened and broke up, but still the two waiting women could see nothing.

Then Terrence burst through the last of the fog and a wall of smoke, wild-eyed. "For pity's sake, ride, *ride!* Everything aboard ship on four legs is following your mares!"

They were right behind him. A slim gray mare burst through the fog and shot in between Tuberose and Lilly's mare.

Tuberose, thinking it a race, was after her in an instant. So was Byrne's Blackberry. Not to mention a bull, several sheep, three cows, and the rest of the Eastern mares.

The dappled gray could run. And *did*. With her head start, she showed a clean set of heels to Tuberose and downright disgraced the noble-hearted Blackberry.

Tuberose at last drew abreast of her. Viveca hauled him to a hard right so that his shoulder hit the mare once, twice, four times, making her turn away from the dangerous cliffs.

He jostled the mare again—the whipping gray mane was only a foot away. Viveca seized mane and a lead shank flying from the mare's halter, and, recalling her teenager stunts, vaulted from Tuberose's back to that of the mare.

After that, the race was easier to control—the race but not Tuberose, who had some romantic ideas about how to behave himself now that he was riderless. A few ungentle kicks from the mare seemed to change his mind. He ran abreast of her awhile, then pulled in front and disappeared over the next hill as if fired from a cannon.

Byrne at last managed to draw near Viveca. "Whistle that damfool stud in, will you? He'll head for home, but Kensington's too dangerous. I have a house for us near Bromley, we'll head there—at a slower pace, if you don't mind; we're all staggering back here."

An hour after Viveca had thawed out with a hot bath in front of the fireplace, half an hour after she and Byrne had passionately bedded down, some stragglers showed up at the house: three cows and the bull from the ship, lowing hungrily at the front gate!

CHAPTER TWENTY-EIGHT

*The Highway near Bromley, England,
December 1772*

"Stand and deliver!"

The coachman obediently reined in the glossy chestnut German Coachers. They protested, in particular the horse on the right, who crow-hopped a few steps farther, making the timid driver fumble the reins.

In that instant the horse on the right seized the bit between his teeth and took off at a gallop.

Screams came from the lady and her daughter inside the carriage. A deep male voice off to the left boomed, "Damn fool! He's lost control of the horses!"

The second highwayman was laughing in curiously high-pitched tones, rather feminine-sounding, really, the driver thought. Then the two riders came into view, one lean black stallion on either side of the carriage.

The bits in their teeth, each German Coacher tried to go in an opposite direction. The horse on the right, ever perverse, tripped up his yoke-mate, began dragging him along on three legs. Beyond all control, the chestnuts fumbled onward, carriage rocking precariously.

Thundering hooves closed in on them, a dark figure on a darker horse drawing abreast of the chestnuts. The smaller of the two highwaymen vaulted off his mount's back onto the driver's box and, shoving the driver to one side, began gathering in the reins. The other rider reached out, caught the chestnut on the right's bit, tried to turn him. When that didn't work, he struggled from his saddle to the back of the German Coacher.

Between them, the highwaymen turned the twin geldings from their headlong course. "Ho, up there, ho, lads!" cried out the high-voiced one standing up in the box and mightily drawing back on the reins.

The highwayman on the German Coacher caught at the horses' bits, secured them in place. Meek enough now, the two horses allowed themselves to be steered off the road.

Both highwaymen leaped to the ground nimbly, the one in the box bringing the driver down, too. "Oops, there, old lad, didn't mean to knock you down."

"He deserves it," barked the tall, dark horseman. "Worst damned driver I've ever seen. Those women inside might have been killed! Ought to have his hands glued together so he can never hold reins again."

"Not my fault; only been driving these fearsome beasts for a week, since the driver shot himself in the foot during a duel," the coachman whimpered.

"*Jives!*" announced the smaller of the two highwaymen in joyful tones of recognition.

Female! Jives blinked as the rider doubled over a moment, helpless with laughter. "Yes, mum? Do I know you?"

"I tried to rob you years ago. I was wearing a striped dress that had been made for your young mistress—"

"Oh, dear," Jives genteelly mourned. "I seem to recall. Disastrous evening. Smashed crockery. No good *ever* comes of stealing dresses."

Viveca patted him on the back sympathetically. "There, there, Jives, this is my last run, and then I'm leaving the country for good. Now do yourself a favor. When we let you go tonight, you get yourself straight to the smithy and ask for a double-snaffle bit so that right lead horse quits getting a jump on you. And, be good enough to stand at his head so he doesn't try to take off again and kill the lot of us."

Byrne went around to the carriage door and opened it. "Ladies," he said, doffing his hat, "if you would be so good as to step outside a moment—"

The point of a parasol caught him in the breastbone. Byrne reached up, snapping the offending instrument in two with a flick of his sinewy wrist. He yanked out its wielder, a middle-aged pouter pigeon, so quickly that she quite cooed with excitement. In fact, she was leaning against his chest now, panting from his proximity (and too-tight stays, he suspected). Her eyelashes were fluttering fast enough to whip up a storm of rice powder along her humpbacked nose. He unhanded her with distaste—this painted, powdered, creature, reeking of weeks of heavy perfuming meant to cover up a dearth of winter baths.

Just then an eager voice called out from the carriage, and another, younger woman emerged. Viveca, grinning, covered the proceedings with pistols uncocked.

"Oh, merciful heavens, it's the St. James boys, with their wicked dark eyes. I believe I shall swoon," the young woman exclaimed.

"Swoon away, only first hand over that diamond bracelet you're wearing," Byrne ordered, unamused.

"Oh, for you, Black Eyes, anything," she answered, eagerly working the clasp. "What did you say to Jives to cow him so badly? And why doesn't your brother speak?"

"Because his 'brother' is actually his mistress," Viveca informed her with a dry smile.

"Oh, is it you, then?" the young woman asked quickly. "The famous one? They say you're Lady Holland the Younger. Is that true?"

Byrne caught Viveca's eye, and they both laughed. A lot of good their masks had done!

Then the older woman began to go on about what an honor this was, and wait, she would get her bag out of the coach. . . .

Both women were wearing velvet coats lined with ermine— coats that made Viveca's mouth water in remembrance. Byrne reached over, gave her shoulders a slight squeeze. "We'll get you some new clothes before we leave England—something besides my little brother's discarded jackboots and breeches for you."

"Better get me a divorce from William first."

"Perhaps I'll just walk across the ocean and bash his damfool head on something harder than *it*—say, a tub of butter!"

America. She and Byrne were about to leave for America. Brother Bertt St. James had scouted them some land, and soon, very soon . . .

"Ladies, your jewelry?" Byrne called out again, louder this time.

The diamond bracelet came flying from the younger woman. Then, from her mother in the carriage, there followed a shower of earrings, brooches, rings.

"I've robbed them before. Aspiring tennis players," Viveca observed. "Where's the loot bag?"

Byrne groped his pockets angrily. "It's gone. Bartholomew was looking for something to put his tarot cards in; you don't suppose—"

"*Damn!*" they chorused. In a moment Byrne was scrambling about on all fours in the snow, picking up a jewel here, a gem there.

"I hear hooves," Viveca said suddenly, uneasily.

"There's still a diamond necklace somewhere in the snow—a big one," Byrne grumbled, searching.

"Byrne, these aren't mere passersby. I hear *swords* clinking— *cavalry* swords!"

He was up in an instant with the necklace. They whistled in tandem for their horses. "The jewels . . ." Viveca sputtered.

Byrne caught Tuberose's, then, Blackberry's, reins. "I haven't pockets enough to hold them," he said.

Her waistcoat was buttoned tight, and she wore a silk chemise beneath her rough woolen shirt. "Quick, Byrne, down the front of my chemise!"

"Isn't it crowded enough down there already?" he groused, but obeyed.

"Mayhaps more crowded than you know," she dared say.

Their eyes met. "What the hell do you mean?"

"Mount up!" she bellowed, giving him a shove.

He handed her up into her saddle. *As if I need help,* she thought, pleased but irritated with his chivalry at such a time.

"Good-bye, Jives," she called out cheerfully, about to dig her heels into Tuberose's flanks. But Byrne was having trouble with Blackberry, who was dancing sideways at the sound of approaching gunfire. "Byrne, he's gone gun-shy since that wound last fall. I told you to take one of my racers. . . ."

Byrne struggled atop Blackberry and spurred him on.

Snow was beginning to fall once more as they jumped a fence into a fallow field. Tuberose at once broke through the snow's crust into a belly-deep drift and floundered awkwardly. Byrne circled back, caught at the stallion's bridle, and tugged. "Come on, you inbred knothead! Move it!"

But Tuberose was bred for speed, not cunning, and he panicked in the deep drifts. He began to buck uselessly, stupidly. *Damn, damn!* Viveca swore to herself as bullets splintered the nearest fence post. Pistols were spitting yellow-and-blue flame in the weird half-light of night snow. She would have to leave him— leave her darling, her fastest racer, her prize stud.

Byrne had the same thought at the same time. He caught her around the waist, heaved. She sprang lightly to his saddle.

Just as he had done the night he kidnapped her, Byrne put her in front so that any bullets would hit him, not her. Tears, sentimental, irrational tears filled her eyes. And at such a time! What an emotional state she was in, Viveca thought as Blackberry lunged off through the snowfall. She was overwrought because there was a chance she was pregnant at last, and it was stupid of her to have come out tonight on this caper. But she hadn't been certain about it. Still wasn't, in fact.

And, as long as William refused a divorce, her child, hers and Byrne's, would be a bastard. If it lived. If she didn't miscarry. God in heaven, what would a night like this do to her chances? She'd never risk a baby knowingly. Not after waiting all these years for one. And Byrne's baby, especially!

They fled through the speckled night. Blackberry was heavier-boned than Tuberose, and better suited for such rough ground. A cart horse had gotten him on dainty, long-legged Black Rose; he

284

had more native cunning than poor Tuberose and knew this part of the country.

A bullet whined off her elbow, making Viveca cry out. "Hold on," Byrne's voice came at her ear. "Not much farther, we'll lose them at the river!"

The pain was a wasplike buzzing in the back of her brain, not a hot, red haze of dangerous bleeding and agony. Viveca ground her teeth and nodded. He meant they'd turn off into the woods at the bridge, let the thick, bare trees swallow them up. But the troop had split in two; someone was shouting, "Don't let them reach the bridge!" Many riders were pushing in from the north, and the bridge was that way.

"They're damnably well mounted," Viveca observed, teeth still tightly together.

"Blackberry's no Eclipse, but neither is he a plow nag; we'll make it. Is the river frozen hard enough, do you think?"

Her heart lurched. The river was probably all right for ponies and people on foot, but to gallop on it on an overloaded horse?

What chance did they have otherwise? She would rather drop through the ice and drown than go back to prison. A bullet in the back, the icy clutch of the river—anything but the pillar at Newgate, chained so she could neither sit nor stand.

The child, she thought suddenly. *I could plead my belly if I lived to see prison.*

They would string Byrne up the first week, though. And not even for a maybe-mythical child would she ever again leave Byrne. Not after all it had cost to find him. Never. No, never!

They dropped low on the stallion's neck, presenting as small a target as possible. Like limbs on one rider, they coaxed Blackberry with hands and feet, crooned to him with voices joined.

She cursed Tuberose's spun-glass nerves. To make one horse carry two of them at a dead gallop . . .

A dully gleaming surface lay ahead. The snow was thicker now, fast becoming a blizzard. "If the ice doesn't hold—" she began.

"We can't go around. I saw half a dozen of them veer off to guard the bridge. And the turnpikes are only a mile on either side of us. We can't surrender, V'ica. They must have orders to shoot us on sight."

Yes. There would be no quarter. "Throw off your coat and boots just in case," Byrne attempted, but could not say more.

He meant in case they went through the ice. Viveca felt him ripping at her greatcoat. Both of them popped buttons, tore at the garment until it sailed away, flapping like a vast bird of prey. She clutched at the ankle of a heavy boot, kicked it away, then the other boot. An icy dagger seemed to pierce her heart. Jesus wept! They weren't going to make it this time!

Frosty night air chilled her stockinged feet. She hoped Byrne could swim better than Terrence. He had been so busy helping her disrobe that he hadn't time to shrug off his own coat.

The black stallion swooped over the embankment, slowing as Byrne eased back on the reins.

Then they were on the ice.

There was silence now. As if the soldiers had stopped firing out of sheer astonishment at their bravado.

The snow piled atop the ice helped Blackberry find his footing at first. Then he hit a bare patch and began skittering. Byrne had ridden him on ice once before, but did Blackberry remember?

He did. After a panicky moment the stallion's nerve returned. He was off and running.

Behind them the cavalry troop hit the ice and went skidding in every direction.

Blackberry was flying now, barely skimming the ice with the grace of a debutante on a ballroom floor. Long, clean limbs flashed, iron-shod hooves descended, sure and steady. On the ice all bulk was gone, coarse blood forgotten. On the ice he was Pegasus, he was Eclipse or Tuberose, a blue-blooded racer.

Behind them came the sharp report of gunfire. They were shooting into the ice, damn them! Trying to start cracks in the ice!

The troop succeeded. There came a report like bronze cannon: deafening, echoing. A thudding, thunderous sound. Viveca glanced back to see the ice breaking open behind them.

Two soldiers, unable to stop, rode straight into it. There followed the agonized screams of man and animal dropped into burning-cold water.

The vast black rift was speeding toward them. Byrne looked back, too. He had never used his spurs to more than tickle a horse's ribs, but now he used them roughly, in desperation. The bank was so close—dear mother of God, only twenty feet! He took another horrified glance backward at the canyon of black water so near their heels.

The bank was close but the rift was closer.

In the split seconds before the rift reached the stallion, Byrne seized Viveca. He hefted her from the saddle, threw her ahead of them, screaming, *"Run!"* She might at least reach shallower water before the rift caught her.

Viveca hit solid ice at the embankment. She went sprawling, skinning elbows and knees on sharp ice shards.

The horsemen still pursued them but slower now, picking their way cautiously along the broken edges. Their pistol muzzles glinted in light reflected from the snow.

A cool, calculating head saved Viveca. At first she thought it was wrong of her to be safe, that she would rather die with Byrne. Then her old fighting spirit returned. No one need die, not if she kept her powder dry. She would protect Byrne if he could but swim to shore. . . .

All these thoughts entered her mind and were put into action in fractions of a second. She was already loading both guns as she rolled and came up on one knee on the frozen river's brink.

Blackberry was half out of the water, forelegs scrambling to hook onto an ice floe still supporting them. Then a spray of scarlet erupted at the rear of his head as a bullet hit him. Blackberry jerked, arched upward like a sinking ship.

Byrne tried to throw himself free as the black water rushed up at him, but he caught a spur in the stirrup. So he cast his bulky coat off and freed himself of one boot and the treacherous spur.

With drawing-room aplomb, he walked up the sinking stallion's neck and cast himself onto the nearest ice floe.

Then he slipped. The floe shattered into a dozen smaller pieces.

He was in the pitiless dark water now. Troopers were firing at the head bobbing in the black rift.

Viveca drew a bead on the man shouting the orders. Always easy to pick the commander in his red coat. Kill the leader and the others would weaken.

With no more pity than she would have shown a mad dog, she shot the man trying to kill her Byrne. Her own coldness and efficiency did not startle her, for she had always been fierce in protection of her loved ones. It was a feeling Ginny had instilled in her, whether through blood or environment, at an early age.

Their lieutenant down, the men temporarily milled in confusion.

Viveca shoved a pistol into her waistband, reloaded, gripped the other gun in her teeth after roaring, "Byrne, hold on, *hold on!*" Her words cracked like shots in the crisp night air.

She scarcely felt the chill. Byrne's life was at stake; nothing else mattered. Her hand flew, unthinking, to the long muffler Caro had knit for her at Christmas, the muffler flung about her neck several times in an effort to take up its eight-foot length.

Viveca instantly yanked it off. She tied one gun into it, unloading it first. There. Now it would be heavy enough for Byrne to catch hold of. Unweighted, the scarf might float uselessly above the water. Scooting along, snakelike on her stomach, she reached a sturdy edge of ice.

Byrne went under again before her eyes. He could not free himself of the second thigh-high boot, which, full of water, pulled him down, down . . .

He sank to the bottom, brushed against something. Capsized fishing boat? Tree stump? Perhaps there were dead men down here, greedy for company.

Something caught at his arms. Branches? Hands? He was panting with fear and exertion, losing precious air and flailing like a maniac at Bedlam. *Boot.* Free himself of the boot.

Then he felt metal and saddle leather slide along his cheek. It was only poor Blackberry's corpse.

And there was a knife sheath on the saddle.

Byrne wrestled the ungainly weight of the dead horse. Air. *No air.* No time. With white-hot pain piercing his overextended lungs, he dug frantically at the saddle blanket, fingers skidding on leather. Sheath. *Knife.* He found the weapon, drew it, slashed down the side of his thigh-high jackboot.

Water gushed from it. He felt buoyed up. Still, there was such pain. Give up and die.

But Viveca was up there. Up above the ice!

Byrne pushed off from the horse's corpse; they rose together, as they had so often in life. He clung to the floating mane, broke surface in a churning maelstrom of water.

He had air now, but it was cold enough to kill him in minutes. Uncontrollable shivering wracked him.

"Byrne, *catch!*"

Fractured white air, flakes big as a fist. He thrust his hand out, body seeming to make the connection before his mind did. Something hit the water at his elbow. Without thinking he reached for it, caught hold. Something scratchy with a lump in it. Eyelids frozen shut, he explored with his fingers. A gun tied in a knitted scarf. God love her! Sharp as broken glass, that woman, and a fighter to the end. They hadn't caught her. No one could defeat her.

He clung to his lifeline with one hand, using the other to break the crust on his eyelids as she towed him ashore.

Thank goodness she wasn't one of those helpless society women. Praise God for creating a fiery, strong, voluptuous woman named Viveca Lindstrom, a woman who could single-handedly break a three-quarter-ton colt or control a runaway carriage team. A woman strong enough to pull an utterly useless man, crippled by wet cold, to safety.

He began trying to swim, knowing that if he did not move he would freeze and die. But his arms and legs were clumsy as logs. The ice was breaking at the edges as he reached it, smashing through. Not even a woman of Viveca's strength could reel in a more-than-six-foot man like himself, and him soaking wet.

Her hat had come loose in the struggle. He could see the pale peach flame of her hair whipping in the blizzard, and it gave him heart again. As through a film of cotton and wool, he saw a scarlet coat behind her. Byrne pointed, shouted, *"Rear!"*

She threw herself on her back and rolled. Her pistol muzzle spat fire as she neatly took the man between the eyes. There was gore; Byrne's eyelashes were freezing again, so he mercifully missed most of it.

Galloping. And Viveca was kneeling, hands to mouth, whistling crazily. Good, strong, earsplitting blasts. On a snowy night like this the sound seemed to carry for miles. Byrne thought, as hoofbeats neared, *She used to whistle like that for—*

A jet-black figure flashed over his head in the mightiest leap imaginable. For a moment Byrne thought it was Blackberry. Christ, he was a dead man, then, to be seeing a dead horse! No living animal could have made that jump!

Then the stallion landed in a precise placement of expensively shod hooves—those neat, tiny hooves that kept him from being a decent mud runner, for mudders needed big hooves, like snowshoes.

Tuberose was up in an instant from his crouch. And Viveca had waded into the water. Byrne half-swam, half-stumbled toward her. She had him under the arms now. "Tuberose, here, you idiot! You beautiful, brainless, running machine! Oh, you beauty, you beauty—hang on to his neck, Byrne, let him thaw you while I take this trooper's coat."

"You angel," he managed, teeth chattering.

Then she was taking his arms, shoving them into the trooper's coat as though he were some helpless child who could not dress himself because he found he *couldn't.* Together they found the strength to get him aboard the horse, with Viveca swinging up behind, protecting his back. "Home, Tuberose! Gee up, laddy! *Home!*" And for once the stallion had sense enough to take them toward Bromley without a moment's hesitation.

They had a house waiting there, full of St. James boys and their mistresses or wives, a noisy, cheerful household where people came and went at all hours. Surely someone would be there to help them.

Sometimes even Dash showed up—dissipated, drunken Dash,

a bloated specter of his former self. He was a mockery now of the rapier-slim youth whose panache and dash had given him his nickname.

No time for mourning Dash's lost youth; here was Bromley now, identifiable only from the familiar feel of brick streets under the horse they rode. Soon Viveca was leaning from the saddle to pound at the stable door.

Young Dickon sprang down from his nest in the loft where he'd been awaiting them. She saw the horror on his face as he unbolted the door. "Jesus, Viv, what happened? Byrne's a regular snowman!"

"He's froze half-dead. Kick Skiff out of bed if he's here."

"He is, and Luke and Luke's missus, too. I'll have 'em heat water for a bath; let's carry him on up. Your nag's wet as hell, too; we'll get someone to rub him down."

Here came Bartholomew in his nightshirt, rubbing his eyes and smelling of tobacco. "Viv—*Byrne!*"

The brothers took him from Viveca, laid him on the kitchen table. They stripped him, rubbed him down with rough towels while Liza, Luke's farm girl wife, did the same for the shivering Tuberose downstairs.

They fired up all three fireplaces to heat water. Then they sat Byrne in the hip bath, Viveca directing them to start with luke-warm water and only gradually get it hotter, for she was afraid hot water straight off would burn him. He was probably frostbitten, after all, and couldn't feel everything; they might scorch his toes off before he felt enough to yelp. While they labored over him, she told of their adventure. Luke, shaking his head, bandaged her nicked elbow.

Byrne was now awake enough to drink the warm brandy Viveca gave him, and alert enough to smile as she chafed his hands and arms. But that was his only response for more than an hour while they sat around him in front of a blazing fireplace, scooping out the cold water and replacing it with hotter and hotter liquid in the hip bath. Poor Skiff, the youngest, was in tears, and Luke half-paced a path on the floorboards.

His buxom wife, Liza, came back upstairs. "Tuberose be fine now, rubbed down and blanketed. Byrne?"

"Is—" her husband began, but the patient himself interrupted to announce clearly: "Tricks."

Everyone jerked toward him. *"What?"*

"Tricks," Byrne repeated, opening bleary brown eyes. "I'll never again make fun of Viveca teaching her goddamned horses tricks. We're only alive now because she taught that jug-headed, addlepated, basket-brain of a stud to come running when she whistled and—*where are my clothes?"*

Viveca vaulted out of her chair and threw her arms around his neck, kneeling in a puddle of water to do so. The others, laughing with relief, filed out of the room and shut the door behind them.

"You saved my life," Byrne said solemnly as she helped him climb out of the tub.

"Only for purely selfish reasons."

She took a blanket off the hearthstone where it had been warming and draped it about him, toga-style. "How's that?" Byrne asked.

"I didn't think our child should be fatherless."

He dropped the cup of broth she'd just handed him. Quick as a wink, Viveca caught it, scalding two fingers in the process. Byrne didn't notice. *"Are* you, do you think?" he asked.

"I'm not certain, but there's a good chance. If I was sure, I wouldn't have ridden out tonight, now, would I?"

"Well, there'll be no more riding out, then. These few jobs we've pulled this last six months have ensured our buying the land we want in America; there's no need to linger here any longer. Especially not if there's a baby. The child can't have gibbet birds for parents now, can she? He? It? They?" Laughing, she went into his arms. "We'll build you a real house," Byrne said, "not like this shabby old dump."

"Oh, now, it's clean enough, and Liza's a mean cook. I'm not sure I'll enjoy giving that up."

"We'll get you servants for the housekeeping and cooking, for I've more money than you think. It's tucked away earning us a pretty percentage . . . they'll be looking for us, you know. We'd

292

better get away as soon as possible. This week, even. I don't want my brothers arrested in my place, as all of us look alike. They're always arresting one St. James for another's crime. And we'd best speak to your damned husband in person. Mayhaps he'll grant you that divorce so our child isn't branded 'bastard' like my brothers and me."

He was slowly kissing her face and hair. Viveca parted her lips beneath his, drank in hot, brandied kisses. A new home, a new life together in America. No more stealing, a child, perhaps, a son or daughter with her blue eyes and Byrne's ebony hair. "Yes, Byrne, yes," she whispered. "Let's leave this place, build a new home."

"I'll plant your bloody tuberoses all around the walks. . . ."

"We'll put in walkways?"

"Herringbone brick paths in your garden, and brick stables for your brainless stud and his mares . . ."

They sank to their knees, kissing and caressing. There was a sudden jingle, then something clunked to the floor and went rolling. "What the—" Byrne demanded.

"I forgot the loot I stuffed down my shirt. Let me get it."

The jewels fell around them in a blaze of color and sparkle. "Look at you," Byrne said passionately. "You're better now that you're twenty-seven; you're firmer and yet curved where a woman should curve, muscle and silky flesh and something in your eyes of the knowledge and experience you lacked at eighteen. I love you, Viveca. You've been my mate of mates since I first found you in that wrecked buggy."

"And you're my match, my man, my partner in all schemes."

"Ahh, but I'll change when we're married. I'll lay down rules."

"Such as?" she whispered, kissing his muscular throat.

"Such as . . . I'll only let you have daughters. Sons would just turn out rapscallions like my brothers and me."

He was licking the place where her shoulder met her neck; he was touching his tongue to all those familiar places. They were both tired; she knew this would not be their most graceful lovemaking. And yet the very simpleness and directness of it was perfect.

Her body came alive beneath his skillful ministrations. She felt her nipples stiffen against her woolen shirt as his hands cupped her breasts, stroking, unfastening buttons and laces. Fingertips stroked fire-lit skin, making nerve endings tingle with expectation. She was aware of the heat and moisture of herself in his embrace, the vulnerability as he peeled her clothes away to find her most sensitive parts.

Viveca caught him, turned him around that she might reach him, too. He gasped as he saw her elbow wound, but she shook her head to signify that it was unimportant and pushed him down. Byrne protested, but she drew him into her mouth with long, slow strokes. His hands were on her, fingers and tongue teasing, arousing her fires.

She knelt over him, guided him into her. Byrne thrust in solidly, gripping her hips, then unexpectedly sat up. He drew her long legs about his hips, moved her slowly, rhythmically. They kissed repeatedly, Viveca's pleasure heightened by his tongue on hers. Then the sensations began their ascent.

He kept their movements slow, deliberate, unhurried. Tingles began building in her thighs, her stomach. Tightening circles of ecstasy moved closer, closed in on her.

He was thrusting faster now, faster but not too fast. . . .

Viveca never knew which of them broke first. She only knew that there was heat and joy, an ultimate explosion of passion before they tumbled down into blankets and each other's arms. Byrne continued touching her, making more explosions in her body. Through a haze of desire she heard a distant door open, heard a drunken voice downstairs raised in song.

More explosions, deep inside. Christ, she could die of such bliss, such unending rivulets of desire, increasing, increasing like gunfire. . . .

Gunfire. She sat up. "Byrne!"

"I hear it. Get dressed!"

They scrambled for clothes, leaping into breeches, hauling at buttons, at sleeves.

"D'ye think it's the troopers?" Viveca cried out, seizing his arm.

"Could be, love, could be. Gather up the jewels, we might need them. And fetch your cash bag from upstairs."

"I don't have it. I turned everything over to Great Edward for investment last week."

They found boots and shoes, went groping in dark corners for weapons.

Skiff burst into the room. "It's the troopers! They have the house surrounded!"

"Then we'll escape through the tunnel," Viveca said at once.

"No, *you'll* escape while I hold their fire," Byrne snapped obstinately.

"I won't leave you again. Why shouldn't I fight it out at your side?" Viveca demanded, lifting her chin.

"Because nobody's fighting *anything* out. I shall stay up here and keep them busy while the rest of you flee out the tunnel. Then, when I'm sure you're out, I'll follow, post-haste."

"I won't leave you again. I've paid too much for us to give you up. There's no need for me to run while you stay."

"There's no need for me to be first out the tunnel. *I'm* not the one who's probably pregnant," Byrne said grimly, then smiled. "I love you, Viveca. I'll only be five minutes behind you, my lady of the tuberoses. Catch her, Skiff."

"Why?" the boy asked, bewildered.

"Because of *this,*" Byrne said. And, lunging forward, he punched Viveca in the jaw.

She came to in a tight, smoky place, upside down, coughing. She tried to fight, but a friendly voice at her ear said, "Here now. Don't go pounding on Sir Galahad when he's about rescuing you."

"Put me down, Luke St. James."

"I'll shoot him if he does," answered Luke's plucky Liza. "You'd be back up that tunnel into the house in a second. Now, don't you fret, Viveca. We've got the night's haul in jewels and your breeding papers on the horses—and Tuberose, too, and Matchless. We'll go to your Aunt Caro's, she'll take us in."

Viveca heard a whinny behind her: Tuberose, blindfolded, being led by Skiff, and Matchless by the capable Bartholomew.

Luke gingerly set her down. "You can't go back. They've set the house afire. Dickon got out through the bushes, I think."

"Byrne?" she asked, eyes stinging, throat full of acrid heat as Luke and his wife shoved her on down the tunnel.

"We think he's behind us, but we're not certain."

"But if the house collapses on the tunnel and caves it in—if he's caught—if he's still in the house he'll burn or they'll shoot him."

She tried to fight her way past them, but the tunnel was too small, too tight, not much more than a man wide and a woman tall. She was turned back by Skiff and the hot lick of saffron flames.

"My God, if he's in there he's dead," she burst out.

"But you're not, and neither's that baby you're carrying. Now hurry or you'll be the death of all o' us," Liza cried out, tugging Viveca along with her.

There was a rush of heat and wetness on Viveca's lips as her nose began to bleed from the terrific heat. Her clothes, plastered to her, were being scorched dry by the flames.

They were running now. Timbers broke behind them in the inferno. Earth poured into the tunnel, dirt and fire pursuing them. The dirt would kill the fire if the flames did not reach them first.

Tuberose, blindfolded, was no longer shrieking in terror. He ran soundlessly now, hot breath panting down the nape of Viveca's neck.

A blast of snow-cold air pierced the tunnel's thick gloom. There were scarlet and golden flames, and then, as they kicked the trapdoor open and burst out into the night, the last of the tunnel collapsed. Frozen earth smothered the blaze pursuing them.

Skiff barely made it, and Tuberose trampled him in the process. Viveca seized Skiff, helped him up. "Are you all right? He ran you down—"

"I'll—I'll be all right."

Bartholomew, the last one out, murmured that Matchless had been killed by the tunnel collapsing.

No one dared speak of their loss. Viveca stared out, unseeing, at the same river that had nearly killed her earlier. She wished it had. Wished with all her heart that she had died in Byrne's arms, hadn't deserted him, fled through the scorched night like a fox from the hounds—a wounded, possibly pregnant vixen.

"Get her on the horse," ordered the prosaic Liza. "I'll ride with her and control Tuberose. To Kensington, lads. A bit of a walk ahead, but if we move brisk-like we shan't freeze."

"Bless you," Viveca told her hoarsely. "Bless all of you. But you should have left me."

"He was ours as much as yours," Luke said stiffly. "We won't desert you; we're all family now, and you'll never be alone as long as there's a St. James to draw breath. Come on, lads!"

And so they rode on into the night.

CHAPTER TWENTY-NINE

Viveca looked up slowly as Caro Lindstrom entered the bedroom. "Byrne's dead, isn't he?" she asked her aunt in a flat, hoarse voice.

"I'm afraid so, pet. The news sheets are full of how the famous highwayman was caught trying to escape the burning house."

"Did they—did they shoot him?" she asked.

"No, it was . . . the rope, Viveca."

She lifted her chin. "He would have been brave, then. I know my Byrne."

"They say he laughed and saluted his captors."

"Better the noose than fire, he always said. He said hanging wasn't so bad if they did it proper; he saw them hang Benjamin, and he said Ben didn't suffer. He wasn't afraid to die, Caro, I know he wasn't."

"Save that it meant losing you," her aunt answered gently, seating herself at the foot of the bed Viveca lay in.

Viveca sat slowly, stiff, aching, feeling the thick bandage around her elbow. "What did the doctor say?"

"That the arm mustn't be used for most of a month."

"All right," she responded flatly, almost lifelessly.

"He also said that you're pregnant. Just barely. Now you have something to live for, Viveca, if you haven't strength enough to live for yourself. Byrne's son or daughter will be needing you—and so will the damned fool St. James lads, milling about like chickens with their heads cut off. Thank goodness Luke married that Liza, or they'd be useless. Viveca, look at me, lass."

She looked up into the unlined, saintlike face of her dear aunt. "They will come here soon, Viveca, looking for you and the lads.

298

They'll ask around and sooner or later someone will remember that the St. Jameses used to come to the Black Bull. You have to go, and go fast, so I can hide any traces of your visit."

"Have we put you in danger?" Viveca asked swiftly.

"Yes," Caro answered frankly. "I have passage for six booked on a ship heading for the Americas in two hours. You've time to bathe and dress—and I thought we'd break out the dye and give your hair a quick coating of walnut-shell stain so you're a nice, unobtrusive brunette for the next few weeks, till washing fades it all out."

"As you think best, Caro," Viveca answered automatically.

"I do," her aunt responded, patting Viveca's arm firmly. "Now I'll fetch the hip bath in, water's all heated. The servants are all abed till dawn, by which time you've got to be gone. Servants who haven't seen you can't tell tales now, can they? I bribed the ship's captain aplenty to keep his trap shut, and Great Edward's got all your bonds and such cashed in for you. The horses are groomed, fed, blanketed, and ready to go—Tuberose, Brick, the four mares from Turkey, and three foals. As a going-away gift I bought back Moor's last filly foal, so you'll have that good blood to rely on. I don't trust them Eastern nags myself."

"You're an angel," Viveca whispered gratefully.

"No, I'm a Lindstrom, if only by marriage, and we watch out for our own. And, Viveca?"

"Aunt?" she asked listlessly.

"There's something here from America, some letters and papers in a bundle."

"Bring them in, please, and stay with me while I read them— or, better yet, be good enough to read them to me; my eyeballs feel scorched."

Caro sat back down on the foot of the bed, slitting envelopes with a pocketknife, scanning the contents.

"Viveca," she said excitedly, "It's good news. William says the divorce should go through in May, that's a couple of months off, and—*oh*."

Her aunt's voice had changed, sobered vastly.

Viveca glimpsed the black border on the stationery and blinked. "He's dead," she said flatly.

"Yes, darling, William died in a confrontation between his troop and the Colonists. Another letter from him is dated a month before that; he says you thought him a coward and he was determined not to let you go until he'd made up for it."

Viveca shook her head helplessly. "I don't think I ever knew the man at all. It's been little over a year since I told him good-bye, but I hardly remember him. His smile, there's a ghost of that vacant smile of his somewhere in my mind, the way he smiled when he least understood me. . . ."

Caro, unheeding, inhaled sharply. "V-Viveca, he left you property!"

"What?" she scoffed sadly.

"He won it gambling—says here he wanted to try to make it up to you for costing you the farm and house. It's a thousand acres of prime grazing land in the colony of Virginia. It's a good omen, Viveca, being as your mother's name is Virginia."

"I—I suppose it is. There's the land I needed. Now I can spend the rest of my money on a house and horses," Viveca agreed blankly. "If the Colonies are going to make trouble, my land had best be tucked far away in some remote corner of Virginia."

"Bertt will know. I'm shipping the lot o' ye to Bertt St. James first off."

Caro rose to leave, but Viveca caught at her plump wrists. "Everyone always *leaves* me, Aunt Caro. Don't leave me just yet!"

And so until the last possible minute, Caro held her broken-hearted niece, pressed the sobbing face to her ample rib cage, and rocked her as she would have a sick, frightened child.

EPILOGUE

Spring, 1773

She would not stay at Bertt's; she had gone straightaway to Virginia to claim her property.

The Colonies were fighting mad, and there was going to be a full-scale rebellion or her name wasn't Lindstrom. *Viveca Lindstrom-Holland—almost St. James,* Viveca thought emptily.

She stood on a darkly green knoll overlooking the house site at dawn. Down there in those trees—that would be the house. Over there, the stables, and back this way, the herb gardens. She could just make out Luke's white shirt in the dawn. Luke the architect and builder; what a dear little brother he was to her. And his little Liza, who was as pregnant as Viveca herself.

Hands on hips, she surveyed the land that was hers as far as she could see. Viveca made up her mind that the stables and house would be of brick and stone so that no fire could ever again take all she owned away from her. They would set up a kiln right here on her property and dig the clay for bricks. And there must be a smokehouse for meat; she had contracted for swine and sheep and cattle to arrive soon. Perhaps she could afford an icehouse, too.

Viveca had run breeding farms and small estates when married to William; she was confident she could do it now on a larger scale.

Not many horses now, but soon! She had already written to Caro asking her to buy back the two best mares, if she could find them, and have them bred by Eclipse, then sent to the Americas. She had only been here two weeks and had already accom-

301

plished all this. But, oh, she was so empty inside, so dead, so numb.

There were twenty-seven breeding farms already established in Virginia; she would visit them after the baby was born and see what kind of stock they had to crossbreed with hers. With that thought she began to cry hopelessly for lack of Byrne to share the plans, the dreams, the victories with. Byrne and horses. One had always gone with the other until now, until . . .

Dust stirred over to the east where the sun had just risen. A rider? Viveca wiped her eyes on the back of her wrist. Must be Skiff, Dickon, or Bartholomew, deciding to cut short the visit to Bertt, who they'd met for the first time on this journey. He'd been deported here before most of them were born.

The horse and rider turned toward Luke's torch light. Viveca watched dully as the rider spoke to Luke and the others. Then all at once Luke's buxom wife broke away and came up the hill to where Viveca stood, alone in the dawn.

"What is it, Liza?" she asked, reaching out to steady the gasping woman.

"Viveca, I wanted to reach you first, warn you, for fear of injuring the babe—"

"Bad news?" Viveca asked, heart stabbing her.

"No, dear—*good* news. The best! It was *Dash* died in the hanging at Bromley. Poor, old, drunk old Dash, 'twas him they caught and strung up on that tree."

The horse was coming up the hill, rider's shirt oranged and pinked by daybreak.

"Then *Byrne,*" Viveca began, comprehension breaking through the storm clouds in her mind.

"Escaped through the stables on Blackbird and was shot. Not bad, only enough that he fell, unconscious, and neighbors took him in and nursed him."

He was here, seated on the back of Black Rose's last filly, the fine-boned Blackbird. The white mark between the filly's eyes, like the last glimpse of sickle moon in the dawn sky over their heads, seemed the best of all omens.

Liza faded away down the knoll as Byrne slid from the saddle.

302

"I gave you up for dead," Viveca whispered, stepping forward, arms wide. "Dear God. *I thought you were dead!*"

"It was Dash," he said, folding her close to his heart.

"Yes, poor old wine-sodden Dash. There was singing in the stable just before the gunfire; I realize now that it was Dash I heard."

"I came as soon as I was well enough to walk and find me a ship. I got to Caro—she sent me here. Lilly and Terrence sent dresses, and Edward sends stocks and bonds."

"And what do *you* send?" she asked, laughing and crying all at once.

"I don't send anything, darling. I bring *me,* with my slate wiped clean. We'll be honest farmers and horse breeders now, not highwaymen. I'll raise you the finest damned brick house in Virginia, for Edward's investments have made me a good-size fortune. And, Viveca?"

"Yes, Byrne?" she asked, letting him wipe her happy tears with a handkerchief from his pocket.

"I'll plant your damned silly tuberoses along the drive and brick garden paths. But I'm damned if you'll ever be *Mistress* of the Night again! *Wife,* perhaps, but no longer mistress. I intend to marry you before you begin waltzing around Virginia giving birth to my children."

"Yes, Byrne," she said with a kiss.

Black mare cropping grass at their feet, they faced the new day together—and the new life beginning as the foundations for their house were laid in the beautiful valley below.